Y0-CCO-014

THE LAST MISSION

Americans in the R.A.F.

CLIF SANTA

The Last Mission: Historical Novel ©1998 pending by Clifford E. Santa. All rights reserved. Printed in the United States of America. No part of this book may be used or reproduced in any manner whatsoever without permission.

For information, address:

Four Directions Publishing
P.O. Box 18085
Duluth, MN 55811
(218) 729-7509

First Edition

Cover by Rick Kolath; Kolath Graphic
Sketches by Pete Feigal and Gladys Koski Holmes

ISBN 0-9645173-2-9

Four Directions Publishing

The Last Mission

The Last Mission is a work of fiction. Although the time and place are factual, any resemblance to persons living or dead is merely coincidental.

Let this story be a memorial to all those brave souls who have fallen in combat and a tribute to the survivors. Let it be a warning to generations to come, "Lest they forget."

Thanks to my Writer's Digest instructor, John Ruemmler, for the excellent guidance he gave me in my early writing; Dorothy Grohs for taking me back to the English lessons I so detested in school; Bronwyn Pope, Deborah Diggins, and Leonard Ojala for editing and support; Ed McGaa, Eagle Man, Four Directions Publishing, who believed in the The Last Mission from the first day he read it; and Bruce Crabtree for excerpts from "Rite of Passage." And to my wife, Betty, for standing by with encouragement and support while I struggled through periods of writer's block and for editing, editing, editing, formatting and editing.

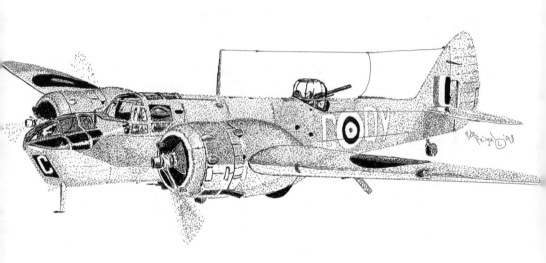

Contents

PREFACE.. *vi*
FORWARD .... *ix*
PROLOGUE .... *x*

First Blood 1
The Team 17
London 31
Under Attack 49
The Channel 65
Joker 81
Missing in Action 99
Marie Claire 117
Wedding Bells 135
A Real Mission 151
Chief 173
We Pledge Our Lives 189
Berlin 199
Detling 223
A Loner 241
The Dream 257
Melissa 277
The Anniversary 285

Epilogue 297
Afterwards 299
Glossary 300
Behind Enemy Lines 304

PREFACE

It was the summer after the Great War, but most of the Lakota (Sioux) remember it as the summer with no rain. Captain Hampton came here from England and grew to love this place, the Red River Valley. He had a vision and bought up many farms before they went bankrupt. Soon he had so many farms he had to hire people to work them. That's how I came to work for the Captain. He had good eyes, like an eagle, but he did not see that I was a half-breed. The Captain only saw a man. The Captain gave us a piece of land to build a home on. No one ever gave Indians anything.

My wife's sister, a full-blooded Sioux, came to live with us and worked for the Captain. Many years later, the Captain told me that when he first saw her, she was the most beautiful thing he'd ever seen. He worshiped the ground she walked on and he wanted her for his wife. She smiled and told the Captain she was Lakota and nobody wanted anything to do with Indians. Again the Captain's eyes were blinded and he said it made no difference. She was the woman he wanted to share his life with, to raise his sons and daughters. She laughed, and said her father was a very important tribal elder; she would cost many horses and cattle.

The next day the Captain went to see her father and a bargain was struck. The Captain gave her father fifty head of prime beef and a dozen of his best horses, and thought he got the better deal by far. They were married in the Lakota tradition, and though they lived in the white man's world, the Lakota heritage was ever present.

Our children grew up together, went to school together, and were like brothers and sisters to each other. Although they lived in the white man's world and went to his schools, they always knew they were half-breeds. Except for sports, there was no place for them; they were Indians. My son Jimmy and the Captain's son David grew to love the Indian ways and would spend the summers with their Grandfather. He taught them the Lakota ways and traditions. How to live with honor. There was no discrimination amongst the Lakota. Nobody called them half-breeds.

The two boys became blood brothers through Hunkapi (Making Relatives), a blood bond that is closer than kinship. Grandfather taught them about the Inipi (Sweat Lodge Ceremony). They learned of their closeness to Wakan Tanka (the Great Spirit) in a Vision Quest Ceremony and they were given their Indian names. They learned of the four directions and the power and meaning of each. Mother Earth took care of them and provided everything they needed.

To most Minnesota boys, Charles Lindbergh was a hero and they wanted to follow in his footsteps, to learn how to fly. With David and Jimmy it became an obsession. The boys had always worked the farms together, and the Captain provided the best machinery for them to work with. They became proficient with each piece of machinery, a seemingly natural ability. To the Captain, the airplane was only another piece of machinery, and he rewarded the boys with flying lessons.

When the boys got their pilots' licenses, they again found themselves in the white man's world -- nobody wanted half-breeds.

England was in trouble and needed pilots. Like David's father, the ancestral homeland did not see any Lakota. England did not see Indians -- they only saw pilots.

Paul Waters, Laughing Hawk

viii

FORWARD

August 1940 -- Germany

"When the British Air Force drops two or three or four thousand kilograms of bombs, then we will in one night drop one hundred and fifty thousand, two hundred and thirty thousand, three hundred thousand or four hundred thousand kilograms...We will raze their cities to the ground."

Adolf Hitler

July 10, 1940 began the Battle of Britain. The first phase was mainly over the Channel and the southeast coast of England.

August 13 began phase two; wipe the British Air Force from the sky. On August 18, the Luftwaffe flew nearly 1,800 sorties aimed at Fighter Command -- its airfields, its ground installations, its radar stations and its aircraft and pilots.

On September 7, 1940, Hitler began bombing London in retaliation for the British bombing of Berlin. At 5 p.m., 626 German bombers and 648 German fighters began bombing London. Successive waves bombed until 4:30 a.m. The next evening the attacks began at 7:30 and continued throughout the night. Some 842 persons were killed and 2,347 wounded.

September 15, 1940 has been marked as "Battle of Britain Day," when Goering threw every available bomber and fighter against London. This was repeated twice more, but on a reduced scale. The Battle of Britain ended October 31, 1940, but the war continued for almost five more years.

PROLOGUE

THE SATURDAY EVENING POST
Editor: Richard Wilson
Waterway Blvd.
Indianapolis, Indiana
June 15, 1940

THE SATURDAY EVENING POST
WAR CORRESPONDENT,
Raymond Burrel
Savoy Hotel
London, England

Dear Raymond,

It has come to our attention that a number of American pilots are going to England and enlisting in the R.A.F. As you well know, it is illegal for an American to join the armed forces of a belligerent nation.

Our reporters inform me that British recruiters are advertising in major papers for pilots. The applicants are instructed to call a New York number collect and are given train tickets to come for an interview. As far as I have been able to ascertain, any pilot wishing to join the R.A.F. as a fighter pilot is provided transport through Canada to England to avoid any F.B.I. intervention.

There is growing unrest in the United States that Roosevelt will involve us in what is considered, by most people, to be Europe's problem. At The Post, there is an undercurrent that it is only a matter of time until the United States will come to England's rescue with more than supplies and munitions.

Ray, locate some of our American pilots. Find out why and how they came to join the R.A.F. Why aren't they in the U.S. Army Air Corps? Something about their families, what they're doing and their lifestyle in general. We need to bring England to the United States, to give the American people an insight into what's happening over there. Good luck Ray, and keep us on top of things in England.

Sincerely yours,

Richard Wilson

Richard Wilson, Editor
THE SATURDAY EVENING POST

xii

First Blood

Sergeant Tommy Tuck poked his head through the doorway of the pilots' ready room. It was an oversized Nissen hut with assorted chairs, benches and tables. While some of the pilots slouched in chairs trying to sleep, others read books or papers. Some were sitting at tables and writing letters home. The painted interior was a drab yellow color, like sun baked mud. "What the hell's those Americans' names?" he mumbled to himself, scanning down the list of pilots on his clipboard. "Oh yeah! David Hampton, front and center."

David marched into Sergeant Tuck's office built on the side of the Nissen hut, closing the creaky wooden door behind him. "Sergeant David Hampton reporting, sir." He stood at attention, his arm snapped up in a stiff salute. The office was grimy, four bare walls, with cracks running across the plaster like spider webs. Cobwebs covered the upper corners of the raised ceiling that had a large piece of plaster conspicuously missing from its center. The single window was sooty, with a crack running diagonally from the top left to the bottom right corner.

"First off, Hampton, I'm a sergeant! Just like you! So don't 'Sir' me and you bloody well don't salute me." Tuck searched haphazardly through a pile of papers on his desk. He pulled a duty roster from the middle of the pile. He studied it for a moment; then crossed off a name and scribbled another in its place. Though short in stature, his soft-spoken voice carried a ring of authority. His wiry build would have looked out of place in an office were it not for his pale complexion. "Flying Officer Duffy is short a pilot in his vic. You'll fly his number two position today. I informed him you were one of the new American Indian recruits from the States; guess it doesn't make any difference who flies with him, it's just a milk run. You'll be flying convoy patrol over the English Channel. Be good learning experience for you new Yanks though, flying with skilled English pilots. Report to him on the flight line, and don't screw up, Hampton."

David slipped his Mae West on and slung his parachute and dinghy pack over his left shoulder. As he walked out to his Hurricane, his step had a certain prideful bounce to it. He was a fighter pilot going up on a mission. He shivered in the damp English fog, but gave no thought to it. Soon, he would be flying one of the Hurricanes now sitting at its tie-down, appearing and disappearing in and out of the drifting fog, like apparitions. David plopped his parachute on the wing and began his preflight check. He couldn't recall such a bone-chilling dampness back home; Minnesota was seldom foggy except in the spring when the snow melted.

"You're one of the new pilots, are yea?" A fitter came walking toward the Hurricane. He was short and stocky with a crop of red hair that said Irish even before he spoke. His eyes sparkled like fiery green embers, imparting an air of authority. Sergeant's chevrons on the fitter's jacket classed him. He stood looking up at David with his hands planted on his hips, seemingly daring anyone to say something about his height. A broad grin broke across his face, and the ruddy complexion changed to a welcome.

"Yes, sir. David Hampton, fresh in from the United States of America. Am I that green?" David grinned back at him.

"It's obvious that you're new; pilots don't preflight their aircraft. That's a job for fitters and riggers. Davie, me boy, we fitters and riggers take pride in always having our kites ready. When there's a scramble, we fitters have the engines running, ready for you to take off. You may only have seconds to get airborne before the Huns arrive. Preflighting your own kite, well, it's kind of an insult. Like we don't know our job, you see? I'm Mac Bolfriend, head fitter. My friends call me Woody, 'cause wid me red hair, they think I look like a woodpecker." Woody chortled, extending his hand. His dark, yellow-stained teeth reminded David of a beaver with two large protruding incisors.

"Sergeant Woodpecker." David winced at the handshake and smiled to let Woody know he was one of the friendlies. "My friends call me Pigskin. That's 'cause back home I was quarterback on our football team. I grew up on a farm. I knew every piece of machinery from top to bottom. That's how I want to know my Hurricane, from top to bottom. Every square inch of her. After all, we're going to be spending a little time together."

Woody chuckled. "Well...yea ain't no limey pilot, that's for sure, but yea Yanks have queer ways, I heared. Pigskin, yea come around and we'll show yea the old girl. Inside and out. When yea get back, I'll be stand'n yea a pint. Guess I better get to know yea. Yea be ah flying one ah me machines."

There were four 303-caliber machine guns hidden in each wing. David checked the bolt on each gun running his fingers over the belt feeding from its ammo box. How different from his 30-30 Winchester back home. Outside of the animals they'd butchered to eat on the farm, white-tailed deer were the only things he'd ever shot and killed. He had never fired a shot in anger. The only time his machine guns had been fired were at targets. In fact, he had yet to see a German plane.

David pondered as to why section leader Lt. Duffy assigned him to fly as his wing-man. He complained constantly about David's sloppy flying. Maybe today we'll see some Germans, David thought, as he crawled under the wing inspecting the landing gear.

"Hampton, are you ready yet?" Lt. Duffy's cutting tone brought David back to the war. It was a British voice, crisp and sharp, like a lord or baron talking down to a servant.

"Yes, sir," David replied squaring his shoulders. He jumped up as though the coach had called him from the bench with a new football play. He stood half a head taller than Duffy and thought how he'd like to meet him in a football scrimmage.

"Saddle up, Yank. Looks like we'll be airborne soon. Stay in formation. Your job is to watch my backside and call a warning if any Hun gets behind us. And Hampton, keep your frigging finger off your gun button. I don't want my ass shot off if we get in a mixup."

Excitedly David put on his Mae West, strapping his parachute on the outside. He climbed up on the wing and struggled into the narrow confines of the Hurricane's cockpit, his ears burning from Lt. Duffy's redress. Well, he'd show'em. He'd fly Duffy's wing all right, like he was attached to it. He had butterflies in his stomach and his mouth was dry.

David fumed as he fumbled with his safety harness and Woody reached in, snapping the buckle into the quick release. David adjusted his seat and began his check list. Brakes set, trim set for takeoff, flaps up, mags off, petrol full, gear down and locked, radiator flaps open for maximum cooling. He plugged in his R/T (radio telephone) jack and pulled his flying helmet on, checking the face mask and oxygen connections. Goggles adjusted, he was ready. His sweaty right hand rested on the control column hand grip and his left on the throttle lever. He worked the controls through their full range, first the elevators, then the ailerons, and finally the rudders. His stomach felt upset -- scared; it was his first operational flight. He buried himself in his checklist, going over each control again and again, locating each instinctively. Undercarriage indicator, green lights on. Hydraulic selector, safety catch across the wheels-up slot. Throttle master switch off, cockpit hood locked open.

Nervously, he wiped his sweaty hands on the legs of his flying suit. Without looking, he placed his thumb over the firing button, feeling and familiarizing himself with its location. He looked through his reflector gun sight and the external bead sight, envisioning a Messerschmitt. He looked up at his rear-facing mirror, adjusting its angle. His left hand found the throttle without groping, then slipped down to the elevator trim-tab control handwheel.

Soon "his" R.A.F. flight would be airborne. He was a fighter pilot, shortly he would be flying in formation, climbing through the low hanging scud and heading out over the English Channel. He felt a rush of adrenaline, like coming out of the locker room onto the football field for a championship game. Now his football was a Hurricane fighter, and the opposing team was the German fighters from across the Channel. David thought about climbing out in formation and being engulfed in the clouds. All he would see was the lead plane, fifty feet away. If he lost sight of the lead, what would he do?

The morning's briefing had been routine: a single 'Vic' formation, three fighters to fly protective cover, circling a convoy steaming up the Channel. A monotonous exercise of boring holes in the sky, but at least he was flying an honest-to-God mission.

A flare arced a fiery trail into the air, bursting in a cluster of a hundred orange stars, signaling the starting of engines. Radio silence was strict; the Germans listened on all the R.A.F. frequencies. The radio telephone transmission could give their position away and would be used only when they were under attack. He heard an engine cough as the Lieutenant started his Hurc. At least the lieutenant had seen action. His ground crew had painted three swastikas on the side of Duffy's kite.

David set the fuel cock to main tanks on, throttle half open, propeller control full forward, supercharger moderate, radiator shutter open. He worked the fuel priming pump until he felt resistance. Ignition switch on, he called "All clear," pressing in the starter and booster coil pushbuttons. The Hurricane groaned, slowly turning the three-bladed propeller. The twelve-cylinder, liquid-cooled Rolls-Royce Merlin III turned through three revolutions, belched dark puffs of smoke from the exhaust, and coughed to life. David released the starter button, still holding the booster, until the Merlin ran smoothly. He screwed down the priming pump. The Merlin gave a deep-throated roar and settled into a staccato tic-tic as David opened the throttle to 1,000 rpms. The battery trolley was disconnected and Woody waved him off.

Rudder trim-tab set full right, elevator - neutral. Propeller control - full forward. Fuel - mains on, auxiliary tank cock and pumps off. Pressurizing cock - atmosphere. Flaps set 28 degrees for short takeoff, supercharger - moderate, radiator shutter - fully open. Check list complete.

David sat waiting for the takeoff flare, his fingers drumming nervously on the control stick. Even at idle power, the Hurricane trembled, waiting anxiously for the moment when all her thousand horses would come to life.

David reveled in the smells of the fighter. Aviation gas lingered on his hands from the preflight check. He savored the aroma of burned gun powder that permeated the cockpit. A lingering scent of wood, fabric and dope remained from recent repairs. The fleece-lined leather flying jacket gave off a pungent odor of wool. He would soon need the jacket for protection from the cold at high altitude. He wiggled his feet in the leather flying boots and squirmed uncomfortably on the seat parachute. Though the tired old Hurricane had seen many hours of training new pilots, it was still new to him. He could almost smell the sweat and fear of other new pilots who had brought the big engine to full power. A thousand horses would be screaming inches in front of him...the cool air from the slow turning prop swirled into the open canopy. David kicked his rudder back and forth in nervous anticipation.

The green takeoff flare arced into the air. The lieutenant's Hurc gave a deep roar as he taxied into takeoff position. David added power, pulling into position off the lieutenant's wing. Three Hurricanes began their takeoff roll together, spread out across the field in a loose formation. David gradually opened the throttle to the gate, feeding in right rudder to correct for the torque. The loaded Hurricanes bounced and slipped down the grassy field looking like hippos in a ballet class. David eased the stick forward gently, and the tail lifted from the grass. With the tail up, he could see straight down the field instead of out the side window. His speed built rapidly and he tested the elevators, adding a little nose up trim. The Hurricane struggled into the air.

Gear up, flaps up, David closed the canopy, marveling at how fast his Hurricane accelerated. Only moments ago he had felt like a helpless, clumsy albatross. Now the Hurc was transformed into a sleek, responsive, maneuverable fighter. Reaching 140 mph, David gradually brought the throttle back. Prop set, he trimmed for the climb at 155 mph and slipped into position off the lieutenant's right wing.

They entered the clouds in tight formation. David's palms were sweaty on the controls. Rivulets of water from the moisture ladened clouds streaked his windshield. The fighters climbed in a tight formation. The clouds thickened, and David eased in tighter. He strained to see the lieutenant's wing tip only forty feet away. Climbing at a hundred and fifty-five miles per hour required constant corrections to hold his position. One screw up and he'd be greeting Wakan Tanka, the Great Spirit of his Sioux ancestry. Their fiery wreckage would be spread over miles of the English countryside. David's Hurricane rocked in the lieutenant's prop-wash. He felt tense, like a banjo string tightened too tight. David could barely make out the lieutenant in his cockpit, concentrating on his instruments. He envied lieutenant Duffy's blind flying and vowed to become proficient at it himself. Someday there wouldn't be someone to lead them out of trouble. David thought, I've always been the quarterback, the leader. One day I'll be the one leading the flight.

The sky brightened and they broke out into brilliant sunshine. David relaxed and dropped back slightly from the lieutenant's wing, still climbing in formation. The lieutenant leveled the flight at eight thousand feet. The Cliffs of Dover appeared below through breaks in the clouds. The white clay cliffs could be seen from miles away. They stood like silent sentinels against the dark blue sea, a homing beacon to returning pilots. Only scattered cloud layers remained as they headed out over the Channel. Smoke from the convoy below revealed its position.

They relieved the flight flying protective cover and began orbiting the convoy. At least he was flying and adding hours to his flight log. The Hurricane was new to David. He was awed at its power and speed and how rapidly it responded. Nothing he'd ever flown compared to it. He caressed the round grip on the control stick, his thumb resting on the firing button. He remembered firing his 303s for familiarization and the toxic smell from the burned cordite. The Hurricane had bucked as if he'd flown into severe turbulence, a thunder storm from eight machine guns firing simultaneously. He outgunned the rest of the squadron. Maybe that was why the lieutenant had picked him for his wingman.

Lieutenant Duffy had three kills, so he must be doing something right. I haven't even seen a German, David thought. What was it they'd told us in briefing? "Beware the Hun in the sun." David squinted up at the sun and saw spots before his eyes. The spots increased in size. David froze, unable to move. He watched the German Messerschmitts rapidly build in size. White streaks came reaching for them. Tracers. Deadly little balls of fire.

"BANDITS!" David screamed into his R/T. Bullets tore into his Hurc making popping sounds when they punctured the fabric. The bullet-proof windscreen was hit, slamming him sideways. His head was thrown against the side of the canopy. A ball of fire erupted directly in front of him where Lt. Duffy's plane had been.

David felt the searing heat from the explosion of Duffy's fighter. His head hurt and he thought it odd that there was no sound. His Hurricane shuddered violently. Black smoke engulfed him, and a strong smell of burning fuel stung his nostrils. Chunks of flying debris banged into his Hurricane. He jammed his throttle to full power, rolled hard right and jerked the stick back into his lap. All in a fraction of a second, for that was all the time there was between life and death. David reacted automatically, as he'd rehearsed a thousand times during practice and in his mind. Enemy aircraft were coming down on them from everywhere.

Blood trickled down David's cheek, cut by a splinter from his shattered canopy. He twisted around in the narrow confines of the Hurricane's cockpit, scanning the skies. Below him, three Junker dive bombers were streaking toward the convoy. He switched the gun's arming master switch to on. David pushed the control forward none too gently, nosing the Hurc over into a steep dive. Wind shrieked in his broken canopy. The German pilots hadn't seen him. At full throttle, the Hurricane screamed as the propeller tips went supersonic. His hearing was coming back. The Ju-87 silhouettes grew rapidly in his sight pip. The unsuspecting Huns were concentrating on attacking the convoy. David maneuvered into position behind them. He worked the stick and rudders until the trailing Junker centered in his gun sight. All his training, all his preparation had been for this one moment, and yet he had never fired at another human being before.

The Ju-87s were straight above the convoy. Telltale streaks in the water marked the violent evasive maneuvers the ships were taking to elude the attackers. At two hundred yards, the trailing Junker's wings filled the bars of his site pip. David squeezed the firing button. His Hurricane bucked from the recoil of eight 303s firing. The cockpit filled with the pungent smell of burning cordite. Tracers arced across the short span, disappearing in the Junker.

He'd never seen the effects of his guns on another aircraft. David watched his bullets striking the Junker's wing. Holes appeared where his bullets ripped the wing open. He danced on the rudder pedals yawing the nose of his Hurricane, spraying the Hun with 303s. His bullets stitched a line of holes up into the engine. The dive bomber was trailing white smoke. Flames came shooting back from the engine cowling. David closed to finish the stricken Junker. He had no conscious thought of killing another man, only destroying the machine. The canopy flew open. The Hun tried to bail out. Then a wing weakened by David's 303s snapped, folding back on the cockpit.

David instinctively jerked back on the control stick, rolling around the burning Junker. The next Junker filled his sight pip and he squeezed the firing button for three seconds. The Hurricane slowed from the recoil of eight 303s firing at once. White smoke poured from the engine of the Ju-87 and David danced on the rudders until the third Junker grew in his sight pip. He fired again and watched white streaks of his tracer shells disappear into the tail of the Hun.

White streaks shot past David's head. He heard a snapping sound as they passed inches away. Bullets slammed into the armor plating in back of his seat. Helpless, he was thrown about the cockpit like a child's rag doll. The impact left him dizzy.

David rolled hard left, pulling the stick back into his lap. He chopped the throttle and dumped his flaps. The Me-109 shot past so close David could see oil streaks on its belly. The Messerschmitt filled his gun sight; David squeezed the gun button. The cockpit filled again with the stink of burning cordite. The Hurricane buffeted from the recoil, as if it'd hit a wind sheer. The Messerschmitt dove for the Channel. Full throttle, flaps up, David rolled on his back and followed. After Lt. Duffy's redress, David was determined to out-fly the Hun. David owed one to the lieutenant, his flight leader who'd chosen him to fly in his vic.

The ME-109 again filled his gun sight. White smoke was pouring from its engine. Must've hit a glycol line, he thought, as he squeezed the firing button. "This one's for Lieutenant Duffy, you-son-of-a-bitch!" David screamed. His tracers arced into the engine of the Messerschmitt, then his guns were silent. They dove, paired, screaming downward, closer to the Channel. Inky blue water, crested with snowy-white tops, rushed up to meet them. David eased the throttle back and leveled his Hurricane.

The propeller stopped turning on the Messerschmitt. David could see the German struggling to open his canopy. Flames shot out of the cowling, lapping at the wings and fuselage. The ME-109 rolled on its back, and the pilot dropped clear. David circled, watching the parachute stream out of the German's backpack and pop open. The ME-109 hit the water in a flat spin, sat there for a moment, then disappeared beneath the waves.

Out of ammo, David looked around. The skies were empty. He turned towards the Cliffs of Dover. David felt drained, though the action had taken only minutes. Half his canopy was missing. He checked his controls. They all worked, though he noticed several bullet holes in his wings. Then he realized the lieutenant had been killed. He was not coming back. What had happened to the other pilot in their flight? Fate was on David's side today. He'd taken the ball and ran -- now he was out on the field alone. But this was not a football game back in Minnesota. Here the penalty for error was death. He'd witnessed death; in a fraction of a second he had seen his section leader killed, and he had killed. It had a permanence to it that David had never experienced. He felt hollow and drained of emotion.

Lt. Duffy was dead, his flight mate was missing, and now he had blood on his hands. He'd struck out and killed in anger. David thought of the pilot he'd just killed. What was that young German like? Did he have a girlfriend? A wife? Maybe he had children back home.

David day-dreamed about his mother and father at home on the farm, working, doing their chores — then someone in uniform coming up to the house; "I'm sorry to inform you that your son was killed in action over England." For the first time he realized what death meant and what he was really doing. It began to weigh heavily on David. He could see the German trapped in his burning plane. The man he'd killed. Did that make him a murderer? How was it that war sanctioned killing? David recalled the argument he'd had with his father. How he was going to fly. Just doing a job and flying; that's all he wanted.

"War's killing and dying," his dad had argued.... He had fought in the Great War and knew what he was talking about.

David had shut out everything his Dad had said. He didn't care; he would do anything to fly. He was certain nothing would ever happen to him...after all, wasn't he the quarterback, the best pilot in their squadron?

David thought, "I'd be dead along with the lieutenant if I hadn't fought back. It's kill or be killed; strike first, strike fast and hard, and live again for another day." David felt played out, weak. It seemed to take forever to get back. Where was the field? The checkerboard pattern of farms slipped rapidly behind him. They seemed so small compared to the vast acreage they had at home.

It was comforting to be back over land. He'd never been a good swimmer. He passed the training area and three Hurricanes flying in close formation. He descended toward his home field. It seemed to take so long, like he was in slow-flight.

David circled the field checking the wind sock and turned downwind. He ran through his check list: Brake pressure - minimum 100 pounds, air speed 120 miles per hour, he dropped his landing gear and flipped the red hydraulic flap handle up. Undercarriage - down and three green lights, propeller control - fully forward, supercharger control - moderate, flaps - down full. A green flare rose in the air flashing in a showery burst. He brought his throttle back, reduced his airspeed to ninety-five miles per hour. He slid the remains of his cockpit hood open, flipped the locked open latch and turned on final approach. The smell of fresh cut hay filled the open cockpit wiping away the stench of fear, death and vomit.

10   *The Last Mission*

Crash trucks waited on the end of the field. For what? He lined up on final approach, the field blurred. He struggled to sit up, to stay awake. His airspeed dropped, 90, 85, 80. He shook his head to clear his vision. A stabbing pain shot through his head. The Hurricane settled gently skimming the grass. He closed the throttle. He felt dizzy, everything looked fuzzy. The Hurricane bounced once, and David eased the stick all the way back.

His right gear collapsed, digging into the turf. The Hurricane spun around, ripping the left gear from the plane. The propeller struck the ground tearing clumps of sod from the field, flipping them into the air haphazardly. The thumping propeller blades hitting the ground sounded like a sick horse gasping its death lament. The Hurricane slid to a stop in the middle of the field. The smell of steaming glycol rose in a cloud around the crumpled wreckage. David slumped forward in the small cockpit. He heard sirens screaming and thought he saw lights flashing.

David heard someone talking. "We'd better get him out of there before it blows." Someone was on the wing struggling with the broken canopy. He tried to look up. Someone shouted, "Oh my God! Medic!"

Hallucinations of a football game flashed through David's mind as he drifted into unconsciousness: he dreamed of a tied football game and the last two minutes of play. He'd been sacked on the last play and slammed to the ground.

The coach wanted to pull him from the game. "You're hurt too bad to play."

He insisted he was okay. Third down and fifteen. "We'll run another quarterback sneak. They'll never look for it again," David said.

"You can't run on that leg, Pigskin," warned Chief, his closest friend and number one blocker.

"Hut-one! Hut-two!" The center snapped the football into his hands, and he faked the hand-off to Chief. Pain shot up his leg as he turned and headed into the hole that'd opened for a brief second. Head down, he bulled his way forward -- struggling, fighting, clawing and kicking. He twisted as someone tried to tackle him, jerking free. Driving forward....

"Strap him down on the stretcher! He's out of his head," a corpsman called. "Give him a shot of morphine."

David struggled as they loaded him into the ambulance.

White lights blinded him. He tried to raise his hand to shade his eyes. He couldn't move. He struggled, and a nurse held his shoulders. "Easy, airman. You're in the hospital. You'll be okay, Yank."

"What happened?" David still had visions of a football game. "Did we get the first down?"

"Sorry, Yank. I don't know about any first downs. You're in the hospital at Biggin Hill. You've just had a plane crash. Looks as though you were banged about some."

"Oh yeah. Where's my plane?" David tried to recall what'd happened. "I was coming in to land. I hit hard. That's all I remember."

"You need your rest, Yank. This shot will put you to sleep and help with the pain."

"No. No more shots. I'll be fine with a little rest...and something to eat." It smelled like a hospital, antiseptics and alcohol. David felt tired and closed his eyes to rest for a few minutes. He didn't feel the cold needle....

A brilliant shaft of sunlight hit David in the face. He awoke with a start. He looked around, confused. The room had a noxious stench like disinfectant. The walls, the ceiling, even the window trim was white. There were several other beds in the room, all of them empty. He looked for his clothes, but they were nowhere in sight. He felt the bandages wrapped around his head and remembered the crash. This was the Biggin Hill hospital. He took inventory of his arms and legs. Everything intact. Thank God! He considered calling out when the door flew open and a nurse marched in.

"Good morning, David. I'm nurse Emma Hoffsteader. How we feeling this morning, Luv?"

She reminded David of his old maid aunt. Her glasses were black and ugly and looked small on her round chubby face. Her white nurse's cap was perched on her head, and her uniform dress was two sizes too small.

"Hungry and sore. Feels like the whole football team ran over me," David said. A groan escaped him as he tried to roll over.

"Relax, Luv. I've got a nice warm bath for you and some clean sheets. Then we'll see about a big bowl of porridge," she said.

"I was thinking more like a beef steak and some eggs and a plate of fried potatoes with four or five slices of toast and a pot of coffee," David replied.

"Sorry, Luv. You're not in the States now. There is a war on, you know." Nurse Hoffsteader scrubbed him more roughly than necessary. The coarse, rough scrub cloth brought the blood to the surface as she scrubbed his backside. "Roll over, Luv."

"Ouch," David grumbled. "I could give myself a bath. After all, I've been doing it for twenty years."

"Are all Yanks complainers, or just you?" Emma added an extra dig. "There, Davie. Just like a new born baby. If only I had a soft, cuddly comforter," she teased. "Now for your porridge"

David grimaced, but there was a grin on his face as Emma left.

Nurse Hoffsteader popped back into the room with his breakfast. Her high-pitched voice almost sang as she announced; "David, got someone here to see you if you feel up to it? A news reporter or something. From the United States, he is. Say, are you someone important? Maybe I should get your autograph." She smiled. "He sure is tall, and good looking."

"If he doesn't mind watching me eat." David worried about who could be coming to see him from the States. Maybe the FBI coming to take him back. He didn't know any reporters. Might as well get it over with. "Send him in," he mumbled with his mouth full of porridge. "This stuff tastes like wet boxes."

"Okay, Mr. Burrel. You can come in now," nurse Hoffsteader called.

"Hi David. I'm Raymond Burrel with The Saturday Evening Post." The tall civilian had to stoop as he stepped through the door. A black, long-stemmed pipe hung precariously from the corner of his mouth. His sandy hair was brushed back to reveal a receding hair line. From his tanned complexion, he'd obviously spent a considerable amount of time outdoors. His round wire-framed glasses slid down to the middle of his long straight nose. He wore a sweater-vest and a tweed jacket with an open-collar shirt.

David relaxed and returned the reporter's smile. "Hello, Mr. Burrel. I'm David Hampton." David extended his hand and was surprised at the firm grip of the reporter's hand. "What brings you to England?"

"I'm doing a series on the Americans flying with the R.A.F." Burrel paused to let him digest the information and studied David's face for a reaction. David's eyes were deep blue pools, watching him with a penetrating intensity. Burrel noted his square chin and black hair. Raymond liked him instantly -- the bushy eyebrows and twisted nose. Raymond thought of his football days. He'd liked to have had David on his team, with his broad shoulders and powerful neck....

"Well, not much of a story here. Guess you kind of bombed out on me, Mr. Burrel," David said. "I'm a nobody, a hick from the sticks."

Raymond pulled a note pad and pencil from his leather briefcase and pushed his glasses back on his nose. His wide mouth pulled up on one side in a lopsided grin, as he struck a match and sucked on his cold pipe. Taking a couple of long puffs as the pipe lit, Raymond let it hang from the corner of his mouth as he opened his note pad. "David, tell me about your life at home? Where did you go to school? Any girlfriends, buddies, what sports were you in?" He'd crossed his right leg over the left and was leaning forward, resting his elbows on his knee. Raymond wrote something in his notebook, then stopped and looked up at David expectantly.

David began: "I was the first string quarterback for the Moorhead Minnesota High School football team. They called me 'Pigskin.'" David smiled at the memory. Thinking back, he put his hand up to his nose. The break had left his nose with a twist and he felt self-conscious. It seemed like it was just yesterday. They were playing Fargo. The sack was one he wouldn't forget. How could he? He had a twisted reminder right in the middle of his face.

"Mind if I use your nickname in my stories?"

"What? What stories?" David came back to the present.

"I want to write a story about your life, and how you came to the R.A.F.," Raymond explained. "I'll call you David, if that's okay? You can call me Spike if you want. That's what my teammates called me." A smile came to Raymond's face. "I was the number one receiver on the University of Minnesota's football team. They called me Spike because I spiked the ball after I scored a touchdown."

"Spike! Hell, I remember you! I've been to a couple of your games." David's face beamed; he groaned as he tried to sit up in the bed. He was stiff and sore as he struggled into a sitting position. "Jeez. So what can I tell you?"

"Why? Why did you leave the United States and come to England to fly with the R.A.F?" Spike's pencil was poised, waiting for David to begin.

David thought about the day he'd been working in the barn with his dad. He hadn't rationalized the why since the quarrel he'd had with his father. "Joker, Chief and I had just gotten our pilots' licenses. We were ready to conquer the world. The only trouble was, nobody wanted us. We tried the Army Air Corp. They said we weren't qualified. You see Spike, I'm half Sioux and Chief is three-quarters Sioux. Then I read this ad: 'Pilots Wanted'. You could call collect to New York, and I did."

"Sioux Indians?" Burrel's eyebrows raised in surprise as he wrote rapidly. "Now that's interesting. Who's Joker and Chief?" Raymond asked while making notes.

"Joker's Ralph Burton. A real joker. Always playing practical jokes on someone. He's the number one receiver on our team. We grew up together with Chief. Best damn football players," David paused, remembering the action on the football field. "Joker has a pair of hands like magnets. Anytime the football is close to him, he catches it. Even upside down."

"What about Chief? Who's he?" Spike asked while his pencil flew across the note book.

"The Chief's my cousin and also my blood brother. We made the Sioux Hunkapi rites together."

"Wait a minute there, David. What's a Hunkapi?"

"That's a Sioux blood bond that binds two people closer than family even. Together, we are brothers and children of the Great Spirit, Wakan Tanka. Chief's name is Jimmy Waters, and he's built like a brick shit-house. I sometimes think we should've called him ox. He ran interference for me, blocked rushers; the two of them made me look good. I mean, a quarterback is only as good as his teammates. Right?"

"They need a leader. That's what you are, David. A leader." Raymond waved his protest off. "You were the leader yesterday. When your flight leader was killed, you took over and broke up the German attack. There are a lot of men on that Convoy who owe their lives to you, David. You're a hero. You now have two confirmed kills and two probables. Not bad for your first encounter. Tell me more about this call to New York?"

David smiled, "Off the record?"

"Anything you don't want printed or might be embarrassing is off the record," Raymond assured him. He smiled easily, often.

"The three of us got together. We knew we didn't have enough hours, so we made some up."

"You padded your log books," Raymond said, jotting a few notes in the note book on his lap.

"I guess you could say that, but I don't think we should let that out," David said.

"So you called New York. Then what?"

"The man on the other end was pleasant. He took some information, and asked if we wanted to enlist in the R.A.F. and fly fighters out of England." David grinned. "Foolish question. We would have signed right there if we could have done it over the phone. He sent us train tickets from Minneapolis to Detroit. We were to cross over into Windsor, Ontario, individually and at different times of the day. You see, Spike, it was against the law for us to join the armed forces of another country. So we had to enter Canada secretly and then we were free to head for England. Jimmy was meeting with Indian leaders. Ralph had a briefcase and told them he was going to Toronto on business. I pretended to be visiting relatives in Windsor."

"So you entered Canada. Then what?"

"The spooky part was going through customs. The FBI was there and had two guys in handcuffs. We'd met them in Detroit the day before. They were headed for England, same as us. We were lucky; the F.B.I. never figured two Indians could fly an airplane, and Joker bought an extra thick

pair of glasses. The F.B.I. never looked at us when we crossed into Canada.
After clearing customs, we met at the Norton Palmer hotel in Windsor with
other recruits. We were given train tickets to the coast and boarded a ship for
England."

The door banged open and nurse Hoffsteader marched in. "I see
you're feeling better, Luv." She gathered up his breakfast tray and straightened his bed covers. She stood beside the bed. "Anything else, Luv."

"Just my clothes, so I can get out of here."

She turned, picked up the tray and marched from the room. "Yanks,"
she said banging the door closed.

"What about your family back in Minnesota?" Spike asked as he continued writing.

"I've got three sisters and two brothers besides my mom and dad.
Dad was mad when I told him I was going to England to fly in the R.A.F.! We
had quite an argument. You see he'd been in the Great War, in France. He
knew what war was. He said, 'It's not our fight. Let'em fight their own
battles!'"

"He wouldn't listen and I was too stubborn. I'd made my mind up to
fly, no matter what. I reminded him that he was English, but he never heard
me or ignored it as he ranted on. 'You know, you'll be expected to kill people?
Hell, you could just as easily be killed yourself! Then what? Think of what
it'd do to your mother!' He wouldn't stop. I guess he knew I was going and
was nothing he could to do stop me. But he kept right on trying. Now, I'm
beginning to realize what he was talking about."

"He came to the train station to see me off the next morning. He had
tears in his eyes and wrapped his arms around me. 'Take care of yourself, son.
We'll be listening to the news. Your mother and I are damn proud of you.'
That's what he said. Dad's a great guy."

"I would have been going to the University of Minnesota now if I'd
stayed home," David said.

"You can always go back to school after the war is over, if that's what
you want."

"That's what I'm planning. But, you know how plans are." David's
voice sounded bitter. "I'd planned to get married after the war," David remi-
nisced.

"You said planned to. That sounds like history."

16   *The Last Mission*

"Spike, you know what a 'Dear John' letter is, don't you?" David's face was tight and strained. "That's what I got. 'I really like you a lot, Davie, but I met this really neat guy. We never planned it. It just happened. We're engaged.'"

"You have three days of leave coming. A little R & R. Why don't you come into London and live it up a little?"

"I don't know anyone in London."

"You know me," Raymond said. "We'll go over a few football plays and I'll show you around. I'm staying at the Savoy. How about looking me up?"

"Deal." David smiled and shook hands with the reporter. A new friend in London.

The Team

David groaned as he rolled over in the hospital bed. Momentarily confused, he looked around the bare room. It looked like a prison. The walls were bare and steel bars crisscrossed the windows. All the beds were empty but his. The smell of antiseptic reached his nostrils and he remembered where he was.

The door banged open and nurse Hoffsteader brought his breakfast. He thought that she had on the wrong uniform as she marched around the room like a drill sergeant. She was stiff and David thought maybe she'd used too much starch in her uniform. He poked at the bully beef and what appeared to be scrambled eggs. "Jeez, I ordered a steak and fresh eggs with potatoes and coffee!"

"Not today, Luv. Eat up, yea'll be leavin' us in a wee bit. There's a couple ah ya chums waiting ta see ya back to base." The nurse marched from the room, banging the door open like a linebacker charging at the snap of the ball. "Ee's awake," she called down the hall.

"Hey, Pigskin! Hear you claimed a couple scalps," said Chief, strolling into David's hospital room with his bowlegged swagger.

"Hey, Chief. You know what they say. If you've got it, you've got it. Who's the beanpole who has to duck to get in the door?" David chuckled. "What have you got there, Joker?"

"It's a leather bag filled with air, to match your head." Joker laughed, chucking the football at Pigskin.

David reached out for it with one hand.

"He hasn't lost his touch," said Chief, relieved to see his friend wasn't hurt.

"We'll see. Wounded in action, he's got a three-day pass and London's loaded with pretty wenches. Time to get off the reservation, Pigskin," said Joker. Chief chuckled and cast a knowing glance at Joker.

"It's about time he quit mourning his lost love and scored." David drilled the football at Chief. Chief caught it with both hands, whooping a chant as he danced around his blood brother's bed.

18   The Last Mission

"Tell you what, Davie, my boy," said Joker. "I'll go to London on your pass! When I get back, I'll tell you what a good time you had."

"All right, you guys," David replied, thinking about the offer made by Spike. "All right, so I'll go to London."

"Okay, Pigskin. Here's what you do," Chief said. "After you check in, make the Eagle Club your stomping ground. It's loaded with dames. You won't have any problem making a score. With your good looks and hawk nose, they'll be taking numbers to get at you. Just wink at them with those deep-blue pools you have. One look at those eyes and...."

"Sounds like you're jealous," David smirked, batting his bushy eyebrows seductively. "What about my kite?"

"That piece of scrap metal you brought back to the field?" Joker asked.

David's face took on the look of a quarterback who needed the next play to save the game.

"The fitters said they couldn't find one salvageable part. I mean, that kite's riddled from one end to the other," Chief elaborated.

"Jesus," David said. "I suppose they'll ground me, now that I busted up one of their war birds."

"Are you kidding?" Joker said. "You know, Pigskin, you're the biggest jerk around. You just happen to be the hero of the day. Two confirmed kills. Two probables, and you busted up the Krauts' attack."

"You just saved a couple thousand souls on that convoy," Chief added. "So I guess the Brits aren't worried about scratching one of their toys. In fact there's a surprise waiting for you back at the field."

"What kind of surprise?" David asked suspiciously. He didn't exactly trust his two friends, the biggest practical jokers around. He certainly wasn't the hero they'd portrayed him to be. All he did was his job. Nothing more than anyone else would have done in the same circumstances. Not only was his Hurc in the scrap pile, but two pilots and planes from his flight were gone. Replacements were nothing but numbers.

"On your feet, Davie, me boy," commanded nurse Hoffsteader as she duck-walked into the room carefully balancing her ponderous body with each step. "Doc says you're out of here. Besides we need the bed for some other heroes." She smiled a toothy smile and hummed a Benny Goodman tune off-key while she laid out some new clothes for him on the bed.

They inhaled deeply of the moist foggy air as they left the hospital. "Jeez am I glad to get out of this stinking place," said David, limping between his two friends.

"Let's swing by the hanger first," Joker said. "Got a little something to show you."

"What are you guys up to?" David asked. "Something's going on. I've been with you clowns too long. You're up to some kind of crap!"

"Let me get the door for you, sir," said Chief jokingly as he sprang ahead to slide back the hanger door.

"SURPRISE!" The squadron stood around a new Hurricane. A football had been painted just below the canopy, with 'Pigskin' inscribed across it. Two swastikas painted on the engine cowling depicted his kills.

David stood dumbfounded. "What the hell's going on?"

"Congratulations, Sergeant Hampton," said Biggin Hill's squadron leader, Brent Simpson. He stood ramrod stiff, a riding crop under one arm. His right hand nervously polished the brass shell-case handle. His uniform was spotless, typical British, trousers creased and shoes shined to a mirror finish. The thin, pencil-line moustache gave a nervous twitch, as if he wasn't sure he was going to speak. "When you make your first kill, you may designate your own kite and personal logo. Chief and Joker figured you'd like the ah, football thing."

David was speechless. He turned to his squadron leader. "Sir. Can I take'er up for a spin? I mean, an operational check. I should at least know how she'll handle, for the next time we get in a scrap." David could see his squadron leader's moustache twitch and was afraid he'd say no. "It's like football, sir. You have to practice, practice, practice. That's what made us good," he almost pleaded.

"I suppose a training flight is in order," the squadron leader said. "You're restricted to the training area only. When you return, you're on leave for three days."

David began his preflight check, running his hand along the aircraft's fuselage, admiring his new fighter. The fuel tanks were topped off, and the oil had been changed after the initial flight tests. New guns were nestled in the wings and loaded. Rubber covers over the gun ports protected the barrels until fired. The controls felt stiff as he lifted the aileron, observing the opposite aileron drop. He felt an intimacy with the new kite, his kite. The football, painted white, stood out against the camouflage paint on the side of the fuselage. He stood back admiring the black letters, 'PIGSKIN.' He'd been baptized.

"Pigskin, if you treat the girls in London like you preflight that kite - - they'll be standing in line to get at you," Chief said.

20 The Last Mission

"Sir. How about Chief and I escort him?" asked Joker. "I mean we've been a football team for so long. We'd be the top flight team in your squadron. Hell, the whole group!"

"Swede, you take them up for some maneuvers," Brent said.

"Okay," grinned Swede. "Pigskin, you lead off and climb to twenty-thousand -- I'll be the Hun, so keep your eyes open. And for Christ's sake, don't shoot. Just maneuver. See if you can get away from me and get behind."

David lowered himself into the Hurricane's narrow cockpit. It was new, right from the factory, smelling of metal, dope and fabric. It hadn't been blooded yet. No sweaty hand on the stick. No smell of fear or burned cordite. No gas or oil leaks, yet. No fumes in the cockpit. The controls were stiff and positive.

"Bloody nice bird, aye Pigskin?" Mac stood on the wing, a grin splitting his round face. The bill on his cap turned straight up and was cocked to the side. "I checked 'er over me self. Finest kite we've gotten from the factory."

"Howdy, Woody. I'm just going up on a short test hop. I'll meet you at The Station when we get back down. I missed our last appointment, so I'm buying."

"I'll be waiting for you, Sarge. And, no shenanigans with me new kite." Mac's chortle echoed through the hanger as he jumped down from the wing.

David taxied the new Hurc into takeoff position. Chief tucked in close on his right rear and Joker off to his left. It was a rare day in England, not a cloud, just bright clear skies. It couldn't be better: a new bird, his pals, and all the flying he wanted. David gave the thumbs-up signal, and the three Hurricanes raced down the field.

The new kite felt light. It wasn't a tired, old worn-out bird and responded instantly to his touch. A quick check and his team mates were pulling into close formation. He closed the canopy and pulled his gear up while circling the field. He lined up to do a buzz job of the airdrome. Running in full power, he dove down on the field. The Hurricane dropped like a rock and he felt the vibration in the controls. Wind howled outside his canopy sounding like a willi-waw howling through a canyon in the badlands. He was leading and felt a power he'd only known playing football. Three Hurricanes raced down the field, line abreast. More than three-thousand horses, at full power, made the buildings jump. They crossed the end of the field in seconds and pulled up in a steep climbing turn. David laughed at everyone running outside. "Pigskin flight airborne, heading for the testing range," he called over the R/T.

The controller's response crackled in the ear phones. It was a tight, strained voice, not the fun bantering of close friends. "Pigskin flight, Swede, fifty-plus bandits south of Fairlight heading north, angels twenty, vector 150, bluster."

David acknowledged, "I hope we have a few more blockers! Looks like a blitz." Jeez, fifty enemy aircraft and in minutes the four of them were going to attack? David felt his stomach doing flip flops. No chance of their coming out of this without a scratch. The boys wanted action; they were going to get it. Angels twenty — the Huns were at twenty thousand feet. Death was waiting above them. "We'll climb to twenty-four thousand to get above them," David thought, his mind racing ahead of their flight. His initial fear behind him, he concentrated on the attack.

"Roger, Pigskin." The controller came back. He was another Yank. Although he didn't play football, he knew the game. "It'll be a draw play; we have two squadrons scrambling."

Oxygen on, they passed twelve thousand feet. David could see a blanket of brown smog hanging over London, but they were climbing above it. Bluster demanded they use full power. We've got less than ten minutes to get above them, David thought. The thousand horses sure took a lot of oats, but they were climbing as David never dreamed. Twenty thousand feet and no sign of the Hun. Still climbing on a heading of one-hundred and fifty degrees.

"Pigskin, Swede, pulling behind you -- you keep the lead Pigskin, I'll cover your backside."

"Roger, Swede." David trimmed the nose down as his flight approached twenty-four thousand. A quick glance confirmed Chief tucked in on his wing, grinning like a Cheshire cat. The rear-view mirror filled with the Swede, covering their backsides. David scanned the sky for Joker. "Where the hell is he," David thought.

"Tally ho!" Joker called. "Bandits ten o'clock, below us."

David flipped the R/T switch to transmit. "Okay," he called, "here's the play: Joker you and Chief streak in and hit the bombers, Swede and I'll cover your back. HIKE!"

Joker had already nosed his Hurc over, and Chief tucked in tight behind him. Throttles at full power, they screamed down on the attack. The bombers were unaware of the diving Hurricanes approaching from above and behind. "Pigskin flight engaging bandits." David watched tracers from Joker's 303s arcing into the wing of a trailing Heinkel. Smoke poured from its engine. Streams of tracers arced in crisscross patterns across the sky, searching for the diving Hurricanes.

Joker and Chief pulled straight up, trading their excess speed for altitude. "Let's split at the top of our loop, Chief, and come in from both sides," called Joker.

"Okay. I'm splitting right." Chief gave a whoop and rolled in on the attack.

A mile away Joker called "TALLYHO!" and dove on another Heinkel.

David eased the nose of his Hurricane over, rolling left and right, Swede tucked in on his right wing. Where were the Messerschmitts protecting the bombers? David saw two chutes open behind a stricken Heinkel. The HE-111 plummeted in a spin, flames lapping around the left wing. A fuel tank exploded and pieces of flaming wreckage drifted lazily downward.

Three ME-109s closed on Joker's tail. David slammed his throttle through the gate, to combat boost. "Joker! Cross left and pull up," David called.

Joker pulled his Hurc up in a hard climbing left turn. The Messerschmitts turned trying to follow. David had a crossing shot as they turned in behind Joker. "Swede, take the one on the right, I've got the left!" David closed on the Hun. The wings of the Messerschmitt filled the bars on his gun sight. He punched the firing button. His Hurricane bucked from the eight 303s firing simultaneously. David's nose twitched from the pungent smell of the burning cordite. Tracers arced across the rapidly closing airspace and disappeared into the ME-109. David was so close, he saw his bullets cutting a line on the Hun's wing. The impacting explosive DeWilde bullets found the weak wing root in the Messerschmitt, and the wing snapped. The ME-109 plunged earthward in a gyrating spin.

David pulled up, and saw a Messerschmitt above. David sighted on the bluish-white belly, silhouetted against a brilliant sun. He noticed the Messerschmitts' nose painted a bright yellow. The Hun, unaware of David below, was still trying for a shot at Joker. David closed to one-hundred and fifty yards. He could see the black cross on the stubby, square tipped wings.

The German rolled to the right and filled the orange circle dot of Pigskin's reflector gunsight. David punched the firing button on the control column, sending a stream of tracers arcing into the Hun. The Hurricane shuddered as the sharp chatter of the 303s sent eight grayish-white streams of tracers streaking into the tail section of the Messerschmitt.

David jinxed left and right on the rudders spreading his pattern of 303s all around the ME-109. Acrid fumes from the burning gunpowder stung David's nose. The smell of the burned powder made his blood race. The ME-109's rudder disintegrated. Pieces off the Messerschmitt came flying back. Engine oil splattered David's windscreen. The German pulled back on the elevators pointing his nose up. His tail snapped off, narrowly missing David.

David looked around for Swede. An ME-109 trailing smoke rolled, twisted and tried to evade Swede. Swede closed on the Hun, firing another long burst into the stricken craft. The Messerschmitt exploded in a ball of fire. Swede disappeared in the firestorm.

David heard a whoop over the R/T, "This one's for the Bull!" Chief was attacking again. David rolled left in time to see Chief pull up from his attack on a Heinkel. The HE-111 was trailing white smoke, a hit in the radiator or coolant line. The Heinkel started a turn towards the French coast, but the engine seized and caught fire.

Joker dove on a Heinkel formation from the opposite side. The Chief rolled out of his overhead loop, diving in on the attack. A perfect scissors action, attacking from both sides. David turned, looking for Swede and felt his left wing jerk. Long jagged rips suddenly appeared. Tracers glowed like little balls of fire as they flashed past his canopy. Oh shit, he thought, my new kite!

David jerked his Hurricane around in a hard left turn. He looked back and could see the ME-109 turning inside of him. He snapped the Hurricane hard to the right, rolling upside down and sucked the elevator back into his lap. He chopped the power and rolled out. The German had disappeared.

"TALLYHO, Pigskin flight. Squadron Leader Brent Simpson here. We're still a few clicks out and low. What is your situation?"

"We're having a turkey shoot! 'Bout time you guys showed up." Must've stopped for tea, David thought. "Come up from below 'em," David directed. "We'll keep'em busy on top."

Tracers flashed by, inches over David's head. He slammed his Hurricane hard to the left, his head on a swivel checking the sky for the attackers. A pair of ME-109s dove on him from above. David jammed his throttle through the gate. Maximum speed, limited to five minutes, but who had time to count?

David hauled back on the elevators with both hands. He felt the blood rush from his head; his vision blurred. G forces jammed him down on his seat pack parachute. He punched the rudder to the floor, rolling the

24 *The Last Mission*

Hurricane out, attacking head-on. The lead ME-109 grew rapidly in his windshield. Lights flashed from the Messerschmitt's wings. The Hun was firing on him.

David jinxed his Hurricane out of the incoming line of fire and attacked. He stomped his left rudder to the floor then the right rudder, slamming his ailerons and elevators against their stops. David left them little to shoot at while pressing his attack. His reflector sight swung across the first attacker. The ME-109 filled the bar spacing and David squeezed his firing button. The Hurricane shuddered as four machine guns fired from each wing. Eight streams of white death, a hundred bullets a second, converged on the Messerschmitt. Still, David held his firing button down. The burning cordite seemed to fill the cockpit as though it had nowhere else to go. His nose and throat stung from the pungent odor.

For a moment, he felt the chill of death, like a cold hand clutching his heart. This is it, he thought, I'm dead. That's not supposed to happen. A vision of his mother and father flashed through his mind in a fraction of a second. Adrenalin erupted in his veins, and he fought off the chilling fear of death. He was a survivor, a Sioux descendant of a tribe of survivors, a fighter.

David put his head down. All he could see was the Hun's aircraft in his windscreen. He held his firing button down, but his guns were silent. He jabbed the elevator forward. There was a loud bang. His Hurc shuddered from the impact. His canopy shattered in a shower of glass. He'd grazed the belly of the Messerschmitt. David felt the controls. Everything worked but the rudder. The Rolls-Royce engine was vibrating violently. The Hurricane was shaking like a dog coming out of the water. David pulled the throttle back, and the vibration eased. His canopy was gone; broken glass littered the cockpit. The wind whistled into the cockpit. His headset had been torn off and lay on the floor. He cut his hand groping for it. "This is the Pigskin. I'm out of ammo and have a little damage. Heading back to base. My engine's running pretty rough. Don't know if I'll make it."

"Joker here, with Chief. Got you in sight. We'll escort you back. Where's the Swede?"

"I don't know," said David. "He was firing on a Messerschmitt, cutting it to pieces. It blew up. He just disappeared in the firestorm."

They flew alongside and examined David's damaged Hurricane. "Boy, oh boy. Are you in trouble," chirped Joker.

"What's the problem?" David tried to smile as he looked through the shattered canopy at his two teammates flying one on each wing. "We got the touchdown! What else counts?"

"Wait'll that fitter gets ahold of you?" Chief imitated Mac's chortle.

"I'm losing altitude; may have to bail out. The engine's running rough. I can't use any more power or it'll tear itself from the plane." David began looking for emergency landing fields in case the engine seized.

"Biggin Hill control," Joker called. "This is Pigskin flight coming in on a wing and a prayer."

"Pigskin flight, what's your position and damage?" questioned the control.

"We're all three sucking air and one's losing power. He may have to bail out or put'er in a field," said Joker.

"Pigskin flight, control here. We have you in sight. The wind is right down the field. You're cleared to land straight in. Crash trucks are standing by."

"Oh shit," muttered Chief. He never was one for words. Just short expressions. "How dry I am," he sang over the R/T. "This kite glides like a brick!"

"Hang in there, Chief," Joker called. "You can make the airdrome."

"Not today, ol' buddy. Didja ever notice how small a field is when you get right down to it. Shit. Save me a cold one. See you at The Station," Chief said as he broke away.

"Joker, I'm not going to make the airdrome!" called David. "I'm barely in the air as it is."

"Hey, Pigskin. Try that ol' leap frog trick you showed me. Dive 'er down and pick up a little speed. Then, yank 'er up and hop over that tree line."

"Sure as hell was easy in practice. I won't have any power to save my butt if it doesn't work," David called.

"It's just another quarterback scramble," coached Joker from above. "Let's see if you can dance your way through that line of tacklers coming at you?"

"This is it! The last play of the game!" David dove his stricken craft, sacrificing his remaining altitude for a little more air speed. His bird responded sluggishly, almost grudgingly. The last row of trees leaped out at him. "That is a damn tall tree," called David. His voice sounded a couple of octaves higher than normal. "Here goes nothing!"

He pulled back on the stick and the nose responded immediately, like a fighter. David struggled over the trees on the verge of a stall. He jerked his flaps in full and dropped the nose to keep from stalling. Gear down, David dropped out of the sky, hitting the field and bouncing back in the air. David sucked the stick back into his lap. The Hurricane bounced again, then stayed solidly on the ground. "Touchdown," he shouted. The Hurc rolled to a stop at the side of the field. Joker landed down the field. David sat in his shattered cockpit, shaking. First Duffy and the third pilot in their vic -- Christ, I didn't even know his name, now Swede. Shit, it could just as well have been any one of us.

"Davie, me boy. Yea all right?" Came a familiar voice.

"What's all the noise about?" David smiled shakily as Mac's red head poked over the edge of the broken canopy.

"Yea ah have'n ah hell of a time getting these kites back to the field now, aren't yea? How many did yea get? Where's the Swede?" Mac's smile turned to a frown as he fired questions at David without waiting for an answer.

"We're okay, but Swede didn't make it," said David. "The last I saw, he was on the tail of an ME-109 and it blew up. All I saw was a ball of fire, then I had one firing on me."

"What about yea friend?"

"Chief ran out of petrol a couple clicks from the field. He was trying to land in some farmer's field. I don't know, I was a little busy trying to get back myself."

"Hop in this hard-arsed lorry. It'll get us over to control. Yea boys tell'em you're okay and we'll go look for Chief."

The day had turned hot and muggy. The dirt road, not much more than a cart path between farms, was dry. The lorry stirred up a cloud of dirt that billowed up around them like a Dakota dust storm. Their sweaty bodies were soon caked with a crust of mud. A vineyard crowded the road on one side and a pasture of dairy cows the other. The smell of fresh manure drifted across the road. "Makes me feel like I was home on the farm," said David, taking a deep breath.

"That's the smell of gold, Laddie," said Woody. "The farmers may not be rich, mind yea, but they always eat the best."

"That's the farm on the left, Woody. The one with the blue-roofed barn," Joker said from the back of the lorry. "There's Chief's Hurc standing on its nose. Now, how in the hell'd he do that?"

"Looks like the lad hit a ditch at the end of the field," said Woody. He was calculating the work he'd have to do before the Hurc would fly again.

"Come on," called David jumping from the still-moving lorry. "Chief might'a got hurt!"

They heard Chief's yell from the far side of the Hurricane. He was bent low dancing on first one foot then the other around the damaged Hurc.

"What'n the 'ell's he doing?" asked Woody. "Come on, boys: the lad's hurt'n worse'n we thought."

"Whoa there, Woody. That's a Sioux war dance. When my brother's wielding that twelve-inch Bowie knife, you don't want to get too close." David said, hanging on the back of Woody's jacket.

"What'n the 'ell's he doing with that knife?" asked Woody as he crawled back into the lorry.

"Chief and I both carry a Bowie knife strapped to our legs when flying. Our grandfather taught us to survive with it and nothing else," explained David, letting fly with a blood curdling scream of his own.

"Two scalps," yelled Chief as they approached.

"Come on," shouted Joker over their war cries. "I'm getting so thirsty, my throat is swelling up."

"Let's head 'er down ta The Station, boys," called Woody as he ground the lorry into gear. "'Bout time yea met the old man and got initiated proper like."

"What's the old man like?" said David. "Everyone talks about The Station and the old man, so what's the big deal?"

"Hap's one of the greatest fighter pilots ever flew. Fought in the Great War. Sent more Krauts back to the fatherland than all yea hotshots put together. From the way he talks, he was a real hell raiser in his time. And I'm not ah doubt'n ah word of it." Woody pulled the lorry to a stop in a cloud of dust. "Here we are boys." Woody led the trio into The Station. The front was covered with weathered boards and looked like an old barn.

David followed Woody into the darkened interior and stopped just inside the door, letting his eyes adjust to the dark. Chief and Joker crowded in behind and followed Woody up to the bar.

"Hap. Drag three more mugs out," ordered Woody, banging his hand down on the bar. "Got yea some Yank plane jockeys to join the club."

They stepped up onto tall stools and bellied up to a long narrow bar. The bar was polished mahogany running the full length of the room. It looked like a mirror. Someone had spent hours polishing it and working to keep it that way. Off the end of the bar was a back room with a snooker table and a dozen booths. The room was dark and smoke-filled with only a single light over the snooker table.

Photos and emblems from different squadrons adorned the walls. On the end, in a place of honor, His Majesty's picture hung, with a light shining on it. A model of a Hurricane hung from the ceiling, nose down in a steep dive. A dozen models of fighters from the Great War were scattered around the bar like a trophy room.

28 The Last Mission

The bar stools had real leather seats, and the front of the bar had a padded leather lip for the patrons to rest their arms on. A polished brass rail ran around the outside of the bar for a foot rest. A quiet hum, like a plane high overhead, filled the room as pilots sat huddled in quiet conversation. All eyes turned toward Woody and the three new pilots as the bartender's sharp voice shattered the tranquility.

"I take it they've paid their dues, qualifying for membership?" questioned Hap Wiggins, the bartender. A battered fatigue cap sat askew on his head with the bill turned up. Hap cocked his head looking down his hawked nose at them. A three-day stubble covered his wrinkled face as he scrutinized his subjects. A twinkle in his eye gave him away before he turned for the mugs.

The conversation began to dominate the bar as the patrons focused their attention on Hap, Woody and the three Americans.

"What'll we do to qualify?" David asked.

Hap popped his upper false plate out with a finger, inspecting it for some irritant. He then slipped it back in, wiping his hands ceremoniously on his apron before he continued. "When you bag your first Kraut, you get your own personal mug." He pulled three mugs out from under the bar, checking them for flaws then handed one to David. A hush fell over the bar as all eyes turned watching the new club members. "Well? Is it okay or not?" questioned Hap with a growl. One eye seemed to bug out of its socket, observing David like a British bulldog.

David turned it over inspecting it reverently. "Hell, no!" He handed it back to Hap. "It's empty."

"Well, I'll be damned!" Hap muttered, turning to fill the three new mugs. A cheer went up around the bar when Hap placed the three mugs of ale on the counter.

Woody raised his mug and called for quiet. "Hear yea, hear yea, hear yea! His Majesty's court is now in session. 'Tis time fer the mug naming ceremony." Woody strutted back and forth, the full length of the bar. He seemed to swell with authority, his height was no longer a factor. Everyone sat at attention -- honoring the occasion. "I, as head fitter, and duly-appointed knight of His Majesty's court, now dub you, David Hampton, half English, half-blooded Sioux warrior...claims his people, the Sioux, were the toughest warriors right up next to them Appatcheys...to be known hereafter as 'Pigskin.'"

A chorus of hear, hear's went up around the bar and every member took a deep long drink of ale from his mug.

"So noted," said Hap as he wrote the new name for inscription on David's mug on a bar pad. "What's your insignia, Pigskin?" asked Hap. He used David's new name. The only name that would be used at The Station.

"A football," David answered immediately.

"What the hell's a football?" stammered Hap, a blank expression on his face.

"Back in Minnesota, I play football." David said. "They call me Pigskin 'cause a football's made from pigs' skin."

"Oh, well. That explains it," said Hap, turning with a puzzled expression on his weathered face.

"Hold it down," shouted Woody, trying to quiet the noise in the bar. "Naming court's still in session. Next Yank candidate, Jimmy Water, is a cousin. Ee's called 'Chief.'" Everyone raised their mugs and confirmed the naming with a swig of ale. "What shall be yea coat-of-arms?" questioned Woody.

An ear splitting scream came from Chief, the Sioux, as he brandished his twelve-inch Bowie knife overhead. "I'm after enemy scalps," he said and laid his Bowie knife on the bar. "This is my insignia. When the Huns see it, they'll know it is me coming for them. They'll turn and run in fear."

Hap's smile split his face as he made due note of the new inscription.

Again Woody had to shout down the celebrants. "Last, but not least, I give you Ralph Burton. Commonly called Joker. What, may I ask, will be your insignia?"

"Hell, that's easy," said the Chief. "It's a Joker. Always pulling practical jokes."

"So be it!" declared Hap, taking note of the last inscription.

A cheer chorused throughout the bar. All mugs were raised in salute and promptly chug-a-lugged, a ritual confirming the naming and welcoming new members.

"Hey, Hap. What are all those mugs upside down on the top shelf, back of the bar?" questioned Chief. The shelf was a weathered board a foot below the ceiling and running the length of the bar. It was lined with inscribed mugs turned upside down. Many were covered with dust.

"They're members of the top shelf club," said Hap quietly. "They've flown their 'Last Mission.'" Hap turned, raising his mug in a silent salute to the departed heros.

A deathly quiet came over the bar as each member raised his mug in a silent salute to their departed comrades.

"Holy Shit," muttered Joker. " There must be more than fifty of 'em!"

30 The Last Mission

"Yesterday we put Duffy's mug on the top shelf," said Woody quietly. "That makes fifty-seven so far!"

London

David stood outside alone, waiting for the train. A cold wet fog blanketed the English countryside. He turned his collar up to ward off the chill. The crowded, smoke-filled station was too confining; he liked the outdoors and fresh air. He thought of the last letter from his father telling of his brothers out working the farm. He longed to be back in Minnesota. If he were back home, he'd probably be taking Bettsie out to a movie tonight. Well, that was history, a passing stage in his childhood. He was a man now and had put childish things behind him. He'd killed. Not in anger, but still he'd killed and that bothered him.

David heard a clicking on the tracks and the hissing and chugging of the steam engine approaching. A single head lamp beamed a narrow pencil light through the blackout hood. It glowed eerily in the misty shroud. Puffs of coal smoke belched from the behemoth, hanging heavily in the moist air and stinging his nose. The screeching of steel as the engineer applied the brakes made him shiver. The locomotive crept by, wheezing and puffing like a tired old man, and came to a stop at the station. An oiler jumped down with a long-spouted oil can and a hand full of rags and began oiling the slides on the engine.

A few passengers disembarked and a black-suited conductor called, "Boooard." Everyone rushed from the warm station house, pushing and shoving. A narrow aisle ran down one side of the car leading to enclosed compartments. Each compartment had its own door with straight-backed, hard bench seats facing each other. David found one that wasn't filled and managed to sit next to a sooty window. It seemed like everyone was talking at the same time, and he only caught parts of conversations.

"Do you actually believe they're going to attack London, ol' man?"

"As I see it, Professor, it's not a matter of if, it's a matter of what day. I recall a line written by Kipling, 'Stand up and take the war, the Hun is at the Gate.'"

The train lurched, moving slowly from the station. David wanted to see some of the countryside, the farms, but could only see a few feet in the dense fog. The stench of sulfuric coal smoke permeated the passenger cars.

31

The rhythmic clicking of wheels on the tracks increased in speed. The swaying of the cars and the warm compartment soon lulled David into a fitful sleep.

Approaching Victoria Station, the locomotive's shrill whistle woke David with a start. The train followed a maze of tracks, switching from one to the other. Through the dirty window, he saw the board shacks alongside the tracks slip slowly by as they crept into the station. The cars bumped into each other until they finally lurched to a stop. The people outside moved across the platform like ghosts, stepping down from the cars and disappearing into the fog. He picked up his kit bag and stepped down from the passenger car. Instantly he was caught up in the drifting crowd. Everyone seemed to be going someplace in a hurry. The noise level was like a vic of Hurricanes starting their takeoff roll. The pack of passengers rose en masse climbing the wet stone steps from the tube station. Cabs honked, jockeying for position next to the curb.

"David! David Hampton!"

David heard someone shouting from the crowd. "Spike. What are you doing here?"

"I came to pick you up. Chief rang me up and told me what train you'd be on. I figured you could use some blockers to find your way through this mess."

"Thanks, Spike. I don't know where I'll be staying!"

"How about the Union? It's modestly priced and friendly," suggested Raymond. "Check in and we'll go over to the Eagle Club for something to eat and a couple of drinks. That's where most of the American servicemen hang out. It's the only place in London where you can get a hamburger and a coke."

David smiled, "That's American! A hamburger and coke. We'd always pick up the girls after a game and go out for a burger and a coke. Maybe London won't be so bad after all. I'd better write the address down so I can find it again."

"The Eagle Club is at 28 Charring Cross Road," said Spike. "There's free cigarettes, donated by tobacco companies or the Red Cross, for our American boys. Volunteers from several women's groups in London help run the club. You may meet some very respectable ladies. Here's the Union hotel. I'll wait while you check in."

David took the steps two at a time. Entering the hotel, he looked around the lobby. It was like a sitting room with big stuffed chairs and carpeted floor. From the high ceiling hung a chandelier made of thousands of pieces of cut glass. Plants adorned the room and the outer walls were built-in book cases. A small table, with a copy of the London Times, stood adjacent to each lounge chair. The room was trimmed with dark mahogany, feeling warm and friendly. He saw the registration desk, straightened his uniform, and walked over. "Would you have a single room available for two nights?" David still felt conspicuous in his R.A.F. uniform.

"Yes." The brunette said, smiling up at David. Her voice was soft, almost a whisper. "Please sign our guest register. Our serviceman's rate is twenty shillings."

David signed the register, blushing as he looked up and into the girl's eyes. They seemed inviting and reminded him of his former girlfriend back in Minnesota. Her rich brown hair was sleek and hung to the middle of her back. Her eyes were deep brown and seemed to sparkle when she looked up at him. He finally stammered, "I'll just drop my kit; I've someone waiting."

She handed David the key to his room. Her hand lingered over his momentarily. He felt a tingle at the contact. It was something he'd forgotten about or had tried to shut out of his life. "Up the stairs and the third door on the right, David." She smiled warmly. It almost felt like home.

Stepping outside into the damp air, David breathed a sigh of relief. Maybe there was some normalcy in all the craziness of war. "All set," said David, out of breath from having run up and down the stairs.

"Sounds like you just ran the hundred yard dash," Spike observed.

"I met a girl at the registration desk. She was so friendly, I chatted with her for a couple of minutes. I told her I had someone waiting in the car, or I might have been there yet." David's eyes sparkled, glowing from the encounter.

"Looks like London's going to set well with you, David. We'll be at the Eagle club shortly so save some of your energy. You'll need it before the night's over," Spike said.

"This is the first chance I've had to come into London. We've been busy training in the Hurricane," David replied.

"Not to mention having seen action twice in a week," said Spike, turning the conversation back to flying. "What's that make, four kills now?"

"Yeah, and two wrecked planes. Besides it was just dumb luck. We lost three men from our squadron, Spike. It could just as easily have been me, or Chief, or Joker."

"Remember the game, David. There can only be one winner. You're still here to fly again another day. Winning is the only important thing, no matter what the cost. Remember that game we played against Madison?"

"You mean the one in the snowstorm? The one where you broke your shoulder, Spike, diving into the end zone?"

"That's the one. Only my shoulder was broken a couple of plays earlier. I had them tape me up tight. Didn't know it was broken at the time. It just hurt like hell. It was the last play of the game and we were down by three. The blitz was on. The quarterback made a line call. On the snap of the ball, I jumped two steps ahead and turned. The pass was thrown. The ball was in my hands as I turned. It was snowing so hard, I don't think anyone actually saw the pass." Spike paused, thinking back, "When I turned down field, I had forty yards to go for a touchdown. It looked so far. I stood there for a second, then took off running. All the defenders were behind me except the two deep men. I ran right at them, angling to the right. I faked a jog further to the right then cut hard left and slipped in the snow, wrenching my broken shoulder. I eluded them by rolling further left then cutting back right, literally diving into the end zone."

"I was at that game. Chief, Joker, and I drove down in my dad's car. I would never have known you had a broken shoulder after watching that play you made. It was snowing so hard, the roads were closed, and we had to stay overnight in St. Paul. We read about your broken shoulder in the paper the next day. I figured you broke it when you dove into the end zone," David said.

Spike smiled, "Remember, David, no matter what it takes, winning is the only thing that counts."

"I was at the game, remember?" David said with a deep admiration for the writer.

"Here's the Eagle Club, David. You go in and find a table. I'll park the car."

David stepped out of the warm car. The damp fog crept into his jacket as if he'd left it open, sending a chill through him. Shivering, he stepped quickly through the door into the club. He gave his coat and cap to the check girl. The music from the club was playing, "There'll be Blue Birds over the White Cliffs of Dover, tomorrow, just you wait and see." The only Blue Birds he'd seen were the Luftwaffe shooting at him, thought David.

"May I help you, sir?" a young lady asked.

David turned, surprised by the woman's musical voice. The fragrance of her perfume and her closeness left him lightheaded. He stood, stammering, "Yes. I -- uh -- I'm waiting for a friend. Could we get a table?"

"Sure can. Follow me. You're an American?" she asked as they headed for a vacant table near the bar.

David couldn't help but notice her well-rounded figure as he followed closely. "Yes, I guess I talk kind-ah funny," he said, apologetically.

She laughed and her voice was definitely English, though it had an Irish brogue. "We get a lot of Americans in the Eagle Club. It's kind of a gathering place for all the Yanks. I'm Millie Bolfriend." She turned, facing David and held her hand toward him. He took her hand gently in his as though it was a fragile piece of porcelain. It was soft and warm and he blushed, embarrassed, but he still held her hand. "I'm in the WAAFs and fill in as volunteer worker in my off-duty hours. We all do our part to help the war effort, you know."

"David Hampton," he stammered, still holding her hand. She had a sparkle in her voice when she spoke and David wondered if there was such a thing as love at first sight. She had round freckle-covered cheeks. Her nose was small and slightly turned up and her lips were moist from a nervous habit of licking them. Her strawberry-blonde hair came only to her shoulders. The accent and reddish hair made David think of Woody, but it must have been coincidental. He felt foolish asking, "You wouldn't be related to Mac Bolfriend, would you?"

She stopped, turned, and looked him directly in the eyes. Her face was shining happily, inches from his. "Yes! He's my brother. How is it that you know Mac?"

David was momentarily stunned, then he laughed. It had to be the war, he thought. "It's a small world. Mac's my fitter. I'm stationed at Biggin Hill, flying with the R.A.F."

Raymond spotted them, still standing together, holding hands. He worked his way around the patrons. "Hi, Millie. I see you've met David."

"Mr. Burrel. What a surprise," said Millie, her face reddening as she released David's hand. "When sergeant Hampton said he had a friend -- well, I thought it was a, ah..." she stood blushing.

"Millie. Here's your golden opportunity. David just happens to be as unattached as you can get. And it's time you got back in circulation for real. Just working all the time is no good. You've got to get out and live a little!"

David, crimsoned faced, finally found his voice. "Maybe when you finish work. I mean, I could buy you a drink or go dancing? Whatever, I would like to see you again."

Millie's freckles stood out on her flushed face. "I, I don't know, ah. I'm afraid I'm not really very good company, with the war and all that's happened."

"I'm a good listener," David responded. "Besides, I need someone to show me around London."

"Well, we'll see," Millie said. "I'm off the duty at twenty-hundred hours. That is, if you'll still be here."

"That's great, Millie. I can keep him occupied until then," said Raymond. "David and I, we've got a lot to talk about, including football."

"Ta-ta. See you later Mr. Hampton. Nice to see you again Mr. Burrel," Her smile turned to a frown as she turned and walked back to her post.

"You know, Davie, that's the first time I've seen her happy since the accident," said Raymond.

David slid into his seat, a puzzled look on his face. "What accident?"

Raymond had a strained look on his face. "Millie was engaged to a squadron leader from another base. Really a swell chap. I became very good friends with them both. Binkie's squadron got into a good mix up with the Huns somewhere around Dieppe. Binkie was shot up pretty bad; his Spitfire took a pounding. On his R/T he said his fuselage fuel tank had taken a hit and fuel was leaking into the cockpit. The engine was overheating and he was coaxing it along just to stay in the air. His chum, flying alongside, told him to jump, but his canopy was jammed. The chaps in his vic escorted him to the first airfield across the Channel. A little grass field at Hawkinge."

"Millie was on duty at Fighter Group Headquarters that day and talked to him on the R/T. The last transmission she heard was, 'I have the field in sight and am landing. See you at the Church, my love.'"

Raymond struggled to find the rest of the words. "His Spitfire had only one gear leg down. He hit the ground hard and the gear collapsed. Fire broke out instantly. A crash crew raced to his rescue, but the plane was an inferno. They watched helplessly as Binkie struggled to open his jammed canopy." Raymond sipped at his ale. "She's a spunky one. This is the first time I've seen her happy and smiling since Binkie's accident. David, I think you're just what the doctor ordered."

"I don't know about that, Raymond, she just seems like such a nice lady. So easy to talk to, bubbly and happy -- I never would have guessed!" David thought of the pilots that were killed from his squadron, but they were only names. He could hardly remember their faces. Except for Duffy.

"Tell me about your family," Raymond asked.

"My mom's a full-blooded Sioux, very strict and proper," said David. "Pop's English, maybe that's why I kind of feel at home here; so that makes me a half-breed. I have two brothers and three sisters, all younger. Susie is the baby. She'd always come and sit on my lap with one of her story books. I must have read each of them a hundred times, but she never tired of hearing them again."

"Sounds like they looked up to you for direction and comfort," said Raymond. "Big brothers are like that you know, especially when they're high school football stars."

"I never thought about it before. Mom was always so busy in the house cooking and cleaning and mending clothes and Dad worked outside in the fields or the barn. Dad and I had some long discussions out in the barn when I told him I was going to England and enlisting in the R.A.F."

"He didn't want you to go?" asked Raymond.

"Not at first. I wanted to fly more than anything, and this was a chance to get some real flying experience. Indians don't get a chance like that back home, even half-breeds. And don't forget the pay." David laughed at that. "Besides, being half English, I feel like England is my second home. Dad was a landed immigrant, so he understood. He was in the Great War and after that he came to the United States and became a citizen."

"A fighter pilot sounds pretty romantic, but it's also very danger-ous." Raymond made notes as he spoke. "Of course, the flying is the prime reason for your being here. Tell me how it came about."

David paused as he thought back to his first flight. "It started with the flying. When we first got our licenses, no one would hire us, especially being half Indian. I tried to justify my going. When Pops and I sat down to talk about it, I told him flying was what I wanted more than anything!"

"What about Ralph and Jimmy?"

"When I told them I was going to fly with the R.A.F., they had their bags packed. We've been together even before we started school. They wanted to fly just as much as I did."

"Did you ever consider that you would be killing people or that you could be killed?" Raymond asked.

"Pop and I talked about that too. Pop was in the Great War. Funny though, he never would talk about the killing. It was always a possibility. I guess I never realized what he was talking about until Duffy's Hurc blew up. Here one second and gone the next. The young German I shot was killed trying to bail out; I wonder if he was married or had kids or a girl...I mean, whatever he'd had, it's all over now, only...." David chewed quietly on his hamburger and sipped his coke. "You know Raymond, this is the first burger and coke I've had since we left the United States three months ago. I never realize how much I missed them."

"David, I think duty of another kind is beckoning you" said Raymond, putting his notes in his brief case. "If you'll excuse me, I'll leave you two youngsters alone. I have a lot of typing to finish up my next article for the Post."

"Hi, Mr. Hampton. I see you're still here," greeted Millie with a wide smile. "Do you like to dance?"

"I'd like that, Miss Bolfriend. I must warn you though, I'm all feet. And, you can call me David."

"In that case, David, I'll be watching out for my feet," she laughed. "Let's head for the Dorchester. It's only a short walk, and I feel like some exercise and fresh air, and no more of this Miss Bolfriend stuff; it's Millie."

"Okay, Millie," David laughed as he helped her with her coat. "Better wrap your scarf around; it's foggy and damp out. It cuts right through."

"You're just not used to our weather, David," she said.

Outside it was an inky black overcast night. The city under blackout seemed somewhat sinister. The fog surrounded and seemed to swallow them up as they walked quietly. David, shivering, jammed his hands deep in the pockets of his flight jacket. Millie walked close by his side in the dark, though keeping her distance. Her steps were short and fast, and David had to stretch to keep up. "Raymond told me about your fiancee's accident. I'm sorry." David said, unsure of what to say.

They walked in silence for a distance before Millie answered. "Binkie was something really special." Her voice choked. "Right from the first time I met him. Have you ever felt that someone you saw for the first time was the one meant for you? We felt a oneness right from the first. He made me laugh. Everything we did was fun. When we were apart, I'd dream and wait for that moment when we would be together again. Oh," she gasped. "Here I am, boring you."

"No, please go on. I'm a good listener. You have such a beautiful voice, and I do want to know more about you," David said turning and smiling at her in the dark.

"Only if you promise to stop me when you get tired of my incessant chatter," Millie replied.

David stopped and placed his hands on her shoulders. "Millie, I don't want you to ever stop talking, just being here with you...I mean, I felt that spark when I first saw you tonight. I don't know what it was, but when you were talking about meeting Binkie, I felt the same way."

"David," she stopped, then continued. "Don't get me wrong, but I didn't feel any sparks. I've been so lonely. With Binkie gone, the whole world crashed in around me. I don't want to get involved with anyone right now. I just need a friend to talk with. To laugh with, and have a few drinks with, and go dancing, and dinners, and maybe even the theater."

David lowered his voice. "Well, little missie, I'm just the one to laugh with and have a few drinks with now and then. I don't dance too gracefully, but if you'll put up with this farmer, I'll dance until you cry uncle." She looked up, smiling. "And furthermore, I think dinner tomorrow night and the theater would be in order."

"So, David, is this a date or what?"

"Well, little missie," he said, "it's a date, with a friend."

"Okay, friend! Shake on it," Millie said.

Her warm, small hand slipped into his big calloused hand, and he felt a flush of excitement he'd never known. When he felt her hand pull back, he released it reluctantly. "I guess we better get on to the dance and out of this cold," David said, poking his hands back in the pockets of his flight jacket.

"David...I have a feeling that something very dreadful is going to happen. I don't know what, but ever since Binkie's accident, I've had this feeling."

"I think I know what you mean. Until last week we hadn't seen action. All of a sudden we were attacked. My flight leader and wing man were killed. I've never intentionally harmed anyone in my life. Now I've killed four Germans and maybe more. They may have been just like us. Maybe they were married and had families. Now they're dead, because of me." David felt relieved at having someone he could confide in. Someone who would listen. "I shouldn't be putting my burden off on you, Millie. I'm sorry."

"Don't be, David. That's what friends are for. You listened to my silly chatter. You don't have to feel guilty. They were attacking you. Everyone thinks it's just a matter of time now before Hitler's planes and troops will invade London. A lot of people will be killed if that happens. Here we are, Luv. Enough of this serious talk. We're going dancing."

David held the door of the Dorchester open for Millie. "Hey, Millie! Someone shut out the lights."

"Feel your way along, Luv. Just be careful how you feel!" They laughed, groping toward a dim light shining around the edge of the blackout curtain.

"Wow," said David. "It's so bright, just like the football field when they turn the spotlights on for a night game."

"You look absolutely smashing, David. Your cheeks are all red. A good match with my hair, don't you think?" Millie asked, as she shook her head scattering water droplets from her hair.

The ballroom was large with a high cathedral ceiling and tapestries hanging from the walls. The center floor was filled with couples dancing. Tables lined the sides of the room and the orchestra sat up on a raised platform in one corner playing, 'I Don't Want to Set the World on Fire.'

David said, "Wouldn't be a bad idea on a cold night like this to have a few fires going." David helped Millie off with her coat and pulled a chair out for her.

"Such a gentleman you are, David. I may learn to enjoy your friendship, even if you are a Yank," she added with a grin.

"Shall we dance?" David smiled back, extending his hand in invitation. "This is one of my favorites." David placed his hand lightly on Millie's waist as she stepped into his arms. The smell of her perfume left him a little heady. He held her closer and their bodies bonded naturally into one, moving in harmony with the music. Millie snuggled her head against his chest. He crooned softly to the music. "It seems we stood and talked like this before, we looked at each other in the same way then, but I can't remember where or when. The clothes you're wearing are the clothes you wore, the smile you are smiling you were smiling then, but I can't remember where or when. Some things that happen for the first time, seem to be happening again. And so it seems that we have met before, and laughed before, and loved before, but who knows where or when?"

The music stopped, but they stood quietly, and David felt Millie's arm tighten around him. "I know the feeling, David," she looked up at him. "I wish we could stay just like this forever." They turned, with an arm around each other and strolled back to their table, each lost in thought.

"What are you thinking, David?" Millie asked smiling, but with a serious look on her face.

David seemed to swell with pride, then dropped to his deep bass voice, "Well, missie, it's like this." Then his tone changed to a serious note. "It's funny. That song I mean. It's like I've known you before. I can talk to you. I mean, I feel that I can tell you anything. There are no secrets between us."

"I know what you're trying to say, David. Since Binkie's accident, I've shut out the world. I've been existing from day to day and everything was closing in around me. I don't know what you're doing to me, David, but tonight for the first time, I've felt alive. I don't want it to end." She looked up at David with tears in her eyes.

He placed his hand gently on her cheek and brushed away the tears. "It doesn't have to end, Millie. Life goes on and so can we. I'll always be your friend, to listen when you need it. With a shoulder to cry on if necessary and to hold you when you want."

"I don't think so, David. When you leave, I'll be alone again. This is only a fairy tale. A dream. When I awaken, you'll be gone and the bombs will be falling. I hate this war. It's eating our guts out."

"Millie, I can't promise you that something won't happen to me, but as long as I'm alive I'll be here whenever you need me. When I'm not here, I'll phone and when I can't phone, I'll write so you'll have me with you always," David said.

"Oh, listen. That's Bing Crosby. Let's dance."

The band played "Moonlight Becomes You," and they danced. It was a slow dance and they clung to each other, like survivors of a shipwreck having found a life raft. Millie laid her head on his chest and David cuddled his cheek against her hair. The band played the closing song and David sang softly, "We'll meet again, don't know where, don't know when. But, I know we'll meet again some sunny day."

"David, let's not let this evening end. I don't want to be alone," said Millie as they swayed more than danced to the sound of the music.

"What would you like to do, Millie?"

"Talk! I've got a bottle of scotch at my flat. Would you like to have a drink, and we can talk?" She'd never had anyone but Binkie up to her flat before. Would he think her too forward? "No strings attached, David!" She added hastily.

"What little time we have, I'd like to spend with you, Millie. No strings." He held the coat for her.

She looked up into his eyes. Her radiant face said more than words. She put her arm in his and they headed toward the blackout curtain. The London fog no longer felt so cold.

"It's a wee bit of a walk, Luv, if you don't mind. I kind of like walking in the fog at night. It hides the hurtful things. You know what I mean?"

"Yes, I think I do. It's like being in another time and place, but since I met you tonight, Millie, I've felt that way without the fog."

"That sounds like a lot of rubbish, but please don't stop. What will you do after the War, David?"

"I want to go back to school and finish my college degree. I want to get my law degree and go into business. What about you, Millie?" David asked.

"That sounds so wonderful. I can close my eyes and picture you with a nice suit going to work to defend the innocent, a knight in shining armor on a white stallion. And a beautiful farm home in the country with a white picket fence and lots of kids running around playing.... Whoa, here's my flat, David, almost walked by. Not much to look at I'm afraid, compared to your big farms and houses in America."

"As long as it's warm and dry, you don't need much until you marry and settle down."

The flat was nondescript, like every other, and different only in the number on the front. Millie unlocked the outside door, and they slipped around a blanket that had been hung over the entryway to block any light. They turned up a steep stairway and began climbing three flights of stairs. Dim lights showed in the hallways, and all the windows were covered.

The flat was small, two rooms. The kitchen was in one corner with a table and chairs in the middle. Against the far wall sat a chesterfield of unknown vintage and a small wooden rocker. There were no knickknacks, pictures or things people always seem to collect. It was Spartan, and felt empty, evidence that Millie spent little time here.

"The facilities are down the hall, David. Just lock the door, Luv. There's just the one for each floor."

"Can I help you with something?" David asked.

"Would you be a dear and hang our coats up? There's hangers just to the left in the bedroom."

The bedroom was also bare except for a bed and one straight-backed wood chair painted white. Next to the bed was a night stand with a small lamp on it and a picture of a pilot in uniform standing next to a Spitfire. David looked at the smiling face and called, "Is this a picture of Binkie?"

Millie stepped into the room with two glasses of scotch, handing one to David. She picked up the picture from the night stand and inspected the smiling, happy face of a man standing beside a Spitfire. "That's Binkie. He loved to fly, more than he loved anything else. Even more than me, I think," she laughed nervously.

"I would have liked to have flown with him. He looks so cocky and full of confidence. I'll bet he handled that Spitfire like a maestro." David stood next to her admiring the man and machine.

"You men are all the same," said Millie with a laugh. "Planes, planes and more planes. That's all you guys talk about. I want to know more about you, David, and what's this football thing Raymond was talking about?" She laid Binkie's picture face down on the night table and took David's hand and led him to the chesterfield where they sat close, but facing each other.

The dawn came suddenly. They hadn't noticed it getting lighter until the sun shone around the edges of the blackout curtain hung over the window. "David!" Millie said as she jumped up and removed the curtain from the window, "We talked all through the night. I never realized how late it was. We really must get some sleep, you know."

"It's going to look scandalous my leaving your flat this time of the morning," he smiled, standing and stretching.

"Don't worry, Luv. It'll give the old fuddy-duddys something to wag their tongues about." She stood, holding his flight jacket.

He slipped the jacket on and cocked his hat on his head. "Well, missie, when shall I pick you up?"

"How about noon, Luv? We'll have some crumpets and tea and I'll show you about London." She looked up at him beaming. He bent down, his lips brushing her cheek.

"Till noon," he said and slipped out the door.

Millie was tired, but the events of the evening and the song, "Where or When," kept spinning through her head. She picked up the picture of Binkie on the night stand and tears formed in her eyes. Burying her face in the pillow, she wept. Her body shook with spasms of grief as she struggled to put her past to rest. She tossed and turned on the bed, finally drifting into an exhausted sleep.

David lay awake on the hard mattress at the Union hotel. Everything happened so fast and seemed so final. Was it fate that had brought him to England or just a coincidence? Why had Duffy and his wing-man been killed and he was allowed to live? And how did Millie fit into the scheme of things, or did she? Maybe when he went back to his base he would never see her again....

A pounding on the door woke him, and he felt as though he'd just gotten to sleep. He sat up in the bed confused, trying to remember where he was. The pounding came again and he called out, "Yes. Who's there?"

"Room service, Mr. Hampton. You asked to be awakened at eleven o'clock, sir."

"Oh, Yes. Thank you. I'm awake now." David stumbled into the bathroom and opened the shutters on the window. Bright sunlight streamed in through the window, blinding him momentarily, and he stepped back, blinking his eyes and stretched. He showered and shaved, liberally sprinkling on aftershave lotion. He never concerned himself with how he looked, but now it seemed important. Outside he hailed a cab and read the address to the driver from a slip of paper Millie had given him.

"You must be a Yank pilot?" the driver asked, glancing in his mirror.

"Yes, but how'd you know?" asked David.

"By your accent. You're not from hereabouts. Besides, the Union hotel is very popular with you Yanks. The address someone you know?"

"Well as a matter of fact, yes. A good friend, who's offered to show me around London."

"It's a great city, London. Lots of good clubs, and, needless to say, some very nice girls. Well here you are sergeant and the fare is on me. We appreciate your helping out in these bloody times. Cheery-O."

David opened the outside door to the complex with a key Millie had given him and took the steps two at a time. Almost out of breath, he tapped lightly on the door. There was no sound from inside, so he rapped his knuckles harder and it echoed in the empty hallway like someone beating on a drum. Two doors down, a head popped out of a door, then hastily retreated. David had raised his knuckles to knock again when he heard a sleepy voice within.

"Who-is-it?"

"David."

The door opened suddenly and Millie stood sleepily clutching her robe in front. "Oh my gosh. David. What time is it? My bloody clock didn't ring. Oh, I'm a mess. David, don't look at me like this," Millie stammered. "You had better come in, Luv. You can't very well stand out in the hall; all the neighbors will be talking."

"Well, missie, I think it's too late. Someone already took roll call. I'm afraid your reputation's been tarnished," David said.

"Bloody good thing. Wouldn't want them thinking I'm a virgin." The kettle of water on the stove began whistling and Millie turned to prepare the tea and crumpets. "Sorry I don't have more, Luv, but I never eat much in the morning. I must be up and about for a while before I eat." Millie sipped her tea and then lit up a cigarette. She sat cross-legged on one side of the chesterfield, her robe half covering her bare legs. "Bloody bad habit, smoking. Do you smoke, David?"

"Only cigars, and then only on rare occasions. Our football coach was dead against it. Said if he caught anyone smoking, they were off the team. So we never got started." David flushed, sitting so close to Millie with only a nightgown on.

Millie ground her cigarette out in the ash tray. Yawning she stood up stretching, "Give me five minutes, Luv, and I'll be ready."

London was exciting. From Buckingham Palace and the changing of the guards to Piccadilly Circus. Maybe it was just being with Millie. She talked perpetually and David proved a good listener. They dined and went to a theater, then danced to the wee hours of the morning.

Millie nestled her head against David's chest. They swayed to the music, clinging to each other. "David," she said, her voice almost a whisper.

"Yes."

"You'll be leaving, returning to your base in a few hours and I'm back on duty. We may not see each other again or at least for a very long time." Millie stopped and stood back looking up into his eyes. "Will you stay with me tonight, David? At the flat? I couldn't stand to be alone."

"Yes, Millie. I'll stay with you." He took her into his arms and held her close. Secure.

They walked quietly, arm in arm through the dark, damp fog, each engrossed in thought. For the first time since he'd met Millie, she seemed at a loss for words. "A penny for your thoughts."

"What?" she stammered. "What is that, David?"

"A penny for your thoughts? It's an American expression we use when someone is deep in thought."

"Well, I should think they'd be worth more than a penny," said Millie laughing. "Besides, what if they're embarrassing or obscene? Well, we'll see. Maybe I'll tell you about them later," she teased, as they turned and headed for her flat.

The stairs did not seem so long as David followed quietly, trying not to awaken the curious neighbors. Millie latched the door to the flat, and David took her coat and hung both their coats in the closet.

David slipped his shoes off and tiptoed up behind Millie as she was mixing drinks. He slipped his arms around her, and she tipped her head back, snuggling into his arms. He bent and kissed the top of her head, and she turned in his arms, stretching up on her toes, her face upturned. Her lips were poised, moist and trembling, and David met them with his own.

It was a gentle kiss, soft like a close friend's. It was a promise and yet seemed to be crying out for something. Something that was empty, lost and seeking a direction, a fulfillment. Their lips ground together answering that need.

"Wow," said Millie, resting her head on David's chest. "I poured us a couple of scotches. Let's go sit and talk." She handed him a glass and picked up her own, taking his hand in hers and walking toward the bedroom. She plopped a couple of pillows up at the head of the bed and turned the lights off, leaving only a small night light in the kitchen.

David sat on the bed resting his back against the pillows, and Millie curled up next to him sipping her drink. "Well, little missie," David drawled, "You sure are pretty sitting here. Like a rose alongside a cactus."

"Okay mister," she laughed, and sat up turning halfway to face him. "Cough up that penny."

"Well here you are," said David, digging in his pocket for the penny. He sat up a little straighter and pulled his knees up.

Millie folded her hands over her knees and rested her chin on them looking eye to eye at David. "Do you ever do things impulsively?"

"Why sure I do. That's one of the reasons I was a good quarterback. Many times I could feel that something wasn't quite right and changed a play. Most of the time I was right. The coach never questioned my judgement, even if it didn't turn out." David sipped his scotch, looking intently at Millie. "If you're having second thoughts about tonight...."

"No. It's just that, sometimes I come on too strong and scare people off."

"You don't see me running, do you?" He brushed his lips lightly against the back of her neck, exploring the texture of her skin with his tongue.

"Oh David, you keep that up and you're going to be in trouble soon."

David set his glass on the night stand beside the bed, then took Millie's glass and placed it with his. He slipped his arm under her shoulders as she stretched out alongside of him. He could feel the warmth of her breath as he leaned over her, his lips seeking hers. Millie's partly opened mouth met his, testing, teasing. Her tongue darted out probing and met his own, then they came together in a hard deep kiss. One that brought out all the deep longing. The need for each other. For the moment, it wiped out all the fear and grief each had suffered. That one passionate moment healed their open wounds, promising a new beginning.

David's hand slipped down and cupped her breast and she moaned. He kissed her neck and she turned her head. Millie unbuttoned his shirt and her hands explored his bare chest. David fumbled with the fasteners on her blouse and she loosened her bra, letting it drop to the floor alongside the bed. David felt her hard nipples against his bare chest while his hand groped clumsily removing the last of their clothes.

Her body telegraphed her need and she hugged him to her tightly. He slipped his leg between hers and felt her moistness. She spread her legs pulling him on top. He pushed into her and felt her thrusting to meet him. "I love you," she murmured softly. They thrust against each other, driving deeper and deeper until he felt himself blossom inside of her. His toes curled against the sheets as he came in hot spurts. She felt her own orgasm welling up inside her and thrust upward to meet his deep driving, throbbing thrusts. "Oh, Oh," she cried out and thrust again, her body racked with orgasmic spasms.

She wrapped her arms and legs around him, clinging to him almost desperately. "I love you David, just don't leave me."

David promised, but thought of how unjust it all was. In a few hours he would dress and return to base, to fight and kill again or be killed. They dozed fitfully in each other's arms.

David dreamed restlessly. The Huns were diving on him from out of the sun and he struggled with his Hurricane, trying to get out of harm's way...he drifted in and out of the clouds...he heard a desperate cry over his R/T, "I'm on fire. I can't open the canopy...." Pictures of Binkie flashed before him...accusing...burning. David woke, dripping with sweat, and sat up in the bed. The room was still dark. There was a slight greying of first morning light showing around the edges of the curtain. He sat up in bed remembering Millie and last night. He looked around, but she was not there; he heard a soft crying from the next room.

David groped in the dark, pulled his shorts and pants on and walked into the room. Millie was curled up on the chesterfield, a blanket wrapped around her dressing gown. She clutched a pillow in her arms. Even in the dark, David could see the picture of Binkie clutched in her hands. He knelt beside the chesterfield and gently stroked the back of her hair, "Millie, honey. What's the matter?"

She buried her face deeper in the pillow, not looking at him. "David. I'm sorry. I wasn't ready for this yet. Will you please leave? I want to be alone."

Confused, David finished dressing quietly, not knowing what to say. Maybe last night didn't happen. Maybe it was all a dream, he thought, as he slipped quietly from the flat. He did not notice the cold as he stumbled numbly through the wet, cryptic fog.

He packed his bags hurriedly and checked out of the hotel. He stood outside Victoria station, alone, shivering in the damp cold, waiting impatiently for his train. Suddenly he wanted to leave London behind. Wanted something familiar like The Station and friends. The base was starting to feel like home.

A locomotive whistle blew somewhere out in the fog, sounding muffled, almost as though it were lost. The massive, black locomotive came huffing and puffing tiredly into the station as if the fog was an extra burden. Brakes squealed and cars banged against each other, jerking to a stop. A sulfuric smell of coal smoke hung heavily in the fog-shrouded station. The engine sat quietly hissing, sending little cloud-puffs of steam into the cold, and waiting in readiness.

"David! David! David!" cried Millie running up to him. She stopped an arm's length away. Her eyes were red from crying, and she wiped her nose with a hankie that was grasped tightly in her hand. "David, I wanted to give you this for good luck. Promise me you'll wear it."

David looked at the St. Christopher medal she'd placed in his hand. He searched her face, looking into the depths of her eyes, her soul, "I promise."

"It's good luck David. As long as you wear it, I know you'll come back to me." Tears ran down her bubbly cheeks, and she threw herself into his arms; her lips crushed his, then she was gone. David stood alone, confused. He looked at the medal in his hand.

The locomotive whistled, expelled a large cloud of steam and lurched forward. One at a time the cars jerked and began following obediently as the train began moving slowly from the station. David turned and raced to climb aboard.

Under Attack

The Station was crowded with pilots rehashing their latest action. David sat alone, nursing a scotch; the hum of conversation sounded like the drone of distant bombers.

He wondered what he'd done wrong. What had turned Millie against him? He smiled to himself thinking of their evening together, her body snuggled next to him. He fingered the St. Christopher medal hanging around his neck, trying to understand why she'd given it to him. What was it she'd said? "It'll bring you safely back to me!" And the kiss, almost desperate.

He hadn't noticed Ralph and Jimmy working their way through the crowd until he felt a slap on his shoulder.

"Okay Pigskin, let's have it. And, don't spare any of the details," said Joker, grinning like a fox. "I want to smell those beautiful London wenches, to taste them! I want to feel their hands groping at my horny body." Joker turned and called to Hap, "Couple of ales for Pigskin and Chief."

"Coming right up, boys," Hap called. They were his boys and he watched over them as if they were his family. He served them in their own personal mugs, foam running over the top. Hap clicked his false teeth up and down with his tongue, wiped his hands on his apron and rested his elbows on the bar, "Well. Didja sow your oats, or what? We ain't got all night, so let's have it."

Chief gave a whoop and raised his mug. "How many broads do we paint on the side of your kite, Pigskin?" He took a deep swallow from his mug, leaving a foamy mustache on his lip. He was looking at Pigskin quizzically, holding up two fingers.

"Okay, animals. I guess I'll have to enlighten you on the finer cultural aspects of London." David chuckled, watching their pained expressions. "First, stop drooling on the bar! I registered at the Union hotel; what a grand old lady. It had a sitting room off the lobby with big stuffed chairs and cases of books and all sorts of plants all around the room."

"Come on with the gibberish. We want to hear about the conquests," said Chief, in his deep guttural voice. His brown eyes came to beady penetrating points, as though he could see what was inside a person.

"Okay, David," Joker explained, speaking very slowly, as if he were talking to an excited child who'd just been to the fair. "We don't want to hear about the climb up the mountain. Just tell us about the summit!"

"Relax, guys. I was just going to tell you about this exquisite beauty at the registration desk." David sipped his scotch. "She had dark brown hair, sleek as a mink, and it hung down past the middle of her back. It was glossy as silk, and when she turned her head, it swept around like a cape. She looked up at me with large brown eyes that reminded me of a young doe. Innocent and trusting. Her skin was light brown, and her face was full and round with a smile that would melt your heart. When she looked up at me and spoke, I swear there was a twinkle in her eye. Her teeth sparkled as white as fresh laundered sheets hanging in the sun. Her hand touched mine and I felt a tingle...right then I knew...."

"Knew what?" said Hap impatiently.

"Knew what room I had when she handed me my key."

"Jeez, Pigskin. I don't have time to listen to crap," said Hap, turning and stomping off to wait on someone else.

"Well," Joker prompted. "Did she come up to your room or not?"

"Am I too late to hear all the details of our hero in London?" chortled Woody, as he climbed on a stool and called for an ale.

"Aw, we can't get anything out of him but gibberish," said Chief, taking a long swig of ale.

"Well now, Davie, me boy. What's the main event of this here trip to London?" asked Woody, sipping his ale and turning to David expectantly.

"There I was having dinner with Raymond in the Eagle Club, and I met the most exquisite lady. She was somewhat shorter than me and had fiery red hair. And when she looked up at me, her green eyes sparkled. Her smile was bubbly and her cheeks were covered with freckles...." David had a dreamy look on his face as he closed his eyes trying to recall every detail about her.

"Come on, Joker, we've heard that line already," said Chief disgustedly, motioning to Joker and heading for the snooker tables in the back.

"David," asked Woody. "Did yea say she had fiery red hair and was a volunteer worker in the Eagle club?"

"Yeh. We went to the Dorchester that evening and danced till almost daylight. Then she showed me around London." David relished watching Woody squirm.

"What the bloody devil's her name?"

"Claims that she has a red-headed brother called Woody!" David turned grinning.

"Well, I'll be. The Saints have heard me prayers," said Woody, smiling. He shook David's hand, his wide mouth spread into a grin that looked as though it would split his face. "That's the first Millie's gone out since Binkie's death. Yea danced all night and toured London? Did yea go the theater?"

"She gave me a St. Christopher medal, said it was good luck and would bring me back to her." David slipped it out of his shirt holding it reverently in his hand. "She is every bit a lady. I hope I can see her again." Slipping the medal back inside his shirt, David felt an emptiness.

"The Saints are with yea, David. She must think a lot of yea to give you a St. Christopher medal." Woody turned to David, smiling. "And now for some more good news. Your kite's back on the line -- good as new she is! Me boys worked the clock around getting 'er ready, seeing as yea'll be leading the flight."

"What? Leading what flight?" David asked.

Woody drained his mug of ale. "See yea at the field, Davie, me boy," said Woody, giving his funny chortled laugh as he waddled off.

That night, David tossed restlessly in his bunk. He slept fitfully, dreaming of Millie; aroused, then rejected. He stretched out his hand to her, and she faded like an illusion. A burning Spitfire came spiraling out of the clouds. He heard screams and woke in a sweat, only to lie back exhausted, afraid to sleep. The dawn came slowly. Tormented with nightmares, David couldn't sleep and dressed quietly in the darkened barracks. He slipped out, closing the door behind him. The sky was turning pink as he headed for the operations shack.

Tommy, the night duty sergeant, turned and jumped, startled when the squeaky door opened. His short, wiry build made David think of his cousin, Jimmy. Even sitting in the office all night, his uniform looked as if he'd just put it on. His big nose looked out of place on his small face, and the shadow of his whiskers was the only thing that made him look like a man instead of a school boy.

"Oh, Pigskin. Didn't hear you coming. Scared the bloody hell out ah me," said Tommy in his heavily-British accent.

"Couldn't sleep," said David, as he poured a cup of tea. "Anything going down for today?" he asked.

"Nothing much, sir," said Tommy, grinning.

"What's this 'sir' crap? First Woody, now you? As I recall, not too long ago, you were ragging on me for calling you sir. What the hell's going on?" asked David, sipping his hot tea.

Tommy just stood there grinning. He enjoying watching David squirm for a moment. "Well, sir, you've left the class of peons. They're promoting you to flying officer."

"Holy Shit," exclaimed David. "So that's what all the secrecy's about."

Tommy mocked a salute and shook David's hand. "Congratulations, sir, and you'd better look surprised. We're not supposed to let on. And, that's not all. You'll be the first American squadron leader to boot."

David stopped his pacing and looked up, "Squadron leader?"

"Yes, sir. Guess they figured with four kills, you must be doing something right."

David didn't hear Tommy talking. He thought, how could he be a squadron leader? He didn't have enough experience blind flying. Now he'd be leading a squadron who relied on him.

David walked through the dew-covered grass to the dispersal area where their Hurricanes were parked. The sun, a bright red ball, sat momentarily on the horizon then leaped into the sky. He spotted his Hurricane with a football emblem inscribed with "Pigskin." He walked around his kite admiring the repair job. Except for the fresh paint and the smell of freshly doped fabric, he could hardly see where the patches were. The bullet holes were gone. David checked his guns, the smell of cordite was still strong. Four swastikas had been painted below his canopy. His kite was blooded now. The sun was fully up, and the warmth on his back felt good. David jumped off the back of the wing, satisfied that Woody and his crew had more than rebuilt his Hurc.

"Sergeant Hampton."

David looked up and saw Tommy waving from the operations shack. He turned, heading for the shack. "What's up, Tommy?"

"Squadron leader Simpson wants to see you in his office right away. Sounds like he's in a wee bit of ah bloody tiff."

David felt tense as he headed for the office across the field. Squadron leader Brent Simpson hated his guts. David knew that he would have been the last one promoted if Brent had anything to say. Brent was all British and had a hard-on for all outsiders, especially American Indians. David checked his uniform before knocking on the squadron leader's door, then rapped sharply.

"Come in," came the high-pitched summons from behind the closed door.

David entered briskly, doing his best to emulate proper British protocol. "Flying sergeant David Hampton, reporting as ordered, sir." David stood at attention before squadron leader Simpson's desk, waiting for recognition.

Simpson took a file from the side of his desk. Without looking up, he opened it. He read from a memorandum in David's file: "For performances rendered in His Majesty's service, you are hereby promoted to Flying Officer." Simpson's moustache twitched in nervous displeasure as he finished reading the promotion order. "Furthermore, for your leadership role intercepting and deterring the latest attack, you are now assigned as squadron leader. You are to take over the Pinetree Squadron. Any questions?" Simpson closed the file with a snap. As he looked up, revulsion showed on his face.

David stood at attention. "I'm appreciative of the promotion, sir. But, as far as leading the squadron, I have very few blind flying hours." David wanted to lead the squadron, but he had no practical experience. Eleven pilots were putting their lives on the line, depending on him.

Simpson looked up, "If you can't hack it, Hampton, we can find a British officer who can! Do I make myself clear?"

"Yes, sir. I can handle it!" David spoke the words through clenched teeth.

"Get your squadron operational. They're bloody riffraff. I don't know how any of them ever got through flight school. Obviously it wasn't a British flying school. Well, there's your task. I can only allow you three days for training. Though, God only knows, you should have far more than that," Brent muttered. He made a few notes in David's file then looked up. "Three days then and you'll be operational. Carry on!"

David saluted, did an about face and marched out of Simpson's office. Three days to put a team together. As quarterback, everyone had looked up to him. He called the plays and they executed them. He wasn't sure if these boys even knew any plays. The only way to find out was to have a scrimmage. He'd tell them about his experiences. Make them feel, touch, talk, and most of all encourage the inexperienced pilots to follow his example. They had three days to master the single-seat fighter. For some, the lessons would be swift and tragic.

David entered the operations room. A blue haze of cigarette smoke hung in the air, and a small coal stove in the corner drove the dampness from the room. A BBC broadcast went unnoticed. Pilots lounged around reading or playing poker, waiting for the morning flight orders.

David called, "Pinetree Squadron, fall out with your flight gear." They shuffled out one at a time, with their parachutes dangling over one arm from the shoulder strap. Some wore their leather helmets with the goggles cocked on top.

"Gentlemen." He was greeted with a few snickers. "For those of you who don't know me, I'm flying officer David Hampton. I've been assigned as leader of this squadron. I've been told that you're a bunch of misfits. I personally think that's bull. With teamwork, we'll show'm they're full of crap. I want to meet each one of you individually, but that'll have to come later. We're going to start practicing like a football team. I'm the quarter-back, and I'm calling the plays. Anybody who doesn't want to be a part of the team will have to deal with me."

"I'm known as 'Pigskin,' and from now on, we'll be known as the 'Pigskin Squadron.' I'll be leading the Red vic with Hans and Storm'n Norman. Chief will lead the Yellow vic with Billy the Kid and Glen. Joker will take the Green vic with George and Robert. Dixie will lead the Blue vic with Mickey and Dick. The vic leader will be number one, his wing man number two, and the last number three. I'm Pigskin, Red-one." David looked his men over. They stood slouching, uniforms awry, some talking and joking with their buddies, uninterested -- three days to put this squadron together?

David needed to get their attention. "Three things I've learned when we engage the enemy. Shoot the Hun first or you're going to be shot. Never turn away from a head-on attack, make Jerry turn first. Failing all else, fly through on a collision course."

"What happens if the Krauts have the same information?" asked Billy the Kid.

"Well, you've just earned your flight pay the hard way." David looked at each pilot, noting the now serious expressions on their faces. They would make a team.

"In the next three days, you're going to learn how to fly combat. Formation takeoff and climb out. When we get to altitude, we'll split and practice some attacks and evasive maneuvers. Watch your tail at all times. Learn the tricks of combat. Never climb or dive in front of a Messerschmitt or you're dead. Turn and turn and turn. This is how you'll evade an ME-109. We're a team now and this is a team game. No show-offs and no dead heros. Cover each other, and use your proper call signs. Okay, Pigskin Squadron, training starts now."

They climbed into lorries, riding to the dispersal area. David hopped out beside his Hurricane and laid his gear on the back of the wing. "How's she look, Woody? Got some hard flying to do the next three days."

"Yea mean harder than the last two trips yea flew?"

"Jeez, I hope not. We're going up training. Good old Brent gave us all of three days to make up a fighting squadron, then he's putting us on the line. I plan on using every minute of that time training."

"Me boys'll be waiting on yea," said Woody, helping David on with his parachute.

David slipped down into the narrow confines of the cockpit and fastened the safety straps. He plugged in his radio jack and turned on the oxygen, checking the mask. He signaled his squadron to start engines. He felt a rush of excitement, like the opening kick-off in a football game, only this wasn't just any game, it was like the play-offs for the state championship. It felt good, he was quarterbacking, leading a team again. He taxied down the line of waiting Hurricanes and they each pulled out in line behind him.

David spun his Hurricane around into the wind and gunned the throttle. The formation staggered into the air. "This is Pigskin, Red-one. Tighten up, tighten it up. Fly your leader's wing as though we're climbing in the clouds," David needed all the blind-flying practice he could get and put his head down, concentrating on his instruments. Sweat ran down his forehead and into his eyes. The squadron had formed on him, flying on his command and actions. If he made a mistake, they would all screw up. David flew the artificial horizon, cross referencing it with the needle-ball and air speed. He trimmed the nose to a cruise climb, set his throttle for climb power and adjusted the manifold pressure. His eyes were moving constantly. Engine too cool, he closed the shutters on the radiator. Heading drifted five degrees, he gently made a half needle width turn, on his needle-ball instrument, keeping the ball centered. Climbing on heading, on course, he checked his instruments for the thousandth time. Passing ten thousand feet, David stole a glance outside and was impressed with the sight of the two Hurricanes in formation off his wing. The rest of the squadron lined up behind them, like a row of dominoes.

David flipped his R/T to the transmit position. "Pigskin, Red-one. We'll make a turn, in formation, to heading three-six-zero degrees and climb to twenty-thousand, then turn to two-seven-zero degrees and level out at twenty-five thousand. Check your oxygen masks for moisture."

"In other words, don't drool," said Joker.

David leveled the squadron at twenty-five thousand, still flying his instruments. "This is Pigskin-leader. Yellow vic will follow me. Green-one, take the lead with Blue vic and spread out. Keep'er in tight, stragglers are the first to be shot. We'll be the Hun, so be ready."

"Roger. Green-one has the lead," called Joker, turning his section south.

David pulled up in a steep climbing turn, into the sun. Minutes passed and they leveled at thirty-five thousand feet. David began jinxing -- turning, climbing, diving, never staying in any one position for more than a few seconds while scanning the sky in all directions. Chief was off a safe distance with his two wing-men, performing the same maneuvers. David turned, placing the sun behind him and searched below for Joker and Dixie.

A flash of sunlight reflected off a wing below and David grinned in his mask. He signaled to Hans, pointing ahead and below. David checked the sun, it was now behind and above them. If only those were Square-heads down there!

David rolled in on the attack, adding a little power and dropping like a hawk on unsuspecting prey. David glanced behind him; his two wing men were tucked in tight. Off to the side, Chief led his vic in the attack. They closed to 500 yards, 400 yards. Their guns were loaded with blanks so they could experience attacking and firing. David wanted his men to see an enemy grow in their sight pip. At 200 yards, David armed his guns and fired.

"Pigskin, Red-one. Green and Blue vic's are dead," called David as they shot through the surprised formation. Planes broke in all directions. The radio turned into unintelligent garble, everyone trying to talk at once.

David shouted, "Get off the radio! All right, listen up. I don't want to hear anything but proper calls, damnit, or someone's going to get killed. All right. Let's mix it up, this is Pigskin-leader, bandits twelve o'clock low."

"Blue-one, bandits, three-o'clock high! Let's meet'em head on."

"Green-one, low on fuel."

"Okay, this is Pigskin-red-one; form up and we'll fly formation back to base. Let's show the Brits how to fly!" David looked back, watching his squadron pulling into formation. He was the quarterback again. Misfits? He didn't think so. He had a team. A few more close order drills....

"Green and Blue, you get airborne as soon as you're refueled. You're the Hun this time," David said.

Four times they climbed into the sky, flying every type of interception and evasive maneuver David could think of. He even invented a couple, taking his pilots by surprise. When they shut down their engines at sunset, the men were exhausted.

Entering The Station, David felt the tension begin to unwind. Woody waved and headed down the bar to join him.

Hap carried David's mug of ale over. "Well, how'd the flying officer make out on his first big day?"

"Hap, it's like football. It's a great game, but Jeez am I tired." David took a deep swallow from his mug. "And dry."

"Small wonder, Davie, me boy. Yea run'em pretty hard today. Me boys was complaining themselves for the work'n yea give'em keeping your kites flying all day," Woody said. "It was good for'em, they need it. Been too quiet the last few days. Something big's going on and we'd better be ready!"

"That's what I was thinking," said David. "Simpson's only given me three days -- then he's putting us on the line. I'm afraid some of these boys won't be ready. They're not up to a Hun attack."

"Now, yea'd sure be the one to judge that," admonished Woody. "Why, Davie, me boy, when yea first arrived, I'd hardly seen anyone as green. And now look't yea. Flying officer, with a squadron of yea own!"

"Yeh," said David, finishing his ale. "Well, better hit the sack. Got a long day tomorrow. Got live ammo this time. Going to the firing range so they'll find out what they can really do."

"Sweet dreams," called Woody. "And remember, me sister's a lady!"

David could hear Woody's chortle as he slipped through the blackout curtain.

David tossed restlessly in his bunk. He smiled in his sleep as he watched Millie undress in the dim bedroom light. He dreamed of her warm naked body snuggling next to his as he slipped his arms around her. Her moist lips sought his and devoured him hungrily. Her nipples poked against his chest and he felt himself harden. He kissed her neck and heard her coo. His lips searched for her breast. His tongue tasted the sweetness of her body. As he reached a hardened nipple, she sighed and pulled his head down on her breast. She wrapped her legs around his body and they lay together.

David heard an anguished cry and looked around confused--he saw Millie in the distance, floating like an apparition. He watched breathlessly to see what she was doing. She was wearing a white shimmering gown and he saw the outline of her body through it. In one arm she clutched a picture. She turned and waved good-bye to him and vanished in a misty veil.

David tossed fitfully in his bunk, clutching his pillow in his arms. In his dream, he listened to the steady drumming of the Merlin engine and looked out of his Hurricane. His port wing jerked and several long rips appeared in the wing. Tracers flash by his canopy, glowing like little balls of fire. David slammed his Hurc on its side, rolled, turned and jinxed. He dove but he could not shake the Messerschmitt. Bullets tore into his wing and he pulled into an ever tighter turn. He could feel himself greying out from the g forces. Still, he held the elevators back with all his strength. The blackout brought a calming peace as though he were floating along on top of a cloud.

David saw a diving Spitfire open fire on the Messerschmitt. He watched, fascinated as the Spit's bullets shot into empty space. He saw the Spitfire pilot look up -- it was Binkie. David called a warning, but it was too late. A pair of ME-109s dove from the cloud above, firing on the Spit.

David watched helplessly as Binkie out-maneuvered the pair of Messerschmitts. An ME-109 fell from the sky in flames, but not without a price. David saw Binkie struggling to open his canopy. Flames leaped from the floor, filling the cockpit. The trapped body...burning....

"Sir! Sir! David!"

David felt someone shaking him. Wild-eyed, he looked around the semi-darkened room.

"Sir, it's zero-four-hundred. You asked for a wake-up call at four," explained the nervous night clerk.

"Okay," David stammered. He sat on the edge of his bed, exhausted. He felt as though he'd been flying all night. He grabbed his towel and headed for the showers, stopping to turn on the lights and call his squadron awake. "Thirty minutes to first takeoff."

His attempt at a cheerful wake-up was greeted venomously. A boot came flying through the air narrowly missing him. David smiled as he adjusted the shower. They were going to make a fine team, and he was their quarterback.

A low moan began, like the wind rising. It grew until the wail of an air raid siren filled the barracks. "Air raid!" David screamed, running from the shower. His body was still lathered with soap as he struggled into his clothes. Still dressing, he ran from the barracks heading for the operations shack. It was breaking daylight, and David slipped in the wet grass. He heard the cough of a Hurricane starting, then another and another. David wondered how the riggers and fitters could have beaten him onto the field unless they had slept in the service pits next to their kites.

David hit the door to the operations, running. Tommy screamed, "A hundred plus bogies heading right for the field."

David grabbed his Mae west, parachute, helmet and goggles and ran for his Hurricane. All around him pilots were running for their planes in mass confusion.

Woody stood ready, engine running, and helped David with his parachute straps and safety harnesses. He plugged his helmet into the radio leads and turned on the oxygen mask. David gave the thumbs-up signal that he was ready. A rigger pulled the chocks, waving him off. He gunned his engine and turned down field. There was no time for a warm up. The Hurricane lifted into the air and David retracted the gear and closed his canopy. Looking back, he saw several Hurricanes climbing behind him. At the far side of the field, a formation of Messerschmitts dove at the field firing. White fiery streaks of tracers flashed from their wings. Bullets striking the ground threw up geysers of dirt. Hurricanes on the ground were transformed into funeral pyres. A Hurc lifting off disappeared in a ball of fire. Smoke from burning planes blackened the sky.

"This is Pigskin! Turn on me. Stop those fighters attacking the field." David turned his Hurricane on its wing and dove straight down. A Messerschmitt crossed the field boundary, firing on the planes still parked in the dispersal area. Its wing span filled David's sight pip. He glanced at the needle-ball and squeezed the firing button. His Hurc shook and filled the cockpit with the acid smell of burnt cordite. He did not see the ME-109's wing snap off and plunge into the ground. He'd already turned looking for another German.

A line of Stukas dove toward the barracks on the far side of the field. "Pigskin-leader, Stukas west of the field!" He jammed his throttle through the gate into combat boost and turned into the dive bombers. David centered his sight pip on the leading Hun. A large bomb hung from the belly of the fighter and several small bombs from each wing. He checked his coordination and pushed his thumb down on the firing button. David watched the three-second burst of tracers strike the engine of the Stuka. A white cloud of glycol spewed from the engine.

David jinxed his Hurc, looking for another fighter. He glanced into his rear-facing mirror; clear. He looked below and saw another dive bomber turning toward the field. He rolled and dove, centering his sight pip on the Stuka. He thumbed down the firing button. The Stuka, less than a hundred yards away, filled his windscreen. One of the Junker's bombs blew up. What had been a bomber turned into a firestorm. David threw his arm up protectively. He was thrown against the side of his canopy. Shoulder straps tore into his arms. The heat from the fire turned his cockpit into an oven. He flew clear of the firestorm, as though he'd been disgorged from hell.

David looked around and saw columns of smoke on and around the field. Thick, black smoke from burning planes. Half of the buildings on base were on fire. The Huns were gone.

David circled the field, "Control, this is Pigskin-leader. Is anybody there?" He examined what was left of the field, pockmarked with bomb craters and burning aircraft.

"Pigskin-yellow-one, I'm coming around, forming on you, what'll we do now?"

David searched for a spot he could land without damaging his fighter. "There's a clear spot on the far side of the field that looks like we can land. I'm out of ammo, Chief! You stay up with anyone who's got fuel and ammo and cover us. I'll be back up as soon as I can get refitted. We'll take turns covering the field and going in for refueling and ammo."

David taxied around burning wreckage and bomb craters. Smoke drifted across the field and smelled of burning oil and rubber. Woody appeared, waving the Hurricane to parking.

"Woody!" David shouted. "I need ammo and fuel!"

"The armorers are coming now, did yea take any hits? Everything running okay?"

"No damage," David called back.

A fuel bouser pulled up in front of David's Hurricane. A WAAF jumped out and started refueling David's fighter. "How many planes did we lose?" David asked.

"I don't know, sir. Most of the girls were still sleeping when the attack began. I'd just left our hut when a bomb hit." Her face was smeared with blood and tears ran down her cheeks. "Most of the WAAFs were still inside their Nissens."

"David," called Woody. "Guns loaded and ready!"

"Okay," said David, climbing back into the cockpit. "I'm climbing up over the station and will cover while the rest of our boys come in, one at a time, for fuel and ammo!"

"Pigskin-leader, airborne. What's our status Chief?"

"We got eight Hurcs out of ammo or almost out. I think there's six or seven more that still have full belts."

"Chief, you direct the landing and refitting. I'm climbing over the station to cover. Don't let more than two planes on the ground at a time. The Jerries will be back to finish what they started. We'll make sure that there won't be any easy targets next time." David continued his climb to five thousand. "Pigskin leader, let's form up and keep your eyes open, especially above and behind. String out in a circle, over the station. That way we can cover each other. Let's call in, who've we got up?"

"Joker here, with two pigeons," called Ralph.

"Dixie, and I've got four more Hurcs with me."

"Pigskin flight -- control here, we've just set up a temporary radio in a truck. Eleventh operations reports that the Germans are hitting all of our fighter bases, and we're to expect ongoing attacks ."

"That you, Tommy?" called David.

"Yes, sir, and bloody good show you chaps put on this morning, Pigskin."

"Dixie-one. Bandits east, high. Looks like Messerschmitts!"

"Pigskin-leader, roger that. Bluster, let's climb above'em. Control, better get everything in the air!" David pushed his throttle through the gate to full combat boost. He trimmed the nose up for maximum climb. He opened the shutters for better cooling and turned the propeller control in for best climb. "Dixie, turn right and circle around to come in from behind 'em. Joker, fly my wing. We'll hit'em straight on. Arm your guns and spread out."

"Pigskin, this is Chief. I'm coming up to join you with one little buddy."

"Pigskin-leader, tallyho. Bandits six-o'clock low. It's a flight of Kraut bombers!" Still at full war power, David pushed his nose over in a steep dive. "Forget the fighters," David called. "Stop the bombers." David's sight pip centered on the first Heinkel. The glass nose looked vulnerable, its lone gunner sitting out in front. They'd been spotted. The single machine gun in the nose swung up firing at them. The HE-111 filled his sight pip. David checked that his needle-ball was centered; his thumb squeezed the firing button. The nose of the Heinkel disappeared in a shower of glass. Exploding DeWilde bullets ripped into an engine and black smoke poured from it.

David ignored the stricken aircraft and turned on another. He was so close he could see terror on the face of the gunner in the unprotected nose. He thought of the WAAF refueling his Hurc and her blood-smeared face. He felt nothing as he squeezed the firing button. His bullets shattered the nose, working back into the cockpit. The Heinkel nosed over in a spiral.

"Pigskin, break left!"

David glanced at his rear-facing mirror. A yellow-nosed Messerschmitt filled his mirror. David broke hard left and pulled up in a steep climbing turn. Tracers from the ME-109 flashed harmlessly behind him. David held his Hurricane in a spiraling climb. The German, having smelled blood, pulled up trying to follow. David saw the yellow-nosed Abbeville flyer in his mirror stall and fall off in a spin.

David pulled his throttle back to cruise and did a wing-over looking for the ME-109 or another bomber. He wiped sweat from his face with the back of his hand. He opened his canopy to vent the cordite fumes from the cockpit. Plumes of dirty black smoked marked the broken and wounded planes from both sides. Black puffs of smoke from flak bursts followed the Huns. The air smelled of death, filled with burned cordite, oil and gas, burning tires and debris from the exploding bombs. A Hurricane streaming smoke spun earthward. Parachutes drifting down looked like a miniature snow storm.

"Pigskin, Red-One. Bandits coming up west of the field." David slammed his canopy closed and pushed the throttle through the stops. Black puffs of smoke from exploding flak shells searched for the bombers. David raced to catch up with the bombers before they could release their bombs. The trailing Heinkel filled David's sight pip. He agonized at how slowly he gained on the bomber. He was almost in range of the Heinkel as they approached the eastern edge of the field. The bomb bay doors opened on the bomber. He couldn't wait. He checked his coordination, touched the rudder slightly to center the needle-ball and squeezed his gun button. The Hurricane slowed from the recoil of eight machine guns firing simultaneously. The cockpit filled with burned cordite, but David did not notice. He saw his tracers disappear into the bomber. Still, it flew on.

Was it only this morning that a bomber had hit the Nissen hut full of WAAFs? His thumb froze to the firing button. Eight streams of deadly fire converged on the bomber. Then the cockpit was silent except for the sound of the straining Merlin. His guns were empty. The Heinkel flew on across the field, but no bombs fell. David thought he could see a light inside the bomber. Out of ammo, he watched the Hun nose over.

Flames burned the interior of the bomber. Fed by oxygen streaming in shattered windows, the Heinkel burned white hot, like a blow torch. David brought his power back and began a climbing orbit. A bomb exploded inside the burning bomber and it disappeared in a ball of fire.

"Control, this is Pigskin-leader, returning to the field."

"Pigskin, there's still a clear strip on the west side of the field. Any damage to your kite?" asked Tommy from control.

"Tell Woody to have some new guns available. I burnt the barrels on that last bomber." David turned into the wind, dropping his gear and flaps. He picked out a clear strip on the side of the field and settled into the tall grasses. The Hurricane bounced along the rough ground. David fish-tailed back and forth, taxiing across the field dodging bomb craters. Woody was on the wing beside David before the propeller stopped turning.

"David, me boy. What a show yea put on for the troops with that last bomber. Here, let me help yea wid these straps. How's me kite running?" Woody asked, eyeing the Hurc critically.

David struggled climbing out of the cramped cockpit. His shirt was soaked with sweat, though it had been cold out. "I was at max power chasing that bomber. I fired until I ran out of ammo."

"We'll have some new guns in shortly, sir," called one of the armorers.

"Hop in the lorry, Pigskin; Simpson wants to talk with all the pilots. He's trying to figure what the hell's going on. Maybe someone should tell him there's a war on. We've sandwiches brought in and hot tea."

"Maybe I shouldn't be too far from my plane," David said, a worried look on his face.

"You need a little rest, Pigskin. It's near noon and yea've been flying since early morning. There's two kites up keeping watch." Woody chuckled, "yea're something of a cracker, yea know. Here comes the Hun bomber, doors open, seconds away from killing more people, not to mention planes. There yea come, guns ah blazing to the rescue. Ah-eee, there'll be some bragging going on at The Station tonight." Woody wheeled the lorry around kicking up a cloud of dust in back of a tent serving as the CO's office. "Be waiting right here with the lorry when yea're ready, Pigskin."

David went over his flight debriefing with squadron leader Simpson. Operations wanted to know how many aircraft he'd seen and what kind. How many fighters escorted the bombers.

Simpson was clearly shaken as he spoke. "We lost over half of our operational fighters this morning. We've more pilots than aircraft so we'll be scheduling pilots in shifts. Your aircraft will be flown this afternoon by flying Officer Lawrence Whitehead's crew. Operations thinks we will have some heavy action this afternoon and we need a more experienced British crew in those Hurricanes."

Simpson did not mention that David's crew, going for early morning training, had saved most of the Hurricanes. David hadn't expected it from Simpson.

"Coordinate your schedules with Tommy, in Control." Brent went back to shuffling papers, ignoring David.

David stomped out of the operations tent, fuming. "Hey Woody, need to swing over to Tommy's operations, wherever the hell that is!" He spoke with his jaw clenched tight.

"Now David, you mustn't be too hard on ol' Brent. He's some Lord's rich boy made an officer. He has to look important, you know," Woody chuckled, trying to keep a smirk from his face.

"That pompous ass. He couldn't lead starving people to the chow hall," said David, as he climbed up, seething, and sat beside Woody in the lorry. "I'm the quarterback and just saved the game. Now they want to put me on the bench!"

"What's all this football stuff, Pigskin?" Woody swerved the lorry around a bomb crater as though it were an everyday occurrence.

"They're turning my planes over to British pilots this afternoon. They need 'real' pilots flying today!" David's face was livid, "British pilots!"

"David, me boy. What was that name yea used?" asked Woody, a mocking grin on his face. "Pompous ass, or something like that?"

David laughed. "That's it, Woodpecker."

"This is the new flight shack." Woody stopped the lorry outside a heavy canvas maintenance tent.

David entered the tent and saw Tommy's desk in the back corner, already covered with telephones and stacks of papers. There were rows of cots on one side and several pilots were sleeping or trying to read. "Hi, Tommy."

Tommy looked up, "Afternoon, sir." He shuffled through the papers and came up with his schedule. "Here's what Simpson's worked up, sir. You'll stand down the rest of today and be on call from zero-three-hundred hours tomorrow until noon."

"Guess I'd better get some sleep," said David, resigning himself.

"Half the remaining aircraft are to be in the air during daylight hours," Tommy read from a memo. "The rest will be ready for takeoff in five minutes or less. When a vic returns for refueling, another will take off. Eleventh operations believes the Germans are trying to destroy our bases and fighters."

"Thanks, Tommy. I'll be at the officers' quarters or The Station if you need me." David stepped outside and climbed into the lorry. Air raid shelters were being dug directly outside the operations tent. "Looks like we took a few hits in our Nissen huts also," David said, as he examined the building. Machine guns had stitched several lines of holes up the side and top of the hut.

"Lost four men in yea hut. Didn't take the air-raid siren serious." Woody gave David the names, but they were newer pilots and he hadn't known them. "Back home, Pigskin," said Woody, stopping at the officers' huts. "First thing yea'd better do is find out where the nearest exit is and the closest dugout. Don't want to be carrying yea out in a litter like we did the other boys this morning!"

"Thanks, Woody. Don't worry, I may end up sleeping in one of the holes if this keeps up." David picked his way through a pile of bunks and lockers in the hut. His bed and most of his belongings had been covered from a near bomb hit. Workmen scurried around cleaning up the worst of the damage and making temporary repairs. "How's a fellow supposed to get any rest around here?" David asked of no one in particular.

"Be ah bloody while, sir. Got to clean this mess up some before we can make repairs. You'd best find somewhere else to bunk. We'll be working in here most of the afternoon."

Turning, David headed for The Station, one of the few buildings undamaged.

The Channel

The interior of The Station was dark and cool, and David stood for a moment letting his eyes adjust to the light. He spotted Spike in his favorite spot at the far end of the bar. His clothes were in disarray and dirty. "Hi Spike, how's things?"

"Pigskin. Didn't expect to see you in here today with all the action," said Raymond putting his pen down alongside a notepad he'd been writing in.

"Yeah, well ol' Simpson's got a cob up his butt. Wants his 'Brit' boys flying this afternoon. Someone with more experience." David took a sip of ale, "I've been given the afternoon off. I was going to catch a little shuteye, but the barracks were shot up, and there are workmen all over. This is the only quiet place around."

"Yeah," said Spike grimly. "I spent the morning helping carry bodies out of the bombed WAAF Nissen. Some of the bodies were nothing except pulverized mush. There were arms and legs blown off, and we put them all in one body bag. Didn't know what belonged to whom. I finally had to get out -- all those young girls killed. We found five still alive, but two of them will never make it."

David sat sipping his ale without tasting it. He thought of the girl refueling his Hurricane, blood smeared on her face. She must have been working with Raymond in the bombed out barracks. "We were lucky, Spike. I had my men up. We were getting ready to take off at daylight on a training exercise. Most of us were in the air when the first Germans hit the base. One of my squadron was hit on the end of the runway and another just lifting off. The rest I don't know."

"Any idea how many Krauts we got?" asked Spike.

"Woody confirmed the first Messerschmitt I shot right over the field. We intercepted a flight of Stukas attacking from west of the field. We took 'em head on and I smoked one and had another blow up in front of me." David rubbed his arm where the seat straps had torn into his shoulders. "His bomb exploded. Damn near blew me out of the sky. I was out of ammo so had to slip in between attacks and refit. We were vectored to a gaggle of fifty-plus bombers with fighter cover. There were only seven of us and we hit 'em from both sides. I smoked one, and I guess you've heard about the one I got right over the edge of the field."

"Heard about it," Spike interrupted, "I was still helping bring out bodies when that Heinkel came over the field. I watched the bomb-bay doors open. It was so close, I could see the face of the nose gunner as we jumped into our bomb shelters. When no bombs dropped, everyone crawled out of their bunkers. We watched the bomber fly across the field and explode. There's a lot of people on base that want to shake your hand, Pigskin."

David blushed with embarrassment. "Just doing my job."

"Bullshit," said Hap from behind the bar. "You're a 'GOD AL-MIGHTY HOTSHOT,' Pigskin. We had a couple pilots just like you in the Great War. Natural killer instinct."

"Or maybe self-preservation," added Spike.

"You guys are making a lot out of nothing," said David. "There were several other guys flying. From all the smoking wrecks and parachutes, I can attest to the fact that they shot down a lot more of the enemy than I did."

"Nevertheless Pigskin, you are the one in the spotlight."

"Keep my stool warm. I'm going to try and find a place to sleep. I'll see you tomorrow afternoon." David finished his ale and strolled back to the barracks. The workers had completed the cleanup. David was exhausted and stretched out on his bunk, still in his flight suit.

He thought about his dreams of Millie and then Binkie. He understood Binkie, but it seemed he was trying to tell him something. The more he thought about his dreams the more confused he felt. Why did Millie always disappear? Was something going to happen to her? He drifted into a troubled sleep. It seemed as if he'd been sleeping for only a few minutes when he felt a hand on his shoulder shaking him.

"It's zero-three-hundred, sir."

"Okay. I'm awake." David sat up on the edge of his bed. Where was he? Why was he awakened? He remembered the WAAFs killed in their Nissen. "Oh, Jeez," he said, holding his head between his hands. His head pounded and he ached all over. Had he slept at all -- it didn't feel like it.

David headed for the tent serving as a crew room. He listened to the briefing while munching on a hard biscuit and bully beef. He washed it down with a cup of hot tea. They would have only twelve planes serviceable. Outside, engines barked as crews completed the preflight warmup.

David briefed his team, his pilots. "Our training was cut short. Seems as though Hitler has other plans. We've been assigned a patrol area to intercept any invaders. Formation takeoff and climb on heading one-eight-zero degrees until we break out on top. We'll spread out in our four teams of three and cover our patrol area. You new guys, stick with your leaders; that's the best we can do. Good luck and good hunting."

The Pigskin team strolled through the wet dew-covered grass, each to his own plane. Woody greeted David, "How's the head this morning, David? Yea was ah pouring the suds down pretty fast."

"Do you have to shout so loud?" said David, grinning back. "It'll be fine once I suck down a little oxygen."

"Talked with Millie on the call box last night. She asked how yea were. Wants to see yea again in London."

"Great," said David, "but I don't know her number."

"Here's her tele at operations. Just ring 'em up and ask for Millie. If she's not there, they'll take a message for her."

The start-engines flare burst in a bright flash leaving an eerie glow over the foggy field. David cranked his Merlin. It fired on the first turn, having been run up by Woody. He gunned his engine and taxied down the field into takeoff position. A typical English fog drifted across the field. David was nervous and double checked all his instruments. There was a heavy overcast and no one knew what the tops of the clouds were. This was his first time leading planes in an instrument climb. He didn't have time to dwell on it as the takeoff flare arced into the air. He advanced his throttle steadily, starting his takeoff run down the rough, repaired field. Clear of the runway, he raised his landing gear and closed his canopy. One last look confirmed the squadron tucking into formation for the climb.

David set his power for climb, adjusted the prop and shutters. He tweaked the trim wheel and let the Hurricane take over. He monitored the instruments, making minor corrections and scanning the gauges. He wondered if the rest of the pilots felt the same knot of fear that was twisting his gut. So far, they were encountering no ice and only very light turbulence. They were flying into harm's way. No one knew whether they would live to see another day. Would the Germans be waiting for them? There would be no more surprises. The Germans had stirred up a hornet's nest and now they were ready to fight back. Passing ten thousand feet, David added more power, still climbing on instruments.

If anything else, it was darker. Maybe they were heading into a thunderstorm. God help them if that happened. The formation would break up and it would be every man for himself. Twelve planes milling around in the cloud; it'd be a miracle if there wasn't a midair collision.

David jumped as his earphones crackled, "Pigskin-leader, control, 100-plus bandits east of Dover heading west, angels twenty, vector 130, bluster."

That cleared up any doubts about where they were going or what was about to happen, "Roger, control," David called and blinked his collision lights indicating a change of course. David brought up his throttle to full climb power, trimming his elevators for maximum rate of climb, a hundred and forty miles per hour. He began a shallow turn to one-three-zero degrees. The Hun must be right on top of the clouds.

At twenty thousand feet they broke out into the clear. The air temperature was a minus thirty Celsius and the sky was a brilliant blue. There was no pollution up here. The top of the clouds were bleached white billowy puffs. David continued their climb to get above the incoming Huns. He gave hand signals to spread out. At twenty-five thousand feet David leveled out and began jinxing his Hurricane. His head was on a swivel, looking up, down, behind and then he saw the German formation. David switched his R/T to transmit. "Pigskin-leader, bandits two o'clock low. We'll hold our altitude until we're behind 'em. Everybody pick a bomber."

"Blue-one, bandits three-o'clock high, attacking."

"Pigskin-leader, we can't wait. Tally Ho, let's break up those bombers." David rolled and pulled the stick back plunging into a near vertical dive. His left hand automatically pushed the throttle through the gate to full combat boost. The Merlin responded and the increase in speed made a sharp whistling sound around his canopy. He felt the controls buffet against the increased pressure and the tail became heavy in the dive.

David concentrated on the lead bomber, centering his sight pip on the wing root. If they were spotted, the bombers would duck into the cloud and escape. He armed his guns and rested his thumb on the firing button. He didn't think of killing men, but he saw an image of WAAF bodies lying scattered and broken. The girl refueling his Hurc, a streak of blood across her face. The image was replaced by the Heinkel filling his gun sight. He squeezed the firing button for three seconds. The bomber's port engine burst into flames and the Heinkel dove for the cloud.

David jinxed and found a second target slipping into the clouds. He squeezed the firing button as his sight pip crossed the cockpit. The bomber's windshield exploded in a shower of glass. Pieces broke off the Heinkel and came flying back at him as if someone had thrown a bag of garbage out the window. Smoke poured from the port engine and the HE-111 rolled slowly on its back.

Tracers flashed by David's canopy, inches over his head. He heard a popping sound and holes appeared where bullets punched through the fabric of his wing. He rolled the Hurricane and pulled the elevators back, plunging down toward the protective cover of the clouds. A cannon shell pierced the armor plating on his seat back, throwing him sideways. He plunged into the safety of the cloud and its white vapor entombed him.

David brought his power back and tried to level the Hurricane, but his instrument panel was shattered. He had no idea what his attitude was. He trimmed the nose back to what he thought was level. A warning light flashed. His oil temperature needle was pegged at the redline. He eased the throttle back and trimmed the nose up dropping his flaps and gear. The magnetic compass spun out of control.

David glanced at his radiator temperature. His engine was overheating. Black smoke seeped in from under the cowling. He could feel the heat in the cockpit from the engine burning. A vision of Binkie's burning spitfire flashed before him. He thought of the dream and Binkie screaming at him to get out. His hand wrenched open the latch handle on the canopy. It slid back easily. Wind roared into the open cockpit and David felt the cold wet moisture. He unplugged his oxygen and radio leads and pulled the release pin on his safety harness. His face felt flush from the flames lapping around the engine. He struggled to stand up in the narrow confines of the cockpit. David flinched at the noise and buffeting. He grabbed the sides of the cockpit and kicked his legs upward, hurling himself over the side. His helmet and goggles were wrenched from his head by the wind. The cold moisture in the cloud felt good on his flush face. The rush of noise ceased, and he felt as though he was falling upward.

He heard an explosion nearby, but saw nothing. Was it his plane? He'd barely escaped. How long since he'd left the cockpit? Was it seconds or minutes? Was he over land or water? Where was he? He had been around twenty thousand feet when he bailed out; how long would it take to drop? David wondered if he'd break out of the overcast in time to open his parachute. He didn't think anyone saw him take a hit. Maybe control would have marked the location of their initial engagement and someone would be looking for him when he didn't return to base. With ten to one odds against them, how would anyone come out of this alive. Strike and run; take cover in the cloud. It was the only way anyone could hope to survive.

David tried to remember if they'd crossed the coast and were over the channel. He pictured the dark abyss below, and a chill went through his body. What'd happened? He'd shot the first Heinkel and immediately turned on the second. The attackers must've closed faster than he'd thought. David recalled the tracers flashing past his canopy and the pings of bullets striking his plane. Before he could react, a cannon shell had slammed into his armored seat back and another had destroyed his instruments. The cloud cover was the only thing that'd saved him. It looked a lot darker below. Hell, which way was below? He couldn't see a thing. David didn't know how far he'd fallen or how far it was to the ground, or maybe the water. He grabbed the D-ring and pulled his rip cord. The parachute streamed out of his seat pack and popped open jerking him around. The loose straps snapped tight, sending a searing pain into his thighs and crotch. He'd always left his parachute straps somewhat loose. It was uncomfortable flying for hours with the straps pulled tight. That was a mistake he wouldn't make again.

David thought of all the tight spots he'd led his team through. He'd been their quarterback, and they followed him, unquestioning. Only now he was alone; still, there was a game plan. If he came down over land, would he see the ground before he hit? He pulled his feet up in a semi-crouch to help take up the initial shock of landing. What if he was over water? He'd have to get clear of the chute before hitting the water. Any breeze would catch his billowing chute and drag him under. Once clear of the chute, he could inflate his Mae West. It all sounded so simple, but David was scared. The unknown element left so many questions; he'd tried to prepare himself for anything.

David listened intently. He could hear the sound of rolling and crashing waves. He put his hand on the parachute harness release, waiting. He strained his eyes trying to see the water below him. The first white-capped rollers appeared through the fog. The water looked grey-green, dirty and cold. David had been fascinated with the ocean while on the troop ship coming from Halifax. He looked all around. There was nothing. No ships, no land, just miles of empty sea.

He was alone, on his own. He knew the feeling. A stadium full of people and he stood by himself. All his receivers covered, his blockers behind him and only the opposing tackles coming at him. Now the opposing tackle would be the cold, wet empty sea. The water looked darker as he dropped closer. He watched the rising swells climbing up, reaching for him, then dropping away leaving deep gaping caverns, black holes, waiting to swallow him. White crests breaking at the top of each wave were whipped into a spraying froth by the gusty winds.

David thought he was close. His feet seemed to be touching the water and he turned the quick release on his parachute harness, falling free. He plummeted, his stomach coming up in his throat. The water rose toward him and still he was falling. David felt no sensation when his feet entered the water, only the continuous downward plunge. Bubbles rose up all around him. He looked up and saw a trail of bubbles to the surface. He watched in fascination as the bubbles continued to climb upward, away from him, as he plunged deeper. He didn't know how far he'd fallen before hitting the water. He struggled desperately, swimming up to the surface. His flying suit and gear held him back. His chest hurt and his lungs cried out for oxygen. His feet seemed encased in concrete.

David could see the surface above him and he reached out, but it was beyond his grasp. A face appeared yet he could not make out any of its features. It was clouded in a misty white veil and it called to him, "David. David." It was Millie; he saw her face and reached up toward her outstretched hand. He felt a surge in the waves pulling him away. David kicked and heard Millie calling, "It will always bring you back to me." He lunged up trying to grasp Millie's hand.

David's head broke through the Channel's surface and he gasped for air. A wave crested and rolled over him. He inhaled water instead of oxygen. His body reacted involuntarily, vomiting bile and salt water. He was drowning and yet he struggled wildly in the breaking wave. His head broke through the turbulent surface and he gulped air into his tortured lungs. He remembered his Mae West and pulled on the cord to inflate it. David lay back exhausted, gasping for air. With his Mae West inflated, he bobbed on the surface like a kite on a string in gusty winds, rising and falling with the swells. Shivering, he pulled his dinghy out of its case, found the CO_2 bottle and his cold, numb hands grappled with the inflation cord. He struggled to climb into the dinghy, but every time he was almost in, it flipped over on him. He angrily kicked and finally propelled himself over the side. The dinghy was half full of water, but David was too tired to care.

David felt an uncontrollable urge to urinate and pondered on how he would accomplish that task. He kneeled in the dingy to pee over the side and a wave flipped the dingy. He was back in the water, but at least he solved one problem before he struggled back into the dinghy.

Each time the dinghy reached a crest, David scanned the horizon. The clouds were lifting, maybe an observation plane would spot him. David found a package of yellow sea marker dye in the raft's emergency provisions and excitedly tore it open. The dye spread out on the water. In his haste David spilled some of the dye in the raft. His blue uniform was covered with a green splotch that looked as though he'd thrown up.

The hours passed, and he shook violently from the cold. David wondered what it was like to die. Would the sea become his grave? He'd never faced the realities of death. Not him. He would not die. It was always someone else, Duffy, Swede, the Huns. But David was uneasy. This was real.

How long could he survive floating around in his little dinghy? Soaked, wet and cold, without food or water. How would death find him? Suppose a German patrol boat found him? Would they gun him down in the water or pick him up to rot in prison?

What would happen to his spirit if he was not given a proper Sioux burial; would it roam forever in the dark? He clutched his totem in his hand, seeking a vision, a sign. He had been named Rain-in-the-Face, where was his totem to lead him?

To survive, David reasoned, was to run the risk of dying all over again in a week. Faced with death or survival, instinct takes over and you do whatever is necessary. You fight and struggle because neither life nor death is certain. He sat soaked and shivering in the dinghy. How long would he last wet and near freezing? The sea would decide.

David was startled out of his day dreaming by the chugging of a boat engine approaching. He felt a panic. Was it a British or a German boat? He turned, trying to follow the boat's progress. David pulled his service revolver from the top of his flying boot and checked that it was loaded. Six rounds, not much he could do with that. If it was a German boat and they threatened to shoot, he was determined to send as many of the enemy to the happy hunting grounds as he could before they killed him. He felt a surge of ancestral blood pounding in his veins. He was a Sioux, he would live or die with honor. It seemed to take forever for the boat to reach him. It disappeared below the crests and then surged over the top.

David slipped the revolver inside his flight jacket, out of sight, but handy if needed. The ship looked small and belched forth volumes of black smoke. The sides were a rust color and what little paint remained hung precariously in scaly sheets. Three seamen stood on deck; one threw a rope boarding ladder over the side, while the other two stood guard with rifles. David could not make out the name of the ship, but a ripped and wind-tattered Union Jack snapped in the breeze. The pilot, watching from an open window in the grimy pilot house, slowed the boat to a dead stop in the water.

David heard their excited voices. "Looks like a damn Kraut to me. Keep your guns on him boys. If'n he makes a false move, blast him."

"Hello," David shouted. With numb, frozen hands he paddled the dinghy toward the boarding ladder, being careful not to show his hidden gun lest they mistake him for a Hun. The diesel engine rumbled deep in the bowels of the rusting boat as it labored, ever so slowly, climbing the swells toward David. "I'm David Hampton, R.A.F. 11th group."

"What'n the hell kind of uniform is that?" One of the guards pointed his rifle at David.

David looked at his uniform and laughed. "I got sea dye all over when I opened the dye marker." David reached up, grabbing the boarding ladder. The boat climbed a swell, dragging him from the dinghy. He grappled with the ladder, clinging desperately as a wave surged up behind him. Strong arms reached down and pulled him on deck. "Sure as hell glad to see you guys," stammered David, collapsing on the deck. "I wasn't sure whether you were British or not."

"Come'n below, we'll get you some dry duds. That uniform looks like hell." A seaman led the way down a narrow companionway. The ship was a bucket of rust and smelled of oil, grease and diesel fuel.

The wool navy pants and shirt were scratchy and coarse and several sizes too large, but they were warm and dry. A sailor handed him a steaming mug. David didn't care what it was as long as it was hot. He held the mug in both hands trying to gain what warmth he could from the cup. He took a sip and choked. "What the hell's this?"

"Drink'er up, matey. Good ol' navy blackstrap rum, a hundred an fifty proof she is. Make a man outa yah."

David sipped the hot rum slowly, feeling a rush of warmth from the inside.

"You got to hold your breath when you sip 'er," laughed the seaman.

"Hey, Benny! On deck. Got a couple more fly boys to pull out'a the drink."

"Gotta go, David. Let me fill your mug. It'll warm you from the toes up." Benny filled the mug then grabbed his rifle and headed topside.

The ship rolled from side to side as it slowed and David braced himself in the corner. He felt no pain as he sipped the dark syrupy liquid.

"Got yah some company, David," called Benny from on deck.

David wondered if they were pilots from his squadron, then he heard a clamor on deck and cursing.

Two German flyers stumbled into the galley, followed by Benny with his rifle at ready. They were only kids. Wet, scared and shaking from the cold. Benny motioned them to sit opposite David and handed each a mug of navy rum. "You got your service revolver, David; you can keep an eye on 'em for me. I don't think they'll be givin' you any trouble," said Benny heading topside.

David wondered if they were from the bomber he'd shot down. For them, the war was over. In a few days, David would be back in the air, fighting. He'd fought and killed. Been shot at and bailed out. He'd beaten the sea, but what other encounters awaited?

The ancient, rusting navy ship bucked the seas for twelve hours. David's two companions were both sick. He didn't have to worry about guarding them.

The Thames was calm and smelled like a sewer. The oil slicked water was covered with floating debris and garbage. Sea gulls swarmed around the ship as they pulled into a remote warehouse dock. A WAAF stood waiting with a car to drive David back to his base.

His flight report completed, David found a new uniform and headed for The Station.

"Pigskin," shouted Hap as soon as he entered. "Thought we'd seen the last ah you when you didn't come back with the boys. What happened?"

"I'm so dry, I can't even spit. I'll probably need three or four ales before I can talk proper."

"Coming right bloody up matey," said Hap clicking his false teeth and filling David's mug till it foamed over the top. "Never mind denying it, I heard you were Buddy-buddy with some ah that navy trash!"

"We were vectored for an intercept and topped out at twenty thousand feet. We turned into the sun and climbed to twenty-five, so the sun would be behind us and the Krauts below." David took a sip of ale.

"Come on with the bloody story, Pigskin," prompted Hap impatiently.

"Well, there they were below and the sun behind us. Perfect setup, right? A flight of Messerschmitts bounced us just as we rolled in on the attack. They opened fire trying to divert us, but we were out of range for them to be effective. I fired on a Heinkel from two hundred yards and he dove into the clouds with one engine burning."

"He's as good as dead," said Hap smiling a toothless grin.

"Just as I dove for the protective cover, I see another Heinkel. I pulled up and squeezed the firing button. I watched my bullets punching holes into the port engine. I had to pull up to keep from crashing into him. I heard bullets hitting my kite and rolled over, diving for the deck. A cannon shell shattered my instrument panel before I gained the safety of the clouds."

"Sure sounds safe to me," said Joker. "Shot up, in the cloud and no instruments!"

"My radiator'd been hit. The engine temperature red-lined. About that time I started thinking of bailing out. When smoke and flames shot out of the cowling, over the side I went."

"Jeez," muttered Hap wiping the sweat from his brow. "No wonder you look so funny. You've got no eyebrows!"

"I didn't know how high I was. I knew I was around eighteen thousand feet when I bailed out, so I thought I could count to a hundred and then open my chute. Should have been plenty of time, right?"

"Come on, David. Just give us the important parts," said Joker.

"I decided I'd better pull my rip cord. Wasn't sure how far I'd fallen. Don't know how long I was in the cloud, but all of a sudden I could hear waves breaking. Remember how they told us to release our chutes just before we hit the water?"

"Yeah," said Joker and everyone nodded their heads in agreement.

"Well, I thought my feet were almost in the drink." David sipped his ale. "When I released from my chute, I must've still been fifty or sixty feet up. I hit the water without slowing down. I went down as far as I was up. Swallowed half the Channel and floated around in the dinghy most of the day. I wondered whether it'd be the Brits or the Krauts who found me first. Got picked up by a navy patrol boat that looked like it hadn't seen port in several months, maybe years."

"Probably hasn't," said Hap. "Lot of 'em were pulled out of the bone yard, and except for fuel and supplies, they won't come in unless they have trouble."

"Best damn rum I ever tasted," said David, smacking his lips. "You should have some Hap. Thick as syrup."

"Bloody navy gets it all," grumbled Hap.

"Guess I'll just have to bail out over the Channel so as I can try some," said Joker.

"What's our hero doing sitting here with a three-day pass in his pocket?" chortled Woody, pulling up a stool next to David.

"Just resting up a bit, Woody. You find me a new kite yet?"

"Well, yea're sure tough on me kites, Davie. We'll have to order a dozen more just to keep yea flying. Besides yea'd best be giving Millie a call. She's been worried sick since she learnt yea're missing."

"I don't want to cause her any more grief, Woody, I mean, after all she went through when Binkie was killed."

"Let me tell you some'n, Davie, it's too late for that. Since yea came along, it's the first I've seen her happy. So, whatever yea're doing, keep doing it. Or I may come lookin' for yea wid me shillelagh."

"In that case, I'd best find a telephone!"

"You can use my call-box in back, Pigskin," said Hap, grinning and clicking his false teeth in and out.

David came back to the bar, ten minutes later, and called for another ale.

"Long call?" asked Woody inquisitively.

David sat quietly sipping his ale.

"Well?" said Hap.

David drained his mug and wiped his mouth with the back of his hand, a grin on his face. "See you guys later. I got a date with a lady!"

A heavy blanket of moisture settled in as darkness came. The clanging bell on the engine sounded muted by the fog. David stared out of the sooted, dirty window, unseeing. The train lurched down the track, swaying like a drunk trying to walk the rail. Things happened so fast. Only six months ago he'd been sitting down to the supper table at home. Insistent chatter from his brothers and sisters filled the air, like a swarm of bees buzzing around a hive. His father reviewed the day's work between bites, talking with his mouth full, so as not to waste a moment of the day. Mother scurried around the table making sure there was enough of everything for her family. She always ate after everyone was finished. Funny, thought David, he didn't know of another family that ever ate like that. By the time dessert and coffee had been served, his father was laying plans for the next day's work. It was October, and they'd probably be plowing the north forty before freeze-up.

The long moan of the locomotive whistle woke David from his dreaming. The truth was that he was homesick. He'd broken the ties to home when he struck out on his own, but he still liked to think back to the good times and worried about how they were getting on without him.

The engine's bell clanged as they approached the station following a maze of tracks. Squealing brakes grated on David's ears as the locomotive slowed to a stop in Victoria Station. David thought it must be foggy in England every day of the year. He had yet to see the station when it wasn't blanketed by fog. People disappeared in the fog like spectral beings. He stepped down from the car onto the stool the porter had placed at the bottom of the steps.

"David!" Millie ran towards him. She threw her arms around his neck and buried her face into his jacket.

He held her, yet felt unsure. He could feel her body racked with sobs, shaking, and he tightened his arms around her. "It's okay, Millie. I'm here. Just like I promised."

She looked up into his eyes, still clinging to his arms. "David, I was so scared I'd lost you." Tears spilled from her eyes like large drops at the beginning of a rain storm.

"Millie, I care for you. I was worried that I'd acted stupidly last time we were together."

"No, you didn't, David. I hadn't finished saying all my goodbyes. But, now I have. Only damn it! Why'd you have to be a fighter pilot?"

"I suppose I could ask for a safe desk job. Out of harm's way," said David.

"And you'd grow to hate me. Every time a plane took off, you'd be flying miles away. No, David, the only way I want you is for you to be yourself. If I'm lucky, maybe I can occupy a small part of your world!"

"I've got three days and I'd like to spend it all with you, if I can?"

"I don't know what you're doing to me, David, but I feel the same way." Millie stood with her hands grasping his arms and looking deep into his eyes.

Her eyes were wide, questioning, like David had never seen them before. He felt as though she'd opened her soul to him, and he was frightened. He'd never been responsible for anyone before, and yet for the first time, he felt like a man. In his mind he'd accepted the responsibility and took her into his arms. "Maybe we should go someplace other than the train station? People are starting to stare."

"I don't care, David, let them stare. They'll never enter our world." Millie stepped back, smiling and reaching for David's hand. "Will you stay at the flat with me?"

"Yes." He bent and kissed her, tasting her lips and her hungry response.

The apartment felt familiar, and David dropped his kit bag in the corner of the bedroom, hanging their jackets in the closet. He noticed the new curtains on the windows, and several pictures hung on what had been bare walls. Two plants sat snugly in the window box.

Millie poured scotches and joined David on the chesterfield. "David, we shouldn't be seeing each other. We've so many differences. It'll probably end in a lot of grief for both of us. I don't know why I'm acting so foolishly, but you've done something to me. I can't help myself."

David felt his heart stop for a moment. He held his drink unnoticed. "Millie, I won't let anything come between us -- unless it's because I'm a half Sioux Indian?"

"No, that has nothing to do with it. David, you're of a different class. You're an officer and I'm just a simple Irish girl. A Mick. No family, no standing, I'll only drag you down."

"Millie, you are first class, and besides, in America there are no classes. We can do anything we want. Go anywhere we want. Everyone is equal. That's one of the reasons I'm here. To protect and preserve that freedom. I wasn't an officer when I started, not like some of the pampered English upper classes. I started out as a pilot sergeant."

"David, I'm Catholic, and you're not!"

"My family is Lutheran, but I only went to that church because that's the one they attended. Actually, I really believe more in the Sioux way...the way of my mother's people. There is no separation by classes or religion. So, what other problems do we have to solve?"

Millie's laugh of relief set David's mind to ease. "How are you in the kitchen, my love?"

"A wizard. I was the oldest in our family and helped my mother all the time."

"I've a surprise."

David followed Millie into the kitchen where she unwrapped two large steaks. "Where?" he stammered. "Where did you get those steaks? I haven't seen a steak since I arrived in England."

"I've a few connections in operations. Once in a while, for a really special occasion, I can arrange something. Turn the radio on to the BBC, David. There's usually some good American music playing this time of night."

David adjusted the tuner until most of the static was gone. "This is the BBC, and now we bring you our program of favorite dance music." Perry Como was singing "Lili Marlene." Millie slipped into David's arms, resting her head on his shoulder. They danced.

Millie had set the table with a linen table cloth and fine china she unpacked from a box in the closet. Candles lighted the table, and David opened a mild, dark red wine. The radio crooned, "You'd be so nice to come home to," and with that they raised their glasses in a silent toast to each other.

That night they made love. Freely they gave of themselves to each other, with no inhibitions, no fears and no uncertainties. The morning came without their awareness. It was near noon and they lay snuggled in each other's arms, talking quietly. The war was a long way away. They mutually avoided the subject, like something taboo.

They strolled through the park, Millie holding on to David's arm. "Tell me about Minnesota and the farm and your family, especially your Indian heritage."

"That's a wee bit of telling. Might take a few years," kidded David.

"Then tell me about your family first. They might not even like me," teased Millie.

"Don't you worry about them not liking you. Why, you'd be adopted instantly. Now Dad, he's English, tall and skinny but all muscle. His face is dark and wrinkled from being outside all the time. And, he's as strong as an ox. In two minutes he'd have you sitting at the kitchen table drinking a cup of coffee and telling you how to plant the north-forty or fix some broken machinery. Mom, she's a full-blooded Sioux, kind of plump now and always happy go lucky. I guess, in her day she was a real looker, and my dad was crazy about her...he still is. She'd be all flustered, probably be cleaning the house and fixing it up for months. She'd be making tea and trying to find a recipe for crumpets and wanting to know if you've met the King and Queen."

Millie laughed, "Someday I'd like to meet them. They sound like so much fun, but I certainly hope they won't go to all that fuss just for me. What about your brothers and sisters?"

"Chelsie will graduate from school next spring and is something of a lady. Wants to be an actor. Then there's the twins. Steffanie and Stefan, and the way they work and wrestle around, you'd never know they were brother and sister. Clayton's going to be dad's number one helper. Spends a full day in the fields even though he's only fourteen. I think he'll be the one to take over the farm someday. Susie's the baby, and she'd always tag along with me everywhere I went. Even when I was taking flying lessons, she'd come to the airport with me and wait until I'd finished. She wants to be just like Amelia Earhart and fly all over the world. I miss that little tyke more than anything. We're a typical half-Sioux family. I'm the darkest, and Susie could pass for pure white."

"You're lucky to have such a loving family. Already I'm beginning to feel like I know them. I never had any family except Mac. Funny, I never called him anything but Woody except when our auntie was around. She raised us and wouldn't tolerate anything but proper names. My dad was a pilot in the Great War and was killed before I was born. Funny, I don't even know what he looked like. My mother died giving birth to me. Woody and me, we were charity cases until an old maid aunt took us in. She worked the devil out of us. Got her money's worth she did. Woody was my knight in shining armor. My protector and benefactor. Until Woody enlisted in the R.A.F. as a mechanic, we'd never been apart. When Woody went, so did I. I joined the WAAFs and finally got out in the world on my own."

They walked through the park, arm in arm. The sun shone brightly through tree branches, and birds sang and flitted about overhead. They spread a blanket on the grass and had a picnic with wine, cheese and hard rolls. They talked for hours about their families and never seemed to tire of talking.

The three days passed and had seemed as one. It was time for David to leave. He felt an emptiness, a hollow in his gut. Something he'd never experienced -- another kind of fear -- and he wasn't sure how to deal with it. In his Hurricane, he knew what to do to evade the enemy bullets. At least in his plane there was something he could do, he could fight back. Now he felt helpless, as though he'd been benched by the coach, and all he could do was watch from the sideline.

He needed to do something, needed some assurance to hold on to, to feel deep inside. Some tangible evidence that this weekend with Millie had actually happened, that it wasn't a fantasy of his imagination. "Millie," he started, not knowing what to say, "I've never felt this way about anyone. I want to spend the rest of my life with you."

Millie looked away, staring out the window at the park, into the distance. "Are you asking me to marry you?"

"Yes," he said without hesitation. "Will you marry me?" He was afraid of what her answer would be. He'd made a commitment and felt relieved at finally saying what he felt.

"Where will we live, what will we do? What about children and a home?" Millie's mind raced on, thinking of all the obstacles before them. "David, I love you and we've just spent a fabulous three days together. Let's think about this, apart, for a time. We can talk about it more on your next leave."

David felt dejected. "I'm not sure when I'll be able to get a leave again. With the German attack, it may be some time."

"Call me when you get a leave, David. I can arrange my time so we can be together." There were a lot of differences between them, and yet she knew she needed him as he needed her; maybe that was all that was important. She felt a tingle of excitement from his touch, and a look of invitation sparkled in her eyes as she took his hand and led him into the bedroom.

Air-raid sirens wailed throughout the night. Search lights crisscrossed the skies seeking the Hun bombers. The steady pomp-pomp-pomp sound came from the flak guns sending their deadly shells looking for the invaders. Fire engines raced through the darkened streets, sirens screaming. The wailing sound of ambulances could be heard as they sped to the rescue of bomb victims. The steady thumping of exploding bombs sent shock waves throughout London and rattled windows in the flat.

David and Millie were oblivious to the sounds around them.

Joker

It was dark as David stumbled through the blackout curtain into the barracks. It smelled like a locker room. There were wet clothes hanging around like a Chinese laundry. "Joker, how goes the battle?"

"Hey, Pigskin. We slaughtered'em. How's London and lady love?"

"We had a great time. The shortest three days of my life."

"Seems like you're spending an awful lot of time with Millie." Ralph grinned. "When's the big day?" David didn't answer right away. Ralph began whistling the wedding march.

"Is there a wedding in the making?" piped in Chief, his shower clogs slapping noisily on the floor. Still dripping from the shower, he stood naked except for the towel wrapped around his waist.

"We're just good friends," said David.

"She's breaking up that old gang of mine," sang Joker.

"All right, you guys. So tell me what happened. Any more kills? Any new kites?"

"We lost three guys. Kobby, Baker and Roberts." said Chief.

"Chief and I each got another kill," Joker said. "Maybe we can get you another weekend pass and catch up, Pigskin."

"Fat chance, but I'll take the three-day pass if you can swing it. What's the status on planes? I see we're posted for zero-five-thirty takeoff."

"We've got ten new Hurcs. For the first time, we've gained more planes than we've lost," said Chief. "They want us at altitude before daylight. The Krauts have switched from bombing air fields to civilians in London. We're to be in position to intercept Krauts crossing the Channel."

"Sure as hell glad you're back," piped up Joker. His face looked drawn and tired. "We've had to fly with that prick Simpson, who doesn't know dick shit about fighting. All he wants to do is fly his friggin' formations."

Chief laughed sadistically. "Whole squadron would've been wiped out, but Joker and me saw the Krauts diving on us from the sun and broke to intercept. Simple-Simpson flies everyone else into a Lufberry circle; round and round they go, covering each other's asses. Someone forgot to tell the

Squareheads the rules of the game. The Krauts picked'em out one at a time diving from above. They would've had a turkey shoot if it hadn't been for me and Joker."

"Kobby and Baker both got it on the Kraut's first pass. They were following Simpson like the Pied Piper." The Joker's face was tight as he described the action. "Jerry didn't see Chief and me right away. They were concentrating on the Hurcs circling below. We had a pretty good deflection shot. ME-109s flew through our line of fire. We turned right behind 'em. Rammed the throttle full forward."

"Errr," Chief imitated his Hurc diving, his hands depicting the action. "The Krauts slowed to turn back for another attack. We were right on their tails." Chief used his left hand for the German pulling out and his right hand for his diving Hurricane. "I was less than two hundred yards and closing like a sea gull after a dead herring on the beach. I could see my bullets tearing into the Messerschmitt. Pieces came flying off like leaves in a September wind storm. The damn thing blew up in my face. I was in a ball of fire. Something hit my wing and I was thrown sideways in the cockpit and knocked out. When I came to, I was in a spin. The canopy was burned from the fire, and I had to open it to see. By the time I'd recovered from the spin, I was only a thousand feet up."

"We split up, picking our own targets," said Joker. His eyes sparkled recapturing the event. He held a broom handle in his hand and moved it subconsciously as though it were the control stick. "I opened fire as another Kraut pulled out of his dive. My bullets were punching holes in that Messerschmitt like a woodpecker on a dead tree. His wing snapped and all I could see was that damn wing in my windshield. I hauled back on the control with both hands. I hit that wing and it felt like I'd flown into a brick wall. I didn't know what the hell'd happened. My Hurc was shaking like it had the chills. I popped the canopy open and pulled the power back to bail out, and it stopped shaking. I limped back, but that Hurricane was as spooky as a virgin in the back seat of my Studebaker. When I got out of that Hurc, I saw why. One side of the horizontal stabilizer was missing."

"We've been damn lucky with close shots," said David. "Next time I get close in, I'll give'em a squirt and break. The hell with waiting to see the fireworks. Better hit the sack guys. I left a zero-three-thirty wake-up call."

"Jeez. Why the hell so early?" asked Joker.

"I want everyone ready."

"Ah, Pigskin. That's not a good call," said Chief. "Why not just go with the play from the bench?"

"'Cause I'm not Simpson," retorted David. "Course, if you want to fly with him...."

"Okay. Zero-three-thirty it is," said both in unison.

David slept in a state of confusion. He dreamt of his squadron flying in and out of the cloud tops. At twenty-five thousand feet their windscreens were frost-covered. They flew around building columns of towering cumulus, unaware of the Huns above them. The Germans had positioned themselves directly in the sun. David called out a warning, but no words came from his mouth. The Huns rolled over, attacking. The nose of the lead Messerschmitt was yellow. David rubbed his eyes and looked again. There was a schnauzer on the side of the cockpit. Lights winked from the machine guns in the wings of the Messerschmitts. Why hadn't they listened to his warning?

He dreamt of the game they'd played against Bemidji. He'd sensed the blitz, but the coach had sent in a deep pass play. David called for a time out. The coach wouldn't listen to him. At the snap of the ball, David had turned, faked a handoff and faded back. He turned around to pass, his arm back with the ball. He hadn't seen the blitz coming, even though he knew it was there. He was hit from the side, breaking three ribs.

David felt the pain in his side and rolled over, moaning in his sleep. He tried to signal his squadron to break, but couldn't raise his arm. Helplessly he watched. One by one, his pals were shot and fell from the sky.

David awoke in a sweat. He stepped into his shower clogs, grabbed a towel and headed for the showers. He'd never sleep after that damn dream. The cold shower felt refreshing, washing away the sweat and the dreaded dream.

Returning from the showers, David heard a low grumbling. The troops were awake.

"Here he comes, boys," called Joker. "Attila the Hun."

"You'll laugh tonight at The Station," countered David, "when you tell everyone how I bagged two more Krauts."

"Anyone who bags a Kraut today has free beer on the rest of the squad," said Chief.

A chorus of "Hear! Hear's!" rang through the barracks. David knew he had a good team behind him. They'd show the Krauts how to play ball.

The clammy, cold fog drove a chill through David as he stepped into the night air. It felt like a bad omen. He tried to shrug it off but the feeling wouldn't go away. He heard the cough of a Hurricane starting up in the dispersal area. Fitters and riggers were already warming up the machines for the morning's flight.

David slipped through the blackout curtain and entered the operations room. He glanced at the weather report: solid overcast. They'd be climbing on instruments. The Germans sure as hell couldn't bomb targets they couldn't see. Maybe they'd catch a flight on top. David thought about his bailout and plunge into the black abyss. A chill ran through him.

The pilots gathered around David, like a huddle. It was his team. His play to call and only he would have to answer when something went wrong. He met the three new pilots. Eager, smiling kids. In an hour they could be dead.

"Listen up," called David. "Here's the play. Formation takeoff and climb out. Navigation lights on until we break out. Radio silence until we spot Krauts. Use your call sign and proper radio procedures. When we level out, Joker, you take your vic up five thousand feet above us and cover our asses. We don't want to be surprised again. Okay, men," and they were men, because they flew in harm's way. "There's only a six hundred foot ceiling so form up right away. When we begin our climb, keep it in tight. Questions?"

David looked at each of his team. They were a good team even though three of the pilots were new. The stakes were high. It wasn't just a game anymore, although some still thought of it as such. "Let's go kick ass."

A lorry drove them out to the dispersal areas, dropping pilots off at their planes. The grass was wet with dew, and the Hurricanes looked like it had just rained. Fitters and riggers scurried around the Hurcs making final preparations for takeoff. David jumped down with his Mae West and parachute slung over one arm. He stood admiring the new football painted on the cowling with Pigskin written across it. "Woody, how's the new kite?"

"Good as new she is. Yea got to promise me to bring this one back!" Woody chortled.

"Well, I'll do my damndest. Only trouble is those lousy Krauts keep shooting at me!" David chuckled as he kicked the tires and made his walk-around, his hands in his pockets. "Looks good to me. By the way, how'd you like to have a Yank for a brother-in-law?"

"Yah-hoo," shouted Woody. "Best damn news I've heard since the war started. Yea and Millie gettin' hitched?"

"It's not official yet," David said. "I just asked her. She hasn't given me an answer."

"Hell, she didn't say no?" asked Woody, pumping David's hand. "Yea mark me words, David. I know me sister. She didn't say no, she wants it as much as yea. Just takes her a little longer to make up her mind."

"You don't go blabbing to anyone until she does. Now, get over here and help me get ready, and quit dancing around like a silly goon." David strapped on his parachute and climbed up on the wing. It was awkward maneuvering into the narrow cockpit with all of his flying gear on. He tightened the straps on his parachute. He plugged in the radio lead from his helmet, connected his oxygen line and checked his mask.

Woody snapped the last safety strap into the quick release and tapped David on the shoulder. "Yea mind what yea're about, and get yea arse back here in one piece, brother-in-law." His chortle fell away as he jumped down from the wing.

The start-engine flare arced into the air. David called, "Clear." The engine was still warm and started on the first turn. He brought the throttle back to idle and signaled the rigger to remove the power cart and wheel chocks. David watched his team taxi into takeoff position behind him.

David shut everything from his mind, concentrating on the one and only thing he now had to do. His team depended on him and would follow his leadership. If he made one mistake, it could cost lives. A game was one thing, but this was life and death. David was doing his damndest to make his team winners. Not only was he their quarterback, but they expected him to be their coach, doctor and father. He breathed in deeply, smelling the fresh air. After last night's rain, it smelled like spring.

The takeoff flare hung suspended, glowing in the morning fog. David eased his throttle forward and the Merlin engine responded with a sharp bark in the damp morning air. The squadron moved as one. He set the pace and the rest followed, leveling off at a hundred feet. Retracting the gear and flaps, he regretfully closed his canopy. The rush of fresh air gone, he set the power for a cruise climb, rolling the trim wheel back for the change in attitude. David's world was now crammed into the small cockpit. His eyes scanned the instruments in a revolving, never-ending pattern. The horizon bar was level, the needle-ball centered and his heading steady. A glow from his navigation lights reflected back from the moisture-laden cloud. David, head down, concentrated on his instruments.

The climb was smooth, and David began to relax, still he maintained his rigid pattern of instrument scanning. He could almost feel his wing man tucked in tight, flying on his lead. David's wing tip would be less than a wing span in front of that turning propeller.

Rain pelted against the wind screen. First a few hard drops hitting with a splatter, then a loud hammering. They'd flown into a building thunderstorm. David's Hurricane bucked in the turbulence. He fought to maintain control.

An eerie glowing ball of light appeared on the top of his instrument panel. Like a little gremlin, it grew and danced across the top of his panel. David had never seen St. Elmo's fire before. He'd heard about it and knew what it was, but there was something foreboding about it. David felt the static buildup in the air. His hair felt like it was standing on end. A thunderstorm was building very close to them.

The squadron climbed through ten thousand feet, still buried deep in the clouds. David added more power and boost and adjusted the trim a fraction more to compensate. Lightning flashed, blinding him momentarily. David scanned his panel. Something was wrong. His climb rate had doubled. They were caught in an updraft. The buffeting increased and he had trouble holding his attitude steady. Time to split. David flashed his navigation lights signaling his team to split and climb on their own. He turned fifty-five degrees to his left. His wing man would wait ten seconds and turn fifty degrees and so on down through the squadron.

David fought the controls to hold his climb attitude. It was no longer a matter of procedures; he struggled to hold his plane right side up and on course. There were now twelve fighters climbing on their own in severe turbulence. A stroke of lightning lit up the sky and he saw spots before his eyes. He turned his cockpit lights on bright so he could see his instruments. A bolt of lightning struck his right wing. His skin tingled and he rocked his wings cautiously checking the controls. David tightened the safety straps and still they felt loose. His Hurricane was being thrown around like a tumble weed bouncing and rolling across the prairie.

As he climbed his Hurricane through eighteen thousand feet, the turbulence slackened. The sky lightened, and he broke out in the clear. David leveled at twenty thousand feet and began orbiting. First one, then two Hurricanes broke out and climbed into formation. Powering back to conserve fuel, hoping against hope, David orbited for fifteen minutes. Two of his pilots were missing. Had something happened to their planes and they returned to base? He couldn't use the R/T. The Germans might be listening.

Reluctantly David turned, leading the squadron toward the Channel. Joker broke, climbing up to cover them from a surprise attack above. David jumped as a voice boomed into his headset.

"Pigskin flight, one hundred-plus bogies, twenty west. Vector two-niner-zero, angels two-five, bluster."

David acknowledged and turned to the intercept heading. He added full power and adjusted his boost. Checking his temperature, he opened the shutters slightly and trimmed for maximum climb. The incoming Huns were at twenty-five thousand; if only he could get above them. The clouds below turned pink as the sun topped the horizon. It was so peaceful; if only it could last. He thought of Millie, how he'd like to share this moment with her.

"Pigskin, Green-one. Bogies, twelve-o'clock level."

"This is Pigskin, Red-one. We'll take them straight on. Spread out and pick your target." David trimmed his Hurricane, settling on a bomber still a distant speck. He dropped his nose slightly until he identified it as a Dornier. It was called the flying pencil because of its slim profile. He armed his guns and rested his thumb on the firing button. They were closing at over five hundred miles per hour. Within seconds the Dornier had filled the bars on his sight pip. David checked his coordination, his needle-ball was centered, and he fired a three-second burst. His tracers flashed out in a high arc and dropped into the cockpit of the Dornier. The plexiglass nose collapsed. Fire flashed through the bomber.

David pulled up over the flaming pencil and dropped his nose looking for another Hun. He scanned the sky all around and checked his rearview mirror. No sign of fighters. A Dornier turned in front of David, diving toward safety in the clouds.

Still drawing full power, David overshot his target. He pulled the throttle back and dropped his gear and flaps. The sudden deceleration threw David against his safety straps. He rolled and dropped the nose. The Hun was right below him. David turned in behind the Dornier. He thumbed the firing button. His bullets ripped pieces off the tail, punching their way forward. Black smoke spewed from the starboard engine.

"Pigskin, Green-one. Bogies two-o'clock high. We're intercepting."

"Pigskin, Red-three. Lost my engine. I'm bailing out."

"Pigskin, Red-one. Break off the bombers. Intercept the bogies."

"Blue-one, out of ammo. Going for cover and back to base."

"Green-three, losing glycol, will try and limp home."

"Pigskin, Red-one. They're turning back. Let's form up and head for the base."

"Yellow-one, I lost my two wing men in the climb."

"Green-one, my number three's got a hot engine. I'll escort him back."

"Blue-two, coming up behind with blue-three."

Five fighters formed up behind David. With the two lost in the climb, they'd lost three, maybe four, pilots. The thunderstorm passed and a scattering of cumulus clouds remained. How fast the weather changed over the English countryside.

Entering the down-wind leg, David searched the field for his missing teammates. Their Hurcs were not in the dispersal area. David lowered his gear, brought the mixture in full, and opened his canopy for landing. Crossing the threshold, he closed the throttle and eased the stick back. His feet worked the rudders, straightening the nose, sinking onto the field. The wheels slid smoothly across the grass, and David gunned the throttle, s-turning back and forth as he taxied toward the dispersal area.

Woody jumped up on the wing as David shut down the engine. "Well, I see yea finally brought me kite back."

"Yeah." said David wearily. "It hasn't been a good day; it cost us. We lost two boys in the climb. One had an engine shot up and bailed out. There's another trying to make the field with an engine overheating."

"But yea turned a hundred or more bombers and fighters back. It's a grand play, Davie me boy." Woody helped David out of the fighter. "And look't me kite. Good as new. Patch a few holes and yea'll be back in the air."

David ran his fingers over the bullet holes. He didn't know he'd been hit. It could have been him instead of the Hurc. His debriefing over, his Hurricane refueled and armed, he was placed back on the ready board. David and his pilots tried to rest, waiting for the next scramble. David pulled out a notebook and finished the letter to his folks he'd started a week ago. He told them about Millie and all the things they'd done together in London. Since he'd met Millie, it seemed as if he never had time to write.

"Good news," called Tommy. "Robert's engine seized up, and he landed in a field."

"Any news on Johnny or Billy the Kid and Glen?" asked David anxiously.

"No, sir," said Tommy. "As soon as I hear, I'll let you know, Pigskin."

David paced back and forth across the operations tent. Waiting. There was nothing to do but wait. It seemed as if they spent all their time waiting. Some were reading or writing letters home. He couldn't write any more when any second there'd be a mad rush to get into the air. David knew they were reaching a dangerous state. Everyone was so tired, mentally and physically. It was when careless accidents happened. He wondered if that's what happened to Billy the Kid and Glen.

The phone rang and everyone tensed, waiting, watching. "Scramble!" shouted Tommy, turning to crank the alert siren.

David threw his Mae West over his head and crowded out the door. His parachute flopped clumsily as he ran to the dispersal area. Fitters had the Hurricane's engines started. David slipped into his parachute and climbed up on the wing. Woody helped him into the cockpit, fastening his safety straps then jumped off the back of the wing. Chocks away, David gunned the engine and taxied for takeoff. He attached his radio leads to his helmet, listening for any instructions. He turned his oxygen on and checked his mask. Pre-takeoff check completed, he turned into the wind and waited.

David fidgeted in the cockpit. What was taking so long? They wasted valuable fuel sitting here on the ground, fuel that could be critical in combat.

David thought about the football game when the coach had pulled him and put in the substitute quarterback. He'd paced the sideline while someone else played his position. His team fumbled the ball, and he lost his temper. He'd pleaded with the coach to let him back into the game, then screamed at him. The coach had sent him to the showers, but there was no going to the showers here.

They were all primed and ready to go. What the friggin' hell was going on? David thought. A lorry sped toward them from the operations tent. "Sir, you're to stand down for now. Your mission's been scrubbed."

Exasperated, David taxied to the dispersal area. He left his parachute on the trailing edge of the wing where it would only take seconds to slip into. David lit a cigar with his shaking hands, trying to relax. He headed back to the operations tent. There was nothing to do but wait. He plopped down in a chair to catch a few minutes of shut-eye, leaving his Mae West on.

David wondered when he would go on liberty again. It seemed that they were either flying or getting ready to fly or on standby alert. Day became night and night became day. When was the last time someone had a day off? A pass was something unheard of. He thought of Millie and felt a chill around his heart. He was afraid to think of her, to let his feelings show. Besides, it could jeopardize his performance when he was flying. He needed to sleep, just for five minutes.

"Squadron scramble!" bawled Tommy.

David was already out the door heading for his Hurricane. Settled into the cockpit, he fastened his safety straps when the takeoff flare arced into the air. "Clear!" shouted David. Woody waved him off. He turned into the wind, gunned the throttle and staggered into the air. "Pigskin Squadron airborne," David called on the R/T.

"Pigskin Leader, fifty-plus bandits over the Channel heading west. Angels fifteen. Vector one-two-zero. Bluster."

They climbed at combat boost and were soon above the brown smog layer surrounding London. David felt naked climbing in clear skies. Nervously his eyes searched the sky above and ahead of them. He would not be surprised again, and he signaled his squadron to spread out. David began jinxing, turning, diving and climbing, constantly checking the skies. His eyesight was exceptional. He usually saw the enemy long before anyone else. At fifteen thousand feet, he rolled his nose left, then right, looking for the Germans.

The White Cliffs of Dover were slipping under his right wing, like airway beacons showing the way back. Eighteen-thousand feet and still no sign of the Krauts. Anxiously, David watched the white rollers in the channel below. Unconsciously his hand felt for his parachute's rip cord, and he tightened his harness straps. He jinxed again and caught a flash of sunlight reflecting off a wing below them.

"Pigskin, Red-one. Bandits nine o'clock low. Spread out and pick your targets." David eased the stick forward. Still at full power, he plunged down on the Huns. They were Junker 88s and had spotted Pigskin's squadron. The bombers nosed over and dove toward London. They were at maximum range and David was not closing. David centered his sight pip on the nearest Junker, checked his needle-ball, and armed his guns. He held the firing button down for three seconds and watched his tracers lazily searching for the Krauts. The range was still too great to be effective. David pushed his throttle through the stops and the Hurricane surged ahead. He checked his sights and fired another three second burst. His bullets converged on the Junker and disappeared.

David nervously watched his engine temperature climb to the red line. He turned the cooling shutters full open. He could not maintain full power much longer or his engine would seize. David watched the bombers head for their targets. Who would they kill this time? Another barracks full of WAAFs, or maybe a school or hospital? David checked his sight pip; he was closing slowly. He felt like a snail, but the Junker's wings began filling the space between his sight bars. David's thumb eased down on the firing button, and he let off a short burst. This time he had the satisfaction of seeing smoke trailing back from one of the Junker's engines.

The Junker jettisoned his bombs and began a slow turn back towards the Channel. David let him go; he was no longer a threat. The diving bombers leveled out for the bomb run. A Junker disappeared in a ball of fire. Someone was getting a few hits. David centered his sight pip on another Junker. White flashes arced toward him from the tail gunner. Bullets pinged off the Merlin engine. They were ineffective. David checked his coordination; the needle-ball was centered, and he fired. His tracers arced across the wide gap of space into the wing of the Junker. Fire wrapped around the wing, and the bomber rolled over in a spiral.

"Green-one. Bandits, six o'clock."

"This is Pigskin leader. Green and Blue, intercept the bandits. Yellow, stay with me and keep hitting the bombers."

David raced after the Junkers and sighted on another. He thumbed his firing button down and watched his tracers arc into the tail of a bomber, then silence. He was out of ammo. "Pigskin, Red-one, out of ammo, heading back to base."

"Green-one, I'm hit! Bailing out."

David turned, looking for Joker's parachute. "Pigskin, Red-one. Anybody see Green-one's chute?"

"Green-two, roger. He just popped his chute, he's okay."

"Pigskin leader, I have him in sight. I'm out of ammo; I'll follow him down. The rest of you stay with the action." David flew alongside Joker and saw him wave. "Control, this is Pigskin leader; we have a pilot in the chute coming down about five west of Dover."

"Roger that, Pigskin leader. We'll alert the watchers in that area."

David throttled back and dropped his gear and flaps circling his pal a short distance out. He popped his canopy open, smelling the fresh sea air. The Merlin engine sounded quiet, idling; he watched the propeller blades turning lazily. Joker swung gently in his parachute and David thought of his own bailout. At least Joker had clear weather and was over land.

Suddenly, Joker's body jerked, hanging in his parachute. White tracers ripped through his body. David froze at the controls, unable to move. He couldn't believe his eyes. This was not happening. This was not possible. Nobody shot an unarmed pilot hanging helplessly in his chute. That was murder. Joker's arm flopped loosely at his side; blood and guts spilled from his stomach. David threw up in his oxygen mask. Gagging in vomit, he clawed his mask off his face.

The yellow-nosed Messerschmitt streaked past, observing the carnage. David screamed, "YOU-SON-OF-A-BITCH!" He slammed his throttle through the gate, retracted his gear and flaps. He turned into the yellow-nosed Messerschmitt. He saw a schnauzer painted just below the cockpit. The pilot grinned at him. David squeezed his firing button, but nothing happened. He was out of ammo. He headed for the murderer. He would ram the Kraut. He was closing fast, pointing his Hurricane at the grinning face. He would never forget that face nor the plane that had murdered the Joker. The German waved and then dropped away in a near vertical dive. Not thinking, David pushed his control stick full forward. His engine quit.

The violent force of the dive momentarily starved the carburetor of fuel. Helplessly David watched the Messerschmitt pull away. Safely out of range, the ME-109 leveled out and rocked his wings in defiance.

Despondently, David restarted his wind-milling engine and flew back to the field. He vowed to hunt until he found the German who'd killed Joker. David drove his Hurricane onto the field, pinning the main gear down solidly. He spun the Hurc around and killed the engine. Woody was on the wing before the engine died. "What'n the hell's wit yea? Flying like a madman?"

"Get'er fueled and guns loaded. Bastards killed Joker. I'm going back after them."

"Calm down, Pigskin. How in tarnation yea going to know which one shot the Joker?" Woody's face was grim as he tried to reason with David. "Besides, yea got to go complete yea debriefing. By the time yea finish, we'll have the kite gassed and guns loaded."

"I'll know that son-of-a-bitch when I see him. He's in the Abbeville squadron. Has a schnauzer painted below his cockpit." David left his parachute on the back of the wing, ready to go, and stomped off toward operations.

"Pigskin," called Chief, running to catch up with David. "What happened to Joker?"

"The Krauts murdered him," said David, his face pale and drawn.

"What? I heard that he bailed out and was okay."

"Some German bastard came streaking in and shot him in his parachute."

Chief stopped and turned to face David. "They shot him in his parachute?"

"That's right. And all I could do was watch."

David completed his briefing report. "You can show me back on line, Tommy. I'll take this into Simpson. Then I'm going up." David marched out of the operations office, head down and determined, as he headed for the CO's office.

Simpson read the report quietly, then questioned David about the attack on Joker. He turned and picked up the telephone and called 11th group headquarters. He spoke quietly into the phone, then sat listening.

Simpson's face was haggard and drained as he answered questions. His mustache twitched nervously, and he sat at attention, his back ramrod straight while he held the phone rigidly, as if he were going to salute.

"David, the commander of 11th group wants to talk with you."

"Sir, I want to get back up and kill the bastard."

"You'll have time enough for that. In the mean time you'll report to the Commander, Eleventh Group Operations, then you have a three-day pass."

"But, you don't understand, sir!" David stammered. "They murdered my pal, it's my job to make'em pay for it."

"You have your orders, Hampton. The sooner you follow them, the sooner you'll be back in the air." Simpson's mustache twitched, "I suggest you get on with them. One more thing: as squadron leader, you will write letters home to the loved ones of the men who've been killed from your squadron. Turn them in to me. I'll add my condolences and mail them. Dismissed."

David stomped out of Simpson's office and headed for the barracks. Bags packed, he walked dejectedly toward The Station to kill time. He had two hours before his train left for London. He stood inside the door letting his eyes adjust to the darkened interior, then walked slowly toward a stool at the end of the bar. Raymond was busy writing and didn't see David until he sat down.

"Hi, Pigskin. How goes the battle?" asked the reporter, closing his notebook.

"Not so good, Raymond. The goddamn Krauts murdered the Joker today." David took a long swallow from the mug of ale Hap placed before him.

"What'n tarnation you talking 'bout, boy?" asked Hap, resting his elbows on the bar, opposite David.

"Joker bailed out. The sons-ah-bitches shot him hanging in his parachute." David saw their faces register disbelief as he gave them the details.

Raymond wrote rapidly, asking questions as he wrote.

"It don't surprise me any!" said Hap. "Back in the Great War, we saw a lot worse things than that." Hap stood looking with a glazed look on his face. A tear formed in the corner of his eye and hung precariously on his stubbled cheek. He turned, angrily wiped the tear on his apron and stomped off down the bar. When he returned, he carried Joker's mug with the picture of a Joker on it. Hap turned Joker's mug upside down with the logo facing out, and reaching up, placed it on the top shelf. He turned and raised his mug in a last toast to the Joker.

"Hap, can I use your telephone to call Millie?" asked David.

"You sure can, Pigskin. You don't have to ask to use it," said Hap gruffly, as he tried to mask his grief.

"Spike, I've got to write letters to the families of everyone in my squadron whose been killed. I don't have the slightest idea what to write."

"Pigskin, you write the truth. Tell them that he was a pilot in your squadron. Put in a couple of lines about the personal things you did in off duty hours and what a great job he did for his country. Finish with how you and the rest of the squadron will miss him. If you want me to look them over when you get done, I'd be pleased to help."

"Thanks, Spike. I'd really appreciate that, at least until I get the hang of it. Guess I'd better go call Millie and see if she can get a couple days off."

"Give her my best regards, Pigskin," called Raymond, as David headed for Hap's office.

David waited nervously for his call to go through channels. He was scared and didn't know what to say; then he heard Millie's voice and all his fears were forgotten.

"David, is that you, Luv?"

David choked up for a moment and then answered, "Yes, Millie."

"David, what's wrong?"

"Joker was killed today!"

"Oh no! What happened?"

"I'm not supposed to discuss it until I meet with the 11th group commander tomorrow. I'm just leaving for London now and have to meet with him first thing in the morning. After that, I'll have three days."

"David, I'll pick you up at Victoria Station. Whatever time you have, Luv, I'll be there."

"Millie. I need you. I feel so lost, so responsible. I just don't know what to do. Got to go. Don't want to miss the train."

"Bye, David. I love you. I'll be waiting."

The telephone clicked in his ear. It seemed to have a finality to it. Like life and death. He left the pub and walked back to the barracks to pick up his bag. He felt entombed as the English mist closed in around him. Kit bag in hand, he headed for the train station. The cold, wet dampness isolated him, and he felt alone, as if he was shut out from everything around him. The long, muffled whistle from the approaching locomotive went unnoticed. He boarded the train and sat in the compartment alone, in a daze.

David felt responsible for Ralph's death. If only he'd listened to his father. He'd be back home working the farm, and Ralph would be alive. How could he write to Lars and Heidi and tell them their son Ralph was dead? What could he say?

David did not notice the swaying motion of the train as it sped through the black, foggy night toward London. The locomotive's bell clanged steadily as they passed crossings and switched through the maze of tracks leading into Victoria Station. The smells of the city seemed to fill the passenger car: the coal smoke, someone's cooking, sewer gasses hanging in the low-lying areas. A car sat waiting to cross the tracks showing only a narrow slit of light from its taped headlights.

The train lurched, jerking back and forth as it came to a stop. The engine wheezed and hissed as if it had just run a race and was trying to catch its breath. Passengers crowded and jostled in a rush to leave. David sat alone in the passenger car in a faraway trance. He could not comprehend what had happened, could not relate it to anything real. It was like walking around in the fog trying to find a way out. He held his grief inside. He felt a hand on his shoulder. He turned and saw Millie.

"Millie!"

She put her arms around him. "Hold me, David."

He no longer tried to keep his pain to himself. He felt Millie's arms around his neck, pulling his head down to rest on her chest. He could not hold back and a flood of tears poured out, like opening the irrigation chute on their farm. His sobbing subsided, and he wiped his face shamefully with the back of his hand. "What a sissy. Crying like a baby."

"David, you're more of a man than any I've ever known. You care for your friends and your men. I know why you are their quarterback." Millie clutched his head to her breast, stroking his hair.

He straightened his uniform and looked deep into her eyes. They were large flooded pools, and her own tears ran down her freckled cheeks to drop unnoticed as she gazed back into his eyes. "David, I have something important to tell you."

"What Millie?" asked David, as a show of concern deepened the furrows on his forehead.

"David, I've missed my period. I may be pregnant."

David sat stunned for a moment; then his face lit up with a smile. "Millie! Millie, you mean, you and me, we're going to have a baby?"

Nervously she clutched her handkerchief. "Well, I haven't been to a doctor yet, but that's what it usually means."

"Millie! That's great news. Holy Cow. We've got to get a bigger apartment, and baby stuff, and...first of all, we have to get married!"

"David, my father was killed before I was born. I haven't decided if it would be wise to have the baby. I mean with the war on and all. We could both be killed, and then where would our child be?" Millie bowed her head, crying softly.

David held her tight. "This is our child, Millie. Whatever is done, we will decide together!"

"Okay David." They sat quietly, reflecting. "Let's go home, I feel kind of silly sitting here in this rail car bawling my eyes out."

David jumped up and helped her to her feet. "You're going to have to take better care of yourself from now on."

"What on earth are you talking about, David?"

"You're carrying our baby now, so you have to drink lots of milk and don't do any heavy lifting. That's for me to do."

"Don't be silly. I'm not an invalid, and besides it will be some time before it even shows. I don't think I can stay in the WAAFs, though. When they find out I'm pregnant, I may be out of a job."

"As soon as we're married, you'll have a full time job taking care of our son."

"Daughter, you mean, and I haven't said 'yes' to getting married!"

David laughed, "A girl would be great; I could teach her how to throw a football. Maybe we'd have the first female quarterback."

Millie laughed with David. For the moment they'd put their grief behind them, beginning the healing process. He had shown compassion for his men and tenderness with her. This was the man she would marry! If they lived through this ugly war. "David, let's go dancing."

"In your condition?"

"Don't be silly. My condition is just fine. Besides if he or she is going to play football, the exercise is just what he or she needs."

David consented, noting that Millie was starting to think of the baby as their baby. Woody was right; they would be married. She just needed time to sort things out.

The taxi crept slowly through the blackened streets with only a thin beam of light showing on the street in front of the car. David held Millie snuggled deep in his arms in the back seat. "Tomorrow, we'll start looking for a new apartment, one on the ground floor. And we'll need baby things, and a crib, and...."

"David, we still have a few months to wait. This weekend is just for us, you and me and no one else."

"Which flat?" asked the taxi driver. "Bloody streets are all blacked out! Can't see a thing."

"This is close enough, we can walk a wee bit," said Millie taking David's hand as she stepped down from the taxi.

They climbed the three flights of stairs to the flat, their faces flush from the cool, damp air outside. "Care for a drink, Millie?"

"All I want is you, David." She dropped her coat on the floor. David took her in his arms, meeting her upturned lips with his. It was a kiss of love, of commitment to each other -- one of compassion, comforting, taking, giving, healing. "David, make love to me?"

They lay snuggled in each other's arms, their legs entwined. The feeling of skin to skin contact became more of a binding commitment than any ceremony could ever be. They loved; then lay together talking quietly, sharing, giving, becoming one together.

The three days flew, and David stood on the platform holding Millie in his arms, waiting to board the train back to base. She clung almost desperately to him. She turned her lips up, kissing him passionately. "David, promise me you'll wear your St. Christopher medal. It will always bring you safely back to me."

"I will. And when I get back, we'll get married and find another apartment for you and the baby."

"We'll see, David. We'll see."

"All 'board!"

Millie clung to David's jacket. "You damn well better come back to me."

David looked down at Millie, her eyes red, almost matching her hair. Tears poured from them freely, and David bent and softly kissed each; then turned, picked up his kit bag and boarded the train. He watched Millie waving, until the train pulled out of sight from the station. He tried to concentrate on the letters he must write, but could not. He finally drifted into a troubled sleep.

Missing in Action

David twitched in his sleep. He had recurring dreams of Joker hanging in his parachute. An ME-109 was making passes at him, its guns firing. Joker swung helplessly in his parachute, his stomach ripped open from a 20mm cannon shell. His intestines hung out like tangled coils of a large rope. He heard Joker calling, "PIGSKIN," his hand outstretched for help.

The lights snapped on in the barracks. "Classes at zero-six-thirty," barked the orderly. "Hampton, report for training to Sergeant Meaker before breakfast."

David jumped up from his bunk, a crazed look in his eyes. He spotted Chief sitting on the edge of his bunk. "What's happening? What classes?"

"Welcome back to the real world, Pigskin. We've been reassigned to the 610 squadron. We've moved up in the world; starting today we're flying Spitfires."

"Spitfires! Hell, I was just beginning to feel real comfortable in the Hurricanes."

David showered and dressed, then headed through the blackout curtain to be greeted by a wet, cold blanket of fog. He fumbled along in the dark until he found the operations building and groped blindly for the door. Slipping through the blackout into the light of operations, he stood momentarily blinded, waiting for his eyes to adjust to the light.

"Hi, Tommy," called David, walking over to the operator's desk. "Where'll I find this Sergeant Meaker?"

"Just coming in the door, sir."

"Bloody damp morning, aye. You the flying officer David Hampton?"

"That's me," said David, extending his hand. "Going to start training in Spitfires, I hear."

"We started the ground training yesterday and the boys are checking out the kites today. Why don't you take this Spitfire manual and glance through it over some bully beef and tea? When you've looked it over, sir, come find me on the line and we'll find you a Spit for you to do a few circuits and bumps. Tally ho."

David headed for the mess tent. The sun was breaking on the horizon, turning misty vapors into climbing columns, like pillars in some Colosseum. It looked as though the day would be clear. Why the change? he mused, as he stood listening to the bark of engines coming from the dispersal area. Spitfires? He felt that he had just mastered the Hurricane.

"Hey, Pigskin. You just going to stand there like a little kid behind the fence, watching the planes, or you going to actually fly one?" asked Chief, as he strolled up in his bowlegged walk.

"Guess I'll have to stay home; I don't have the two dollars for a ride!"

"Bullshit. Stick with me, Brother, I'll show you how to fly for free."

"That'll be the day, Chief. Just run through a couple of scrimmages, a few key plays to get me rolling. What'll I need to know about this Spitfire to get it in the air without killing myself? I'm not going to spend the better part of today reading any damn manual!"

"Even YOU got it made, Pigskin. Meaker said any idiot who could fly a Hurc would handle a Spitfire with no problem. Must have been talking about you," said Chief, his teeth flashing white with his Cheshire cat grin.

"Sure as hell hope it holds together like the Hurricanes," said David. A serious frown clouded his face, "I may have a wife and baby to support soon!"

"Congratulations, Brother. Okay, listen up. First of all, it has the same engine as the Hurc with a two-speed, three-bladed prop. So if you want to brake in a hell of ah hurry, just put the prop in fine pitch. And, it has a real narrow gear, makes you feel like you're going to tip over from the littlest bump. On takeoff, if you happen to put it in high boost, you'll be doing two hundred miles per hour by the time you cross the fence at the end of the field. Oh, one more thing. There's only two flap positions; up and full down, so you don't have any flaps to assist on takeoff."

"What about landing speeds and stalls?"

"There ain't hardly such a thing as a stall. Just drop the nose a hair, add a little power and gently add a little opposite rudder. Just watch the nose on takeoff, 'cause they told us the long nose covers the horizon and the sucker has so much power, it'll go straight up. Couple boys pulled 'er right over the top on takeoff, heading straight for the ground. Scared the livin' hell outta them. Anyway, coming in; slow to 140 mph, gear and flaps down. Approach speed's eighty-five miles per hour. Over the fence at seventy, cut the power and she'll drop on about sixty-five."

David flipped through the manual hurriedly while stuffing his mouth, and then headed for the line. Meaker spent twenty minutes going over the controls: fuel system, prop, mixture, and hydraulics. He then went through the complete sequence for a familiarization ride. Undercarriage selector lever - DOWN, flaps - UP, landing lamps - UP, contents of lower fuel tank - FULL. He had the sequence memorized, but he still followed the check list to the letter. Both fuel cock levers - ON, throttle - ONE-HALF INCH OPEN, mixture control - RICH, airscrew speed control - FULLY BACK, propeller - LEVER FULLY FORWARD, radiator shutter - OPEN.

There were little differences from the Hurricane, thought David, as he began the starting sequence: priming, press the starter, and give it another shot of prime. The starter push-button also turned on the booster coil so there was one less button. The Merlin engine caught and he adjusted the throttle to a thousand rpm and locked down the priming pump. He exercised the airscrew speed control, checked temperatures, pressures and controls. Cockpit hood, locked open, and emergency exit door set at half-cock. After warm up, he opened the throttle to maximum boost for cruising with weak mixture and tested the constant speed airscrew. He then opened the throttle to maximum boost for cruising with rich mixture and checked each magneto, the static rpm boost and oil pressure.

David signaled that he was ready to taxi for takeoff. He turned down the field facing into the wind and began his takeoff drill: Trim tabs - elevator, one division nose down from neutral, rudder - fully to starboard. Mixture - rich, pitch - fully forward, fuel - both cock levers on, flaps - up, radiator shutter - fully open. He opened the throttle slowly and compensated the nose swing with opposite rudder. The tail lifted and he held the Spitfire level. He lifted off surprisingly fast and raised the undercarriage holding the lever hard forward until the indicator light came on. He held the Spit level as the air speed built to 140 mph and trimmed the elevators for a maximum rate of climb at 160.

Returning to the field, David turned downwind checking the wind sock. He slid the cockpit hood open and flipped the lock-open latch, then set the emergency exit door at half-cock position. His speed dropped to 140 mph and he dropped the undercarriage holding the lever fully forward for two seconds to take the weight off the locking pins. His gear lights turned green. He turned on base leg and pushed the mixture control to full rich and the propeller speed control to full forward. Turning final, he put the flaps down and trimmed the nose. His left hand on the throttle he sank towards the end of the runway crossing the threshold fifty feet up. He pulled the throttle back and leveled the nose letting the Spitfire settle onto the main wheels while holding a slight forward pressure. Three wheels touched simultaneously and he added throttle to main taxi speed.

David spent the afternoon becoming familiar with the plane that would take him in harm's way. Another day was spent with his Pigskin Squadron ringing the Spitfire out in mock combat. They'd spent ten hours in the air flying combat procedures. They would take turns coming in for fuel so that only three Spitfires were on the ground at any one time. At the end of the day, David was satisfied the Pigskin Squadron was pulling as a team. "Last one to The Station buys the ale," shouted David as he watched his exhausted team stagger from their kites.

Everyone raced for the barracks, no longer tired.

"Looks as though we could have flown a couple more sorties," said Chief, grinning as he swaggered up to Pigskin.

"I was thinking about it, but I was getting so thirsty I couldn't even talk," said Pigskin, his voice starting to squeak.

The Station hummed like a vic of Spitfires all warming up at the same time. David and Chief worked their way through to their chairs at the far end of the bar. "Hey, old man. Couple ales for some thirsty veterans," called Pigskin.

Hap turned, grinning his toothy grin as he clicked his false teeth up and down. "Not till I see a few pounds on the bar. Seems as though your mouth overloaded your ass, or maybe I should say pocket book?"

A chorus of, "Hear, Hear's" came from his teammates holding up mugs of ale in confirmation.

Reluctantly, David counted the money out on the bar and Hap brought them their ales.

David and Chief drilled each other on the new procedures for the Spitfire, planning maneuvers on a bar napkin like football plays. Three ales later, they were played out. They could think of nothing else.

David slept fitfully. They were playing football and Joker went down field for a long pass. David waited, dodged a couple of tackles and stepped back into the pocket. He looked left and right, faked to throw a pass to the right, then turned looking down field for Joker. A Messerschmitt sat in front of the goal post. The pilot gunned his engine, turning the nose of the plane towards Joker running down the sideline. David saw the yellow nose of the Messerschmitt and his eyes caught the schnauzer emblem below the cockpit.

The German looked at David, grinned, and fired his machine guns at Joker. Streaks of white, burning tracers searched for Joker running down field. David screamed, "NO, NO!" and threw the football at the ME-109.

"PIGSKIN!" shouted Chief, shaking his blood brother awake.

"Chief. Oh, Christ. I just had another dream!"

"I know, Brother. Come on, let's shower and go eat."

"Yesterday we started bombing the German fighter bases across the Channel. Three squadrons each of Spitfires escorted a dozen bombers," said Chief.

"Whew, that's some pretty heavy cover for so few bombers," said David, sitting on the edge of his bunk. "Now we get to give the Krauts a taste of their own medicine. What about the Abbeville flyers? Did anyone see the yellow-nosed Messerschmitts?"

"Didn't hear of anyone reporting any, Pigskin."

"I want that son-of-a-bitch for myself. I want him to bail out; then I'll take my time finishing him off. I want him to know who his executioner is," said David grimly.

"Sounded like they had a lot of action. They lost two Spits. Come on, Pigskin. Let's hit the chow line before briefing. And, when we're up there, don't forget that this is a team game. You've got a lot of blockers out there and some good receivers and runners. Think of it as a football game, and the ball is snapped. How about a draw play? I'd like to get my hands on the ball again," said Chief grinning.

They walked through the darkness toward the mess tent. "Look at the stars, Chief. We escort bombers across the Channel in clear skies, no protective clouds."

"Look at it this way, Pigskin; the bombers can see their targets, and we might collect a couple more scalps."

"They just might send up the Abbeville crew if we can bloody their noses," said Pigskin, as he led the way through the blackout curtain into the mess tent.

"Phew! That smell. We must be in the mess tent," said the Chief.

"S.O.S., Chief. At least it's something we can gag down," said David.

"Shit-on-the-shingle. I wonder, Pigskin, if they actually put meat in that gravy and then strain it out or is it just artificial meat flavoring?"

"Complain, complain, complain. Here we are, on a beautiful fog-bound island, early morning wake-up call so we can go flying, free meals, and all the airplanes furnished no charge. Come on, Chief, remember back when you would work all week just to pay for an hour's flying?"

"Pigskin, you forgot the part where we get paid for having all this fun," Chief replied.

"Eat up, Chief. I want to get over to the briefing and find out where we're going."

The mess tent filled with flyers, many still trying to wake up and some sitting sullenly, sipping coffee to sober up.

David and Chief dropped their mess trays and utensils in a rack by the back door and slipped out into the fresh morning air. Engines coughed to life somewhere out in the dispersal area, as fitters and riggers made their final checks before signing the planes fit and ready.

They slipped through the blackout curtain into the briefing room, a large maintenance tent with rows of wooden benches. In the front, two screens stood draped with a cloth cover. The bright lights overhead left them blinking as they stepped inside from the dark. Several pilots were already waiting in small groups, like huddles of football players, speculating on the day's mission. A haze of blue smoke hung in the air.

"Howdy, Pigskin," greeted one of the other squadron leaders. "Sorry about Joker."

David winced at the mention of Joker. "Hi, Cowboy. I hear we're taking the action over to the Krauts now."

"Yeah, nurse maids for a bunch of slow flying whales. 'You must protect the bombers at all costs,'" said Cowboy in his best British-officer voice.

"So, what action did you see? Did the bombers hit anything?" asked Pigskin.

"We had lots of action. Halfway across the channel we were pounced on by a squadron of ME-109s. We had a turkey shoot. We out-numbered them three to one, had good altitude and the sun was behind us. I got one on the first pass. Must've hit his fuel tank. First a wing folded and then, KA-BOOM! Nothing but a fire ball. My boys got three more, and by the time we turned around for another pass, another squadron was all over them. They lost two kites. We never lost a plane."

"What about the bombers?"

"Oh yeah. The bumbees. That's what Jonesie started calling them."
Cowboy laughed sarcastically. In a proper British accent he mimicked, "'The
bumbees were out for a look-see and a spot of tea.' The French coast was
blanketed with fog, so they scrubbed the mission. Not one of'em got so
much as a scratch."

"ATTENTION."

"At ease, gentlemen," the Wing Commander greeted them. "Smoke
'em if you got'em. Sergeant Tommy Tuck will give you the details of today's
mission. Sergeant Tuck."

Tommy flipped the blanket off the first stand, showing a detailed
map of England and France. "Today's mission will be to Cherbourg. If
weather is a problem, your secondary target will be Le Havre. You will be
escorting a squadron of Blenheims whose mission will be to destroy the German airbases there. You will rendezvous with the bombers over Weymouth
at twenty thousand feet, at zero-six-hundred hours. There will be two squadrons of Hurricanes flying top cover. You will be flying three squadrons of
Spitfires, one in the lead and one on each side of the bombers."

"Are those bumbees going to show up this time so we don't waste our
fuel waiting for them?" called someone from the back of the room.

"Sergeant Dixie, I believe," said Tommy identifying the pilot. "Yesterday was one of the problems we're working out. As you know, the lead
bomber blew a tire on takeoff and it delayed the formation taking off until
they cleared the runway. We won't take off today until they call on a land
line giving us the time off of the last bomber. Does that answer your question, Sergeant?"

"Good enough, Sergeant."

Tommy stepped over to the second map and flipped the cover over.
"This is Cherbourg. The airdrome is north of town three kilometers. The
secondary target is Le Havre," Tommy flipped the first map over showing the
backup target. "The airdrome is five kilometers to the northwest of town.
These bases are German fighter bases and we expect them to be heavily de-
fended. If you encounter flak over the target area, stay outside the hot zone.
The German fighters won't fly through their own flak but will be waiting on
the edge ready to pounce on our bombers. Pigskin's squadron will be flying
lead. Any questions?"

"What's the weather over the Channel and the target area?" asked
Pigskin.

"Sergeant Bishop will give you the latest weather. Sergeant."

"Gentlemen," Bishop began. "Our latest reconnaissance shows a scattered cloud cover over the French coast that should dissipate shortly after sunrise. Winds aloft should be moderate from the south. Temperature at altitude will be around minus 20 Celsius. Seas in the Channel will be moderate. That's all on the weather. Sergeant Tuck."

"One last piece of information, we are now flying over enemy-held territory. If you're shot down or forced to bail out, try to make contact with the French resistance. We have been working secretly with them. They will make every effort to hide you until arrangements can be made to smuggle you back to England. Sorry we don't have any better information to give you. You're the first crews flying into German-held territory. Wing Commander Tonsund."

"Gentlemen, today you are taking the war back to the Germans. This is just a beginning, the finish line is Berlin." Cheers and applause filled the tent until the Wing Commander held his hands up for quiet. "Up until now, our aircraft production has been limited to the Hurricanes and Spitfires mainly to protect England from the invading Germans. Our bomber supply is very small. It is of the utmost importance that you protect our bombers at all costs. They are our link to Berlin. One last bit; if you should find yourself in a situation necessitating a bail out, remember that you are British. If captured you must resist giving information to the enemy at all costs. It could be critical to your fellow pilots, and your loved ones, and England. This goes doubly so for our American and Canadian friends who are assisting us in this endeavor, for they represent two countries. Good luck and bloody good hunting."

"ATTENTION," called Sergeant Tuck, as the Commander put his hat on and exited stiffly down the center of the room.

"Expect to start engines in thirty minutes. Dismissed, except Pigskin Squadron," called Tommy. The pilots left in noisy groups to pick up their gear.

The Pigskin Squadron formed a semicircle around David, like a huddle. "I'm David Hampton, known as Pigskin for our new pilots. Storm'n Norman, you're to take the Joker's position, Green-one. Lance, you'll fly Red-three position with me. O'Leary and Robin will fly Yellow-two and three positions behind Chief. Bernie, you'll fly Blue-three behind Dixie. Sorry we don't have time to do a little training together, but they tell me there's a war on. Remember, we're a team, and we work as a team. Pretend it's a football game and follow your leader. No acrobatics or stunts. If we meet the Krauts head on, don't turn or you're dead. Attack head on. If a Hun gets behind you, pull into the tightest turn you can. A Messerschmitt can't turn inside a Spitfire. Any questions?"

"Sir, Lance Barstow from Vancouver, Canada. How'll we know the German planes, sir?"

Laughter filled the room. David bit his lip to keep from laughing. "If they're shooting at you," said David, "they're Germans. Shoot back. You new men, listen up. You're flying the wing position, and that's where you will stay. Don't go off on your own for any reason. When your lead dives in on attack, cover his backside. If a Kraut gets on my tail for example, call Red-one break! That'll tell me I'm in eminent danger. You then dive in on the attack, and number three man will cover you."

"What if we meet them head on?"

"We spread out, Bernie, and everyone picks his own target. In a head on attack, do not turn or pull away or you're a dead man!"

"What happens if the German does the same thing?"

"Well, Bernie, we'll drink a toast to your memory, 'cause you just earned your flight pay the hard way. One more thing, if anyone sees a Messerschmitt with a yellow nose and a schnauzer painted on the side, call it out. He's mine! Okay men. Flight leaders stay for a minute, the rest of you get your gear, and be ready for takeoff. Stay together and good hunting."

"I don't know, Pigskin," said Dixie after the rest of the squadron left. "There's a couple of them won't have much of a chance."

"I don't think so either, but that's the way the cards fall. Besides, they know how to fly, or they wouldn't be here. They'll have to learn the same way we did. They take their chances the same as everyone else."

"Sounds to me as though you're not too concerned about the new guys," said Norman, "since Joker was killed."

"My concern is none of your damn business, Norman. We've got a job to do, and we'll do it the way I see best. If someone gets scrubbed from the team, that's too bad. And, that includes you, Norman. Joker was like a brother to me. We've been together since first grade. The only way these new guys have a chance is if you show 'em the ropes. You, Normie. You make sure they understand that their position is to follow and to cover. If they don't, their flight will be a very short one."

David slipped his Mae West over his head and slung his parachute over his shoulder, heading for the lorry waiting outside. Chief climbed in beside him. "Big game today."

"Those Krauts are going to be like a stirred-up hornet's nest after yesterday. The sooner we get at 'em, the sooner we can knock 'em down."

Chief grunted his approval.

They rode in silence, the way David wanted it. He looked for Joker, as if he'd appear with that silly grin on his face. When they got back from this mission, he would write to Joker's folks. It sounded so final; he couldn't bring himself to accept it. It was as if he were off on leave, and when least expected, he'd pop in with some funny remark.

"Time to go to work," said Chief. The lorry bounced to a stop at the dispersal area.

"See you upstairs, Chief." David turned and headed for his new Spitfire.

"Top ah the morning to yea, Pigskin," called Woody from the cockpit.

"Hey, Woodpecker. How's the kite?"

"Good as new, Davie me boy. So, how are the young lovers?"

"We had a great time. Even went apartment hunting."

"Ah, so when's the day?"

"Well, we haven't made any final plans; in fact, she hasn't exactly said yes, but I think she's getting close. Maybe next leave."

"Ah, what ah grand event it will be. We'll celebrate for three days. What a party. What a hangover. It'll be the talk ah the base, Davie, me-boy."

"There's two of us who won't be at the party. We'll be long away on our honeymoon."

"There's the start-engine flare. Better get crackin', Davie, and mind yea take care ah me new kite."

"Don't you sweat it, Woodpecker. I've got a date with a lady, and wild horses couldn't keep me away. CLEAR!"

The rigger signaled all clear, and David engaged the starter. It turned once, coughed, and settled into a smooth staccato tic-tic. He could feel the pulsing power of the Merlin idling. The slow-turning propellers drove crisp morning air swirling over the windscreen into the cockpit. As he completed his cockpit check and sat idle, waiting, visions of Millie and then Joker flashed before him. David tried to put them out of his mind and concentrate on the Spitfire's controls, but it was not possible. He led his squadron to the end of the field and turned into the wind for takeoff.

The flare came almost immediately; David eased his throttle forward. Man and machine became one deadly killing weapon. David raised his gear, pumping the hydraulic pump until he heard the thump of wheels locking into position. He reached up and latched the canopy closed, then looked back and saw Hans and the new kid, Barstow, pulling into position off his wing.

Why'd everyone think he was responsible for the new pilots? Hell, he'd tell them what he knew and show them as much as possible, but they were on their own. The way Joker, Chief and he'd been. No one had shown any deep concern over them. They'd survived on their own. A fighter pilot was a loner; he flew alone and even though they were a team, each pilot was responsible for his own actions. He played his part and took his chances and some would die...like Joker.

"Pigskin Squadron airborne, climbing on course."

"Roger, Pigskin. Angels twenty-one, vector two-five-zero."

Their rendezvous with the bombers was on schedule at twenty-one thousand feet. He set his power for a cruise climb to conserve fuel. David adjusted the trim wheel, trying to keep busy, to keep from thinking; still, he felt his gut tighten. He feared failure more than anything, and he'd known failure...he'd lost games because of his mistakes...would he now lose teammates because of mistakes? If only he hadn't wasted all his ammo, he could have protected Joker...What action would they find? The Krauts would throw everything they had at them...Defend the bombers at all costs, that was their orders. The Germans would have some costs.

It felt different escorting bombers instead of defending their own bases. They had already flown longer without action on this flight than David had flown since his first training flights. It seemed almost boring, like the convoy patrols. He thought of Duffy and scanned the skies all around. He changed course frequently, jinxing, looking, waiting, and readied for the unexpected.

David leveled at twenty-one thousand and brought his power back, reducing his cruise speed to one hundred and seventy-five mph, extending his fuel for maximum range. They reached the rendezvous and no sign of the bombers. David began a slow orbit; then he saw the bumbees climbing below them. They circled the bombers once and pulled into the lead. David felt uncomfortable flying at a such slow speeds, as if they were targets waiting for someone to take a shot at them. The German bombers had been such easy targets. Now they were in the same position.

David watched the coast line slip slowly behind them as they headed out over the Channel. Subconsciously he tightened his parachute straps. The water below looked so peaceful. Glancing up, he saw the Hurricanes in position above them. On each side of the bomber formation flew another squadron of Spitfires. This was more protection than the German bombers ever had. If they'd had this kind of protection, they'd still be bombing England.

The rocky, sandy beach of the French coast passed below. Small, lush green fields and vineyards passed swiftly. He wished they'd been lower so he could see some of the farms. After the war he would take a trip over here and see what they were fighting for. David started the turn towards Cherboug. He jinxed his Spitfire nervously, marveling at the smoothness of the controls while constantly scanning the skies for Bosch. They should have intercepted the Huns by now. Low clouds had moved in, covering the countryside. Would this be another scrubbed mission where the bombers couldn't see their targets? David continued jinxing, his eyes scanning. Then he saw them, a dozen black specks outlined against the clouds below.

"Pigskin, Red-one. Bandits, twelve-o'clock low." David called on his R/T. "Green and blue flights, cover the lead. Chief, follow me and cover the left side. We'll take the right."

"Roger that, Pigskin," called Chief. "Arm your guns, boys, here's your first kill."

David eased the control stick forward into a steep dive. He added power, and his airspeed climbed until he maxed at the red line. "This is Pigskin. Hans, you take my left wing and Barstow, you stay on my right. Pick a target, boys." David flew until a Messerschmitt showed between his sight bars. It grew rapidly. David saw white flashes from the ME-109 reaching up, searching for them. "Pigskin, Red-one; Hey Barstow, there's your Germans! Hold your fire until their wingspan fills your sight pip."

He heard the pings of bullets bouncing harmlessly off the Merlin engine. A jagged hole appeared in the metal of his wing. David concentrated on his sight pip. White tracers snapped over his canopy, inches from his head. The ME-109 grew in the sight bars. They were closing with the Messerschmitts at over five hundred miles per hour. He squeezed the firing button. One hundred rounds a second poured from the Spitfire's eight machine-guns. The bullets vanished in the Messerschmitt and its wing buckled.

David jerked his elevators back in a steep climb, feeling the blood rush from his head as the g forces increased. The ME-109, already forgotten, spun out of control below. He turned, jinxing, checking his rear view mirror, scanning the skies above and below. His wing men both pulled up safely from the dive. "Pigskin, Red-one. Let's get back to the bombers."

"Pigskin, Green-one, diving on bandits, twelve-o'clock low."

"Pigskin leader, we're coming up from below the bandits."

"Pine leader, red and yellow flights turning in to intercept bandits three-o'clock low."

"Rastus leader, our target's covered, we're turning to the secondary."

"Pine-Yellow-three. My engine's overheating; I'm going to try and make the coast."

"Pine-Yellow-two, fall out and escort Pine-yellow-three home," called Pine leader.

David watched two more Messerschmitts turn away trailing smoke. Then one of the Blenheims dropped from the formation leaving a trail of white vapor. "Victor leader, can anyone send a flight to escort that bomber home?"

"Roger, Pigskin, Red-one. Victor-blue flight, fall back and escort the wounded bumbee."

"Sparkie-leader here, bandits two-o'clock low."

The Spitfires, out in the lead, were barely visible. David jinxed, checking the skies all around. One squadron of top-cover Hurricanes were diving in on attack. A fireball mushroomed where a plane blew up. David saw a dozen black specks heading straight for the bombers.

"Pigskin, Red-one. Bandits twelve-o'clock level." David sighted on a closing Messerschmitt. The Hun, sensing David's attack, turned into him. David checked his needle-ball for coordination and squeezed the firing button. White flashes arced up at him from the ME-109's returned fire. A hail of bullets were striking his engine. A pinging sound came as bullets punched holes in the metal wing and fuselage. The Messerschmitt grew until it filled his windscreen. David jammed the elevators full forward. For an instant the sky above him was a dark blur. The impact threw him forward against his safety harness.

David felt as though he were drifting in space. Like the time he'd parachuted out and was inside the cloud. Protect the bombers at all costs. Well, he'd protect them, he wouldn't let his team down. He'd lead them right up to the final whistle. Nobody could ever accuse him of not being a leader, of letting his team down.

"Pigskin! Bail out! Pigskin, Pigskin, bail out!"

It was Chief calling. What was he calling? "That you Chief? Where you at?"

"Pigskin, bail out! The tail on your kite is gone!"

David shook his head. He'd blacked out from the crash. His Spitfire was spinning out of control. David tried the controls, nothing. The engine raced wildly. He chopped the throttle and cut the ignition. Centrifugal force of the tumbling plane pinned his arms to his side. He struggled to open the canopy, but did not have the strength in his arm to reach the release. David felt the forces of gravity pressing his body against the side of the cockpit. He lapsed into a gray-out.

"Pigskin, bail out! Bail out!" called Chief.

The Spit rolled and threw David upward. Desperately he lunged for the canopy latch and wrenched it open. He grabbed at his safety harness, ripping the quick release open. The Spitfire tumbled and flipped him out. Floating free, he saw the tops of the clouds below. David thought he heard Joker; "Don't open your chute yet!"

David watched his new Spitfire looping wildly as it plummeted earthward. Free-falling, he rolled and tumbled. He saw fighters and bombers far above him, then the clouds reaching up. Like the waves, his feet seemed to be touching the tops of the clouds, yet he waited. He would not provide them with a helpless target like Joker had been.

David had his hand on the D-ring of his parachute. Safely inside the cloud, he jerked the rip cord. There was a rustling of silk as the chute trailed from his pack. The parachute popped open with a bang followed by a bone-crushing jerk. He was thankful for having tightened his parachute harness straps. Drifting silently inside the protective cover of the cloud, he breathed in, filling his lungs with fresh air, free of the confines and stagnant odors of the cockpit and the oxygen bottle. He felt he was swinging back and forth in his chute, but there was no sensation of motion. David heard a soft sound, like the wind whispering in the pines, but it was the chute billowing in the wind.

What would he find on the ground? Most likely German troops. If he was lucky, the cloud might conceal him right to the ground. Surely the French farmers would be sympathetic and help an R.A.F. flyer. He crouched in a semi-tuck position in case he hit the ground before he saw it. If there were no Germans around, he'd bury his parachute, try to find a farm and hide out. How would he ask for help? He couldn't speak one word of French. He wished he'd taken French in school. If he got out of this, David vowed to study French, at least enough to tell someone what he needed or get directions.

Through a thin spot in the clouds, he caught a glimpse of green. The cloud thickened and he lost sight of it. He heard an explosion. Was it his plane or were the bombers making their drop? He listened intently, but there was only one explosion. It must have been his Spitfire. The ground appeared. He was much closer. He drifted toward a vineyard. A farm couple, working a short distance away, turned to watch his descent.

He dropped over a row of grapevines and pulled his feet up in a tuck position. He broke through the canopy of vines, hitting the soft tilled soil. David tried to roll, but he was tangled in his shroud lines and the grape vines.

He heard excited voices in what he supposed was French. He tried to turn toward the voices while untangling himself from his parachute. He heard the sound of running feet behind him and turning, looking up into the eyes of an angry farmer. David felt something hard and pointed against his chest. The farmer was holding a pitchfork, pinning him to the ground. He was short and fat and had a round face with puffy cheeks. His face was dark red, a lifetime of working outdoors. David came from a farm and knew the look. The farmer was breathing hard from the run, but his muscular arms held the pitchfork, like a spear, unyieldingly against David's chest.

"Regardez! Ce que vous avez fait? Allez vous payer pour cela?"

David felt his skin prick from the tines of the pitchfork bearing down on his chest. "I'm not German," he shouted. "I'm American. I fly with the English."

"Qu'es que vous dites?"

"Venez vous de Britannica?"

"I'm an American. I fly with the English." David used his hand to simulate an airplane. "R.A.F.," he said slowly and pointed to the unit symbol on his uniform.

David couldn't understand their rapidly spoken French, but the hand signals were universal. The farmer lifted the pitchfork from David's chest and stuck it in the ground. The couple began helping him untangle the shroud lines and cut him loose from the grape vines. David rolled his parachute into a bundle, took one quick look around making sure he left no sign of his presence, and turned to follow.

They entered a barn and David stood for a moment letting his eyes adjust to the darkened interior. The farmer called and motioned for him to follow. They entered a small storage room in the back that had harnesses hanging on the walls. There was a work bench on one side and a dusty, cobweb-covered window above it looking out on the farmyard. The farmer motioned him to sit on a chair in the corner and wait. He left David alone, closing the door behind him.

David heard the latch drop in place on the far side of the door. He checked the door, it was locked from the outside. He examined the room and found an attic door leading to a store room filled with old equipment. It looked as though nothing had ever been thrown away. David thought of his father. He was the same. "You never know when you might find a use for something," he could hear his dad saying.

David found a couple of loose boards on the side wall and pried the bottoms out. There was enough room to slip between them if necessary. It led into a manger and he found a manure chute he could squeeze through and slip into the vineyard to hide. He pondered whether to wait and take his chances or slip out now and make his escape while he had time.

He removed the revolver from inside his flying boot and checked that it was loaded. He would wait and watch the farmyard. He had an escape route if he needed it, but he didn't think he would. He felt he could trust the farmer and his wife. They were living off the land. The Germans were the invaders. Even though he couldn't speak the language, there was a bond between them, these tillers of the soil. He heard a door bang from the farm house. He looked around the cluttered storeroom and finding a box to stand on, looked out the dirty window. The farmer and his wife stood in the yard, arms waving and both talking excitedly at the same time. They gestured wildly with their hands as they spoke. Then the farmer turned and headed down the road, and his wife stepped back inside the house.

David closed his eyes for a few minutes trying to comprehend what was happening. The tension of combat and his crash had drained him. He heard the squeak of hinges and sat up with a start. Someone had opened the barn door and was sneaking towards the storeroom. He listened to the quiet, soft rustle of footsteps in the fresh straw. He stood to one side, pistol drawn, watching the latch handle on the storeroom door lift and the door open slowly. "Anglais," called the woman. "Anglais?"

David stepped forward from the shadows, slipping the pistol into his waistband. The woman was old beyond her time, her face wrinkled and dark from the sun. Her back had a permanent bow from long hard days working in the field. Her clothes were old and had patches on patches. She wore a black shawl and though she carried a cane, she was surprisingly agile. She handed him a basket filled with food and wine. A toothless smile reminded David of his grandmother, but when she spoke, he saw sorrow in her eyes.

He couldn't understand her words, but the fear on her face and the urgency of her gestures left no doubt that he must escape. Yet, if he left where would he go? The Germans would find him before sunset. He would spend the rest of the war in a prison camp or worse. His mind raced ahead, thinking of how to escape. He was half Sioux, and he felt the impulses of his Indian blood, of his mother's people. He would use his natural instinct to escape, to evade. He must think like an animal, hide, run; if he could escape into the forest, he would be in his own element, and then he would be the hunter instead of the hunted. Deception was the key to escape; what would the Germans expect him to do? Run. That would be natural, what they expected. He must not let the Germans suspect the good woman who was helping him.

Excitedly she kept repeating something in French. He felt she was upset about something, but he did not know what.

David showed the woman the loose board and how he would slip out of the room. He gestured to her to lock the door. He would escape. He would leave his parachute in the room as evidence that he had been there. The woman locked the door, leaving the barn. David watched her cross the barn yard and enter the farm house. He wished he could have communicated with her.

David was hungry. He took a large chunk of cheese and a roll from the basket, biting off chunks and washing it down with wine. He pulled the bottom boards loose to slip through. The sound of a vehicle driving into the farm yard and voices shouting drew David back to the window. An army truck rolled to a stop in a cloud of dust. David saw a swastika painted on the door of the vehicle.

The farmer stepped down from the cab of the first truck. German troops jumped from the back of the truck, carrying rifles with long bayonets attached. Two of the troopers had German-Shepherd dogs on leashes. There would be no escape. Even if he had left, the dogs would have tracked him down in minutes. An officer barked commands. Troops ran to surround the barn with rifles at the ready.

Playing football back in the states, David had seemingly been trapped countless times. Through deception he had eluded the opposition. He pulled the boards apart and slipped from the room. He could hear the troops in position outside the barn. In a couple of minutes it would be all over. Desperately, he looked around the inside of the dairy barn.

A large manure bucket hung from an overhead track. It was four feet long, deep and wide at the top. It had a rounded bottom that opened like a clam. It was similar to one on their farm in Minnesota. It could be lowered on a chain hoist and then filled from the stanchions on both sides. When it was filled with manure, it was raised with the chain hoist, pushed down the track to the outside, and dumped.

David threw his food basket up into the bucket. Grabbing the edge of the trolley he vaulted up and dropped inside. It was raised up to the top of the overhead track so someone walking by could not see in unless they stood on a stool or lowered the hoist. He curled up in the bottom of the bucket. It was still wet from the morning's chores.

David heard the barn door crash open and German voices shouting as they ran toward the store room. He heard the latch open on the store room door and someone shouting. "Kommen sie hier, Englisch. Vee vill not shoot!"

From the sound of voices, they'd found his parachute and the torn boards he'd escaped through. He'd left the boards askew to let them think he'd escaped. They'd brought dogs; he could hear them barking and whining as they circled the barn looking for his scent.

David had always liked the smell of the barn and the cows, but the odor of the fresh manure he was lying in was overpowering. His uniform was soaked, yet he dare not move. A fly crawled across his nose, but he lay still as death, barely breathing lest they hear the sound.

David closed his eyes and listened; he felt the concussion of thunder overhead and rain beating against the barn. The squall was of short duration, but a sign of his totem. He had been named Rain-in-the-face, and a vision came to him of the ancient medicine man sitting cross-legged in his tepee on a buffalo skin, in the Badlands of North Dakota.

Chief and he were receiving instructions in the Sioux Vision Quest ceremony (Hanblecheyapi). The old medicine man's gray hair shimmered in the light reflecting from the small fire in front of them. His bare chest sagged and skin hung in loose fat rolls at his side. His fringed buckskin breaches were grease stained, owing to the many times he had wiped his hands across the soft leather.

The medicine man puffed quietly on the sacred red-stone pipe, exhaling slowly and turning to watch the smoke disappear overhead, calling to Wakan Tanka, the Great Spirit, for a vision. He thought of the old man's low guttural chant, "To the four quarters, nature's power and wisdom, you shall run for help, and nothing shall be strong before you."

David felt his sacred totem bag and silently his lips chanted the medicine man's words to Wakan Tanka for wisdom and for Mother Earth to guide his feet. He would follow the path of his ancestors; he would trust in his totem. He was Rain-in-the-Face. He heard the thunder rumble in the distance as the squall moved by, then he saw a vision of a White Buffalo. It stopped, turned and bowed its head to the four quarters of the universe, and then disappeared into the storm.

A great calm came over him as he silently waited. The White Buffalo, a most sacred symbol to the Sioux, had been sent as a sign. Wakan Tanka had heard him. His totem was strong and with it he would survive to fight again another day.

Marie Claire

David could hear voices talking excitedly as they searched the barn. The dogs whined, running around sniffing, their handlers shouting out harsh commands. He couldn't understand what they were saying. He lay as low as possible in the manure shuttle. He saw the top of a German's helmet, inches away from where he hid. As the soldier walked past, he could have reached out and touched him. The German continued. The tip of the soldier's rifle barrel and bayonet moved by his hiding place and disappeared. He shuddered at the thought of an encounter with the German and the bayonet. He wondered what it felt like to be stabbed with a bayonet. The soldier would be twisting and turning the bayoneted rifle, struggling to embed it in his stomach or chest. The thought of it was terrifying. A chill of fear ran through him like a current that he had no control over, and he began to shake.

It seemed as though hours had passed since he'd crawled into the manure shuttle. His muscles cramped from being confined in the small, cold steel bucket, and he shivered uncontrollably. His clothes, soaked with urine and cow manure, hid his human scent from the dogs. He hardly breathed. He lay as immobile as possible, like the living dead. He thought of his grandmother lying in her casket, cold and stiff, and that's how he started to feel. He squeezed his nose with two fingers and clasped his other hand tight over his mouth. If he sneezed, it would give his hideout away. He'd be caught for certain; maybe beaten, imprisoned, shot or even bayoneted.

He heard crashing and banging about as the Germans searched methodically in every corner of the shadowy barn. David could hear scraping noises in the loft above him. There came stabbing sounds as they probed the hay with bayonets. How soon before someone looked up and noticed the manure shuttle hanging suspended from the overhead track? With only a pistol, he had no chance. If one of the soldiers saw him with the pistol, he would be shot. David listened intently. The sounds coming from the barn faded. Had they finished searching the barn and moved outside? Minutes dragged by, but he dared not move.

David could no longer hear anyone inside the barn. His whole body felt numb and he doubted he could stand. Still, he waited. A few minutes waiting would be better than years in a German prison, or death. David thought of the many times he'd called the draw play. He'd fake a hand-off to Chief and fade back with the ball tucked out of sight. The opposing team would pile on Chief, and he'd slip back unnoticed. He'd had lots of time to spot the receiver. Joker would be downfield, waiting. His blocker, thinking the play was dead, would be walking back up the field. The ball came singing through the air to Joker, wide open. Six points!

David passed a couple hours reliving old football plays and analyzing them. What made them work? Deception. Most of the really good plays were built on deception. If he were to survive, get back to Millie and fly with his team, he needed to invent new tricks, ones that weren't in any book. He'd had a lot of time to think and plan. With the Germans searching the countryside for him, none of the neighboring farms would be safe.

Cautiously David shifted his body around in the shuttle and peered out. It was getting dark. The farmer would be coming in to do his evening milking. He heard the barn door open and held his breath, listening. He drew his service revolver and held it ready. Soft footsteps came shuffling through the loose straw lying on the floor. David eased himself back down in the bucket and thumbed the hammer back on his service revolver.

"L'Angleterre?"

It was the farmer's wife. Could he trust her? She'd already warned him and brought him food. He needed help if he were to escape.

"Here," he called softly, struggling to sit up in the shuttle.

Startled, she jumped back for a moment, then ran up pulling the chain hoist. The chain drive clanked noisily as the bucket dropped slowly to the floor.

David flexed his cramped muscles. He had no idea how long he'd been hiding in the bucket, but it was dark and the woman carried a kerosene lantern. The woman spoke excitedly in French, keeping her voice low. She practically lifted David from the bucket, ignoring the manure that his uniform had absorbed like a sponge.

She took David's basket from the bucket and hoisted the shuttle back where it belonged. Smiling, she looked at David and pointed to the bucket, then to her head, implying he was smart. The woman picked up his basket and motioned to him to follow. She opened the barn door and looked around, then shuffled off toward the house. It was the dark of the moon, and the lantern cast long shadows across the farmyard.

David followed closely, keeping one hand on the pistol in his waistband. He heard a cowbell in the distance. It must be her husband bringing the cows in for milking. They entered the house. The woman lit a coal oil lamp sitting on a large round table. It was a farm kitchen just like many back home. The room was large, with painted board cupboards covering two walls and a sink large enough for a small restaurant. A round table stood in the center of the room with a dozen chairs around it. Sugar lumps and a creamer sat in the center with salt, pepper and a dish of butter. Canning jars stood on the counter waiting to be filled. There was a milk separator in the corner and pegs on the wall behind the door to hang their barn clothes when they came in. It smelled like a farm, and David felt at home.

It must have been a big family from the picture hanging above the door that led into the parlor. A dozen children gathered around the young couple. Where had they all gone?

The woman pulled on David's sleeve impatiently and led him into a bedroom off the kitchen. She dug through a large steamer trunk in the corner and pulled out a dark wool suit and shirt. She held it up to David, checking his size, and shook her head. It was big, but he needed some different clothes. She put them on the bed, motioning for him to change.

David stripped off the smelly uniform and put on the dark wool suit. It felt scratchy but it was clean and warm. He pulled the belt tight to hold the pants up and pulled a black wool sweater over his head. He slipped a shortcut, black jacket like a pilot's leather jacket over the sweater. It was too big around and the sleeves and legs were short. The cap sat on his head like a dish pan, but in the dark or from a distance, he would be inconspicuous. He slipped out his knife, cut his R.A.F. crest off the uniform and stuffed it in his pocket for identification, if he needed it. He slipped his sheathed knife into the top of his boot and tucked his service revolver in his waistband under the coat.

David noticed the picture on the dresser and picked it up, studying the young man in it. A soldier. These must be his clothes. He placed the picture back on the dresser, then noticed a folded flag lying alongside. Her son must have been killed in the war. Maybe she was a part of the French Resistance.

David stepped into the kitchen. The woman turned, eyed him closely, then placed a hand over her mouth to cover a smile on the weathered face. She motioned David over to the table and handed him a slip of paper. David opened it and the name, MARIE CLAIRE, was written on it in bold penciled letters. She took it and folded it carefully, tucking it in his shirt pocket, then took a scrap of paper and began drawing a map. She pointed to David and placed an X on the map. Then she drew a road leading from the farm to a town. She drew several buildings and one she circled. She wrote a name on the side and pointed to the building. All the time she was drawing the map, she spoke in French. David nodded, understanding the map.

The map completed, she gestured that he was to follow the road she'd marked. He memorized the name of the building with the X. She pointed to the note she'd given him, then to the building. Finally he made the connection; he was to go to this building and give them the note. It must be some kind of a code the underground used. Then she took the map and burned it in the wood stove. She waved him away, and as he turned to leave, he saw tears in her eyes. He bent and kissed her cheek then turned and disappeared into the night.

It was black outside, the dark of the moon. A dim light showed from the barn where the farmer was tending his cows. David wondered what'd happened to their son. Had he been killed fighting against the Germans when they invaded France? Now the farmer was helping the Germans while his wife was working with the Resistance behind his back. War!

David walked quietly toward the town, as though he were stalking a deer in the Badlands. It was a dark night with no moon, and his eyes adjusted quickly to the dark. Light from stars twinkling overhead like fire flies cast just enough light to make his way. He shuffled slowly along, feeling the road with his feet, like a blind man. He could smell the ripened grapes in the vineyards along the road. There were no lights showing from any of the buildings he passed. He took note of the distance and bearing from the farm by the stars overhead. After the war was over, he vowed to come back and find the farm and the peasant woman who'd risked her life to help him. By then, he would at least know enough French to understand her. He wanted to know about her son whose clothes he was wearing. What had happened to him?

He heard a vehicle coming slowly down the road in the dark and slipped into the ditch. He slid to the bottom, stopping momentarily in a puddle of water. Stealthily, he crawled out of the water, up the opposite bank and into tall grass, like a fox stalking a pheasant. With his Sioux heritage, it came to him naturally. Mother Earth was guiding his footsteps. He now became one, bonding with the earth. He felt a keen awareness. But for the passage of time, he could have been with his distant Grandfather, waiting on the prairies of Montana for Custer. David pulled himself into a row of grape vines and hid in the shadows. He watched as a scout car idled slowly along the gravel road.

The headlights were taped leaving a tee slit in the center, allowing a sliver of light to shine directly on the road. He heard tires crunching gravel as the jeep came closer. Through the tall grasses, he watched the lighted ends of two cigarettes, glowing in the dark, move by slowly. Low guttural voices came softly to him in the still night air. German soldiers. Were they looking for him or just on a routine patrol? He was thankful for the dark suit.

David reached up and picked a bunch of grapes, savoring them while waiting for the Germans to pass. He judged that fifteen minutes had passed before he slipped back through the ditch to the road. He walked as though on moccasined feet in grasses along the road, so as to leave no sign of his passage.

He came to the small village the farmer's wife had marked on the map. It consisted of a dozen two-story buildings. Everything was blacked out. He had difficulty making out the signs in the dark. A cat meowed and he jumped. He slipping his hand around the handle of his pistol and walked by the storefronts, feeling his way in the dark. Music and voices came from a building ahead and light showed through cracks under the window. A painted sign, with a plate, silverware, and a bottle of wine, hung in front. It was the one he was looking for. He entered the pub cautiously. The lights, though dim, seemed bright when coming in from the dark. The room was small with only two tables. There were four Frenchmen sitting around one of the tables, with a bottle of wine in the middle, and dirty plates in front of each. They'd just finished supper and were drinking wine and smoking long skinny black cigars.

His eyes adjusted to the dimly lit bar. The air was tinted blue from the smoke. The bar was L-shaped and had half a dozen stools standing vacant in front. Several rows of bottles lined the back of the bar, many covered with dust.

The bartender sat behind the bar half asleep. He was short and fat and had large arms folded across his stomach. David slipped up to the bar, sat on a stool, and cleared his throat quietly to get his attention. The bartender stood slowly, and speaking in French, waddled over toward David. David couldn't understand. He didn't know what he should do, then remembered the note. He pulled the rumpled paper from his pocket, unfolded it and handed it to the bartender. The fat man put his cigarette between his lips and cocked his head to the side, as if to see around the smoke.

The bartender's eyes opened wide as he looked at David. He said nothing but quietly poured a glass of wine, then set the bottle and glass on the bar, indicating David help himself. He shuffled into the kitchen, returned with a plate of pasta covered with tomato sauce, cut several slices of cheese from a large block under the bar, put half a dozen hard rolls in a basket, and placed them in front of David. Though he shuffled slowly, his eyes were now alert, glancing suspiciously around the bar.

He gestured for David to eat and be quiet, fully aware of the danger they were in. One mistake, one slip and they could all be taken prisoners, tortured and eventually killed. Of this he had no doubt. The bartender turned and slipped out from behind the bar. Going to the first table he began picking up dishes then headed for the kitchen. David had his jacket open, the pistol tucked under the bulky cardigan where it would not show. He cautiously checked to be sure he could free it in an instant if needed.

He was hungry, slurping the pasta noisily. He bit large chunks of cheese and bread with his teeth, ripping them off and washing it all down with red wine. It was a feast. He poured a second glass of wine from the bottle the bartender had left on the bar and sipped slowly.

The door opened and two German soldiers came in. They glanced at David and the Frenchmen, then stood their rifles against the wall. They dropped heavily into chairs at the second table. David sat, hunched over, sipping his wine and munching his bread and cheese. He didn't know what else to do. If he stood up the baggy clothes might give him away. The soldiers had obviously been drinking. It was another draw play, deception was the name of the game. He would sit quietly at the bar, sipping his wine and looking half asleep, though he was ready for instant action.

The bartender entered. David motioned with his head. There was a look of surprise or maybe anguish on the bartender's tired face. He wiped his hands on his apron and picked up a bottle of wine and two glasses, heading for the soldiers' table. He greeted them in German and joked with them for a moment, then headed back to the kitchen. David slipped his hand under the sweater, around the pistol.

He didn't know where the bartender had gone. Was he with the underground? Or had he turned David in to the Germans like the farmer? He would use his pistol only as a last resort. He must not jeopardize any members of the underground who were risking their lives to help him.

The door opened, and a young woman came in. She was short and had a black shawl wrapped around her shoulders and dark scarf over her head hiding her features. She stood for a moment letting her eyes adjust to the light then spotted David.

"Ah, Pierre. Mon cherie," and came over to David climbing up on the stool next to him. She put her arm around David's neck and kissed him on the cheek. Surprised, he turned toward her and was about to ask who she was when she held his face in both hands and kissed him. His lips hurt and she still held him tight. As soon as she let him go, she started talking rapidly. She talked excitedly, gestured with both hands. David had no idea what she was saying, but sat pretending to listen, nodding his head occasionally.

"Fraulein, kommen sie hier," called one of the German soldiers drunkenly.

She leaned back looking over David's shoulder, "Non possible!"

The Soldier stood drunkenly and staggered toward the bar. David slipped his hand under the cardigan, around the pistol. He would not be taken by two drunken Germans. The girl saw his move and placed her hand over his, holding it tightly. She snuggled up to him whispering in his ear, but he could only guess at what she was saying. He felt the tenseness in her body next to his and he relaxed somewhat, but did not release his grip on the pistol.

"Komme fraulein."

David stiffened as the German stood, unbuttoned his jacket and stumbled toward them.

One of the Frenchmen at the table stepped in front of the drunken German. David listened to the argument without understanding. Then he heard what sounded like "fiancee." The soldier began to argue with the Frenchman angrily. The Frenchman, speaking broken German, steered him toward the bar ordering two cognacs.

David felt that he was on the sideline watching a dangerous play. There was a scramble and the quarterback sidestepped the tacklers, but he was still behind the lines. He had to scramble to escape. He felt the girl tugging his arm. She wanted him to leave with her while the German was distracted. He slipped from the barstool, as though he'd had too much to drink and she put her arm around him and steered him toward the door.

Outside she grabbed his hand and ran into a darkened alley. He stumbled along in the dark, trusting her. They came to a church, and she led him around to the back. They stumbled down stone steps groping their way to a basement entrance. She knocked softly on the door and waited. There was no answer. Impatiently she pounded again and a muffled voice came from inside. The door opened. A small candle inside gave enough light to reveal a priest standing in the doorway. He was tall and appeared to have dark features, but David could not be sure in the poor light.

"Monique?" the priest greeted her.

"Pere Paquette," he heard her call the priest, then something about, "Anglais."

"Come in, my son," the priest said. His voice was soft, but deep like Chief's.

"You speak English," David said startled.

"Yes. Hurry. Come inside so we are not observed. You never know when the Bosch is watching. So, who are you and how can we help?"

"I'm David Hampton, an American, and I fly Spitfires with the R.A.F."

"Ah yes. A fighter pilot. But you look so young. You're from the United States? It's been a long time since I was in the U.S. I spent two years in New York going to school, but I didn't like it there. Too crowded." The priest's face looked worried and tired, yet his eyes sparkled. "We'll need to get you back to your unit in England. We are operating a secret underground against the Germans. Any disturbance will bring attention to us. If they find that we are helping you, we will be shot. So, for your own safety and ours, you must remain as inconspicuous as possible. If you are discovered by the Germans, you will be on your own."

"Why are you risking your lives?" David asked.

"Why? This is our country. Monique's husband was either killed or taken prisoner somewhere. Many of our sons and daughters were killed during the German invasion. They come into our towns and take whatever they want. Rape our women and girls. If we interfere, they shoot us. If it takes a year, or ten years or a hundred, we will fight in any way we can until we have our country back."

"The farm where I got the clothes -- her son must have been killed in the war. I saw his picture on the dresser next to a flag."

"We do not speak the names of people. It is too dangerous. If the Germans should capture one of us, everyone who is known to that person would have to go into hiding for his life. I only have one connection, and that person will only have one or two connections. This way the link cannot be broken."

"How soon can I get back to England?"

"I don't know, my son. I must make some inquiries tomorrow and arrange for the next leg in your journey back. It may be a couple of days or a few weeks. You must be patient and stay hidden. But first you must have some clothes that fit and a bath. Phew, you must have been living in a barn." The priest spoke to Monique in French, gesturing toward David. David heard something like, "merde." "Monique will bring some of her husband's clothes for you. You are about his size."

She came up to David, stood on tiptoes and kissed him before fleeing out the door. David turned to the priest. "Why is she doing this? If her husband is a prisoner, they might kill him if they found out."

"Monique is a very attractive woman. When the Germans came to our town, they took her by force. There were a dozen or more who took turns raping her. After several days, when they grew tired of her, she made her escape. Now she fights them in any way she can. You fighter pilots sleep in a clean barracks every night, have good food and never see the atrocities that are committed."

David bristled for a moment, then told him about Joker. "From the clothes and the smell, you can see I've been getting a closer look at the other side."

Father Paquette laughed. "You are so right, my son. Come with me and I'll fix you a bath. You can wear one of my robes until we have some new clothes for you."

David lay back on the mattress the priest had laid out in a store room. With a bath, clean clothes, and having contacted the underground, he felt safe, but it was strange wearing the priest's robe. Deception, he kept telling himself, was the game. The people in the underground were masters at it. It had been a long day and he fell into a restless sleep.

Visions flashed before him of Monique being dragged off by a German flying a yellow- nosed Messerschmitt. David clearly saw the schnauzer emblem on the side. He could see Monique through the canopy, fighting and screaming for help. The German waved at David then turned and tore her clothes off.

David awoke with a start. The priest was shaking his shoulder. "Wake up, David. You've had a bad dream, son. Here are some clothes that Monique brought by for you. Put them on, and then pull the priest's robe over the top to cover them. Come, I've prepared some morning tea."

David stepped into a pair of sandals Father Paquette had set by the bed for him. He headed into the next room, his sandals flopping noisily on the stone floor. The room was almost barren. A cross hung on one wall and a picture of the Virgin Mary on another. There were wooden benches and a plain wooden table on each side. A pair of mugs stood steaming on the table with some hard rolls and a slab of cheese. "I like the outfit Father, but I don't know how a priest is supposed to act."

Father Paquette laughed. "Keep your head down and carry the rosary beads in your hands. Everyone will think you are meditating and will not disturb you." David had a hard time thinking of the Father as a priest. His face looked wrinkled and weathered as though he'd spent most of his time working in the field instead of a church. A ragged scar ran from his high cheek to his jawbone. His nose had been straight at one time, but a break had left a large lump in the middle. The Father's hands looked out of place. They were massive. They reminded him of his father working on the forge at home, making horse shoes on the anvil. The backs of the priest's fingers and hands were covered with black hair, but that did not hide the many scars. Nor could his muscular build be covered by a priest's robe.

"You haven't been a priest all of your life," David said.

"No," he paused for a moment then continued. "I was a longshoreman for several years. During the Great War, I was in what you Americans would call the Commandos. We spent most of our time behind German lines sabotaging supplies, bridges, trains, anything that would bring the war to a close."

"So, after all that, you just stopped and became a priest," asked David?

"Something like that." Father Paquette smiled. "It was a calling to serve God and help the people. This is how I can best serve both."

"What do I do now, Father? How do I go about getting back to England and my unit?" His face hardened as he thought of Joker. "I've got an appointment with a certain German."

Father shook his head. "Vengeance is mine, sayeth the Lord. You must give up this vendetta or it will be, 'chant du cygne,' your death song."

"He was my best friend, Father. I will not rest until I have avenged his death."

"I know, my son. I know." His face looked bitter as he thought back to his own past, then he beamed. "But now we priests must go to work. We are going to visit an orphanage today."

"I don't speak French. How can I go?"

"You are a priest with a twisted tongue and cannot speak. All you have to do is listen and nod your head. The children will love you. Besides, there is a nun who will take your picture for your new passport."

"What new passport?"

"You are going to be Damettreis Reggis, a Greek sailor. You will be boarding your ship in Cherbourg in three days and sailing for Crete."

"How'll I get to my unit from there?"

"Someone along the line will direct you. That is all I know. Secrecy is necessary to protect the underground from the Gestapo."

David sipped his tea and munched worriedly on his hard roll and cheese. "Where is this orphanage we're going to?"

"It's several kilometers away, and the countryside is crawling with Germans. Are you a good actor?"

"I've never done any acting, but I'm a quick learner. I was the quarterback on our high school football team back home."

"Ah, football. It's the one thing I really miss about America, that and hot dogs. But today we will pass through three German check points. You will be my brother, Dominic, who has been retarded since birth. So, all you have to do is look stupid, let your bottom lip hang low on one side with your tongue out and drool a bit. Can you do it, Brother Dominic?"

David contorted his mouth sideways letting a dribble of spit trickle out the corner. He crossed his eyes and clung to Father Paquette's arm, mumbling and slobbering.

Father laughed. "Monique was right; you are a fighter and definitely an actor. Come, Brother Dominic, this is going to be an interesting day."

David climbed into the ancient Renault while Father set the throttle and spark, then walked around the front with a crank. It started on the third turn. Father threw the crank in the back and jumped in. "It's not much of a car but it works. The Bosch let me keep it to make my rounds to the orphanage and some of our shut-in people. I'm rationed to five liters of petrol a month so it's not like I'm going anyplace."

"As long as it works," said David. "We've got a Model A back home, just about like this. We use it a couple of times a month to go to town for groceries. Joker had a car," David said bitterly. "We used to drive to our football games. Afterwards we'd pick up girls and go to town for sodas."

"Checkpoint coming up just around the bend, Brother Dominic."

"Okay Father. I'm ready." David patted the pistol tucked out of sight in the waistband of the suit Monique had provided.

"Only as a last resort," Father said. He pulled up his robe revealing a pistol strapped to his leg.

"Halten Sie hier!" called a German soldier standing in the middle of the road pointing his bayoneted rifle at them. Father Paquette produced his papers, speaking in German, and pointing at David.

The guard walked around the car and looked in at David who had his head turned away. He reached in and grabbed David by the front of his robe jerking him around.

David had relaxed his muscles and let himself be jerked around as though he had no control over his actions. He looked up at the guard with his eyes crossed, slobbering spit on the guards arm.

"Vas!" exclaimed the guard jerking his arm back and wiping the spittle on David's robe. He turned and signaled the barrier open, waving them on.

As soon as they were out of sight, Father Paquette broke out into laughter. Tears were rolling down his cheeks as he tried to imitate the guard checking David. "Brother Dominic, if you weren't a valuable fighter pilot, I would recruit you to work with us in the underground."

"I'd love nothing better, but I have a mission to complete."

"I wish I could talk you out of it, but I know better. I've been there myself. The Bosch killed my family because they wouldn't let them take my sister." David thought of his own family and how his father and brothers would defend his sisters and mother if the Germans came marching into their farm.

They rode in silence passing through the next two checkpoints. David wondered how these people, who'd suffered so much, could maintain their composure after all they'd been through -- the deaths, the rapes and degradation of human values. The Father was right; the pilots never saw the atrocities that went on below them. They had their own world, locked in their cockpits high above. Except now. Now he was one of them and would do whatever was necessary. Deception and deceit were their weapons and he would use them to the best of his ability.

"Brother Dominic, that's the orphanage on top of the hill. Remember you are deaf and dumb. The children will flock around you, just nod your head and smile."

A short, chubby nun with small, wire-rimmed spectacles on her round nose came running out to meet them, her black habit flopping in the wind. A circle of small children surrounded her. "Pere Paquette. Vous ami?."

"Oui, Sister Teressia," said Father Paquette, switching to English. "This is my brother, Dominic. Unfortunately, he cannot speak. He has a twisted tongue."

David smiled at the sister, twisted his face trying to form a word, but only a gurgling sound came out.

"As you can see, Sister, Brother Dominic needs to be taken care of. He wants to travel to Crete to visit relatives and needs some sailing papers."

"You've brought him to the right place, Father. It may take a day or two, but I'm sure the good Brother will be happy staying here with the children."

"I must be on my way, Sister." Turning he whispered, "David, you are in good hands. Good luck and Godspeed, my son."

David grabbed the priest's robe and bent his head whispering. "Thank you, Father, for everything you have done. Thank Monique. After the war, I will be back."

David followed the sister into the orphanage. At first the children were shy, but intrigued with David. They seldom had visitors except for the priest and the sisters. David wished he could speak, but he must play his part at all costs. He kept reminding himself that all their lives were at risk for helping him escape. He felt a deep obligation not to endanger them more than he already had. If the Gestapo ever questioned them, all they would remember was the deaf and dumb priest.

David felt depressed as he looked at the bleak surroundings of the orphanage. They were as sparse as Father Paquette's room had been. Bare plaster walls with a large crucifix hanging on the far end. A picture of Mary and Jesus. The room doubled as their class room and dining room. David saw the children working in their school books occasionally sneak glances at him. They were all dressed in the same dark blue uniforms.

Sister Teressia entered and motioned David to follow her. Once out of the room, the sister spoke in broken English. "We have need to make picture for passport. Not much time. Be ready to leave in morning."

They entered a dark storeroom. Sister Teressia took several boxes down from the top shelf, then opened one and removed a camera. "You take off robe. We take picture in work clothes."

"How come you're working in the underground, Sister?" David removed the priest's robe. He felt uncomfortable in the dark wool suit Monique had brought for him, but he knew he would blend in with the farmers.

There was a long silence. The sister worked quietly, setting up the camera. David thought she hadn't heard or understood him. Then she stopped and turned to face him. "Monique, my sister!"

"Oh. I'm sorry. I didn't know. There's a lot about this lousy war I don't know, but I'm learning."

"You must learn; you are, Damettreis Regis. You are sailor, on Greek ship, Andrus. You not speak. In morning, Sister Astel come, take you to market. You dress in robe, other clothes under. In market you take robe out. Two sailors from ship come, take you. They no speak English. You, not speak. You understand?"

She reminded David of his English teacher in school. She was strict and to the point. There was no humor in her eyes and her voice was hard and bitter when she spoke. "Yes sister, I understand. I have three sisters and two brothers back home. If I can help stop the Germans, then they won't have to suffer the things your people have."

"Come Damettreis, it is time for our evening meal. If you miss sitting on time you will not eat until tomorrow morning."

David sat with the children. A sister dished a bowl of soup and handed him a roll. He watched the children and followed their example eating. It was a plain soup made with what vegetables they could pick from their garden. There was no meat in it or seasoning and it tasted quite bland. It was not like back home in America. There were no fat children.

David was shown a mattress rolled out on the floor in the store room. He lay down thinking it was early to go to sleep. The next thing he knew someone was shaking him awake. The nun handed him a wallet and motioned him to follow. She seemed in a hurry. She was tall and thin an moved in jerky nervous motions. Like all the sisters, dressed in their habits, she reminded him of the penguins in the Minneapolis Zoo. He assumed that this had to be Sister Astel who would escort him to town and his next contact in the underground.

David opened the wallet and saw his passport along with several papers he couldn't read and a few worn, crumpled bills.

The sister placed several empty baskets in a three-wheeled cart. There were two big wheels in the front and a single bicycle wheel and seat on the back. Sister Astel stepped up unto the bicycle and started pedaling down the road. She motioned David to follow and did not look back to see if he were there.

David had to jog to keep up with the sister. Rounding a bend in the road, they came to a German check point. Sister slowed until he could walk alongside her. There were two guards; one walked back and forth in front of the gate across the road with his rifle slung from his shoulder. The other sat inside a guard house his rifle standing against the wall. David felt the pistol stuck in his waistband. It would be clumsy trying to get it out from under the robe if he needed it. The guards opened the gate for them without asking for papers and turned their backs, ignoring them as they passed through the gate. David never looked back.

Sister Astel peddled her bike harder and he walked at a rapid pace, breaking into a sweat. They passed farm after farm, some with cows while others had a variety of pigs and chickens. David played a guessing game of which animals were on the farm from the smells. Every farm had its own vineyard. Some were small, probably just for the farmer's own use, while others were obviously for business. The grapes smelled tempting and David wished he could stop and pick a bunch, but it was all he could do to keep up with the sister.

The market square was bustling with activity when they arrived. It had a strange smell, a conglomeration of odors, many David couldn't place. There were stands of cooking food and stands with potatoes and carrots, onions, cabbage, lettuce and tomatoes, plus racks of chickens, bled and plucked. Trays of fish added to the odor of the market, along with the mob of farmers and townspeople all haggling over prices. The sister left the cart and signaled David to wait. She returned shortly from out of the crowd, carrying a basket filled with produce, placed it in the cart and disappeared back into the crowd.

David felt conspicuous standing there with nothing to do, but knew he blended in with the crowd and that was the only thing that counted. A pair of German soldiers walked by with rifles slung on their shoulders. David leaned against the back of the cart. He crossed his eyes and drooled spit out of the corner of his lip. The soldiers glanced at him and continued on their way.

Sister Astel worked her way through the crowd and carried another basket of produce to the cart. She motioned with a nod of her head for David to follow as she pushed her cart through the market square to the far side of the street. There she left the cart and, with a basket under her arm, ducked into a narrow doorway.

David followed into a dark passageway. It opened into a dimly-lit bar with several small tables. Two men were sitting at one of the tables and a fat man was behind the bar. The sister greeted the barkeep and he pointed to two gruffly dressed sailors sitting at one of the tables. Sister Astel approached them and said something in French that sounded like a password or code to David. They answered back and stood laughing and joking with Sister Astel like old friends.

The tall one was skinny and his cheeks were hollow, making his face look like he'd been starved. His eyes were sunken, and they beaded up to piercing dark points. His friend was short, fat and had a face that was round and full. He was jovial and laughed all the time.

The sailors looked at David. The taller of the two said something in French, shaking his head negatively. Sister gestured for David to take the robe off. He pulled it up over his head and handed it to the sister who folded it carefully and placed it in the bottom of her basket. David pulled a flat hat from his jacket pocket, shook the wrinkles out and put it on. The sailors appraised David, smiled, and asked for his papers.

David didn't understand until the skinny Frenchman took out his wallet and showed him his papers. David pulled his wallet out and rummaged through the contents, finally producing the new identification card the sisters had made for him. They grabbed the card out of his hand and together examined the picture and studied David. Then one of them threw it on the floor and stomped it with his boot. He picked it up and rubbed the shiny finish with his dirty hands. When he handed it back to David, it looked wrinkled and dirty. The Frenchman held his passport alongside of David's. David understood and nodded his head. He would show them that he knew the game. He crossed his eyes and slurred his speech.

The sailors relaxed and smiled. "Bonjour, Monsieur Damettreis Regis." He extended his hand and David shook it limply, keeping a blank look on his face. The Greek sailors laughed and clapped him on the shoulders. They pulled up a chair for him and motioned he sit with them and have a glass of wine. David looked around the room for Sister Astel, but she was gone.

David compared himself and his clothes to his two new friends; both had a three-day stubble on their faces, and their clothes looked like they'd slept in them for the last couple of days. He looked at his own and they looked the same except they were clean. David pointed to his jacket and then theirs and they didn't make the connection. David went to the back of the bar and lay down, rolling and squirming around on the dirty floor. Then he got up, brushed the excess dirt off, and sat back with the seamen.

The bartender watching the proceedings motioned for David to follow him. They entered a store room in the back and the bartender showed David an old greasy engine. The bartender took one of his hands and held it next to David's. David rubbed his hands over the dirty engine and scrapped his finger nails across it. He worked the dirt and grease deep into his hands and then wiped his hands on his pants and across his face. The smile of approval from the bartender showed he'd pass.

They spent the afternoon drinking wine. They weren't in any hurry. He hoped they knew what they were doing. The bartender brought them plates of spaghetti covered with tomato sauce, and again David watched Skinny and Fats, as he labeled his traveling companions, eat and copied their manners. They slobbered spaghetti sauce on their faces without a care. David tore pieces off one of the hard rolls and stuffed in his mouth followed by a fork full of spaghetti he sucked down noisily.

It was dark out when they left the bar and they staggered down the street, half on the walkway and half in the street. Fats turned into a small doorway; David had to stoop to enter. It was a bicycle shop and a young man sat on a stool in the back working on a bicycle. A stack of bicycles stood against the back wall. Wooden bins containing various parts hung from a third wall. A dozen or more bicycles hung by their wheels from hooks in the ceiling. Against the side wall was a work table and on the wall behind it hung an assortment of tools. Everything was clean and in its place. Obviously the mechanic took pride in his work.

"Bonsoir, Monsieur. Comment allez-vous?"

"Très bien, merci. Avez-vous un taxi?"

"Oui."

"Concuisez-moi a Cherboug, au navire Andrus."

David heard them mention Cherboug and the Andrus, but could understand nothing else. Then the shop owner replied, gesturing with his arms and mentioning Bosch several times.

Both Skinny and Fats produced wallets and started counting bills. Skinny poked David with an elbow indicating that he contribute some money. Fumbling, David dragged his wallet out and produced some bills. The driver selected bills from each until he was satisfied. He turned and entered an adjoining garage and motioned them in. David and Fat crawled into the back seat of a black Fiat and Skinny sat up front with the driver.

The afternoon's wine and spaghetti topped with a couple of cognacs were starting to catch up with David. He opened the window just in case his afternoon's activities decided to leave him. The countryside sped by, but it was dark out and he felt too ill to watch where they were going. "Bosch," called the driver. David didn't understand and didn't care until he saw the gate across the road and soldiers on both sides of the car.

"Alt." Soldiers shined flashlights inside the car, shouting harsh commands. The driver got out of the car and was talking loudly, gesturing with his arms.

A soldier held out his hand demanding papers. Two Germans on the far side of the car unslung their rifles pointing them at the car. "Alles drau ben. Jetzt." They opened the door and dragged Skinny out by the front of his jacket. He showed the German his papers then stood by the car. Fats was next and managed to extract himself from the car without assistance. His papers checked, he stood next to Skinny.

The soldier was shouting at David as he tried to climb out of the back seat. A hand reached in and grabbed his jacket jerking him out of the car. David threw-up. Vomit shot out of his mouth and over the German's uniform. The soldier jumped back screaming and struck David on the side of the head with his rifle butt. David fell to the ground and struggled to get up. His two friends tried to help him but the soldier ordered them back to the car. David felt the point of a bayonet on the rifle pressing down on his chest. He could not move. He had his wallet clutched in his hand and held it up.

One of the German guards took the wallet and walked over to the lights in the guard shack. He examined the papers, pocketed the rest of David's money and walked back, throwing the wallet on the ground beside him. The bayonet was removed from his chest and his friends picked up his wallet and helped him into the car. The gate opened and the Fiat sped through.

David sobered up fast after the encounter with the Germans and his stomach was now empty. He put his hand to the side of his head and felt his cheek swelling where the rifle butt had hit him. They were in a town traveling up side streets and alleys. David wondered if it was Cherboug and then something large and dark loomed alongside the taxi. David looked up. It was their ship.

They climbed the gangway in the dark, Skinny in the lead and Fats behind. David crawled up the steep steps, one at a time. He looked below into a black abyss. He felt sick again and tried to vomit but nothing came up. Fats, waiting behind, urged David on quietly. It seemed as though he would never reach the top when a hand reached out and grabbed his jacket pulling him over the last step unto the ship.

David could feel the deck pitch gently even though the ship lay tied to the dock. They entered a narrow hatch and went through a passageway into a room with bunks. There were grimy-looking steel bunks, probably crew bunks, against one wall of the narrow room and metal lockers on the opposite wall, leaving a narrow walkway in between. The room smelled more like one of their football locker rooms after a game played in the rain and mud than a ship. The walls and ceiling were all painted the same color, an off-white that made him feel sick again. Skinny showed David a bunk and motioned to him to lie down and wait.

David lay back on the bed and passed out.

Wedding Bells

David felt someone shaking his shoulder. He looked up and saw Fats motioning him to get up. He tried to sit but his head was pounding and it hurt to even move. Fats handed him a cup of black coffee and he tried to swallow but it was so strong he gagged on it. He sat on the edge of the bed trying to sip the hot liquid and wondered where they were. The ship rolled gently and he could hear the steady thumping of the engines. They must be out to sea.

For the first time since his bailout, David felt as though he would actually escape. Skinny stuck his head through the hatchway and spoke excitedly to Fats, motioning David to come. He stood shakily, head pounding, and followed them out. Moisture filled the air and he pulled his jacket tighter around his neck. A light fog hung over the water. The sky turned a dark pink, then lightened as the sun poked over the horizon. The fresh salt air felt good to David and he breathed in deeply. From out of the fog a smaller ship appeared traveling in the same direction as theirs. It closed to within fifty yards of the big ship and someone threw a light line across. A sailor grabbed the line and pulled it over, dragging the heavy line attached to it down on the deck. The sailors worked without speaking, as if they'd rehearsed the procedure a hundred times.

Skinny fastened a sling around David then clipped it onto the large rope. A line was attached to the sling and two burly sailors would play it out slowly so David would slide across to the steamer. He dug his pistol out from under his shirt and handed it to Skinny. "You will have more use for this than I." He looked at the churning water below, grimaced and climbed over the side rail, turned and saluted his two friends.

"Au revoir, Monsieur Regis."

David looked down at the dark sea reaching up for him and shuddered. Unconsciously he pulled his feet up and looked away. The steamer was coming closer and he tried to turn facing it. It was a naval ship flying the British flag. David didn't know much about ships but from the cannon and machine guns on deck it must be some kind of patrol boat. They obviously had some connection with the underground.

David hit the deck solidly and two sailors grabbed him, unbuckling the harness. In seconds the ropes were released and retrieved. An officer came up, and David saluted. "Sir, David Hampton, flying officer with the R.A.F."

"Welcome aboard, Hampton. Come on below and we'll get you a clean uniform and some food. Those are strange clothes you have."

"You should have seen me in the priest's robe," said David, laughing. "I've been hiding out with the underground for a week. The country is crawling with Germans. We slipped through several checkpoints and everywhere you turned there were German patrols."

"Here's your quarters, Hampton. This is Seaman Bartlow; he'll fit you with a proper uniform and show you the galley. You can roam the ship as you like. We'll be on patrol for another five days before we're scheduled to dock. If we go to quarters, you're to come back to this room and wait here. We don't want to lose you after all the trouble we've gone through to get you back." The officer turned and left.

"You must be somebody important for us to leave our patrol just to pick you up," said Seaman Bartlow.

"Just a Spitfire pilot with the R.A.F. Collided with a Messerschmitt and had to bail out."

"You're some bloody lucky chap. Here's some clothes should fit. May be a wee bit bulky but they're warm and dry."

David folded the clothes he'd gotten from Monique and pocketed the wallet with his Damettreis Regis passport. The clothes he would package up and drop sometime if he could make a pass over the village where Monique and Father Paquette lived. It would let them know he had survived, that their efforts were not in vain. "How about the mess hall, Bartlow? I'm starved."

"It's not a bloody mess hall Yank, it's a galley. This way and watch your head."

David followed as they wound their way through a maze of narrow passages and down a couple of steep stairs. "How in the hell do you ever find your way around down here?"

"She's a pretty small ship Yank, under sixty meters. After you've been on 'er a few months, cleaning and scraping and painting, you'll know every rivet and seam."

They stepped into a galley that was brightly lit and Bartlow called one of the cooks over and introduced David.

"What'll you have, mate? Most anything you want, we can fix."

"Steak and eggs and some fried potatoes and a gallon of coffee." The cook smiled and headed for the stove.

"So Bartlow, what kind of a ship is this? I mean what do you do out here?"

"We're a destroyer. We hunt down subs, sir. Most the time we're fixing and cleaning the ship. But when we get on a German sub, it's all hands on deck. Then we start dropping depth charges. Got us one last month. Blew 'er right in half. Should have seen the bloody garbage come floating up."

"Anybody survive?"

"Are you kidding? That damn sub must've been down three hundred feet. One of our depth charges caved her in. She collapsed like you stomping an empty tin can." He stomped his foot on the floor for emphasis. "Sent every one of them murdering Kraut bastards straight to hell. Got to run, sir. Will there be anything else you'll be needing?"

"No, I'll finish eating and then wander around." David turned to his steak and eggs; he never expected to actually get a steak and real eggs. He cut a piece of steak, put it in his mouth and began chewing slowly, savoring every bite. He poked an egg yoke with his toast trying to remember when he'd last eaten a real egg. It was at home, before he left for England. His mother had fried them in butter, just for him. Several slices of side pork fried crispily just the way he liked it along with potatoes from their garden. Almost everything they ate came from the farm, either grown or raised.

David left the galley and headed down a passageway to the first stairs heading topside. After the third set of stairs, he stepped out onto the deck. The ship smelled of fresh paint everywhere he went. There were no rusty, scaly flakes or grease and oil sloshing around like the steamer that had picked him up when he bailed out over the channel. He took in a deep breath of the fresh sea air.

He stood letting his eyes adjust to the bright sunlight. The waves were short and choppy and the ship rolled very little, as they were traveling in the same direction as the waves. David wandered around the deck watching the sailors working on their equipment. He stopped to watch a sailor stripping and cleaning his machine gun. "How d'ya know where all those parts go?" asked David.

"Hello, sir," said the sailor, looking up. "You're the flier we picked up."

"Yeah. Bailed out over France just before my Spitfire blew up. Spent a week hiding out and dodging Krauts."

"This baby's my whole life," he said patting the gun affectionately. "I can bloody well tear her down and put her back together blindfolded." He placed a belt of ammo in the magazine and closed the cover. He pulled the bolt back and let it snap forward. The steel mechanism clicked softly, chambering a round in the barrel. The seaman called on his intercom, "Port waist gunner back in service." He turned to David. "Sir, you want to sit up here an see how she feels? Just don't push these two thumb-buttons; they're the triggers. She's loaded and ready to fire."

David climbed into the sailor's seat and gripped the double handles of the machine gun with both hands. The smell of fresh gun oil made him think of his father -- how they'd always cleaned and oiled their guns the night before deer season opened, even though they hadn't been fired since the previous hunt. It was a ritual they always performed, like a pep-talk from the coach before a game. He wondered what his dad was doing now. Probably out in the barn with his brothers, tending to the morning chores. He'd probably have a couple letters waiting for him when he got back to base. David sighted the machine gun, checking the swing and how the gun turret turned.

"Fighters!" someone screamed from the bridge. A bosun's whistle blew the call to battle stations.

"Sir, get down! Enemy fighters coming in." He climbed into position swinging his gun forward, looking for the attackers.

The ship heeled hard to port and David stood behind the gun turret looking for the fighters. Then he spotted three black specks diving from out of the sun. "They're coming out of the sun!" he shouted up to the gunner.

The turret turned. The sailor sighted his gun momentarily, then thumbed the two firing buttons down. The machine gun shook on its mounting, spewing hot smoking cases onto the deck. David smelled the burning cordite. The air around the ship turned into a cloud of blue from the burning powder. Seamen rushed to their battle stations. The machine gun firing overhead hurt David's ears. He'd never noticed the sound when he fired the eight guns in his Spitfire. Bullets striking the heavy steel deck made metallic sounding pings as they hit and ricocheted about the ship. He stood as close to the heavy steel of the gun turret as he could get, but still felt exposed.

David felt a tug on his pant leg. A bullet narrowly missed him. A sailor fell holding his chest, then rolled on his back. A stream of blood shot out of his chest, like a water fountain. A medic ran to his rescue and suddenly fell holding his leg. The deck turned red with blood.

"Medic!" screamed the sailor with blood running from his leg. He was pulling his wounded chum by the collar and dragging himself towards a companionway.

David could feel the fear around him. He smelled sweat, blood and the acidic fumes of burned cordite. Screams from the wounded ran together with the staccato of rapid firing machine guns. Someone screamed for a medic, another for ammo. The odor of burned paint, where hot lead from incoming bullets had strafed the ship, stung his nostrils. It was a game. Every member on the team was on the field and there were no time-outs. It was a life or death struggle and when a player fell, the game went on without him. The penalties were wounding or death unless you were one of the lucky ones.

"Ammo!" Two ammo bearers ran forward carrying cases.

"Torpedo!" The ship heeled hard to starboard. David felt the vibration in the deck as the throttles were advanced to full power. He watched the two white streaks heading for the ship. He agonized at how slowly the ship responded, as if stuck in slow motion. Had he survived two bailouts and a rescue from France only to be blown out of the water? It didn't seem fair. He couldn't fight back. He was like a bird in the barnyard with a broken wing, waiting for one of the cats to find him. There must have been a sub lurking somewhere in the Channel. David gripped the railing waiting for the explosion. The ship continued its turn toward the speeding torpedos. Ever so slowly the ship turned, and the torpedoes passed harmlessly to the side. "Hooray!" came a cheer from someone on the bridge.

"Attackers, port beam!"

Two Stukas were coming at them, skimming the water. The sailor above David swung his gun around and sent a stream of tracers reaching for the dive bombers. Return fire from the Stuka sent tracers back to the ship in a two-way stream.

David heard a gagging sound and looked up. The sailor above stood grasping his throat with both hands. Blood shot out between his fingers. He stumbled, falling from the turret. David jumped from his protected shelter and caught the sailor.

"Medic!" David screamed. The sailor looked up at him with unseeing eyes. He put his hand over the hole in the sailor's neck trying to stop the flow of blood but it was no use. David had long worked with his father butchering animals on the farm and recognized the signs of death.

David felt a tug on his jacket sleeve. His arm burned where a bullet creased him. He jumped into the turret and swung the heavy machine gun toward the attacking Stukas. He thumbed both firing buttons down and the gun bucked in his grip. He saw his tracers arcing into the water in front of the attacker and struggled to raise the barrel. It seemed to take forever before he saw the tracers center on the Stuka. Smoke came from its engine and it nosed over, hitting the water. It cartwheeled back into the air, breaking up and falling in pieces.

David swung the gun to bear on the second Stuka. His hands, covered with the sailor's blood, were slippery on the gun's handles. His mouth was dry and tasted salty, like the taste of blood. The ship was encased in a haze of blue smoke and heat from the guns firing. Sweat ran down his forehead and his eyes and nose burned from the smoke. He was oblivious to the sounds around him -- the screams of pain, the calls for medics or more ammo. The ship's hammering guns sent a continuous rain of fire at the attackers. He screamed at the attacking Stuka, his own gun firing continuously.

Streams of tracers left the ship coming from every gun on the port side. And still the Stuka came. David saw his tracers disappear into the Hun aircraft. Black smoke poured from the engine and flames lapped back around the cockpit. He saw the pilot slumped forward in the cockpit. The Stuka hit the ship. David was thrown from the gun turret.

Burning oil and burnt flesh stung David's nostrils. Dense black smoke poured out of the hole in the side of the ship where the plane had hit. The deck was hot. He struggled to get up, coughing and vomiting. He fell to the deck and began crawling across the burning steel. Water poured over him from a fire hose and two sailors ran to his rescue. They grabbed both his arms and ran, dragging him across the deck.

David sat gulping mouthfuls of fresh air. He wiped a sleeve across his face and struggled to his feet watching the sailors fighting the fire.

"Over here, Mister," called someone to David. "Take the hose. Keep a stream of cold water pouring on the deck."

"Okay, I got it." David swung the nozzle back and forth. Steam poured off the hot steel. Fire burned out of control below deck. Smoke billowed from the hole in the side of the ship where part of the Stuka's tail protruded. Burning paint, oil and fuel crossed the deck and he gagged for fresh air. For the first time David noticed a sister ship steaming alongside. Where it came from, he didn't know but was glad to see help that close in case they needed it.

The smoke stopped pouring out of the hole in the side of the ship as the fire crews below brought the fire under control. David worked his way across the burned deck spraying cold sea water before him, cooling the hot steel.

An officer walked up to David as he shut his hose off. His rugged features seemed out of place on a ship. He had a hawk nose that looked more like the rudder on a sail boat. He extended a hand that seemed large enough to wrap around a football. Like everyone else, his white uniform was torn and smudged with soot and blood, but he had a sparkle in his eye. David knew where that sparkle came from. They had just defeated a superior enemy, and the adrenaline was still coursing through their veins.

"Commander Bennington. Most of my friends call me Ben. We couldn't help but notice how you took over Smitty's gun. We're grateful to have you aboard, Yank," greeted the tall lanky officer.

"Beg your pardon, sir, ah, Ben. But they were shooting at my ass. I guess I tend to get hostile when that happens," said David, with a grin on his face.

"You're a natural leader, Mister Hampton, and a hell of a fighter. I'd be proud to have you serving aboard my ship if you'd consider switching over to the Navy."

"I'm a fighter pilot; I always wanted to fly. I'd just as soon keep flying my Spitfire."

"I understand. If there's anything we can do for you while aboard, it's yours."

"If I could let my base know where I'm at. I've been missing in action for a week."

"We've already passed that information on to group. They'll have notified your unit. Carry on, Mister Hampton."

"Thank you, sir." David saluted and went back to helping the sailors clean up. He scraped, cleaned and painted and his time aboard ship seemed to fly.

The sea breeze was blowing a mist of salt spray moderately across the port quarter. Gone was the burned paint, the blood, the screams, and David, eyes closed, stood at the rail breathing it in deeply. He was getting his sea legs and stood easy as the ship rose on the crests and plunged into the blue troughs. A bow wave would roll away as the ship knifed through a crested swell, sending a fine mist drifting back. David squinted his eyes in the bright sunlight. The only time he'd seen it so clear and brilliant was when they'd climbed their Spitfires through the overcast and left the city smog below them. The Cliffs of Dover stood like white sentries welcoming them home. The sun was reflecting off the white clay cliffs, sandwiching them between the dark blue sea and the bright blue sky. Heat waves rose from the water and the cliffs shimmered like a mirage.

"Officer Hampton, sir?"

"That's me," said David, turning from the rail.

"Seaman Hamshire, sir. I'm the radio operator. We just received a message for you, sir. When we dock, there'll be a WAAF with a car waiting to drive you back to base."

"Thank you, Hamshire. I was wondering how I'd get back, with no money and only my I.D. tags for identification."

"Good luck, sir. We'll be docking in an hour."

The seaman left David standing at the rail alone. Entering the Thames estuary he watched the water turn to a dirty brown. Flotsam drifted past the ship as they headed for their dock near London. David wrinkled his nose at the smell coming from the water. It was a combination of everything that ran or was dumped into the river. It smelled like the locker room the time the sewer backed up. A dark gob of something black drifted by, and he smelled crude oil.

The small ship maneuvered under its own power into the narrow confines. Refuse covered the stagnant water in the slip. David looked down from the rail and saw a bloated rat floating belly up. He half expected to see a body floating among the debris.

Seamen threw light lines down to the men waiting on the dock, and they grabbed them, pulling the heavy hawser lines across and slipping them over the bollards. The lines tightened and the ship came to a rest. David saluted the ship's captain standing on the bridge. The salute was returned and he turned, heading down the gangway.

David walked toward the WAAF waiting beside a car at the end of the dock. He felt strange not having a kitbag to carry. He looked up and saw the WAAF running towards him.

"David!" she shouted.

"Millie?" She was in his arms, smothering him with kisses. Her perfume made him a little heady. He'd been gone for two weeks and the smell was almost foreign. She seemed to melt against him and he relished the warm softness of her body.

"Oh, David!" she cried, tears streaming down her rounded cheeks. "You're back."

"It took me a little longer than I'd planned." David wiped the tears from her cheek. "Do you have a wedding dress picked out?"

"Yes, David. Yes. I not only have one picked out, I bought it."

"How long've you been planning this?" asked David, grinning like a kid at the county fair with his first cotton candy -- he couldn't get enough of looking at Millie; holding her and listening to her happy, bubbly voice.

"Since I first saw you, David," she teased. Then her face grimaced as she thought back two weeks. "When Woody called me and said your plane went down over France, I told him to start planning for our wedding; we would be getting married as soon as you came back. Then I bought my dress."

"First, I'd better get some different clothes and probably report in."

"Everything's arranged. We'll swing by the new apartment and pick up your things."

"New apartment? What things?" David asked.

"With the baby coming, we needed something bigger and better. Also, all of your things from the base are at the apartment. When you were reported missing, your belongings were put in storage. I had Chief and Woody smuggle them out. I have everything at the apartment," said Millie.

"How'd you get the car and manage to be its driver?"

"I have connections. Working at headquarters, everything that happens comes through us. When I heard they'd picked you up on a ship and asked for a confirmation on your identification, I started doing a little maneuvering on my own." Millie smiled smugly.

"Still, I should report in. Simpson's not going to be happy."

"If Simpson doesn't like it, he may end up at headquarters dumping secretaries' waste baskets and cleaning latrines," said Millie through clenched teeth. Her eyes sparkled and her shoulders were squared and rigid. She gripped the steering wheel with determination and the knuckles on her hands turned white.

Millie wheeled the sedan around piles of rubble that once were buildings. She cut in and out of side streets, bypassing many that were still blocked off to traffic.

"I'm glad I'm on your side when you get your dander up." He lowered his voice and added, "Little Missie."

"You'd darn well better remember it Mister," she said with a smile on her face. "Here's the apartment. It's the only block that wasn't bombed," Millie said. She pulled to the curb, parking in front of a large brick building. "We have the front half of the second floor, two bedrooms and a bath."

"How'd you manage that trick, Millie? I mean with the war on and everything." David got out of the car and stood looking at their new apartment. It had cut stone steps leading up to a veranda. Ivy grew up the sides, clinging to the red brick walls as if it was rooted there.

Millie joined him looking at their new home. "It's only two blocks to the trolley line and look at the lawn around back, Luv. White picket fence and a sand box for our baby to play in."

"Looks like you have everything, Millie. I can lay back with a scotch and a cigar and listen to the BBC while you fix supper."

"Haw! Is that what you think?" said Millie, taking his arm and handing him a key. They walked arm in arm up the steps to their new home. "We have our own outside entrance. Won't have a bunch of geezers peeking out the hallway to see who I'm with." She smiled up at David.

He turned the key in the lock and opened the door.

"Well, are we going to stand around in the hall?" she teased.

"No. My bride to be." He swooped her up in his arms and carried her across the threshold.

"David, what are you doing? You'll hurt yourself!"

"I'm carrying my bride across the threshold into our new home," said David, setting her down gently.

"But, we're not married!" she stammered.

"We are as far as I'm concerned." David held her close looking deep into her eyes. "You're not the only one who's had plans since we met." He kissed her long and deep, a kiss of commitment, binding them to each other.

"Come and see our new bedroom," she whispered.

"I haven't seen the rest of the apartment!"

"We'll have plenty of time for that. Later."

David felt a chill when she said later. What were their chances of surviving the war. How many "laters" did they have? He felt like a cat who's used up half of its nine lives. How many times had he been shot at in combat? Was there a bullet with his name on it? Twice he'd bailed out. He'd survived the sea and escaped from German-occupied France. What next?

Millie'd turned the sheets and blankets back on the bed and unbuttoned her blouse. "Okay, Mister," she said in a deep voice. "Do you need an invitation or an instruction manual?"

David laughed. "Neither, Missie," he countered, throwing his wool navy jacket on the floor and stepping out of his trousers.

Millie dropped her bra and slipped between the sheets. "I should call you freckles," David said, as he kissed her neck and nibbled his way toward her breast.

Millie moaned when she felt his erection throbbing against her leg and pulled him over. She wrapped her legs around him tightly. "David, David."

Later they lay entwined in each other's arms talking, whispering. "David, I was so scared I'd lost you."

"Not a chance. I have my Saint Christopher's medal. It kept me safe just like you said it would, and brought me back to you. Along with a lot of people who risked their lives to help."

"What people?"

"Ordinary people. People like us, resisting the Germans. Fighting for their lives, trying to survive. First there was a farmer's wife, who'd lost a son. Then a bartender and a girl whose husband was missing in action."

"Tell me about the bruise on the side of your face."

"In a minute. There was this priest who took me in and fixed me up in a priest's robe. Then I hid out at an orphanage run by a couple of nuns. My next escorts were two Greek sailors from one of the merchant ships. I had to spend the afternoon drinking with them."

"You did what? You mean I'm sleeping with a drunk," she teased, softly kissing the bruise on the side of his face.

"You know the axiom. When in Rome, do as the Romans do. The two sailors were my escorts. I called them Skinny and Fats. They smuggled me through German checkpoints to a ship. So, when I met them we were killing time and spent the afternoon drinking in a bar. We had big plates of spaghetti and more drinks. After dark, we took a taxi back to the ship and were stopped by a German patrol along the way. One of the guards grabbed me and I got sick all over his jacket. He clubbed me with his rifle butt and knocked me down. They checked our papers and let us go."

"Poor darling," she crooned. "Let me make it better," and kissed his bruise gently. Then she straddled him as he lay on his back.

"Oh, yes. That's better. Much better." He thrust upward meeting her gentle rocking motion until they lay exhausted in each other's arms.

"You should be getting back to base and check in, my dear. The sooner we get started, the sooner we get married."

"I just want to stay here with you, Millie. The hell with the war."

"I know David. But, that's not how the script was written. You just rest here, Mister. I've got another surprise for you."

"What?"

"You'll see." Millie slipped from between the sheets and headed into the bathroom.

He heard water running. Then Millie called, "David, can you come lend a hand, Luv?"

He threw back the sheets and put his bare feet on the cold floor. "We need some rugs on the floor, dear," he said as he hurried toward the bathroom. Millie was sitting in a large iron, claw foot tub, filled with hot, steaming water up to her neck.

She turned and smiled coyly at him. "Hey mister. How 'bout jumping in and scrubbing my back?"

"And baby too?"

"And baby too," she teased through poised lips.

"Well, missie," he said in a deep voice. "Let it never be said that I didn't help this lady in distress." He slipped into the tub behind her. "Is this the spot?" he asked massaging her neck and shoulders.

"That's one, and there's lots more. I think you're going to be busy for the rest of the evening Mister."

"Damn! Now I'll have to wait until morning to check in at base."

She turned in his arms and kissed him long and hard. "I don't think they'll know the difference. Besides, you have an appointment as soon as you turn in your flight report."

The dawn was one David had grown to associate with England, foggy and damp. "How can you see where you're going?" asked David nervously as he strained to see the road in front of their car.

"Relax, my love. I've lived here all my life. I know this part of London like our apartment. Don't you have fog like this where we're going to live after the war?"

"We have fog, but nothing like this. Most of the time it's dry and the sun is shining and in the winter the ground is white with snow for three or four months."

"Oh, that sounds awfully cold. When we have snow, it's only a short time. Then it's gone."

"Ours is a dry cold. You don't feel it like the damp cold in England, besides we'll have a big warm house and lots of kids running around."

"Well now, do I have anything to say about this?" Millie asked with a smile on her face. "A real home in the country. I can hardly wait."

"It'll be a two-story house with all the bedrooms on the second floor and a large bathroom with a big claw-foot bath tub."

"And a big lawn with a white picket fence around it for our children to play and I want a flower garden. I always wanted to have my own flowers."

"You'll have lots of flowers, my dear. All around the house, and across the front of the garden and along the walkway coming from the driveway."

"Living out in the country, Luv, I suppose we'll have to have our own car."

David laughed. "In America, everyone has a car. We'll probably have a big Ford sedan. Dad's partial to Fords. Knowing him, he'll probably have one picked out for us when we get home. And, I think the Wilson farm may be for sale soon. I'll write dad and ask him to check for us."

"Is it a nice farm? If we're going to have a big family, we'll need a big farm, won't we?"

"The Wilson farm isn't big. Not much land, but it's one of the nicest around. It has the richest bottom land in the Red River Valley. We'll raise beets, and we can always buy more land once we're settled."

"What in the world would you do with beets, David? Sounds like something we feed to pigs."

David laughed. "These are sugar beets. We make sugar, my dear, and ship it all over the world."

"Oh," Millie gasped. "We're going to be important. I mean, we'll be helping feed people all over the world. We'll need lots of boys to help you with the farm. We'll have to practice a lot at making boys," teased Millie.

"Well we'd better practice making girls, 'cuz girls are just as important on a farm as boys. Can't have one without the other or you'll end up going in circles."

"All this talk about practice. We may have to pull into some secluded patch of woods so we won't get behind," teased Millie. "Now that the fog has lifted, it's warm and sunny."

"There's a spot and our khaki colored car will be well camouflaged," said David.

"I was kidding," said Millie, as she turned the car into the grove.

An hour later they were back on the road. "Better brush the grass out of your hair, David. Everyone will know what we've been doing."

"I don't mind." He snuggled up to her as she drove.

"Keep your hands to yourself, mister. After all, good English girls don't do those things. A girl must be proper, and...." David kissed her on the cheek and sat back combing his hair. "And decent. Here we are, David. You'd better check in."

"Where'll I meet you?"

"Woody's got everything arranged, Luv. See you at the Church." David stood on the wooden sidewalk for a moment before he shouldered his kit bag and headed for Simpson's office. He stood his bag on the floor in the corner and was greeted by the clerk.

"Good morning, sir." He came around the bare desk, his hand extended. "You're the luckiest son-of-a-bitch in the whole R.A.F. Congratulations, sir!"

"Thanks. Guess I'll be the first to agree with you on the luck. The CO in?"

"Yeah, and you'll probably need a little more of that luck, sir. He's pissed that you didn't show up yesterday."

"Here goes," said David, knocking on the door.

The door jerked open. Simpson stood glaring at him. "Where the hell've you been, Hampton?" His voice was squeaky as though he swallowed a whistle. "You were supposed to be here yesterday." The door slammed shut and Simpson stalked around the desk dropping heavily into his chair. His mustache twitched nervously and his upper lip turned up in a sneer. "Your ship docked yesterday morning. You had a driver that was to bring you directly here."

"Sir, I had to go by my apartment and get one of my uniforms and clean up a bit. We'd started out, but the fog was so thick and with the curfew still on in London, they advised us not to drive until morning. Sir!" David still stood at attention trying not to smile.

"You're to go over to operations and report to Sergeant Dennis Bickers in Intelligence. When they're finished, file your flight report and you have a ten-day leave. We'll settle this when you get back. Dismissed!" Simpson shouted. The chords on his neck stood out. His face was livid, dark-red, as if his collar was too tight.

David tried to hide the smirk that was growing on his face as he did an about face and marched from the room. He found the spy, as everyone called intelligence officers, and Dennis began the debriefing. He began with the note the farmer's wife had handed him, "MARIE CLAIRE."

"That's the code name for the French underground. They are very secretive about the underground. This is the only solid lead we have to make contact with them," said Dennis, as he continued to write in his notebook.

"Sergeant, from what I learned, that's the way they want it. No one knows anyone in the underground except one link each way. Nobody knew where or how I would get out of France except that I would be turned over to their next contact and they would take it from there. It seems as though they know best. If the Germans catch one of the underground, they can't torture it out of them if they don't know it. That way the link won't be broken."

"Sounds logical. So, you're saying that if our flyers bail out over France and are not captured, to write 'Marie Claire' on a piece of paper and give it to the first friendly Frenchmen they encounter?"

"That's it, Dennis. That seems to be their connection to the underground."

"That should be all we need for now. You're to be married, I understand. Congratulations. Off with you now. If we need anything further, we'll find you when you get back from your honeymoon."

David stepped out and blinked his eyes trying to adjust to the bright sun. "Give yea ah lift, sir?" came a voice from the sedan parked in front.

"Woody! How in the hell didja know I'd be here?"

"Me sister's been driving us nuts ever since yea went on vacation in France. New apartment, bring your things from the base. We've been planning your wedding and didn't even know if yea were still alive. Yea're a sight for sore eyes, Davie, me boy. Me brother-in-law!"

"Sorry about your new kite, Woody, but those damn Germans keep wanting to bust'em up."

"Not to worry, Davie me-boy. We got lots ah new kites coming every day now. It's the pilots! It's murder sending those new kids up. They're scared shitless ah the plane let alone flying combat. Some ah them only have thirty or forty hours in a Spitfire. I tried to tell ol' piss-face Simpson, but he's only interested in sending a full squadron up. Couldn't care less if any ah them make it back."

"You got to have a team and fly as a team. That's the only way they have a chance. Follow the leader and cover his back side. That way they'll get a little more experience with minimum exposure."

"'Nuff ah that bullshit. Got some ah yea things and a dress uniform back to the barracks. Yea get shaved, shined and we'll head for the church, and don't be taking a nap. We only got an hour to get ready," Woody ordered.

"Boy, she's got this timed to the minute."

"Couple more hours, Davie me boy, and we'll be off the hook. Then she's all yours," chortled Woody.

David showered and shaved, dressing excitedly. On the way to the church, Woody filled him in on the squadron's activities. The church was old and covered with vines clinging to the cut stone sides. The windows were stained glass with pictures of Jesus and Mary inlaid in the glass. At the front of the church hung a large cross with a Christ statue hanging from it.

Organ music began and Millie stood in the doorway. Sunlight shining through the doorway radiated her wedding gown as she stepped into the darkened interior of the church. She looked like an angel descending from the heavens with the sun's rays streaming in behind her. David stepped forward and took her arm and they walked to the altar together.

"Do you, David Hampton, take this woman, Millie Bolfriend, to be your lawfully wedded wife until death do you part?"

David froze when the priest said, until death do you part. He felt a chill, a dark omen. Millie squeezed his hand, and he squeaked, "Yes, I do."

Millie responded to the questions.

"I now pronounce you husband and wife. God be with you."

A dozen men from the squadron formed an archway with drawn swords as they left the church. "Just married," had been written all over their car. Old boots and tin cans hung from the back bumper, clattering behind as they drove away.

They had ten days alone in a secluded Irish cabin, locked in the sweet embrace of each other's arms. Ten days seemed like an eternity compared to what they'd had so far. Tenderly they coaxed every secret from each other and learned the mysteries of their bodies. They made love as though each moment could be their last.

A Real Mission

The Station hummed like a flight of bombers passing high overhead. Smoke suspended in the air gave the pub a blue haze. The sound of snooker balls clicking together came from the back room.

"Hey, Hap. It's the honeymooner and he looks like he's got a powerful thirst," said Chief, draining his mug and banging it down on the bar.

"You're right, Chief. Poor boy sure looks wore right to a frazzle, don't he?" said Hap clicking his false teeth in and out.

"That he does. Probably so worn out from honeymooning he won't be able to lift a mug of ale. Howdy, Pigskin. Welcome back to the real world," said Chief, raising his muscular arm in the greeting symbol he and his blood brother used.

"What's new, brother?"

"Well, Pigskin, minute you turn your back, all hell breaks loose. Wasn't anyone to piss and moan, so I guess we were stuck."

"Stuck with what, Chief?"

"All the Americans are in one squadron now. Eagle Squadron."

"So big deal. We spend a few days playing around with new pilots seeing what they can do and assign them a position in the squadron. Sounds okay to me. What else is going on?" asked David suspiciously. "You guys look like you're up to something. How about hustling me up an ale, Hap, and while you're pouring, wipe that silly grin off your face, ol' man."

"You'd best show a little respect for your elders, Sonny Boy. Now tell us all about the honeymoon. And none ah the bullshit."

"Hap, you're nothing but a dirty old man. We're married and plan to live happily ever after and have lots of kids. That's all you're going to hear," said David, smiling. He reached over and affectionately brushed the old man's sparse grey hair away from his bald spot. "Now, how about my ale? A guy could die of thirst around here."

"Here's your bloody ale! Oh Jeez. Here come two more clowns. We're going to have a regular circus in here," mumbled Hap. "Maybe I should charge admission," he said in a loud voice.

"Hi, Spike. Hey Woody, pull up a chair. Grouchy here, is pouring ales," said David, grinning.

"How's me brother-in-law, an' me sister after their fabulous honeymoon in sunny Ireland?" said Woody. "Ah to be back in the land of shamrocks and Irish whiskey."

David took a sip of ale and puffed on a cigar. "Ireland was the most beautiful place I've ever seen. We had a cottage on the bluffs above Dunglow. Ours was the only one for over a half a mile. Our nearest neighbors were a couple raising sheep. What a fantastic view of the Atlantic. We spent hours watching the waves washing up on our beach."

"Not to change the subject, but how about telling us about your vacation on the French Riviera," asked Raymond.

"Yeh," said Hap. "You meet any good looking girls?" he asked, grinning like a Cheshire cat. "Now back in the Great War, us pilots would have women fawning all over us."

"Well as a matter of fact I did meet a very nice French girl," said David, puffing on his cigar and slowly sipping his ale.

It was quiet except for the squeaking of chairs as those listening moved closer. Someone banged his empty mug on the bar and Hap filled it while listening to David. The BBC was playing music, 'You'd be so nice to come home to.'

"She had a body like you can't imagine. Well you probably know, eh Hap?"

"Yeh, she had tits out to here," said Hap, holding out his two arthritic hands cupped in front of him.

"That's about it, Hap. Her face was angelic. It seemed to radiate when she looked up at you and smiled. Her eyes, they were brown and soft like a fawn's and seemed to say, 'come to me.' Her teeth sparkled like pearls held up to the sun. Her hair was dark brown, silky and hung down over her shoulders. Then she wrapped her arms around my neck and kissed me, and our lips melted together. Her body molded against mine and I could feel her breasts pushing against my chest."

"Holy shit," said Hap hopping back and forth from one foot to the other. "Now that's more like it. Now tell us about how you laid 'er."

"Whew. Better not tell your wife about that one or she'll be put'n ah ring in yea nose," said Woody.

"It's one of the first things I told Millie. After the war she wants to go to France with me and meet her."

"Hell," said Hap. "I'd like to be a mouse in the corner when that happens. Them French babes are something. I remember back in the Great War when we were flying against the Huns...."

"Pigskin, what was her connection and how'd you meet her?" asked Raymond, anxious to hear about David's escape.

"I'd just made contact with the French underground and was sitting in this little bar drinking a glass of wine and eating a plate of pasta with cheese and hard rolls, when in came two German soldiers. They stood their rifles against the wall, took their helmets off and sat down."

"What the hell, were they blind?" asked Chief. "Didn't they recognize your uniform?"

"I didn't have my uniform, Chief. I had on a farmer's old clothes that were several sizes too large. Sitting at the bar, they never noticed. So there I was with two Germans sitting in the bar less than twenty feet away. I wondered whether I'd have to shoot my way out with that puny little service pistol when in comes the French girl I'd mentioned. She marches right over to me, saying something in French, wraps her arms around my neck and kisses me, like I was Charles Friggin' Boyer!"

"You shot the German bastards and saved her life," said Hap grinning and clicking his false teeth up and down. "And, she took you home to show her gratitude, right?"

"Not quite. One of the Germans was pretty drunk and decided he wanted some of the action for himself. A Frenchman, sitting at one of the tables, intervened. While they were busy, she grabbed my arm and hustled me out of the bar. We slipped through blackened alleys to my next connection in the underground."

"You mean you never got laid?" asked Hap, an disappointed look on his face.

"Hap, for Christ's sake. I'm a married man."

"Well," Hap said indignantly. "You weren't married then!"

"Sorry old man, but since I met Millie, there never was anyone else. Nor ever will be."

"Hear, hear," said Raymond. "I'll drink to that. I'd like to hear some more about your escape from France."

"I can only talk about things that happened. I can't tell you anything that will identify anyone in the underground. They risked their lives to help me escape. I owe it to them not to betray that trust."

"I understand, David. Besides, everything I write goes through a censor board before it's transmitted."

David told of his escape, from his bail out until Millie picked him up at the dock.

"Joker'd probably be here right now if he'd done the same thing and hadn't opened his chute so soon," said Chief.

"'Tain't so," said Hap. "Back in the Great War, I shoulda got kilt ah hundred times, but didn't. Then some new guy come along an got his-self kilt first time out."

"When your number's up, it's up," said Chief making a cutting motion across his neck with his hand.

"I don't think so," elaborated Raymond. "You're a victim of your circumstances and background. Look at Pigskin, a quarterback. He's used to scrambling, trying to fight his way out of tight places. When flying, he's twisting, turning, looking around, behind, ready to act instantly."

"Attacking," said Chief, his eyes sparkling. He pulled the Bowie knife from the top of his boot, feeling the edge of the blade with his thumb. "That's how we got most of the cavalry. Always attacking. Germans ain't no different. Just don't wait for them to find you. Get them first, then they are on the defensive."

"Chief's right," added Pigskin. "Get high and run in front of the sun. They'll never see you coming out of the sun. I found that out when Duffy got it. A stationary target is just asking for it, you got to be jinxing all the time. When you least expect it, Jerry's going to be lining you up in his sights."

"Don't you ever get scared, Pigskin? I'd be scared shitless with someone shooting at me," said Raymond laying his pencil and notebook aside and filling his pipe with fresh tobacco. He struck a match with his thumb nail and sucked in noisily on the pipe. A stream of blue smoke rose and hung suspended over their heads like a cloud layer.

"Only a damn fool wouldn't be scared. The worst is the waiting. When you have time to sit and think about all the close ones you've had, you start thinking that maybe this time you'll screw up. It's like the time we were playing St. Paul State. The coach pulled me and put in the substitute quarterback. It was pouring rain, like we were playing in a lake. The sub went out and fumbled the ball. St. Paul recovered and ran it in for a touchdown and all I could do was sit there and watch. Like watching that Kraut bastard murder Joker and there wasn't a thing I could do about it."

"Yea guys can bullshit all night. I've got me ah new crew to train and get yea Spitfires ready. Be seeing yea." Woody tipped his head back and drained his mug.

"Wait up, brother-in-law," said David, "I'll walk back to base with you. Better try and get some sleep myself. See yah Chief, Spike. Keep the mugs full, Hap."

"Night, Pigskin. Good hunting and don't take any more French vacations," called Raymond, chuckling more to himself than to anyone left in the bar.

"Hell, he wouldn't know what to do anyway," grumbled Hap as he filled Chief's and Raymond's mugs. "Back in the Great War, we'd drink and party till dawn, then go kick Kraut asses. These kids now-ah-days don't know how to fight...."

David tossed fitfully in his sleep. Monique came running through a field of ripened grain, their golden heads shining in the sun. She tripped and fell. Four German soldiers grabbed her. She struggled, kicking, biting and scratching, almost breaking free. A hairy fist clubbed her alongside the head and she fell dazed. They threw her down on her back. Each soldier held an arm or leg, so she could not move. Piece by piece they ripped her clothes off. She struggled against their brute strength. David wrinkled his nose in his sleep, smelling their dirty, sweaty bodies and the stench from their breath. Monique lay helpless, her naked body shining white and pure against the ripening grain.

A German soldier came strolling up unbuttoning his pants and grinning. It was the German that had dragged him from the taxi at the checkpoint. He spit tobacco juice and spittle dribbled down his chin. He was fat and greasy and smelled as though he hadn't taken a bath in months. Naked from the waist down he knelt between Monique's legs and flopped heavily on top of her. She screamed and tried to kick but was powerless against the four soldiers holding her. The greasy Hun on top of her was fumbling clumsily between her legs when she sank her teeth into his ear. He screamed striking her in the stomach but she sank her teeth deeper and tore his ear half off.

David watched helplessly as the German placed both knees on her stomach, driving them into the soft white flesh. Blood poured from the German's ripped ear, splattering Monique's naked body. The greasy Kraut held one hand around her neck strangling her while he beat her face with his other fist. Blood and broken bones showed where moments ago a beautiful face had been.

"Pigskin! Pigskin!" David woke screaming.

Chief had him by both shoulders, shaking him. "Hey Pigskin, you having another bad dream, or what? Sounds like you're going on the warpath, Brother."

David sat on up on the edge of his bunk, soaked with sweat from the dream encounter. "Must've been the ale, Chief. Maybe I'll have to quit drinking. Damn dreams. I'm afraid to go to sleep."

"Hell, just go to the dispensary and get some sleeping pills. That'll cure your problem. Unless there's someone trying to get a message to you. The old medicine men would have dreams all the time. Mom said their dreams would tell us when to plant our crops and when to go hunting."

"These are pretty violent dreams, Chief. I don't think there's anyone trying to pass messages. Most of the time there's someone I know real good or care about and they're in trouble. They always call out to me for help, but I can't do anything to help them. I feel so helpless, like watching Joker get shot to pieces and I couldn't do anything."

"When I go to bed, I think of good things. Like when Sitting Bull and Crazy Horse wiped out Custer. Then I sleep like a baby. You should try it sometime."

"Will you two shut up so we can get some sleep?" shouted a sleepy voice from the darkened barracks.

"Good advice," said Chief. "See you in a couple hours," and he padded off to his bunk.

David could not sleep. He was terrified of having another dream. Showered and shaved, he slipped through the blackout curtain and the cold wet fog encased him like a cocoon. A chill ran through him and he walked briskly toward the dispersal area, his hands tucked deep in the pockets of his jacket.

"Halt. Who goes there?"

"Flying officer David Hampton."

"Advance and be recognized."

David walked toward the sentry and a shielded flashlight shined in his face. "Sorry, sir. Kind of spooky out here in the dark, with this fog."

"Couldn't sleep. I wanted to take a look at my new kite. Haven't been up flying since I bailed out of my wrecked Spitfire over France. Shouldn't be long."

"Your kite's the fifth one down, sir."

David climbed up on the wet wing and opened the canopy. After spending ten days with Millie, it seemed strange sitting in the cockpit. He settled down in the seat and rested his right hand on the stick with his left hand on the throttle, getting a feel for the new Spitfire, fresh from the factory.

It smelled brand new. Fresh paint, oil and aviation gas. A slight hint of burnt cordite. It had never been used except for test flights. He would be the first one to put it to the test. He hoped Mother Earth would continue to guide his foot steps, or in this case, his flying. He needed it, for now he was a husband and soon would be a father.

The new kids. They looked so young, he thought. They should be home going to school. What the hell, he was only a year older. God, he was starting to feel old. All these kids, they were his responsibility now. It was his fault that Billy the Kid and Glen were dead. If he'd only called his squadron to split and climb on their own a minute earlier, they'd be flying today.

His hands moved across the instruments and he turned the sight pip on, checking the orange aiming dot on the windscreen. He began to hear voices, "Pigskin, break right. There's one on your tail." He moved the controls unconsciously.

"Bandits, twelve o'clock high."

"I'm hit! Bailing out."

"Hold your fire till the damn Hun fills your windscreen."

David rested his finger on the firing button.

"Hey, open up," shouted Woody tapping on the canopy.

"Now you've done it. I was just about to open fire on an ME-109 and here you come climbing up on the wing," said David, grinning at his brother-in-law.

"Haw. Would've like to see that," chortled Woody, grinning like a leprechaun. The bill on his cap was turned straight up and the cap pulled down to his ears. "If yea'd cut loose wid them 303s, everyone on base would've been in the bomb shelters in their skivvies. Come to think on it, give me five minutes to get over to the WAAF barracks and yea can cut loose a couple short bursts."

"Go on with you, Woodpecker. You're starting to sound like Hap. Maybe you've been hanging around that dirty old man too much; now you're beginning to talk like him," said David, smiling up at Woody.

"Yea'd best trot your mangy carcass over to the slop shop or yea'll miss breakfast."

"Now what in the hell'd I be missing?" asked David, as he climbed out of the cockpit.

"Well, if yea'd been wid us during the famine, them so called slops might be looking pretty good," said Woody. "Off wid yea now, I got me work to do."

"Any way you can squeeze a few more belts of ammo in there? I got a feeling there'll be a few Krauts going to the fatherland soon," said David, stuffing his hands deep in his pockets and strolling off through the fog toward the breakfast tent.

They flew for a week, checking out the new American pilots forming the Eagle Squadron. They fired on drone targets pulled behind another aircraft and practiced strafing on ground targets, putting the Spitfire literally through the wringer. David worked his squadron during every minute of daylight on every day they could fly. When they felt comfortable with their position in the squadron, he took them up for mock dogfights.

Exhausted, David slept little. His nights were plagued with dreams, but not all bad dreams. One night the White Buffalo, the sacred symbol of the Sioux, appeared in his dreams. Leading him on, a soft woman's voice spoke to him. First in Sioux, "Mitakuye oyasin, we are related to all things. Rain-in-the-Face, listen to the wisdom of Mother Earth. To the four quarters and nothing shall be strong before you. Place your body, your mind, your spirit within the wisdom of Mother Earth, for she will provide you with the earth you walk on, the air you breath, the water and food you take nourishment from." Thunder crashed and lighting flashed in the distance and the White Buffalo turned and ran toward it.

Lights flashed on in the barracks. "Everybody up, everybody up. Mission this morning. Everybody up, mission today," the sergeant went through the barracks bawling like the town crier.

The briefing room buzzed as pilots stood in groups, talking nervously, smoking, and trying to pass the time.

"Attention." Everyone stood as Wing Commander Tonsund marched briskly to the podium.

"At ease, gentlemen. Smoke'em if you got'em." Commander Tonsund spoke with a heavy British accent. You had to listen closely to understand what he was saying. There was a shuffling of chairs and a low grumbling as pilots not yet awake sat back down. The blue haze of the room became deeper, as a dozen or more cigarettes were relit. "Our targets today are the aircraft factories at Le Mans. Backup targets will be Cherbourg or Le Havre. Flying officer David Hampton, from the Pigskin Squadron, has just escaped from Nazi-held France. Officer Hampton will brief you on how he contacted the underground."

David worked his way through the crowded briefing room to the platform. He turned, looking back at his fellow pilots. All faces looked to him, to their quarterback. It was as if he had some new magical game plan.

David cleared his throat noisily. "My first contact was with some French farmers. I was hidden in their barn, fed and given civilian clothes. They wrote the name 'Marie Claire' on a piece of paper and drew a map to a pub where I was to go. When it was dark, I walked into town and found the pub. I handed the note to the bartender and he made the necessary arrangements to pass me on to the next contact in the underground. I was passed on from contact to contact until I was put on a ship and transferred to a British frigate."

"How'd you know they wouldn't turn you over to the Krauts?"

"I didn't. All you can do is trust them and hope you made the proper connection," said David, thinking of his close encounter with the farmer.

"Do you speak French? I mean how do you tell them who you are and what you want?"

"I kept the insignia from my uniform and used a lot of hand signals. Once I got started, word was passed on from contact to contact. I did meet one person who could speak English. I'm studying French now, at least enough so I can speak a few words and tell them who I am. They'll handle the rest."

"Thank you, Officer Hampton," said intelligence officer Dennis Bickers, standing and walking toward the podium, cutting David short.

David stepped down and worked his way back to his seat. Several pilots shook his hand, congratulating him on his return.

Officer Bickers began in a monotone, "The target today is Le Mans. We'll be hitting six buildings that are known aircraft factories."

David didn't particularly like the intelligence officer. He reminded him of a weasel with his dark little beady eyes that were always nervously looking around. When he spoke, it was in a high-pitched nasal whine that grated on your nerves like a piece of chalk squeaking on a blackboard.

"They're turning out several ME-109s a day, so you can see it's an important target. There will be three squadrons of Blenheims, led by the Pine Squadron with Victor and Oak covering each side. Sparkie Squadron will fly top cover. Today, we're trying something new. Pigskin's new Eagle Squadron, the Seventy-first, will be flying Spitfires. The Eagle Squadron will arrive over the target area thirty minutes in advance of the bomber formation. I'm hoping they will draw the fighters up and engage them. By the time the bombers arrive, the fighters will be out of ammo and low on fuel. Coordinate your watches. On my mark, the time will be zero-four-thirty. 'Mark.' Sergeant Bishop will brief you on the weather."

At least they wouldn't have to escort the bumbees, thought David. Or maybe weasel-face is hoping we won't come back. It wouldn't be the first time someone was set up in order to get rid of them.

Bishop marched smartly toward the podium, then tripped stepping up to the platform. He apologized, loosening his shirt collar with a finger, as though he couldn't breathe. He looked old compared to the pilots in the room. He pushed his round-rimmed glasses back up on his nose and placed a clipboard under his arm.

"Good morning, gentlemen," said Sergeant Bishop in his squeaky voice. A couple of calls of endearment greeted him back. "Good news today. The weather over the target area should be clear. We have a large high pressure area ridging down from Finland and pushing into the Channel. It will be an instrument takeoff and climb and should be clear the rest of the way. We expect the weather to be clear by the time you return. The bombers have plenty of fuel. The Spitfires will be cutting it close on fuel. You'll have minimum time for engagement. When you become critical on fuel, you'll have to break and head for the Channel. We've alerted Hawkinge, near the town of Folkestone. It's the first field after crossing the Channel where you can safely land for fuel. I recommend everyone check your maps and know exactly where it's located."

"Thank you, Sergeant Bishop," said Commander Tonsund, taking over. "Pigskin's Eagle Squadron will take off at zero-six-hundred hours and head directly to the target. With their higher cruise speed they should arrive on target thirty minutes in advance of the bomber formation. The rest will take off fifteen minutes later. The bombers will already be airborne and you will pick them up over the Channel just off Dover at angels twenty. Gentlemen, this operation is different from any you've flown so far. No one will wait for you; this operation is based on timing. If you're not in position on schedule, they will go without you. If that happens, I'm afraid our losses may be staggering. Good luck and good hunting."

The Commander stepped down heading for the door. Bishop jumped up calling, "Attention."

After the briefing, Pigskin gathered his squadron to one side. "Chief, I want your vic to fly top cover two thousand feet above us. Dixie, you fly your vic one minute behind the Chief and a thousand feet higher to cover him. Storm'n Norman, you'll fly one minute behind me and a thousand feet higher with your vic and cover our backs. We'll make a formation takeoff and split after we reach the Channel. It's going to be thicker than flies on shit with Messerschmitts, so you new guys stick with your leader and keep your eyes open. Okay, let's go kick Kraut asses."

David climbed into the front seat of the lorry. He breathed deeply of the fresh air, thankful to be out of the smoke-filled room. The sky was dark and the base of the clouds almost hid the tree tops. The lorry came to a stop in the dispersal area. David was anxious for his new pilots. "Let's go, men. We don't have much time before engine start. Watch your spacing in the climb. If you lose contact, turn ten degrees right and continue the climb on your own and we'll meet on top." That was all the advice he could give them; they were on their own.

"Davie, me boy," called Woody, walking out from under his Spitfire. David chuckled to himself as he watched his brother-in-law come strutting toward him in his arrogant swagger that was more like a duck waddle. "Couldn't get any more ammo in but did something else I think yea be liking."

"Okay, what's this that I'm going to be liking?" asked David. He slipped the parachute straps over his shoulders, pulling the straps up between his legs and fastening them loosely.

"We loaded yea 303s mostly wid DeWildes, mixing in a few armor piercing and incendiaries."

"I thought the DeWilde bullets fouled the barrels?"

"Makes ah hell of ah mess out ah them," chortled Woody. "That's the armorer's problem. Should ah heard them screaming when I told them what I wanted, but then I told them they'd be working on Simpson's kite and that shut'em right up."

"I don't suppose there's any way you can get me some extra fuel, maybe slip a couple hundred gallons in someplace?" said David, as he placed his hands on the sides of the cockpit and settled into the narrow seat. He adjusted the seat pack parachute and tightened the straps. He pulled the safety straps up between his legs and fastened the straps into the metal catch. Woody fastened David's shoulder straps and gave each a tightening jerk.

"We run'em up and I had'em all topped right to the cork after. Lot ah screaming but what the hell, it might get yea another ten minutes in the air. Off wid yea now and bring me new kites back," said Woody as he jumped off the wing and strutted around front to pull the chocks.

David pulled his helmet on and plugged in his radio leads. He turned the oxygen valve on and checked its flow. He pulled his gloves on and sat nervously drumming his fingers on the side of the stick.

Five minutes to six, the start-engines flare arced up. The low cloud base glowed an eerie green until the flare dropped back below the cloud. David started his engine and brought the throttle back to idle. He taxied from the dispersal area, s-turning back and forth to see around the nose. Pigskin glanced back as his squadron lined up behind him, ready for takeoff. It was his squadron, his Eagles. They had a real mission, drawing up the German fighters. Only live combat would prove the new replacements' worth. They were all Americans, seasoned pilots, with fighter experience. David thought how fitting it was for them to be called Eagles. For once, they were not baby-sitting the bumbees.

Zero-six-hundred. The takeoff flare arced up and disappeared in the cloud. David began easing his power forward. The Spitfire rolled slowly and he swung the nose left and right, looking past the engine, down the field. He eased the stick forward and the tail lifted, heavily at first, then it began to fly. He rolled the trim wheel forward and fed in right rudder to compensate for the engine torque. As he reached takeoff speed, the Spit bounced lightly a couple of times, then flew. Clear of the ground he leveled out, tapped his brakes to stop the wheels from spinning and brought his gear up. The wheels banged into the wheel wells, locking into place. He released the canopy catch, sliding it closed. He flew the full length of the field, skimming the ground, while his team jockeyed into position for the climb. He trimmed the nose up and was swallowed by the overcast. His wing tip lights glowed like halos off the moisture-laden clouds. Rivulets of water ran up his windscreen in a series of narrow winding streams.

David began a gradual turn toward the Channel. He had his engine throttled back for an economy climb. The Merlin's engine quieted to a whisper, like wind blowing gently through the pine trees. There was no rush to get to altitude. So what if it took them twice as long to get on top? Conserving fuel was more important. If they ran out of fuel over France they would lose both the plane and the pilot.

David scanned the instruments without thinking. He flew by instinct. The vibrations of his Spitfire sent signals which he received and stored or used immediately. He adjusted the throttle, screwed in the prop pitch a hair, added a touch on the mixture. As they continued the climb, he rolled the trim a fraction, and turned five degrees back to his heading. His team was flying on his direction, on his command. If he screwed up, the whole team would screw up.

He did not fear for his life. He felt a certain immortality, an indestructibility. Joker had been the same way, but he had been murdered. A cold-blooded, calculating murder. It could have happened back home with some crazy man.

Chief thrived on the danger of combat. He looked forward to it, the challenge. It was in their blood to prove themselves in battle, to honor their Sioux heritage. To count coups in battle. David thought of the braves sitting around a campfire, telling of their daring encounters. He could almost smell the smoke from the fire. Chief and he would sit in a place of honor with the braves of his great-grandfather.

Chief was David's teammate, his back up, his blood brother. He was an extension of David, like an unseen arm. When David was trapped behind the line, Chief was there throwing a critical block. He'd carry the ball through a line of tacklers, shaking them off like a dog shakes off water when coming from the lake.

Chief wielded his Spitfire around in battle like a Sioux warrior would have ridden his war pony, brandishing his scalping knife. He was glad Chief was his teammate, his blood brother. David thought of the Hunkapi ceremony in which they had become blood brothers. A blood bond that is closer than kinship.

The wrinkled old medicine man had dressed in his ceremonial deerskin breeches. His chest was bare. A necklace of bones strung together and decorated with flattened porcupine quills hung from his neck. A single eagle feather stuck up above his head at a forty-five-degree angle from the ball of white hair knotted in back of his head. Even though there had been a clear sky, the campfire cast eerie shadows against the blackened woods -- like a party of warriors dancing in a circle. David thought of the old man's words. "There are three ideals of peace. Peace comes to your souls and their relationship to the universe and to the Wakan Tanka. Second, peace between you two brothers to recognize the kinship of all people. Third, peace is between nations who recognize that all people are family and children of the Great Spirit. You are now brothers, in blood and spirit. You are one and will look out for each other as brothers, now and when you journey to the spirit world."

David recalled the ancient one taking his ceremonial knife and making a cut inside of each of their right arms. He'd felt nothing as the knife made an inch-long cut. Then the medicine man had placed their arms together, the cuts one against the other. He bound their arms with a piece of deerskin. "Now your blood will flow from one to the other. You are blood brothers forever."

The sky lightened around him and they shot through the top of the overcast. It was as if someone lit a lantern in a darkened room. David squinted for a moment as his eyes adjusted to the sunlight. He glanced in his rear-facing mirror and saw his squadron hatch from the cloudy incubator one at a time, pulling into formation behind him. They were eagles, the Eagle Squadron. How many times had he stood behind the center for a moment, admiring the team, waiting for the snap of the ball? On his command they would engage the opponents in a struggle for each yard gained. Now, on his command they would kill or be killed.

David leveled at ten thousand feet, adjusting the power and trim to hold his altitude. The clouds dissipated and he could see white caps on the dark blue Channel below. For once, Bishop had predicted the weather correctly.

He should make landfall just south of Le Havre, giving him the needed fix for their heading to Le Mans. They would stay low to draw up any German fighters. They were the decoys.

It was like the draw play, his favorite. He took the snap from center, slipped the football to Chief unseen, turned and ran back ten yards as if to turn and pass. David loved the look on their faces when he turned and the tacklers realized they'd been duped.

They were flying the draw play. Get the Germans to come up after them, expending their fuel and ammo. They'd look damn silly sitting on the ground refueling and arming when the bombers hit the factories. Deception -- that was the key to any successful play. Get them thinking you were doing one thing, then do the opposite.

Halfway across the Channel, David rocked his wings signaling his team to split into four vic's. He saw the smoke from Le Havre blowing at an angle and he changed his heading five degrees to correct for the wind drift. It was such a short flight across the Channel in the Spitfire, less than ten minutes even at economy power. David watched the waves race up on the beaches in long white unending rows -- crashing into rocks, shooting up geysers of spray, then subdued, sliding quietly back into the ocean from whence they came. They crossed the beach into France. It won't be long now, thought David. The coast watchers would be phoning their position and scrambling fighters to intercept.

It was the snap of the ball from center; time to execute the draw play. David turned his radio switch to transmit, "Pigskin, Red-one, arm your guns and keep a sharp eye out for bogies. Loosen up your formations. Let's start jinxing." He pulled his Spitfire into a hard left turn, then back to the right climbing a hundred feet. He looked all around him and then checked the rear-facing mirror, jinxed right and left and dropped a hundred feet. His head was on a swivel, turning, looking, constantly alert for the teeniest speck -- one that was out of place, that did not belong. He looked at the sun, never staring directly at it, but looking around it. He jinxed, again looking down, and saw a dozen or more specks climbing up to intercept them. At first, they were like specks of pepper stuck to his windscreen, though with each passing second they grew.

"Pigskin, Red-one, bandits six-o'clock low. Looks like twin engine, probably ME-110s. Wait'll they get closer and we'll dive on'em. Storm'n Norman, you attack when they turn to follow us. You'll have a broadside shot."

"Green-three, bandits six-o'clock low, climbing."

"Yellow-one, bandits three-o'clock level."

White streaks shot past David from below. The ME-110s were firing on them but they were still too far for an accurate shot. David rocked his wings signaling his wing men and rolled hard left pushing the throttle lever full forward. The Merlin engine growled back with new found energy and the Spitfire surged ahead. He watched the airspeed needle climb toward the redline. Inverted, he pulled the stick back with both hands, plunging the Spitfire in a vertical dive. The controls were hard and the tail buffeted from the increased pressure. He half-rolled and checked his sight pip. The Messerschmitt's wings filled the bars on his sight pip. "Red, two and three, pick your targets."

The Messerschmitt was near a stall, trying to climb at a steeper inter-cept angle. David centered his sight on the wing root and fired his eight 303s. A steady stream of fire erupted from each of the Spit's wings. The cockpit filled with the odorous acidity of burnt cordite. Tracers arced down into the Messerschmitt like fourth of July rockets. The ME-110's wing snapped like a match stick. David rolled hard left sucking the stick back in his lap. The g forces pushed him down in his seat and he felt himself blacking out. He eased the pressure on the stick and pulled the throttle back. The wind whis-tling around his canopy softened.

"Yellow-one, intercepting ME-109s behind you, Pigskin."

"Red-one, roger," said David, rolling hard left, then pulling up and rolling right, looking for his attacker.

"Green-one, bandits five-o'clock. Attacking."

"Blue-one, Chief, hard right. One on your tail."

There were enemy aircraft coming at them from all sides. The radio was a solid chatter of voices. Every fighter in his squadron was engaged in a dogfight. David saw a flash of fire off to his left. Parachutes blossomed below them. The sky was filled with criss-crossing streaks of tracers.

David stood his Spitfire on its starboard wing, turning in behind an ME-110. The blood drained from his head and he felt himself greying out. He slacked off on his back pressure, trading his excess speed for altitude. He closed on the ME-110. The rear-facing gunner swung his single gun toward David.

The German knew David was behind him and began jinxing. David turned with him, four hundred yards and closing. He wanted to conserve ammo...the closer the shot the less he would use. Three hundred yards...the Messerschmitt filled his sight pip. The rear-facing gunner opened fire. David watched the white tracers reaching toward him, almost in slow motion. The gunner's bullets pinged, glancing harmlessly off the Merlin engine. One hit his windscreen shattering the glass. The gunner was good. David moved his controls, centering his sight pip on the gun turret. He skidded and slipped following the big heavy twin-engine Messerschmitt, like a pair of ballerinas. David rolled and turned with the big fighter as though they were paired. The gun turret slid into his sight pip and he squeezed the firing button for only a second. Eight streams of DeWilde bullets shattered the glass turret. The gunner slumped forward, his gun drooping at an odd angle.

The fifty-three-foot wingspan filled his windscreen. David closed to a hundred yards. He skidded the Spit, centering his sight on the left engine and fired a three second burst. The Spitfire bucked, filling the cockpit with powder fumes from the guns. The heavy DeWilde bullets ripped into the engine cowling. Black smoke trailed from the engine. The Messerschmitt rolled, no longer taking evasive action. Pieces of the wing came flying back. David slammed the controls hard right, jerking the stick back. The Messerschmitt exploded. David was thrown sideways in the narrow cockpit.

"Pigskin Squadron, this is Red-one. Break off and let's head for home, we're getting low on fuel."

"Blue-one. You want to tell the Krauts the game is over? Bastards keep wanting to shoot at me!"

David looked around and saw Dixie circling, trying to get behind an ME-109. "Keep'er tight Dix. Pigskin red-one, I'll swing by and give'em a squirt."

A ball of fire streamed through the cockpit, shattering David's instrument panel. His head snapped forward and he began to lose consciousness. The Spitfire rolled and David's hand fell from the control stick. He struggled to reach the stick, but the Spitfire spun out of control. Centrifugal force held his arm pinned to the side. He saw a blur of blue, then a blur of green; a death spiral. So, this is how the indestructible pilot would end his flying career. So much for an evaluation on the draw play. He thought of Millie and mumbled, "Honey, I'm sorry," before he slumped, unconscious.

"Red-one, roll out!" screamed Chief into his R/T. He pushed the elevators forward, plunging the nose of his Spitfire straight down. Chief rammed the throttle forward to full war power. "Pigskin, pull out. Hey Brother, come on. Get ah hold of that stick, roll out." The ground came rushing at him in a blur of green. "Pigskin, fumble. Come on Brother, there's a fumble. Get the ball! Pigskin, fumble!"

David heard Chief calling fumble, but his head hurt and he tried to shut it out. He kept hearing fumble, fumble. Oh my God, the ball's loose. His eyes opened and he saw a spinning blur of green rushing at him. It looked like the toy tin top he'd had at home when he was five years old. Wind whistling around the canopy sounded like the top spinning. It felt as if he was inside the top looking out.

"PIGSKIN, FUMBLE!" screamed Chief into his transmitter. "FUMBLE, PIGSKIN. FUMBLE! "

Fumble. They had to get the ball back. He struggled to sit up, but the centrifugal force held him hard against the side of the cockpit.

"FUMBLE, FUMBLE, FUMBLE!"

David kicked down with his left foot jabbing the rudder to the floor. The rotation slowed, but his airspeed needle was pegged at redline. He lunged for the throttle and jerked it partially back. He heard his blood brother's war cry.

"Come on, Pigskin, pull'er out. We're getting too close to the goddamn ground. Pull'er up, Brother."

David struggled with the stick, but the controls were hard like they were stuck. He wrapped both hands around the stick and pulled. It would not move.

"Pigskin, drop your flaps."

David chopped the power and rolled the trim wheel back. He pulled the flap handle and heard a wrenching noise below him. He strained on the stick with both hands and the Spitfire bucked. The plane buffeted from the high speed, but the nose rose grudgingly. Trees passed in a blur. He had the impression of flashing green treetops. He thought of riding the train back home, how he'd sit with his nose to the window and try counting telegraph poles as they sped past.

"Ah, Pigskin...you're scaring the shit outa me flying so damn low. You suppose we could pull it up just a bit?"

David pulled his flaps up. Something was banging against the bottom of the Spitfire. Gingerly he brought his power back to cruise and adjusted his trim.

"Wires!"

David looked out the damaged windscreen. Power lines. He pushed the nose forward and hit them dead on. The wire stretched, singing with the increased tension. The three bladed metal propellers cut the wires like tinner's shears. They snapped, like whips popping, jerking the Spitfire downward. A brilliant white flash, like a photographer's flash powder igniting, left red spots before his eyes. His reflex action automatically jerked the stick back. The nose came up slowly. A tree sprang up in front of him. He slammed the throttle forward into full war power and hauled back on the controls. He was too close to turn. The tree seemed to come at him in slow motion. David remembered a football play. His mind raced so fast, the players stopped in place. The tree seemed to be climbing with him. He braced for the crash.

The Spitfire leaped upward, like an eagle rising on a thermal of warm air. They really were eagles. David looked upward at the sanctity of space above him. His instructor had drilled it into him. One of the most useless things to a pilot was altitude above him. He held the stick back in his lap with both hands, literally hanging on the prop. He prayed the Merlin wouldn't miss a beat; he needed every ounce of power he could get. Then he hit.

The metal propellers chewed their way through the top of the tree. Leaves and branches flew past David as if he was in a September windstorm. He felt the plane buffet, then he was in the clear. Reluctantly he lowered the nose to a normal climb angle and adjusted his power. The Spitfire was indestructible.

"Jeez, Pigskin...you should be flying for the circus," called Chief. "I sure as hell thought you were laying claim to some of that French territory."

"The grapes weren't ripe or I'd have brought some back for the boys," said David. "Maybe you'd better fly alongside and give this kite an eyeball. Seems as though we have a stretch of water to cross yet."

"It's a good thing Woody's your brother-in-law," chortled Chief, trying to imitate the mechanic.

"That bad, eh?"

"Let me put it to you this way, Pigskin. If'n it was me, I'd bail out when I got to the other side and tell'em the engine seized up. Be a helluva lot simpler."

"This ol' pony's taken me into battle and brought me back out, I can't abandon 'er that way. Anyway, I've got to make out those evaluation reports and I promised Woody I'd bring her back. Better eye-ball the weather build-up over the English coast."

"Good ol' Bishop blew it again. We were supposed to be clear when we got back. What you think, Pigskin? Going over the top or duck under?"

"Let's see if we can duck under, Chief. I'll have to follow you though, my instrument panel is gone and I can't see much out of this busted windscreen."

"This is going to be fun. The quarterback out on the field, fair game."

"Just remember I only got half a kite. I'd kind of like to walk away from one for a change."

"You and Woody both," said Chief.

David slid into position off Chief's wing and closed in to within twenty-five feet as they entered the soup. "Pretty thick stuff, Chief. Think it'll be clear under?"

"Could be," said Chief. "Let's take a look. Going down."

David adjusted his power and trimmed for a gentle descent through the milky haze. He was flying within a plane's length of Chief's wing tip. His eyes followed the navigation light, ready to make any adjustment necessary to maintain his position. His actions were automatic. He adjusted the trim and power as needed, his right hand rested lightly on the stick, the left hand on the throttle. Like their blood bonding, they groped their way downward together, looking for the sea, for a break between the clouds and the water. He thought of Glen and Billy the Kid, trying to climb in formation in a thunderstorm. If you lost your contact for a fraction of a second....

How long had they been in the cloud? It could have only been minutes, but to David it seemed like hours. He studied his shattered panel where the cannon shell had destroyed his artificial horizon and needle ball. Without instruments, he was dependent on his blood brother. A couple of inches over and the shell would have hit him. Some Kraut would be painting another British flag on the side of his kite. He'd never thought about himself, but now he had Millie and the baby to worry about. What would have happened to them if he'd been killed?

There was little forward visibility and they descended slowly, watching for the water. David was afraid to take his eyes off the Chief's wing. Suddenly he saw the glare of water ahead. "Pull up Chief!" Because of their angle of descent the water had appeared to be above them.

Instinctively the Chief leveled out. "Jeez Pigskin, did you see that? It looked like the water was above us!"

"Just keep'er level, Chief. If we don't break out in ten minutes, we'll climb on top."

"Then we could at least bail out if we had to. Sure as hell hope we don't run into any ships out here."

All David could see was Chief's wing tip, and nothing else. It was like a dream. They were suspended inside a cloud of fleece. It almost looked like the cotton candy his dad had bought him at the circus back home. He felt bug-eyed from watching the navigation light in front of him. His muscles were tight and he tried to flex them in the narrow confines of the cockpit.

David felt as if he'd fumbled the ball and everyone from both teams had piled on him in the scramble to recover it. Time dragged, like players peeling themselves off the pileup, one at a time. He lost all track of time. How much fuel did they have? Another five minutes? If they were lucky, maybe twenty minutes. If they ran out of fuel this low, they would have to belly-land on the water.

David thought of one snowstorm they'd had at home. They were dismissed from school before lunch. Walking home with his brothers and sisters, they stayed bunched together so they wouldn't lose sight of each other. His sister had lain in the snow ahead and when he walked by, she'd jumped out hollering "Boo," and thrown powdery snow in his face.

"Pigskin, looks like it's starting to thin out a bit."

David could now see all of Chief's Spitfire. Looking ahead through the fog, he saw a small fishing boat. Sitting on the mirrored water, it looked as if it were suspended in space. "We must be pretty close to the coast for that small of a boat to be out here."

"I think I can see the beach ahead. Yeah, that's it. But where the hell are we?"

"Head in the direction of the base, Chief. If we run out of fuel, we can land in a field." David moved back from Chief's wing as they flew clear of the fog. A hundred feet up, the ground passed in a blurred mirage of colors. Fields, farms and small towns merged as though they were condensed into a miniature child's play set. He saw people wave at them and in a brief second they were gone.

"About ten degrees right, Chief. Let's get a little more altitude."

"It's your play, Pigskin, but I think we'd better land somewhere for gas or we're going to end up walking."

"Gas isn't going to do me much good. I'm overheating. Temperature's almost red-line." He throttled back and checked that the coolant doors were wide open. The Merlin engine began vibrating. At first David thought it was one of the engine gremlins pilots always imagine, but it grew steadily. He opened the canopy, ready to bail out if necessary. He'd bail out only in an emergency; there were too many people and houses to risk letting the Spit find its own way down. Besides, they needed the Spitfire in one piece or as close as possible. "I'm going to have to put'er down. The ol' Merlin's sending signals and I'm afraid it's not morse code."

"There's the field, Pigskin. Two more minutes. Coax it along, you can make it. We've just been given the two minute warning and we're down by three points. You've got to get the touchdown. We can't settle for a field goal."

"Easy for you to say, they're not trying to sack you. Fire a warning rocket, Chief. Don't want anyone on the runway when we get there. That's if we get there." David glanced at the temperature needle. It was pegged solid on the red-line. The vibration from the Merlin turned into a heavy knocking. David thought about the time they'd rode their bikes down the railroad tracks. His hand tingled on the control stick and he eased the power back. The controls were mushy and unresponsive. He smelt a pungent acid odor of something being too hot, but not yet on fire.

David lined up on the field. He saw the flashing lights of crash trucks rushing onto the far side of the field. "You'd better land ahead of me, Chief. No telling what's going to happen when I put this Spitfire down."

"Just ran out of gas, Pigskin! I think I can make the field though. I'll take the left side and you take the right and the first one to The Station gets free ale."

"Gear won't come down, Chief, I'm belly landing." David cut the fuel and feathered the prop. He shut the ignition switch and brought the nose up. The propeller hit, throwing clods of sod flying through the air. The Spitfire cocked sideways, tipping up on one wing and the nose, then lost its momentum and settled slowly to the ground. David released his safety harness and jumped out, running from the damaged kite.

Black smoke poured from the engine. Orange tongues of fire flickered from the engine compartment. A mushroom ball of flame rose above the Spitfire. An empty fuel tank blew up. Parts of the engine cowling were launched by the explosion and drifted back to earth like lost feathers drifting downward from a sea gull. The explosion lifted David and dropped him as though a two-hundred-and-eighty-pound tackle had picked him up and slammed him to the ground. He'd been sacked many times playing football, but nothing like this. He lay on the ground trying to get his breath. He felt himself jerked around by the harness straps of his parachute, as if his chute had popped open. Someone was dragging him away from the burning wreckage. He struggled to get up, but his arms and legs hung uselessly at his side.

"Relax, Brother. You finally got to walk away from one," said Chief.

"That don't count, Chief. I didn't walk, I was running like hell."

"Shit, I thought you had a football and were running for a touchdown."

A lorry slid to a stop in the grass alongside them. " 'Ave yea no respect for me kites?" asked Woody, as he stepped from the lorry. "Now what didja think I'd be doing with that mess?"

"Well," said Chief. "The guns should still be good."

"As I recall," said David. "You said to bring your kite back for a change. So here it is," said David, grinning at his brother-in-law.

"May the Saints preserve us. What'd me sister get us into? Outside ah yea brain being a wee bit addled, is the rest ah yea okay?"

"I've one hell of a headache, but ain't nothing a mug of ale wouldn't cure," said David, struggling to unbuckle his parachute.

"I'll be dropping yea off at operations. When your reports are finished, stop by The Station an' I'll buy yea an ale. Yea sure as hell brought me kite back," said Woody shaking his head.

Chief

"Come on, Chief, let's grab an ale. I've got a couple of hours before my train leaves for London and three days with Millie."

"You buying, Pigskin?" asked Chief, as they stepped from the barracks. A chilly wet fog encased them and they walked rapidly to keep warm. "It sure as hell would have been nice if they'd built The Station a lot closer to the barracks," said Chief.

"Maybe they'd build an enclosed walkway for you Chief. Ol' Sitting Bull himself would roll over in his grave hearing you whimpering like a little puppy about the cold," David said.

"Hell, the only time we see the sun is when we climb through the fog and get on top. Besides, after I practically carried your ass back today, the least you could do is arrange for a car to pick me up and drop me off."

"You're right, Brother, I'm sorry. I screwed up but it won't happen again," said David, grinning affectionately at his blood brother. "You still planning on going back to school after the war?"

"Sure am. Got a letter from the tribal council yesterday. They're going to pay most of my tuition so I can go to law school. After I get my law degree, I'll do all the tribal legal work. What about you? You still going to farm?"

"That's great news, Brother," said David. "Matter of fact, we are going to farm. I wrote Dad last week and asked him to see if he could buy the Wilson farm for us."

"You couldn't do any better. The best bottom land around. Hell, anything you plant will grow there."

"We're going to raise kids and sugar beets and in that order. Millie wants to have lots of kids and she's all excited about the farm. Say, why don't you come into London and have supper with Millie and me? You've got three days, same as me, and we'll show you around the town. Maybe even line you up with one of her girlfriends. I'll ring Millie up from The Station."

"Why not? Don't get a free meal very often," said Chief holding the door of The Station open for his blood brother.

173

The Station was quiet with only two pilots sitting at the bar. Hap stood behind the bar wiping glasses and humming to himself. The Station was dark except for a single light behind the bar. David sniffed. "Hey, Chief. I think we're in the right place; I can smell ale!"

"I might'a known it'd be you two clowns," wheezed Hap as he shuffled down the bar, slipping his teeth back into his mouth. A three-day stubble failed to cover the wrinkles on his weather-beaten face. "The minute I saw the plane come in smoking and then the fire, I said it had to be you two. Could have made some good money too, but the chicken-shits in here wouldn't bet me," grumbled the old veteran as he filled their mugs. "Well? How many Krauts?"

"Got three," said Chief. "An ME-110 and two ME-109s."

"Hot damn," said Hap slapping the bar and skipping back and forth from his left foot to his right foot. "How about you, hotshot?"

David held up two fingers, "ME-110s."

"Adolf, better get your bags packed. We'll be sending your ass on a permanent vacation," cackled the old man. His eyes were piercing and sparkled in the low light of the pub. Wisps of white straggly hair hung out of place across his face and he wiped his sweaty brow with the back of his crippled hand. He set the foaming mugs on the polished bar and gave each a gentle push, sliding them down the bar to stop within an inch of their respective benefactors.

David sipped thirstily, leaving a foamy mustache on his upper lip. "Damn, does that taste good or what?"

Chief grunted his approval and wiped his sleeve across his mouth. He wasn't one for words except when they were alone. "Better go call Millie, Pigskin. Don't want to miss a real meal."

"Use the call box in back," said Hap, plopping his elbows on the bar. "Gimmy all the gory details, Chief, and don't leave out any of the good parts."

"We were decoys," said Chief, letting Hap mull over this tidbit of information while he slowly sipped his ale.

"What in tarnation you talking about, Chief?"

"We led the formation by thirty minutes and drew up all the fighters," said Chief smugly.

"You mean you guys went out alone and drew up all of Krautsville on your own?"

"That's 'bout it."

"Holy shit. What'd you do a dumb thing like that fer?"

"We are the Eagle Squadron, what more'd we need?" said David, slipping back onto his stool and cocking his feet on the foot rests. "Should have seen those Krauts swarming up like hornets out'a the nest."

"Yeah," smiled Chief. "We had the height and were spread out, attacking from both sides, in a cross fire. Had five of them smoking before they knew what happened."

"Caught'em with their pants down," cackled Hap with a hoarse laugh.

"Not quite yet," cautioned Pigskin. "'Bout the time everyone was out of ammo and low on fuel the bombers showed up. Jerry was back refueling and arming. The bumbees waltzed in and bombed their target and got out. No fighters to interfere. They never lost a plane."

"Jeez. I'd ah given anything to be there," said Hap, his eyes misty and his jaw set.

"Damn near lost Pigskin though," said Chief in his guttural manner.

"Just taking a little evasive action," added Pigskin, raising Hap's curiosity level about even with the boiling point. They chuckled to each other as the old man sputtered.

"Let's have it. You're holding back on me."

"Just keeping the best for last," added Chief dragging it on as long as possible.

"Well, I took a minor hit. A Kraut cannon shell wiped out my instruments and blew half my windscreen out. I kind of blacked out for a minute."

"Minute, hell!" said Chief, swelling with pride as he told of the dive and his calling Pigskin to pull out.

"Kie-rist. If'n we'd dove a plane like that back in the Great War, we'd 'ave ripped the wings off 'er." Hap wiped the sweat from his bald head, pushing the trailing wisps of hair off to one side. "How'n the hell'd you pull'er out?"

"I tried everything. Even pulled the flaps down. I think I shredded them. The ground was coming up in a blur of green. I don't know how high I was -- didn't make any difference though, at that speed I couldn't possibly have bailed out. The last I saw, my airspeed was pegged at the redline. Finally I rolled the trim wheel back and the nose responded."

"Not until you cut a power line and tore out a bunch of trees," corrected Chief, draining his mug.

"Guess we'd better catch a train or we'll miss supper, Chief."

"Hey, you guys can't leave now. We're right in the middle of a major combat operation."

"Got a wife, Hap. Fill you in on the rest when we get back. Come on Chief, best not keep your sister-in-law waiting. You'd be setting a bad precedent."

.   The train station was packed with travelers headed into London for the weekend. The air inside the station house was blue with cigarette smoke and the noise sounded like a distant thunderstorm. David and Chief stood outside shivering on the platform rather than endure the mob inside as they waited for the train. "Sure beats floating around the Channel in a dinghy," said David, trying to push his hands deeper into his pockets.

"Or buried ten feet deep in a French vineyard," said Chief. "One thing for sure, there weren't any Krauts crazy enough to try following us in your suicide dive."

"Could be a good evasive tactic."

"You wouldn't mind if I didn't join you next time?"

A long, low whistle announced the arrival of the train. A single head lamp, seemingly suspended, came slowly toward them from out of the fog. The locomotive crept slowly into the station, huffing and puffing like a tired old fat man trying to climb a flight of stairs. Brakes squealed and steam belched out in clouds, hiding the engine. A sulfuric odor stung their nostrils from the coal smoke, and trailing dots of black soot settled all around them. The cars banged to a stop one at a time, pushing into the one in front and then jerking backward, only to be pushed forward by the one slowing behind, until all were at rest.

A brakeman jumped down carrying a large oil can with a three-foot-long spout and began lubricating the slides on the side of the locomotive's drive wheels. A conductor in a black uniform hopped down from the passenger car and placed a stepping stool directly in front of the steps. "Board!" he bellowed, and the crowd of passengers behind them surged forward. Like a cresting wave they rose up the boarding stairs. A fat woman dressed in a black full-length coat and wearing a black scarf tied around her head pushed in front of David. Her arms were loaded with shopping bags and boxes, and she looked like a sculpture an artist had created in a junk yard by adding whatever pieces he could attach to it. David stepped back to make way lest he be trampled.

"You fly boys are so nice," she said, forcing her way up the stairs. David heard Chief's quiet chuckle behind him and had to bite his lip to keep from laughing. The conductor stepped up to help the woman who had become wedged in the stairway with her parcels.

The only compartment with a seat open was already occupied by the fat woman. David and Chief slid in on the seat opposite her. "I suppose you'll be looking for a party in London," said the fat woman. She reached into one of her bags and brought out half a cooked chicken and began stuffing it into her greasy face. The train lurched and stopped, then jerked forward and pulled out of the station, rapidly building speed.

"My wife is picking us up," said David, hoping that would keep her quiet for a while.

"My sister-in-law," added Chief, in a noncommittal tone.

"Well, land sakes. You don't look like brothers." The woman ranted on about relatives and David turned to the window, leaving Chief to entertain her.

Their reflections in the window looked like ghosts staring back at them. Maybe it was the ghosts of their lost comrades trying to commune with them. David thought how fate had brought him through today or he'd be in the spirit world.

Shanty shacks whipped past in the fog as they approached London. The tracks split and split again until it seemed as though they were entering a maze of one hundred different tracks. He wondered how they could possibly find their way through and come in on the right track, and then the roof over their arriving platform loomed out of the fog.

David nudged Chief, "There's Millie. Let's go." They both jumped up and barged from the compartment before the ponderous woman could get in front of them.

"David. David," called Millie from the crowd jostling and pushing. David forged ahead, unmindful of the crowd around him. He picked Millie up in his arms and held her close. Reluctantly he let her down and she looked up at him with a questioning look. "Something happened today?" she asked, more of a statement than a question.

"Just missed you, Millie," David said, trying to hide his emotions. "I almost forgot our company," he said, turning to Chief.

"Hello, Jimmy," greeted Millie. "So glad you could come, Luv. We haven't had much of a chance to have company. In fact, you're the first. And I've prepared a special meal just for the two of you," she beamed, taking David by the hand and slipping her arm in Jimmy's. "Come on, I managed to get a car for the weekend."

"What a sister-in-law. Just what I've been saying all along. 'Pigskin, get a car so I don't have to walk in the cold, wet fog.' I think I'm going to like your choice more all the time, brother," said Jimmy, tossing his kit bag in the trunk and holding the door open for Millie.

"What a gentleman," smiled Millie, climbing behind the wheel of the faded brown sedan. She shifted gears expertly and the car whipped out into the busy traffic. They passed block after block of bombed out buildings, whipping around piles of rubble in the street. "This area was pretty hard hit, Jimmy. We'll be out of it shortly."

"Jeez," said Chief, who was not one to waste words. "How'n the hell, oops, heck, did anyone live through any of this?"

"Most of them went to the underground during the bombing."

"You mean the railroad underground?"

"Right, Luv. 'Bout the only safe place when the Germans were bombing. Even that wasn't always bloody safe. I know a whole block of families that was wiped out when a section of the underground caved in from the bombing." The brakes squealed and Millie parked the sedan in front of the apartment.

It was a dark red brick building, like every other building in the block. A type of ivy covered the sides, climbing the wall up to the eave.

"Be a dear, Jimmy, and bring those two bags from the trunk," asked Millie while she fumbled in her black shoulder bag looking for the key. She held the door back for them as they struggled up the steps with Millie's grocery bags and their kits. "Davie, honey, will you fix us some drinks while I change?" She closed the bedroom door. "Only be a minute."

Chief inspected the somewhat Spartan apartment while Pigskin made their drinks. "Well, what do you think, Chief? Like it?"

"Yeah, pretty nice. Won't take you long to fill it up though when the baby comes."

"Okay, boys," beamed Millie marching into the kitchen. She picked up her drink and looked longingly at David, then fondly to her brother-in-law. "David's spoken of you so often I'm beginning to feel I've known you ever since I first met David. Cheerio Chief, brother-in-law," said Millie, raising her glass in a toast. She felt a little strange calling Chief by his nickname.

"To life!" David said, gently patting Millie's slightly bulging stomach.

"We cheated death again," said Chief, grinning like a Cheshire cat and clicking his glass against theirs. He tipped his glass, draining it in one gulp. "Auf," he gave a shiver from the bite of the strong liquor.

"Okay," directed Millie. "You boys set the table and I'll check our supper. I put everything in the oven before I came to pick you up and it should be done. Jimmy, why don't you light the candles and David please pour the wine." Millie set out a hot dish, fresh rolls and a garden salad.

"I keep eating like this and my uniforms won't fit," said Chief as he helped himself to a second plate.

"By the way, Jimmy, David and I have talked it over. When the baby's born, we'd like you to be the godfather," Millie said.

Chief sat quietly for a moment. "You want me to be the godfather? I'm not real family," he stammered.

"You are to us, Jimmy," said Millie reassuringly placing her hand over his and squeezing it softly. "It would mean so much to us knowing there was someone who cared for our child if something ever were to happen to us."

"Sure," stammered Chief. "But, what's a godfather do?"

"The main thing, Chief," said David, "is if something would happen to us that you would take our child and give it a home. Raise it as one of your own."

"And you have to come to all the birthday parties and eat cake and ice cream with the kids," said Millie smiling.

"Heck, ain't nothing going to happen to you guys. But, if that's what you want, I would be honored," Chief replied.

"Yahoo!" shouted David wrapping his hand in his blood brother's upraised hand, a symbolic bond of their brotherhood.

Millie hugged him and kissed him on the cheek and he bowed his head, embarrassed.

Millie drove them through downtown London where soot-covered, grayish-black limestone buildings lined the streets. Many standing buildings were bombed-out shells. Crews worked day and night clearing the streets. Green parks were scattered throughout the rows of red bricked houses, adding a touch of color. They drove through narrow streets and small tree-filled squares, up winding alleys and broad avenues. They passed theaters playing Shakespeare and Sherlock Holmes. The docks were a zoo of mass confusion as ships from all over the world came in and out of the Thames to unload and retreat before another bombing raid.

Bobbies dressed in blue uniforms stood in the center of cross-circled intersections, stiffly directing traffic with a sharp blast on a whistle and white gloved hand signals. Double- decker street cars clanged noisily through the crisscross streets and broad avenues. Red-coated guards stood rigidly in front of Buckingham Palace.

They spent a day at Hyde Park going to the Zoological Gardens and the zoo. They drove to Trafalgar Square, by the War Office and Number 10 Downing Street. They stopped at the House of Parliament and stood outside as Big Ben boomed out the hour. They ended the third day at Piccadilly Circus, an open paved area, a link between daytime shopping and evening entertainment.

"I've never had it so good," laughed Chief. "I mean, everywhere we go, someone buys us drinks or supper. What gives? Heck, I can save a lot of money for school that way."

"Chief, remember all the bombed out buildings we've seen?" asked Millie.

"Yeah, but those people don't have a thing. I mean most of 'em lost everything in the bombing!"

"They're grateful to be alive," said Millie quietly. "If it hadn't been for you fighter pilots risking your lives to stop the Germans, London would have been totally destroyed. We'd probably have Germans goose stepping up Piccadilly Circus right now. The pilots in the R.A.F. saved us from annihilation, Chief, and you're one of 'em. A Hero. Hell," said Millie wiping her misty eyes. "How can I go wrong? Our baby has a hero for a father and a godfather."

"I might just stay here," said Chief grinning. "Nobody's ever treated Indians like this anywhere we've ever been. Most of 'em look down on us and spit on us."

"Can't let you stay, Chief. You have a greater obligation to your family and tribe. When you get your law degree, you'll have a chance to change that, brother," David reminded him.

"Just dreaming, Pigskin. A fellow needs a dream once in a while so when he gets knocked down he still has something to look forward to. Talking about obligations, I think we have a train to catch," Chief said.

David tossed fitfully in his sleep. "BANDITS, SIX-O'CLOCK HIGH." He slammed the throttle forward to full emergency power. At the same time he sucked the stick back in his lap and rolled a hundred and eighty degrees. He felt himself greying out from the g forces. He struggled to hold the turn. White-hot tracers flashed by so close to the canopy, his face felt the heat from their passing. The sky was black with Messerschmitts dropping on them like fish hawks swooping down, talons extended. A Focke-Wulf 190 filled his sight pip and David's finger cramped around the firing button. His tracers disappeared into the big radial engine of the Focke-Wulf. The FW-190 ate his bullets as an appetizer and wanted more.

Black smoke poured into his cockpit and David lost sight of the German. His engine pounded like a sledge hammer on an empty steel drum. He felt the heat and saw a flash of light between his feet. Flames lapped through the firewall into the cockpit. He jerked the throttle back and shut off the fuel selector. A ball of fire erupted from the forward fuel tank wrapping a sheet of flame around the cockpit. Oil, grease and the fabric skin fed the inferno.

David released his safety strap and pulled the stick back until he was inverted and could drop straight out of the cockpit. His hand grabbed the canopy release handle and jerked, but nothing happened. He jerked again with both hands on the jammed canopy. His feet and legs hurt and he could smell the stench of burning flesh. He crouched on his seat and heaved upward with his shoulders on the canopy.

The Spitfire spun out of control pinning him in the burning cockpit. The fire, fed by fresh oxygen, burned like a blow torch and he felt his legs burning. His flight suit was on fire though he no longer felt the pain. Adrenalin pumping, David kept jerking on the canopy release handle until it broke off in his hands and he fell backwards.

He hit the floor screaming. Lights snapped on in the barracks and Chief was beside him shaking him awake. "Pigskin. Pigskin, wake up! Come on, brother, wake up!"

David sat up holding his head in both hands. He was drenched with sweat and looked around bewildered. "'Twas a hell of a dream Chief. I was on fire and the canopy jammed. I was struggling to get out."

"It's okay, brother. Better go get showered and dressed. We'll go to breakfast before briefing."

Pilots stood huddled in the briefing tent, each with their own groups, smoking and talking nervously.

"TEN-SHUN," barked sergeant Tuck.

There was a scraping of chairs and shuffling of feet in the smoke-filled tent, accompanied by the low grumbling of pilots standing at attention. "At ease gentlemen. Smoke 'em if you got 'em." Wing commander Tonsund marched in briskly, removed his hat and set it on a chair behind him. He snapped his briefcase open and removed the orders for the day. His bald head shined like a reflector and his short waxed moustache sat on his lip like it was pinned on. He adjusted his glasses on his narrow nose, shifted his tie as though it were pushing on his neck and cleared his throat. He wanted his men to feel relaxed and comfortable with him. His chiseled features and brisk military manner suggested that he would not tolerate sloppiness or disregard for military order.

"First, I want to congratulate you on your mission to Le Mans. No losses and a perfect bombing run. Let's hope for more of the same so we can end this war." A round of applause went through the briefing room.

Sergeant Tommy Tuck, standing at ease behind the commander, clapped and then held his hands out, palms down, to quiet the room and let the Commander get on with his briefing.

"Our mission today is to Brest. Our target will be the U-boats and their docks and warehouses. Sergeant Dennis Bickers will give you the details. Sergeant Bickers."

Bickers stepped to the podium smartly and stood rigidly at attention. He talked in a monotone that dulled your brain waves and lulled you to sleep. He could have been talking about bringing in strippers for a show on base and everyone would have been yawning in boredom. He looked as though he'd never seen the sun. His skin was the pale, sickly color of someone who had spent all his life locked in a basement.

"Eagle Squadron will fly a decoy mission," he monotoned. "They will cross to Morlaix and fly toward Quimper, drawing the fighters away from Brest. Takeoff at zero-six-hundred hours. The bomber squadron and escorts will circle at sea and approach Brest from that direction to avoid ground observation. These are the U-boat pens. Our first target will be any U-boats that are tied up. Secondary targets are the adjoining warehouses. Questions?" he asked, without expecting any.

David stood, "Sir, I don't think we'll fool the Germans with another decoy mission. They'll be expecting it."

"Fighter command doesn't think so, nor do we," sergeant Bickers replied, looking down his nose at David. "Very well then," he seemed to close the briefing to any further discussion. "Sergeant Bishop will give you the weather." The intelligence officer, "The Spy," as everyone called him behind his back, stepped down, glaring offensively at the Yank for having the audacity to question his judgement.

Sergeant Bishop jumped up like a puppet on a string. His arms and legs flopped clumsily at his side. He dropped his clipboard, and as he bent down to retrieve it his rounded face flushed red in embarrassment "I didn't need that anyway," he apologized in his squeaky voice, a grin splitting his chubby face. His high-pitched voice seemed to rise an octave as he turned to the weather-briefing map. "Clear skies all the way. We have a big high pressure system over the Channel. There will be some morning fog in the low-lying areas that will burn off at sunrise. There may be some widely scattered cumulus over France that will be no factor," he concluded. He stepped down from the podium happy that for once he was not the bearer of a gloomy weather report.

"Chief," said David, as they left the briefing hut, "I feel funny about this mission."

"What'er you talking about? Be another turkey shoot. We split up and cover each other like before. Hell, brother," said Chief, with his Cheshire cat grin, "only thing you got to worry about is running out of ammo while we still got Krauts to shoot down."

"We never ran the same football play twice in a row for the simple reason that nine times out of ten it wouldn't work. They'd be waiting for it. We've lost the element of surprise. The Germans didn't take over Europe by being stupid. They're not going to fall for the same sucker play twice."

"So what kind of a play you wantta call, Pigskin?"

"I don't know. You can damn well bet they've got something waiting for us, Chief. Let's stack our four vic's at two thousand foot intervals. Green above me and blue above him and you take the top, Chief."

"Sounds like a Hail Mary play. Doesn't work too often. It can turn against us, Pigskin."

"We don't know where they're coming from, so we'll try and cover as much territory as possible. The first sign of bogies, we'll converge and cover each other."

"Okay, Pigskin. A quarterback line call. Once we see what develops, we'll play it from there," said Chief, beaming.

"I guess I just never had anything to worry about before. After our last mission," David paused as if reliving the flight again, "if it hadn't been for the indestructibility of these Spitfires, I probably wouldn't have come back from that one. I'd have left Millie and the baby alone...."

"Will you knock off all that morbid shit, brother? Hell, it's making me depressed listening to you. Forget it. It's behind us. And another thing, Millie and the baby will never be left alone. Not as long as I'm the godfather. They're now part of the tribe."

"Yeah," sighed David smiling at his blood brother. "See you upstairs." He raised his arm half way, his palm extended towards the Chief. They locked hands, a gesture of their blood bonding.

David rocked his wings, checking his squadron climbing in loose formation behind him. They were a good crew, now combat-blooded. He'd tried to distance himself from his pilots, but when you stared death in the face you became part of the brotherhood. A bonding grew between them like a catalyst, molding them together to form one unit, one squadron. The Eagle Squadron. He left his canopy open, thinking back to his dream. He liked the feel of fresh clean air swirling around him and he breathed deeply, filling his lungs. David thought, it wouldn't be long, and the cockpit would smell of gun powder, sweat and fear. Was it a premonition, the smell of death waiting for them?

David reduced power to cruise, conserving fuel. Leaving England behind, the Cliffs of Dover stood like gleaming white sentries in the morning sun, patiently waiting to guide them home. Their route over the English Channel was becoming as familiar to him as jogging from the locker room to the football field. It was no different. They were going forth to meet an adversary on the playing field. It was a matching of wits -- a display of the skill, leadership and bonding the quarterback had with his team.

He shivered, but not from the cool air whipping in his open canopy. He thought about the game against Bemidji. The coach sent in a play from the bench, the same draw play they'd just run. David called a time-out, jogging over to his coach. "They'll be swarming over the line," he argued. "I want a quick, short pass to the left or right. They won't be looking for it. The surprise will catch'em off guard. Be good for at least twenty yards," but his pleading had fallen on deaf ears. At the snap of the ball, the entire Bemidji line swarmed over him. Three broken ribs kept him from playing the rest of the year.

David felt as if he and his squadron were animals locked in a pen at the slaughter house. Now it was their turn to be led inside, for what he didn't know, but he felt he was no longer the quarterback. He was leading, but not calling the plays. There'd be a lot more than broken ribs this time. He slammed the canopy closed.

The picture-card blue waters of the Channel passed below them, unnoticed. Each pilot was engaged in his own thoughts and fears. Only a fool or a braggart would say he knew no fear. The four vics spread out, each taking their respective positions. David scanned the skies in a rapid movement of his eyes. His vision was far above normal and he saw bogies long before anyone else. His exceptional eyesight was one of the reasons he was alive. The ability to see the enemy first gave the Eagle Squadron the element of surprise and they would need it today.

David cleared his mind of everything but the task of finding and destroying the hated Hun. He concentrated on scanning the skies. Flying the Spitfire had become a habit, like putting on your socks or blowing your nose. He scanned ahead, up and down then in a sweep to the left and right, above and behind and began the scan again, all the time jinxing; climbing, turning, diving.

Nothing. Not a single Hun fighter rose to meet them. "Chief, something's wrong. We should've been into'em thicker'n barn flies in July," said David over his R/T. "Why'nt you switch channels, and listen for the bumbees?"

"Gotcha, Pigskin. Switching."

David continued his scanning. Were the Germans on to them?

"Pigskin, Yellow-one. The bumbees are under attack. The frequency is jammed with chatter."

"This is Pigskin, Red-one -- I'm climbing, full power. Form on me." David wondered if they'd be too late to help the bombers. "Pigskin Squadron, switch to "B" channel. Maintain silence until we get into the Huns."

The radio was cluttered with the chatter of voices. Fighters were engaged in every sector trying to protect the nearly defenseless bombers.

"Rastus, Red-one, bailing out."

"Victor, Green-three, turn hard left. You got one on your tail."

"Sparkie, Blue-one, two-o'clock high. ME-109s diving on the bombers."

"Parson, Yellow-three. Snappers three-o'clock high."

Ahead there was a bright flash, just a flash. Someone was blown to pieces. Black plumes of smoke dotted the battle area. White canopies drifted earthward, marking the pilots lucky enough to escape from stricken aircraft.

"Hello, Rastus leader. Pigskin Squadron, be with you shortly."

"Pigskin. Rastus leader. Get'em off our backs or there won't be any of us left."

David spotted three ME-109s ahead and below them. "Pigskin, Red-one, Bogies eleven-o'clock low, pick your own targets," and he dove, advancing his throttle to combat boost. The propeller blades screamed as the propeller tips went supersonic. He closed almost vertically on the rearmost fighter. At five hundred yards and closing, the Messerschmitt grew rapidly in his sight pip. He could see the black crosses bordered with white on the square- tipped wings. The German spotted the Spitfire and nosed over.

David rolled with him, closing to a hundred and fifty yards, lining the Hun in his sight. He glanced at his needle-ball, checking his coordination, and squeezed the firing button. The Spitfire shuddered from its eight machine guns hammering at once. Cordite fumes seeped into the cockpit, stinging his nostrils. The odor was a stimulus. He felt his blood racing, his temples throbbing. He laughed crazily, dancing on the rudders, shifting his field of fire left and right.

Grayish-white tracers entered the Messerschmitt's tail. In an instant the heavy DeWilder slugs shredded the elevators and rudder. Chunks broke off the Messerschmitt, looking like a flak burst. David closed to fifty yards and fired another quick burst. Oil splattered his windscreen. Smoke poured from the stricken craft. He lifted his gloved thumb from the firing button, kicked in right rudder and pulled up into a steep climbing turn.

His left wing jerked, throwing the Spitfire sideways. A jagged hole appeared near the wing tip. Long ragged holes opened across the metal wing. David glanced in his rear-facing mirror and saw his attacker closing from his left rear quarter. He saw the ME-109s yellow nose and his heart stopped. The Messerschmitt was very close, fifty yards or less behind and above. David jerked his throttle back and turned the prop to fine pitch. He jammed the flaps down and skidded the Spitfire out of the German's gunsight.

The difference between life and death is a fraction of a second. The Hun overshot David. The oil-streaked bluish-white belly filled his windscreen as the ME-109 passed within feet of David. He could see individual rivets on the bottom of the Messerschmitt and a black ribbon of oil on the belly running back from the engine. The German pilot had a look of horror on his face, having realized his mistake.

David thumbed the firing button on his machine guns. Almost mesmerized, he watched his bullets stitching rows of holes in the wing and belly of the ME-109. His three second burst ripped holes in the naked belly of the Messerschmitt and he saw daylight through the wing. Smoke poured from the engine and the plane rolled into a spin. The canopy flew open, but the flyer could not exit the spinning plane. David rolled the Spit on its side, watching his second victory of the day, waiting for the pilot. A wing snapped off the Messerschmitt and it burst into a ball of fire.

"Pigskin, Yellow-one, I'm hit! Going down!"

"Chief, where you at?" shouted David into the R/T. He snaprolled the Spitfire on its side in a steep turn. Burning pieces of aircraft wreckage littered the sky, fluttering earthward like autumn leaves in a wind storm. Streams of smoke from spinning, burning aircraft marked the area of battle like the boundary marks on a football field. Several parachutes hung suspended at different levels.

Then David saw a Spit in a steep dive, trailing black smoke. Flames were lapping out around the engine. "Bail out, Chief! Get out Brother, I'm right behind you."

David dove after his blood brother screaming, "BAIL OUT, BAIL OUT!"

Chief struggled, trying to open his canopy. David dove alongside of Chief's Spit and could see flames inside the cockpit. Chief struggled desperately, pounding on the jammed canopy, fighting to escape.

"Chief, pull the hood jettison lever inside the top of the hood!" David screamed into his R/T. "Chief, get out." The smoke and fire engulfed the Spitfire. David smelled burning flesh. He could not see his blood brother in the blazing inferno.

A blinding white flash-fire surrounded the Spitfire. Chief's Spit exploded in a white flash and then a ball of fire. Flaming pieces drifting down from the fulmination were all that remained of Chief and his Spitfire. The force of the explosion threw David against the side of his cockpit. Heat from the blast burned the outside of his Spit. He could feel the heat inside his small cockpit. David ripped his oxygen mask off his face, unable to breathe. "Chief!" he whispered desperately. He circled the falling debris calling, "Chief, where are you? Chief, come on, pull your rip cord!"

"Pigskin. This is Dixie, the Chief's gone. Come on, we're low on fuel. We've got to head back."

"Got to protect Chief when he pops his chute. Can't let the Krauts get'em," he sobbed into the R/T.

"Pigskin, he's dead. You can't do a thing here. We'll come back and get those bastards. Come on Pigskin, let's go home."

David made another turn as pieces of Chief's burning wreck fell to the ground. In a moment, one second in time, his blood brother was gone. This wasn't supposed to happen -- they had a dream -- they'd had their whole life ahead of them. Now it was all gone. First Joker and now Chief.

David turned -- devastated -- toward the Channel.

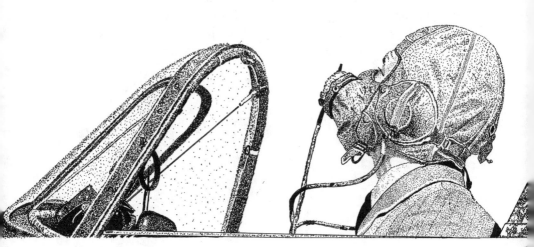

We Pledge Our Lives

"Pour me another drink, Hap," David slurred, intoxicated.

"Pigskin, I think you've had enough for one night," said Hap. His wrinkled face scrunched up. "Why don't you go back to the barracks and sleep it off?"

"Gotta train to catch. Millie's expecting me," David said, swaying on the bar stool.

"Here's a cup ah coffee. Better get some of this down or you're not going anywhere," said Hap.

David sipped noisily. "Christ. What the hell you doing to me, Hap? I don't want that shit. Gimme a drink."

"Pigskin, you've had too much to drink. Now I'm not give'n you nut'n but coffee. Gettin' drunk ain't gonna change nothing. Chief's dead. Gone. Ka-put. Go home and sober up," Hap commanded.

"He's right," said Woody, climbing up on a stool next to David. "'Tain't like when yea disappeared. Everyone saw Chief blow up. Ee's gone, David."

Hap turned and walked dejectedly down the bar. He reached up, took Chief's mug down from its place on the shelf and turned it somberly in his crippled hand. The Yanks were like family to him. The sons he'd never had. A tear sprang to life and ran from his sagging eye lashes, splashing on Chief's mug. He wiped it angrily, ashamed at his weakness. He turned and dragged a stool out from behind the bar. Shakily, he climbed the stool, clutching the mug in his gnarled hand. He steadied himself with his left hand, reached up and placed the mug on the top shelf, upside down. It joined the brotherhood of others who had gone before him, who had paid the supreme price for freedom. Who had flown their Last Mission.

"No!" David cried. He buried his head in his arms on the bar, sobbing uncontrollably.

"Come on, Pigskin, we've got a train to catch," Woody said, placing his hand on David's shoulder. "Let me give yea ah hand, brother-in-law."

"Hell, I can make it. You don't have to baby-sit me," David said, wiping his face with the back of his sleeve.

"Well," said Woody. "Just what good is a brother-in-law if he can't help out once in a while? Besides, I met this redheaded Irish girl that kinda gets me blood pumping," chuckled Woody.

"Now that's more like it," chirped Hap from behind the bar. "And when you get back I want to hear details of a real conquest." Hap's wrinkled face split in a grin and he waved, wiping his eyes as Woody helped David stagger from the pub.

The blacked-out train rocketed through the countryside heading for London, its steel wheels clicking rhythmically on the jointed rails. It rocked slowly from side to side as though it were a boat riding the swells. The smell of coal smoke was stronger in the heavy damp air, as if it didn't have room to escape. "Woody, I don't feel so good," said David, hanging his head between his knees.

"Well, yea not be gettin' any sympathy from me, after the way yea was pourin' em down. And from the smell, yea'd best be ah heading for the water closet," said Woody, his face scrunched up.

David stood, bracing himself with both hands against the sides of the swaying compartment. A long muffled whistle sounded as the locomotive approached a road crossing. Slowly he staggered down the car to the rest room.

Woody worried about his brother-in-law and the risks he took flying. He had a natural talent to fly and seemed to have a sixth sense. Or was he just lucky? How long would his luck last? Woody shuddered at the thought that David might not return from a mission. How would he ever tell his sister if some day David's mug was placed on the top shelf? She had already mourned for one beau killed in action. But now she was married and carrying David's baby.

Chief had been David's best friend, but if something happened to Pigskin...they were family now, with a baby on the way....

"Emptied my stomach. Feel much better now," said David, stumbling into the compartment and flopping down on the seat.

"Whew," gasped Woody. "Yea be ah smelling pretty stout there, Davie, me boy!"

David ignored the comment from his brother-in-law looking at him worriedly. "What'll I tell Millie?"

"I called Millie and told her, Davie. She took it pretty hard and she'll be ah need'n yea to be strong."

David sat, seemingly transported, listening to the train wheels clatter, clickety-clack, clackety-click. "If only I hadn't spread the squadron out so far, we could have covered each other better."

"'Tain't nothing like that. We're at war and these things happen. It's more fate than anything. He was one of the best pilots, had a good flying record and had scored a lot of kills. He was just in the wrong place at the wrong time," Woody said softly.

"I found his totem bag back at the barracks," said David. "He never went anywhere without it."

"What in the 'ell's a totem bag?" asked Woody.

"It's a medicine bag. Everything that brought him good luck, he'd put something from it in the bag. To us Sioux, it is sacred. It was part of our Sioux religion and Chief would never have left without it. He believed it protected him."

"That's a bunch of hooey. 'Tain't no way that bag ah little do-dahs could protect him from Kraut bullets or his kite blowing up."

"You don't understand, Woody. To you or anyone not Indian or at least part Indian, it wouldn't mean a thing, but to Chief it was his life and he believed it. Whether it had anything to do with it or not, Chief believed in it. He forgot his medicine bag. His Spitfire caught fire, the canopy jammed trapping him inside."

"Must ah been a bullet hit the canopy to jam it like that," rationalized Woody, stroking his freshly shaven chin, trying to understand the nature of Chief's Sioux religion.

"It wouldn't have happened if he'd had his medicine bag," said David with a deep conviction. "He was more than just a blood brother. We were first cousins, we grew up together. Everything we did, we did together." They sat in the darkened train, each with his own thoughts. David opened the curtain, staring into the black night. The train wheels seemed to boom a rhythmic thunder. It was as though he was traveling through a tunnel; there were no lights anywhere. "Did'ja ever think about hell, Woody? I mean, this is what it must be like, hurling through a black void, everything turning against you. There's no longer a light at the end of the tunnel."

"Whoa, matey. In a few minutes you're going to step out into the sunshine and clear blue skies," said Woody. "Or did you forget yea got a wife and baby on the way?"

David was silent for a while, then looked up with a half hearted grin at his brother-in-law, "I guess I'm just a foolish drunken hick from the sticks. I was feeling sorry for myself. Won't happen again."

"Well, it'd better not or I'll come give yea ah good shellacking. Now yea'd best get back to the washroom and clean up some before we pull into the station."

The train jerked and creaked as it slowly entered the station. Sulfuric smoke from the engine hung heavily in the damp fog, stinging their nostrils as they stepped from the car. A naked string of light bulbs from which it seemed that all warmth had been drained, hung overhead, dimly illuminating the cold, windy platform. It was winter and icicles hung from the station roof like the teeth of a demon waiting for the kill.

"How 'bout sharing a ride, Pigskin? We'll drop yea by the apartment first, then I've got me lady waiting."

"No. You go ahead Woody. I'll walk."

"Walk like'ell. Yea'll freeze yea gonads off."

"I need the fresh air. It'll sober me up an maybe I won't smell so bad. 'Fraid I made a fool of myself. You go ahead, Woodpecker, and behave yourself. Remember you're going to be with a Lady!"

"Right-O!" said Woody, as he shouldered his kit bag and raced up the stairs two at a time.

David turned and walked down the darkened street. A damp mist closed in around him. He thought of Chief and felt as if he were transported to another time and place. The place was the Badlands, an isolated part of the Sioux reservation. The place where he and Chief became blood brothers.

His meditation became a vision. He saw a shape, a form of a man. The form turned into the medicine man sitting across the small fire from Jimmy and David, puffing slowly on the red-stone pipe, meditating. He passed the pipe to David and while he took a puff, the medicine man began instructing them in Hanblecheyapi, the vision quest ceremony of the Sioux. The medicine man was old and rolls of fat hung loosely at his sides. His crop of white hair sat on his head like a clump of snow on a jack pine branch. A worn and tattered buffalo robe hung loosely from around his shoulders down to the ground. The scent of pine smoke hung heavy in the close quarters of the tepee. The pile of furs they sat on were soft and warm, caressing the body with a feeling of elegance.

The old medicine man sat quietly puffing on the long stemmed pipe. It was the ritual where a boy becomes a man and is thereafter recognized as a man of the tribe. "You have completed the first part of your Vision Quest, the sweat lodge ceremony. Your minds, spirits and bodies are cleansed. You must fast for one day and night or as many as three days and nights," he spoke softly, in a deep guttural voice. "Each alone, on an isolated Badlands butte, with no fire, water or food." The old man stopped, his head down as if in prayer. Then he looked up, staring at each with a deep penetrating look. "Place four sticks around you with pieces of colored cloth on them, representing the four directions. In our dreams we may feel alone, without the Great Spirit. In your Vision Quest, you begin awake and alert and feel the vastness of the universe and our oneness with it. You might drowse. Dreams may come and go. It is much of a mystery, yet I can identify six powers. First is the west power, the blue color, where the sun sets in the west, Wiyopeyata. We are dependent on life-giving rains. Thunder and lightning are powerful tools given by the Great Spirit to let you see and hear. The second power is the north power, the white color. Waziya sends the white blanket of winter snow upon Mother Earth to let her rest. Red is the color of the new dawn. Wiyoheyapa, the rising sun is the power of the east. With each day come new experiences, new journeys. Itokaga, the yellow south, is the fourth power. The long warm days given Mother Earth will blossom into food, medicine and shelter. The fifth and sixth powers are Mother Earth and Father Sky. Every part of your being is a part of Her. Your physical self is fueled from the Sun, Father Sky."

Every feature of his dark wrinkled face seemed to be highlighted by the light from the flickering fire and his eyes were drawn to sharp, beady, penetrating points. "When your hearts and minds are pure, the spirits will send you a sign," he paused, seemingly to sleep for a moment. Then he puffed on the pipe and continued. "It may be a bird or an animal or even a rock or tree. They may speak to you so you will know that the spirits are with you."

In their Vision Quests, Chief had seen a bull and he was thus named, Bull. It was fitting, for Chief was a bull or maybe bullheaded, David thought. He'd taken a chip off a horn and some tail hair, for his totem, from a long-horn steer he'd wrestled to the ground in a rodeo. "Where was your totem when you needed it, Chief? Why'd you go off and leave it?" Had he heard a bull bellow when the Chief was hit, or was it his imagination?

It started to rain, but David walked on in a muse. He saw himself standing on top of the highest butte, naked except for a breech cloth between his legs and tied around his waist. It was his third day of fasting and still he had seen no sign nor heard any voices. He no longer felt the hunger pains, but his mouth was dry. He placed a small pebble in his mouth to roll around and help create saliva. The sky blackened and storm clouds dropped lower and lower in the sky, encasing him in a blanket of moisture. Thunder boomed overhead and lightning flashed, lighting the night sky. The rain fell and he turned to face it, opening his parched mouth to it eagerly. The Sioux were dependent on the life-giving rains, as were all living things.

David remembered how he'd been named. 'Rain-in-the-Face.' Grandfather-of-All, the medicine man, interpreted thunder and lightning as powerful tools of the Great Spirit. The spirits had come to him in their true form. WAKAN TANKA had come to him in the rain.

David walked on, turning his face into the wind, opening his mouth to catch the rain. His body shook with the first stages of hypothermia, but he did not feel the rain or the chill, for he was transported, suspended in time. The spirits communicated with him. He saw a large bull. A longhorn, with a chip missing from the tip of one horn. It stood atop the highest ridge and spoke, "My Brother, I am with you in the rain."

Lightning flashed overhead and the vision was gone. David stumbled on through the dark, drenched and shivering. Ahead, lights shone from behind a shade. Millie was waiting for him, watching from the window. She saw him coming up the walk and disappeared from the window.

"David. Oh David, you're all right." She ran heedlessly through the rain, launching herself into his arms. Her face and hair were wet and her body shook with racking sobs. She clung to him desperately.

"It's okay, Millie. It's okay. I'm okay," David said over and over, his body shaking from the cold.

"David, let's get inside. You're freezing and soaked clean through. Why are you walking? Why didn't you hail a taxi from the station?" They climbed the steps to their apartment. The lights were turned on bright and the radio blared a Tommy Dorsey tune. In the bedroom, David noticed a bassinet at the side of the bed and small dresser piled with baby clothes.

"I had to say good-bye to Chief, Millie. One last time, I had to say good-bye." He held Millie at arms length, shivering with tears hanging precariously in his eyes. "I had to say good-bye to my blood brother," he repeated, trying to make Millie understand.

"David, you can tell me about it later. Right now, get out of those wet clothes and get in bed before you catch pneumonia. She helped him remove his wet clothes, toweled him dry and tucked him into bed naked. "I'll go fix you a hot drink, Luv. Be right back."

David's chilled body shook under the covers. Illusions of Chief still flashed through his mind. Lightning flashed and he saw a bull, through the pouring rain, with a chipped horn climbing a steep hill in the Badlands. Lightning flashed again and he saw a White Buffalo calf on top of the hill waiting for the bull to join him. He could hear the old medicine man's death chant coming quietly from inside his tepee.

"Here, David. Put this hot water bottle on your stomach to warm you." She reached under the covers, alarmed at the coldness of his body.

He held the hot water bottle next to his stomach then let out a yelp. "Holy Toledo, this thing's hot. You got something I can wrap around it, Millie?"

"Here's a towel, Luv, and a hot toddy to drink. It'll warm you from the inside. I'll have to help warm you from the outside," said Millie smiling as she removed her clothes letting them drop to the floor.

David sipped the steaming spicy brandy and felt it radiating heat from the inside through his body. The drink burned all the way to his stomach and the liquor made him feel a little heady. He watched Millie drop the last of her clothes to the floor. She caressed each of her enlarged breasts, teasingly holding them erect. "I can probably help you do that," David volunteered, his teeth chattering as he snuggled deep under the covers.

Millie turned, profiling her stomach to David. She held it gently in her hands, smiling. "I can feel it kicking. I think it's definitely going to be one of your football players. Here, give me your hand," she said, slipping under the covers, cuddling her warm body next to her husband's.

"I felt something," said David, smiling. "Doesn't that hurt when he kicks like that?"

"She," said Millie. "You know it could very well be a girl. No, it doesn't hurt, Luv. By the way, do girls play football?"

"Heavens, no," laughed David. "Football's too rough a game for girls."

"You seem to forget all the things we girls do here in England so you boys can go off to war," she twitted.

"Yeah," said David soberly. "I know. And I'm not too happy about my pregnant wife working in operations, right in the thick of it."

"We all have to do whatever we can to survive. Everyone must work together for the good of all, Luv." Millie thought quietly for a moment, as though she was meditating, then rolled over and kissed David. It was a long passionate kiss. Embracing, seeking, probing, one of compassion, giving and taking. Their legs entwined and their arms surrounded each other, skin to bare skin. Her breasts pressed against his chest. His erection thrust up between her legs and throbbed hard against her thighs.

"Can we still do it?" he asked. "I mean, with the baby, will it be okay?"

"Of course, silly. We have a lot of time yet." Her legs wrapped around him, pulling him into her.

They made love slowly, quietly becoming one, their bodies molded together in a passionate embrace.

They lay quietly in each other's arms, comfortably, secure. Millie whispered in David's ear, "David...tell me all about Chief. Since the very first time you met him and everything the two of you did together. I want to be a part of both of you."

"We go back to when we were five years old. Chief's dad came to work for my father on the farm. Our mothers are half-sisters, but to Indians, we seldom use that term. They were full sisters in Indian custom, so we're first cousins. We gave them a small piece of land and they built a home there. Jimmy's dad always said that someday Jimmy would be a great chief and everyone started calling him Chief. He was on the honor roll at school and had planned to go to law school. He was always pretty serious and had plenty of time to study, since he never paid much attention to the white girls. Being darker than me, their fathers wouldn't let them date him anyhow and Chief knew that. With a law degree, Chief wanted to work for the tribal council and represent Indian claims against the government for broken treaties."

"It sounds so gallant. It's what dreams are made of. Tell me about how you two became blood brothers," asked Millie snuggling in his arms.

David told the story of how Chief and he were named and became blood brothers. Then he explained how, walking from the train station in the rain, he'd seen a vision. He'd seen a bull, Chief's totem, he had spoken to him. "I didn't know how I could write to his father and mother telling them Jimmy had been killed. The dream of his being a tribal lawyer is gone. But, now I can tell them of the vision and they will understand and can accept it. You see, Chief has made the journey to the Spirit World and to the Sioux, his spirit lives."

"Show me the scar where the medicine man cut your arm for your bonding."

David turned his arm, exposing the inch-long scar on the inside of his wrist.

Millie held his hand in hers examining the small scar. Then she bent her head and kissed the scar. Tears poured from her eyes unchecked and she buried her head against David's chest. He held her protectively and after a time her sobbing subsided, yet she clung to him. Finally, she said, "It's going to be a long time before we put the loss of Chief behind us, Luv, if ever."

"I know now what the medicine man was talking about when he said our bodies and our spirits were bonded. Honey, we haven't lost Chief. He will always be with us, watching out for us and his spirit will watch over his godchild."

"David..." Millie asked, pausing.

"Yes, my love. What?"

"David, if something happens to me, I want you to promise that you'll find someone else. I don't want you to let your life go for nothing. The time we've had together is so short, but it's been the best thing that's ever happened to me."

"What? What kind of foolish talk is this? First of all, there isn't anything going to happen to you."

"Listen to me, David. We are in a desperate struggle with Germany. Our survival chances are at best fifty-fifty. Once the Germans cross the Channel, England will be through."

"If. That's if they cross the Channel. The United States will never let that happen. Besides, we've started a turn around, we're taking the war to the Germans."

"David, when Binky was killed I shut out the world. You weren't the first man I went out with since, but you were the only one who'd ever gotten through to me, to break my link with the dead. I know what I'm talking about. David, Luv, I pray to God you never have to go through what I did. I want you to promise that if anything ever happens to me that you'll put me to rest after a time and then get on with your life. You've got too much to live for. You have a dream; don't let that dream die for anything. Promise me, David."

"We are living on the edge of death every day, Millie. Every second of every minute of every day. I'm not going to speculate on what could or couldn't happen. I won't ruin one second of our time together with such morbid thoughts. And, it's not my dream, honey, it's our dream. Yours and mine. We have a baby coming, that's part of our dream and a part of you and me. I won't put that aside, not ever. I love you, Millie, and nothing will ever change that. Not even death."

Millie sat up in the bed letting the sheets and blankets fall loosely around them on the bed. She crossed her legs under her and sat looking down at her husband. "David, I love you more than life itself for you have given me life. Part of our love grows inside of me and there is nothing I would change, unless I could end this ugly war and we could go to our new home in America." Her green eyes burned with fire and her mouth was tight in grim determination. David had never seen her so set in her ways and saw a new side of his wife. Her button nose seemed so prominent when she had her dander up. The freckles on her face, neck and chest blushed a deep red. "But, you must promise me that you will live the dream even if you must do it with someone else."

David closed his eyes trying to hold the tears back. It was unthinkable that anything could possibly happen to Millie. But, they were at war and anything was possible. He'd made hundreds of decisions in his short life. On the football field, he'd made decisions in fractions of seconds, but the most he could lose was a game. This was the first time he'd had to face the reality of life, and death. Ralph was dead and now Chief and there was no end in sight. David could not force himself to even think of someone other than Millie as his wife. She was determined and he'd never seen her so upset. "On one condition," said David.

"What condition?" she asked.

David sat up, looking his wife in the eye. "You must make the same promise to me. Should I not make it through this conflict, you must continue on with our dream. You must put me aside and find someone else to live the dream. You are an American now and our child will be an American when born. You have a farm, and if anything should ever happen to me, you are to live in the house I bought for us and farm the land. My family will help you, but you must also find someone to live the dream with. Promise me that you'll do that, and I'll promise you the same."

"I promise, David. I love you and will be with you always. We will have our dream. This I pledge to you."

David took his wife in his arms and they lay cuddled together. "Just as Chief and I are blood brothers, so are we bonded, husband and wife. Our spirits are one and will always remain as one. This I pledge to you. I want you to have one of my dogtags as a part of me, a totem, and I have the St. Christopher medal you gave me. No matter what, I will always be with you in spirit."

They talked for hours, about their new home, things for the baby, the crops and children. Schools and colleges and David's family and Millie's brother. They speculated on the new girl Woody talked so excitedly about and whether it was just another fling or if he was serious.

Berlin

Lightning flashed angrily across the sky as the train sped through the blackened night. David felt an emptiness he'd never known. A deep burning sensation of fear. Fear of the unknown. He'd never known fear, the word itself was unknown to him. But this was new; a black hole, a vortex he'd fallen into and he was spinning out of control. From his darkened compartment he stared into the rain, the abyss of the storm. He was known as Rain-in-the-Face and now he looked to the spirits of his Sioux ancestry to give him a sign. The night was a dark empty void, continuously streaked with angry bolts of lightning ripping through a troubled sky. A coldness encased him like a chill of death. He shivered. Was it a sign, an omen? Was his fear a groundless product of his imagination?

He thought of Millie and their baby and the life they'd planned together. Then her voice came to him, "If anything should ever happen to me..." Tears streaked down David's cheeks as he sat alone in the darkened train. The wheels pounded on incessantly, clicking rhythmically on cold, wet steel.

The train pulled into Biggin Hill station and David walked down the platform, heedless of the rain. He turned toward The Station. He did not need a drink, but he didn't want to be alone. At least Hap would be there. He was like a father. Not his father, but like a father confessor and he needed someone to talk to.

Lightning flashed and lit up the inside of the clouds, like a sheet being held up with someone shining a torch behind it. Rain stung his up-turned face as icy drops struck. Clouds churned across the sky in blackish-greenish turbulent rolls. It reminded David of a tornado he'd seen crossing the prairie back home. Everything in its path had been sucked up or destroyed, broken, discarded and scattered across the county. Thunder rumbled, turning on its fireworks and there stood the bull. Snorting, it turned, running into the abyss. It stopped and turned, looking back at David. He could feel its eyes burning into his eyes. The bull turned and trotted off, disappearing into the void without looking back.

"Holy tarnation!" said Hap. "If'n it ain't the great Kraut whacker his-self! What'n tarnation you been up to, boy? You taking a bath and washing your clothes at the same time?"

"Hell, Hap. Way it's raining out there, we might have to build another Ark," said David. "How 'bout throwing me one of your grubby bar towels so I can wipe my face and hands and while you're flapping your lip maybe you can pour me an ale?"

"Hut one, hut two," called Raymond sitting at the end of the bar with most of the eagle squadron.

"Hi yah, Spike. Hi, guys. What brings everybody out on a night like this, other'n keeping the old man primed?" laughed David.

"You know me, Pigskin," said Raymond, sliding his clipboard and pencil to one side. "I've got to be where the action is one way or the other. Besides, by the time this war is over, I can write a book on the 'Great War' just from listening to Hap here. You know, for instance, that he'd shot down twenty-one enemy fighters before he himself was shot down and crippled?"

"Whew," said David, wiping the rain from his face and drying his hair. "He must have been some kind of a holy terror in the skies from the way he talks."

"Look at all the pictures on the walls in here and the models of planes hanging from the ceiling," said Raymond. He turned on his bar stool and let his eyes wander around the room. "Those aren't decorations, this is Hap's war museum."

"What'er you bunch of leather heads scheming up now?" grumbled Hap.

"Why, old man, we're just admiring your collection of war relics," David said, grinning at the boys.

"War relics," fumed Hap. "I'll have you know Sonny Boy, those so-called war relics 'ave sent far more Krauts to the Fatherland than you smart-aleck-sky-cowboys have. Or probably ever will," he added with a smug grin on his whiskered wrinkled face.

"Hey, Pigskin," called Storm'n Norman from down the bar. "Did the Woodpecker make his conquest?"

"Hear, Hear," echoed a chorus from the squadron.

"Come on," coaxed Dixie. "What's she look like?"

"Let me close my eyes while you describe her," said Lance in his heavy French-Canadian accent. "Etch her body into my memory with colorful descriptive phrases that'll make my blood run hot with envy, eh."

A cheer of approval rang out and everyone crowded around.

"Ah's so dry, ah can't even spit," said David, imitating Dixie's southern accent.

"Ale come'n right up," said Hap, a wolfish grin on his wrinkled, whiskered face.

The room was quiet as a barracks in the middle of the night. There was only the sound of heavy breathing, as they waited in anticipation for another erotic encounter they could all enjoy.

David took a deep, long pull on his mug of ale. Finally he set his mug on the bar and wiped the foamy mustache from his lip with the back of his hand.

"Well?" prompted Hap. Patience never had been one of his strong points.

David grinned. He thought of Joker, how proud he would have been at the deception. They were all primed and he would carry on the sham as long as possible. "Now, you all know how the Woodpecker is prone to exaggerate just a smidgen."

Heads bobbed in acknowledgment. "Well, I had to suffer through the trip into London listening to the Woodpecker. Why, by the time we pulled into London, Cleopatra would've looked like a dance-hall floozie by comparison." David sipped his ale.

"Well," said David, "when we got in to Victoria Station, there was only one cab outside. So, ol' Woody says, 'guess we'll have to share. Suppose you'll want to go by the apartment first?' I laid a real guilt trip on him, Oh I don't mind, but I don't know what Millie'll say if I'm late!"

"Cut the bullshit and get to the babe," grumbled Hap. A rumble of supportive comments came from the group.

"Being the great humanitarian that I am," said David smugly, "I capitulated."

"You what?" asked Dixie.

"He gave in, dummy. Now pay attention," grumbled Hap.

"Anyway, we pulled up to her apartment and of course I had to go in and meet her." David drained his mug, banging it on the bar. "Well, you could've knocked my socks off. She was the most gorgeous thing I've ever laid eyes on. Except for Millie that is," David added hastily.

"How about the boobs," shouted Hap excitedly, hopping from one foot to the other.

"First of all, she's tall."

"How tall?" asked Storm'n Norman.

"Well, she's got a pair of gazoombas like this," exaggerated David, holding two cupped hands out a considerable distance from his body. "And, when she wrapped her arms around the Woodpecker, there was boobs resting on both of his shoulders and his face was buried between twin mounds."

"Holy Shit," said Hap, doing an Irish jig behind the bar. "Now that's like the good ol' days, during the 'Great War.'"

"Her eyes were green, like green emeralds flashing fire," intoned David, mesmerized with his deception. "Her hair was flaming red, hanging down past her waist in silken billowing clouds and as soft to the touch as cashmere. Her body was trim and sleek as a mink and her face radiated a sheen like an angel's. She smelled like the first lilacs in spring. It was the scent of a woman in need. The scent of a woman ready, willing; a female in heat...."

Raymond smiled, sipping his ale and puffing on his pipe. "You never did meet her, did you, Pigskin?"

"Well, not really," said David sheepishly.

"Krist, Spike. What'd you have to go and spill it fer," said Hap, stomping off down the bar.

Raymond grinned at David and said, "You should be writing fiction stories. You'd make a fortune."

"It could've been like that," said David, trying to suppress his smile.

"And the frigging Krauts will lay down their guns and surrender," retorted Dixie. "See y'all tomorrow, I'm heading for the sack."

"Me too," said Norman, waving as he drained his mug and left.

"Well, Pigskin. Looks like we're the only ones left," said Spike. "You got time, I'll buy you another ale. I'd like to learn more about you and Chief before the war. That is, if you feel up to talking about it."

"Sure, Spike," said David, quietly taking a sip. He lit a cigar, puffing on it, blowing a couple of smoke rings, then he began. "Chief's father came to work for my father when we were only five years old. Chief's mother and my mother were half sisters. We grew up together, like real brothers...."

Sergeant Meaker stepped up to the platform, the chalk board behind him. "Good morning Eagles. Today, Eagle squadron will begin checking out in a new aircraft from the United States. High Command has put a lot of eggs in the basket developing this fighter and I believe they're fully justified. This new fighter is built by North American Aviation. They call it a P-51. We in the R.A.F. have named it, most suitably, the MUSTANG. It has an Allison V-1710 engine, twelve cylinders in line. It will give you eleven-hundred horse power at three thousand rpm. It is equipped with six fifty-caliber machine guns. Two guns are mounted on the lower engine cowling, below the exhaust manifolds, and are synchronized to fire between the three propeller blades. Each of these guns will have two hundred rounds. There are two fifty-caliber machine guns in each wing, each gun having five hundred rounds. There is a gun charging handle to be pulled out. This activates the nose guns only! The wing guns will be live at all times. So don't screw up and hit the firing button on the ground! The machine gun belts will be loaded with armor piercing bullets mixed with a few exploding rounds. Every fifth round will be a tracer. All six guns fire at once, from a single firing trigger. The trigger mechanism is located on the top forward side of the control stick. As you all know, the Spitfire is limited to a two hundred and fifty mile radius from England before it must turn back. The Mustang has a range of over a thousand miles"

Gasps of awe came from the Eagle squadron. David piped up, "I hope it comes with whoopie cushions!" A round of applause and cat calls came from his pilots.

Meaker smiled and continued. "Sorry, but that was a little misleading. The Mustang is equipped to carry two additional seventy-five gallon drop tanks. One under each wing. This added fuel will extend your range to well over two thousand miles. So, you probably don't want to drink a lot of coffee in the morning and maybe take a candy bar along. There are two fuel selectors. The one on the right is for your drop tanks. There are three positions on it, the left tank, the right tank and off. With the auxiliary fuel tanks, you will want to switch from the left to the right periodically to help maintain a balance with the extra weight on each wing. Fuel from these external tanks is fed to the engine by activating an electric boost pump, which creates a suction, thereby drawing fuel from the drop tanks. To drop the external fuel tanks, first turn on the main fuel boost pump and switch the left fuel selector to one of the main tanks. Shut off the auxiliary fuel pump and move the auxiliary fuel selector to off. The red button on top of the control stick activates a solenoid which releases the tank shackles both at the same time. If for some reason the solenoid malfunctions, there is a manual cable release on your lower left-hand side."

"From all the data we have on the Mustang at low altitude, it is least fifty mph faster than anything the Germans have in the air today. It will out-turn the ME-109, the ME-110, and the FW-190. It will out-dive them all, including the Stuka. The Allison engine has a pressure carburetor and will not stall out when you push forward in a steep dive. As you very well know, our fighters have been restricted to a range of two hundred and fifty miles from England. The best you could do was escort bombers to northern France, or at the very maximum, the western fringes of Germany. Unfortunately, most of the bomber targets are four hundred to seven hundred miles from our home bases, which means that the bombers must fly most of their missions unescorted. Consequently the bombers have been taking unacceptably high losses. With the P-51 Mustang, all that will change. Soon we will be taking the war to the Germans and for the first time we will achieve air superiority over them. Eagle squadron, report to the line and begin your familiarization flights and the beginning of the end of the war."

David stood clapping and his entire squadron joined him. "Okay Eagles, let's go to work. I want everyone to go over all the systems again with your rigger. Learn where every switch and control is and be able to put your hand on it without looking. When you can do this blindfolded, we'll get in a few bump-and-runs."

In the next week, David took his squadron up on training flights over the checkerboard pattern of the English countryside. He climbed them through the clouds in formation. They took off and landed in formation until they worked together as a team. He began flying at treetop level, dodging buildings and up and down through hedge rows. He wanted to see fresh grass stains on the tips of their propeller blades when they landed. They ran practice gunnery runs on mock convoys, trains and rail cars, bridges and anything that could help the Germans in any way. Then he broke them into groups and began dogfighting, each trying to outdo the other.

David got permission and took them on a rhubarb across the channel. They spread out into three flight vics. David sighted a string of tanker cars sitting out in the open on a railroad siding. He signaled his wing men to spread out and follow him. He nosed the P-51 over in a steep dive with a wing man on each side. The Mustang responded instantly to David's touch and he centered his sight pip on a black tanker and touched the firing button on his fifty's. The Mustang bucked from the six fifty's firing at once. The recoil of the six heavy guns was much greater than the eight 303s they were used to in the Hurricanes and Spitfires. The smell of burned cordite was like a toxic drug; his adrenalin seemed to rise to its peak and beyond. His tracers arced slowly down, reaching for the black tank cars but not quite finding them. He eased the stick back slightly and the stream of tracers rose up, striking one of the cars. The car exploded, shooting a geyser of flame directly up into his flight path. David jerked back on the controls and the Mustang came over on its back. The P-51 responded faster than anything he'd ever flown. He leveled while inverted and rolled out looking for his wing men. Three tanker-cars were burning fiercely. His wing men slipped down from up above and joined up with him.

"Yellow-one, we have a truck convoy. We're going in on attack."

"Green-one, got a field below me. Looks like ME-109s parked in the woods all around. We'll giv'em a quick squirt. Holy shit; there's flak coming at us from all sides. Green-one, everyone on the deck."

"Pigskin, Red-one. Green-one, you take out the planes, we'll go for the flak positions, from north of the field to the south. Red, two and three, spread out and follow me down to tree top level. You see any guns firing, wipe'em out."

"Red-two, Roger that."

"Red-three, Rog."

"Blue-one, got you in sight. We'll make the same flak pass, east to west."

They each made three passes until there were no more flak guns firing and six Messerschmitts were on fire, sending up columns of thick black smoke.

"Pigskin-Red-one, I'm out of ammo. Let's join up and head for the barn."

David strolled across the field, through dew-covered grasses. The sky was whitening in the east, lighting the green fields with sparkling gems. Creeper vines covered the sides of the red brick houses adjoining the field. They emerged from dark shadows to brilliant shades of green as the sun crested the horizon. The still forms of the Mustangs, painted with British camouflage of dark green and dark earth with sky blue on their undersides, materialized out of the morning mist. They looked ominous with three-bladed props and gun covers in place, ready for the return blitzkrieg. They waited silently, spread out in the dispersal areas around the fringes of the field, with only the clink of tools and an occasional curse to mar the silence as riggers and fitters completed their work. Armorers jumped down off the wings, having finished loading and arming the machine guns. A bouser truck topped off the last fighter and left the field.

David walked out to the low-winged fighter with the football painted on the nose. He called a greeting to Woody and the rigger working on his Mustang. David arranged the straps on his parachute so everything was ready. He stepped up on the main wheel and climbed onto the wing. Flipping back the canopy cover, he slipped into the cockpit, settling down on the seat pack parachute and dingy, fastening his safety harness and adjusting the straps. He ran through his pre-start check list. With the stick between his knees and his right hand resting on the grip, he felt for the rudder and aileron trim knobs with his left hand. He turned both so the white marks for climb were aligned. He set the elevator trim for takeoff, turned on his reflector gun sight, setting the bars to the ME-109's wing span at two hundred and fifty yards. He hung his helmet beside the gunsight and seated the hose from his mask into the oxygen outlet, locking it in place. He plugged the lead wire from his helmet into the radio connection on the right side of the cockpit.

"I hear yea protected my virginity at The Station last night," beamed Woody, climbing up the wing to be alongside David sitting in the cockpit.

"What are brothers-in-law for?" David asked.

"We're riggin' yea wid five hundred pound bombs under each wing. They mount in the same shackles as the drop tanks. It'll give yea a little more snoose on a rhubarb. If yea are escorting a long bomber run, yea've got four hundred and twenty-five gallons of fuel plus your seventy-five gallon drop tank under each wing. So, in a short run, yea get the bombs and a long one, the extra fuel."

"So Woody, all I have to do is push the red drop tank button on top of the stick and bombs away?"

"That's about it, Pigskin. Got time for breakfast?"

"You bet, Woody. Let's go and you can tell me about lady love," said David, chuckling.

"She's tall, yea know. With gazoombas out to here," Woody said, chortling.

"Come on, Woodpecker," David replied. "Now the real thing."

"All kidding aside, Pigskin. She's a lady. Just like I told yea, and we hit it off right from the start. I think this is the real thing."

"So Woody, can you hear wedding bells ringing yet?"

"There's real possibilities," said Woody, smiling.

"Well, next leave we get, how 'bout bringing her over and having supper with Millie and me?" asked David. "After all, if she's going to be family, it's about time we meet her."

"I'll ask'er. I'm sure she'll want to meet yea. I'll call Millie and warn her so she can requisition some ah those beef steaks she so mysteriously comes up with."

"You had to mention that when we're stuck eating in the slop shop, didn't you?" David grimaced at the powdered scrambled eggs, bully beef, bitter bread and goat's milk butter piled in unappetizing clumps on his metal tray.

"Eat hearty, David me boy. Yea going to be up there for a long time before yea next meal."

"Yeah. Nurse-maiding a bunch of bumbees. That'll be as exciting as watching ice melt. I'd better head over to the briefing and find out what new tricks they've thought up for us this time. See you out at the kite, Woodpecker."

The briefing tent was packed with squadron groups huddled together, smoking and laughing nervously. They speculated on the rumored new mission; many held good luck charms and were bragging about their last mission.

"Okay, men, today's mission is one that's never been tried," said Sergeant Tuck, stepping up and flipping the cover over on the operations map. "Our mission today is a surprise visit to Berlin. The first of many more to come." The room was quiet, a deathly silence pervailed, as though they were at a wake. Each pilot digested the startling information in his own way, making peace within himself. "We're going to show Hitler and the Germans they have no safe haven."

Excited rumors swept through the room like a gust of wind blowing in through the door. "You mean, only we bombers are going to Berlin. We're as good as dead," said the pilot from the lead bomber squadron.

"Not this time," continued Sergeant Tuck. "We have three squadrons of Mustangs equipped with long range fuel tanks. They will escort you until German fighters are encountered. They then release their drop tanks and engage the enemy. Any questions?"

"Yeah," said David. "If we release the drop tanks too soon we aren't going to have enough fuel to finish the mission and return to base. Why don't we keep the extra fuel until the tanks are empty?"

"Good question," said Sergeant Tuck. "The tanks are light weight so you can carry more fuel. One incendiary hit in the tank and you'll go up like a Roman candle. As soon as the enemy is sighted, drop those tanks immediately. Besides, the extra weight from external tanks would cut your maneuverability down considerably."

Tuck covered the map and turned to one of Europe. "We should have cloud cover from mid-Channel almost to Berlin. Weather reports are that it will be clearing over the target shortly before your arrival. Back up target is Hamburg. Takeoff for bombers is zero-nine-thirty. Mustangs at ten hundred hours and you will rendezvous over the Channel. Coordinate your watches. On my mark, the time will be, zero-eight-three-zero...Mark. Good luck and good hunting."

Everyone clustered around the maps and photographs, checking details, discussing the weather and debating the relative merits of Berlin as the target. David thought, for the bombers this was more or less routine, but for his squadron, the long-range escort was something entirely new. Something that had never been done, never proven. This was a real mission and a proving mission. He could feel the exhilaration in the air, just like when the circus came to town. Everyone was excited about it and making plans.

Everyone had something to do and David wished he could pitch in and help. The atmosphere before takeoff was a mood of suppressed exhilaration. The drone of the conversation was all about the flight to Berlin. Slowly, the bomber crews booted up and in twos and threes started walking out toward their planes.

The start-engines flare arced into the clear sky. David grabbed his chute, grasped the half belt on his left and brought the safety box around, holding it to his stomach while he fit in the shoulder and leg-straps and closed the catch. He stepped on the main wheel, jumped up on the port wing and slipped into the cockpit, pulling on his helmet. Woody laid the safety straps over David's shoulders. He pulled the side-straps over the peg and fit them in the pin. He pulled on a pair of tan chamois gloves over the white silk ones, then completed his cockpit check: Brakes set, trim -- white lines together for takeoff, flaps up, mags off, petro full, undercarriage down and locked. The rear air scoop had an automatic adjustment on the rear exit door for maximum engine cooling. Oxygen connected and checked, helmet straps fastened.

David began his pre-start check. Mixture lever, forward. Prop, low pitch-high rpm. Throttle, advanced three-quarters of an inch. Battery on, fuel boost pump on high, primer three strokes. He could smell aviation gas as a drop leaked from the primer. A faint odor of burned powder lingered in the cockpit like a container that had held an onion, but was now empty.

David called, "CLEAR," checking forward on both sides of the engine cowling, then flipped the starter switch on. He counted the propeller blades turning over slowly in front of him. When eight blades had passed, he switched the magnetos on both. The engine coughed once and he gave it another shot of prime. It coughed again, turning faster and faster. Alternating white and dark puffs of smoke shot out of the exhaust. The Allison V-1710, V-12 in-line engine caught, sending a cyclone of wind and dust back over and into the open cockpit. David sneezed from the swirling dust and brought the throttle back to idle.

David glanced to the right, toward the rest of his squadron, noting all were ready. The fitter disconnected the battery trolley. Woody tapped his right shoulder, "Good luck," and jumped down off the wing. David signalled to his flight, released the brakes and eased the throttle forward. The Mustang engine roared momentarily, then dropped to a deep-throated rumble as it rolled from the dispersal area.

Woody and his rigger waved, two fingers up, the Vee for Victory. They were the lifeblood that kept his Mustang in top condition. The team that kept him in the air and mothered his P-51 as if their own lives depended upon it. When he had a bad day, they felt it. Anything he asked, they would do. David saluted, and raised his hand giving the victory sign.

David taxied into takeoff position, then closed and locked his canopy, waiting for the flare. He switched on his gunsight and an orange-red circle appeared in the middle of the sight glass. The first circle represented a deflection shot for an aircraft flying perpendicularly at 100 mph, and a two-circle lead for aircraft flying at 200 mph. An aircraft was in range when its wingtips touched the two horizontal bars on the glass in front of his eyes. He checked the scratched nick he'd made in the windscreen which he could use if his gunsight failed. He knew just where to hold his head to sight on the nick.

The armorers had loaded his guns with a combination of armor-piercing and incendiary shells. David thought about the extra work the armorers had in loading and later cleaning the barrels. There was nothing he wanted that they wouldn't do -- it was their war too.

The takeoff flare arced into the clear sky trailing a vapor of orange smoke and bursting in a brilliant star flash. David glanced at the drooping wind sock then gave his squadron the thumbs up signal and released his brakes. His left hand advanced the throttle full and the fighter began its takeoff roll, yawing momentarily, then with a delicate pressure on the rudder, it rolled straight ahead.

David checked his gauges in quick glances; engine temperature, rpm, oil pressure, boost. The ground passed faster and faster, becoming a blur of green. The end of the field approached rapidly and David eased the stick forward, lifting the tail gently. The Allison engine was turning to its max and the Mustang responded slowly in the warm, still, morning air. With the extra drop tanks, they were loaded heavier than they'd ever been. The bumps became lighter and then the wheels were free of the ground. He held the stick back gently, climbing slowly over the field boundary.

David eased the boost back to avoid over-straining the engine, retracted his gear and pulled his flaps up. He missed the fresh air from an open canopy. The Mustang's canopy was in three pieces. The left panel folded down and the top and right panel hinged and folded down on the right side. David relaxed and set the power for a cruise-climb, making a slight adjustment on the elevator trim wheel on his left. The headphones crackled with their rendezvous heading, "Pigskin leader, vector zero-seven-zero."

The green countryside flashed beneath his wings. David led his eagle squadron in a gradual turn to their intercept course. Continuing their climb, the farms began to look like doll houses and animals looked like ants. Ahead, the water in the Channel looked dark blue under the bright sun and no crests showed on the calm waters. David speculated whether he would see them again this day or ever and thought of Millie with a pang of fear.

If only he could send her back to the States; she would at least be safe until the war was over. It would be one less thing he would have to worry about. Well, two, he thought, for soon the baby would come and with it another life to worry about. Maybe they should have waited until after the war. But then he thought of Millie snuggled in his arms and how he'd felt their baby kick. He could picture the smile on Millie's face as she held his hand against her stomach so he could feel the new life inside her.

David increased his boost, adjusted the throttle and turned the trim wheel a fraction as they climbed through ten thousand feet. Ahead and above him he could see contrails from the bomber group still climbing to altitude. Clouds moved in below them as they approached the French coast. The bombers were leveling at the top of the clouds.

"Rastus leader, Pigskin leader. Little friends coming up on your six-o'clock position." David didn't want any nervous gunners taking shots at them as they climbed over the bombers to their cover position.

"Roger, Pigskin. Nice to have your company. We'll try and hold angels ten, that way we can duck under if we get company."

"Gotcha, Rastus. We'll cover you from twelve." David switched to "B" channel to talk with his squadron. "Pigskin leader, arm your nose guns and check your oxygen masks for moisture. Make sure they don't ice up."

"Check your guns, don't drool in your masks," Dixie mocked.

"All right you guys, pay attention. It's minus twenty degrees Celsius outside," said David, reaching up and scraping the ice that had formed on the windshield. Ice always formed on the bullet proof windshield while the plexiglass side windows stayed clear. His goggles misted up and were a nuisance, but they would protect his eyes if there was a fire or he had to bail out. He did not miss the numbing cold, sitting stationary, unable to move for hours, in the Hurcs and Spitfires. The hot coolant ducts ran under the floor boards, and if anything, he now wished he could cool his feet. He worried about his pilots; at altitude, oxygen shortage was always a danger if your line frosted.

David fretted about their position. They were making a long flight on top of the clouds using only dead reckoning. Cumulative errors could take their flight miles off course. They had to rely on the bombers using an astro-sextant for their position. Sometimes, if conditions were good, they could use their radio aerial to determine the bearings of wireless signals from ground stations. Still, David worried about their position. Anyone forced down would probably sit out the war in a German prison camp.

"Hey, guys! I heard a good one the other day about this guy going on a tour to Rome," said Storm'n Norman.

"Better not tie up the radio, Norm," cautioned David.

"Ahh, it's just a short one."

"Yeah," drawled Dixie. "Help keep us awake."

"All right," said David. "Just keep it short."

"This guy's in getting a haircut and tells his barber about his trip. His barber says, 'And I suppose you have an audience with the Pope also? Well, let me tell you about that. You'll be standing in the Vatican square with ten thousand, garlic smelling Italians. The Pope comes out on a little balcony and waves. That's your audience with the Pope.'"

"So, a month later, when the guy gets back from his trip he goes in to get his hair cut. His barber asks, 'How'd your trip go? Did you get to see the Pope?'"

"Yeah," the guy says. "We got an audience with the Pope and boy were you wrong about that. There were only two other couples in there with us."

"The barber got excited and asked, 'What'd the Pope have to say?'"

"The Pope turned to me, looked at me for a long time, and asked, 'Where'n the hell'd you get that haircut?'"

A chorus of laughs and cat calls came back over the "B" channel. "Okay guys," chuckled David. "Pigskin leader. Let's keep the channel clear and keep an eye out for those Bogies."

The clouds began to thin. David watched the German landscape unfold far below, like pieces of a jigsaw puzzle. Through the scattered clouds, he saw bright flashes of German 88-mm antiaircraft guns firing. "Rastus leader. This is Pigskin, you got flak coming up!" Black puffs of smoke erupted below them and David heard a ping from a fragment hitting the metal.

"Rastus leader, tighten up and we'll start weaving. Blue section, pull it in. You know what happens to stragglers."

"Red flak. This is Rastus leader, red flak coming up." Red-powdery flashes ringed the formation of bombers. David could almost smell the burning powder from the flack bursts though they were well ahead of the bombers. "Watch out for Messerschmitts."

David watched the red flak bursts. The Germans used red flak to vector their fighters to the bombers. "Pigskin leader, be alert, we'll start jinxing." He had an empty feeling in the pit of his stomach. In a few minutes his life could be over. Some of his squadron would be killed. On a beautiful sunny day, there were men coming to kill them or be killed.

"Pigskin, Green-one. Bandits three-o'clock high!"

David's head snapped around to the right searching. "Pigskin, Red-one, drop your tanks!" He saw six black specks diving toward the bombers. "Green and Blue, take'em. We'll cover."

"Yellow-three. Shit! My engine quit."

"Pigskin, Red-one, turn your fuel selector to the mains and boost pump on high!"

David glanced in his rear-facing mirror. It was a plain, small flat rectanglar mirror and he had to move his head from side to side before he saw the pilot. It was their new replacement. David hoped it wouldn't be his first and last flight.

"Yellow-three, got it going. I'm okay."

White streaks shot past David's canopy. He jerked the stick back and to the left, jamming the rudder to the floor. His left hand slammed the throttle forward through the gate. He twisted around in a steep climbing turn, looking for the enemy while switching his R/T to transmitter. "Pigskin, Red-one. Snappers, six-o'clock high!"

The attacking Huns had taken a quick squirt at them as they dove through the Mustangs' formation toward the bombers. Off to his right David saw a bright flash. An aircraft exploded. He hoped one of the Mustangs hadn't forgotten to release its drop tanks. Flaming fragments falling from the sky were all that remained of the plane and pilot.

Six Messerschmitts rolled and came hurtling down. The bluish-white bellies flashed in the sun. David saw the black crosses bordered with white on their square wing tips. The noses were painted a bright yellow. The Abbeville Kids.

A vision of Joker passed through his mind and a knot of anger twisted David's gut. He turned to engage the ME-109s. Head on, they closed at over six hundred miles per hour. He centered his sight pip on the lead Hun and fired a three-second burst with his fifties. His six heavy machine guns sent a stream of armor piercing and incendiary bullets into the oncoming Hun. A wing snapped and the Messerschmitt pilot jettisoned his canopy. Out came the pilot. David watched momentarily, then pulled the stick back looking for the rest of the ME-109s.

"Red-three, you've still got your drop tank!"

"It won't release!"

"Red-three. Pigskin. Pull your emergency release cable. If that doesn't work, dive for the clouds and head for home," said David.

David looped over the top. The ME-109s were in front of him. He'd never fired while upside down and held his deflection well above them. A Messerschmitt's wings filled his sight. His finger squeezed the trigger on the stick, firing the six fifty-caliber machine-guns. Tracers flashed out from the Mustang destroying the Hun's elevators and rudder. Pieces of the stricken aircraft came flying back. David ducked instinctively while rolling back to level. Oil splattered his windscreen and the Mustang lurched to port. Something had hit his wing and he checked his controls; they still worked.

A flash of fire erupted below David. "Red-three, Pigskin leader!"

"Red-two. It was Hans that just blew up! He couldn't get his drop tank loose."

"Red-two, form on me," called Pigskin, as he jinxed, turning left and right. It seemed as though they'd been fighting an eternity, but it could have only been a few minutes.

David spotted three Messerschmitts below them. "Red-one, Bogies twelve-o'clock low." He eased the nose over, leading the last Messerschmitt. Still too far, he held his fire. Glancing in his rear-facing mirror he saw Lance, his number two man, pulling in behind. The Canadian was a natural pilot. He handled the Mustang as if he'd been born in it. "Red-two, Pigskin. You take the right, I'll get the left and wait until I fire. I don't want these Hun bastards getting away." The wings of the ME-109 began to fill his sight pip. They were in range, two hundred and fifty yards and closing rapidly. David held his fire. His finger rested on the firing trigger. At a hundred yards the Messerschmitt filled the windscreen and David screamed as his finger clamped down on the firing trigger, "This one's for Joker, you son-of-ah-bitch!"

The Mustang bucked, filling the cockpit with the smell of gun powder. It stung David's nostrils, but it was an odor he'd grown to like. His muscles tensed, blood coursing through his veins. Armor-piercing bullets punched holes into the Hun's wing. The ammunition tray inside the Messerschmitt's wing exploded. From the corner of his eye, David saw another explosion. Lance had scored. David jinxed left and right, rolling left in a climb, then back right diving. The Krauts were gone.

"Pigskin leader, let's regroup," called David as he watched the bombers head in on their bomb run. It was easy to follow their progress from the brownish column of flak bursts.

David circled his squadron outside the flak, waiting for the bombers to complete the bomb run. There would be no more fighters until they were out of the flak. String after string of flak shells streaked after the bombers. A blinding flash came from the middle of the group. A Wellington took a direct hit. There would be no parachutes from that one. Another turned from the formation trailing black smoke and descending rapidly.

David watched streams of bombs fall from the bowels of the bombers. Groups of yellow flashes blossomed on the ground. Clusters of incendiaries wove patterns of flash fires on the buildings below. In the middle of the barrage of bombs came a blinding flash. A column of black smoke erupted like a geyser from a volcano. Berlin was burning.

The bombers turned and the clouds of flak stopped, as if they were in a neutral zone. Helplessly, David watched the lone stricken bomber struggle toward home, trailing smoke.

David flew what was left of his squadron into position covering the other bombers.

"Rastus leader. Tighten up group. The Huns are going to be on us like hornets out of the nest. Pigskin, where are you at?"

"Rastus leader. Pigskin. Little friends are closing on your three-o'clock position."

"Rastus leader. This is Rastus green-two. We've lost an engine. We can't hold altitude."

"Green-two. You'll have to try and make it into the cloud cover. We won't be able to wait for you."

"Rastus Green-two. It's too late. Bandits six o'clock low. Maybe we can decoy'em off you guys for a few minutes."

David scanned the sky, aware that the Huns liked to attack from out of the sun. The sky was clear as they dogged the formation of bombers struggling toward the distant cloud bank and safety.

David glanced up toward the sun while jinxing his P-51 left and right. The thing was not to look at the sun, but around it. Then he saw the specks diving on the bombers. "Pigskin leader. Bandits, twelve o'clock high." David pulled his nose up adding full power. He concentrated his sight on the leader. Then he noticed the large radial engine. Focke-Wulf 190s!

The R/T became a garbled mixture as several fighters began calling targets as they engaged the enemy.

"Rastus leader. Maximum dive. Let's head for cover!"

"Rastus green-two. We're on fire! We're getting out."

David centered his sight pip on the leading FW-190. The enemy gaggle was a large one, thirty or more. There was no time to worry about the odds. The leading FW-190 was in a diving attack, nearly straight down. The Focke-Wulf's wings filled his sight pip. He pulled the trigger. The Mustang bucked as the four 50s in the wings sent their heavy slugs into the Focke-Wulf. His nose guns were silent, out of ammo. David watched the white stream of tracers disappear into the big radial engine. Head-on, the Focke-Wulf offered a slim target. David felt his Mustang jerked sideways. Long tears appeared in his wing.

The two fighters closed at over 600 mph. David danced on the rudder pedals, jinxing out of the line of fire and swinging his tracers into the Hun's wing. His finger locked down on the trigger. Tracers continued to stream into the FW-190; his bullets were scoring. He headed straight for the enemy aircraft. The Focke-Wulf filled his windscreen, a blurred oncoming silhouette. Neither pilot changed course -- neither wanted to present the other with a target. It was a contest of nerves. The FW-190's wing snapped and David jerked back on the controls. He was in the clear, but had no time to look for the Focke-Wulf.

David rolled, inverted, and sucked the elevators back into his lap. A dark form flew up from below filling his windscreen. He rammed the throttle through the gate and rolled in behind a twin engine ME-110. The Messerschmitt banked and David pulled the nose up to lead him. The rear gunner chanced to look up and saw David. A startled look showed on his face for a second, and then he whirled his machine gun around, firing as he turned. David saw the Hun's tracers stream up, reaching toward him. He jammed the stick forward and kicked his left rudder pedal to the floor, throwing his Mustang out of the line of fire. Too late. He heard the thumps of the enemy fire striking his bulletproof windscreen and he ducked instinctively. He glanced through his sight pip. The ME-110 filled his windscreen. He jerked back on the trigger of his 50s, ignoring the shells ricocheting off his windscreen. His four remaining fifty caliber's out-gunned the single machine gun. The glass bubble of the rear gunner's compartment exploded in a shower of glass and the gun swung harmlessly to the side.

David was on top of the Messerschmitt, less than a hundred yards. The ME-110 no longer took evasive action. David fired a three second burst from his much heavier machine guns. His shells ripped into the port engine. Smoke poured from the engine and it burst into flames. David pulled up and rolled right to avoid a collision.

David saw a Mustang in a steep dive, flames shooting out of the engine. There was no parachute. He felt sick thinking of Chief.

Something smashed into the back of his seat. David felt a pain in his back. He was taking hits in the armor plating behind his seat. He glanced in his rear-facing mirror. A yellow-nosed ME-109 was behind him, both wings firing. David jerked his throttle back and pulled his flaps in full, pulling his prop back to fine pitch. He'd used this ploy before to throw a German gunner off and get behind him. Tracers tore through his wing. The Hun had not fallen for his trick. The yellow-nosed Messerschmitt loomed ominously behind him, maneuvering for another shot.

Desperately, David rammed the throttle through the gate, changed to coarse pitch and jerked his flaps off. He slammed the Mustang into a hard left turn, pulling the stick back in his lap. He felt the blood rush from his head and his vision turned grey as he started to black out from the g forces of the turn. The Mustang shuddered, shaking the airframe in a pre-stall. He slacked off on the back pressure a fraction to keep from blacking out, yet holding the P-51 in as tight a turn as possible.

David glanced up at his mirror trying to find the Hun. To his horror, he saw the yellow nosed Messerschmitt tightening the turn and closing in on him. What was going on? The P-51 was supposed to have a tighter turning radius. He tried to think. Another turn and a half and the Abbeville flyer would have him in his gun sights. Then he saw the schnauzer logo below the canopy of the Messerschmitt. This was the pilot who'd killed Joker! If he didn't do something soon, he'd be next. He had to get behind the German. This was the pilot he'd been looking for. David never thought about killing people, only the machine. But this was different. This was the murderer who'd shot Joker hanging helplessly in his parachute. More than anything he wanted to force the German to bail out, to avenge Joker.

David kicked his right rudder to the floor and pulled back on the elevator, climbing steeper. His left hand pushed the throttle through the gate and full coarse pitch on the prop. It was his last desperate ploy. An ME-109 could never follow in a tight climbing spiral. The Messerschmitt would stall and drop out the bottom. Inevitably, the Abbeville murderer would have to push over and dive to escape. In a steep dive, the Mustang could overtake the murdering Hun.

David looked in his rear-facing mirror. It was not possible, he thought. The yellow-nosed Hun was climbing up behind him and closing. An ME-109 could not follow in a tight climbing spiral and yet this one was. He must be the German ace of aces. To be flying with the Abbeville symbol, the yellow nose, he had to be one of the best. It was only a matter of seconds and it would be all over. David felt the blood rush from his head as he tightened the spiral even more. He glanced in the mirror. White flashing lights winked from the Messerschmitt's wings. It looked as though the Hun's prop would chew his tail off.

Desperately, David yanked the stick back and kicked in opposite rudder. His head slammed against the side of the cockpit. The hood ripped off the Mustang. Wind screamed into the open cockpit ripping at his helmet and oxygen mask. He glanced in his rear-facing mirror: the German was gone. He probably figured David had killed himself and went looking for an easier target.

David held his vertical plunge, heading for the safety of the cloud bank below. He eased the throttle while scanning the skies ahead for the bombers.

Tracers snapped by inches above his head. Without a canopy he could feel the heat from their passing. Instinctively, David jammed his left rudder to the floor, throwing his Mustang out of the line of fire. He glanced in his rear-facing mirror. It was the yellow-nosed ME-109.

David rolled inverted and sucked the stick back in his lap. The P-51 plunged recklessly toward the earth. Metal ripped open from hits he'd taken in the side of his fuselage, vibrating in the wind with a harmonic warning. Wind screaming in the missing canopy felt as though it would tear him from the cockpit. The force of the wind tore at his goggles and helmet. The oxygen mask was pulled from his face, but he no longer needed it.

David felt the Mustang shudder. He had to slow the dive or he'd shed his wings. He pulled the power back and checked his mirror. The German was behind him and closing, but he was not firing. He was well within range. What was he waiting for? Maybe he thought David would still kill himself if he let him. Or, he was out of ammo. Why was he still following?

David tested the elevators. They were heavy and he couldn't move them. He used both hands on the stick. It would not budge. The ground was coming up alarmingly fast. His elevators were frozen and would not move. He couldn't possibly bail out of the P-51 at the speed he was traveling. He tried rolling the nose trim back and there was an immediate response. He rolled it back some more and the Mustang began to level out. As his speed dropped, the elevators became effective.

David glanced in his mirror. Nothing. The German was gone. Then he looked out the port side. The yellow-nosed Messerschmitt was fifty yards off his wing. The schnauzer on the side seemed to be grinning at him. The German saluted and rolled on his side, streaking for home. David sat, paralyzed, unable to move. He couldn't believe what had happened.

Ahead he saw the bombers skimming the base of the clouds. His head phones had been torn off his head and he groped around the floor feeling for them.

He tried his R/T, "Rastus leader. Pigskin, Red-one. I'm six-o'clock low, about five miles behind you."

"Pigskin, Rastus leader. We've got one wounded duck back there. Can you keep an eye out for him?"

"Roger, Rastus. Pigskin. Can do." David slowed his P-51 to minimum cruising speed and began a series of wide sweeping "S" turns, looking for the bomber. He was alone and almost out of ammo. If the Huns jumped him now, he was almost certain to not make it back. David thought about Millie and wished there was some way he could send her back to the states. She was stubborn for sure and deep in his heart he knew she would not go without him.

David made a sweep to his left, his eyes moving constantly up and down, left and right. He searched an imaginary block, then moved onto the next block. Nervously he watched the sky and automatically jinxed his P-51. He did not want to be surprised. He could not relax his vigil for a second. He was close to the cloud base and could always pull up to safety as long as he spotted the Jerries first.

Without the canopy, David was glad he hadn't lost his goggles. He needed their protection for his eyes from the wind. Something flashed in the distance and he bracketed the area with his eyes. There was the bomber limping along almost at ground level. He switched his R/T to "B" channel, "Lone bomber from Rastus group. This is Pigskin, Red-one. Do you copy?"

"Pigskin Red-one. This is Rastus blue-two. We're shot all to hell. Everyone's wounded or dead. The pilot's dead. I'm the copilot. All our instruments are gone."

"Rastus Blue-two. Can you keep'er in the air?"

"We've still got one good engine, Pigskin. Don't know how bloody long it'll keep turning though. We've got no compass, or any instruments, including air speed. You don't suppose you could point us in the right direction, old Chap?"

"Have you home in time for afternoon tea," said David, as he did a wing over and flew alongside the Wellington. On the starboard wing the engine was missing. A gaping hole showed where the engine had been wrenched or blown from its mounting. Half the tail was missing and the bomber was riddled with holes. David gasped when he saw the nose of the bomber or what once was the nose. It was gone. A gaping jagged hole was all that remained.

"What'n the hell's keeping you in the air?" asked David, as he flew ahead, leading the bomber toward the Channel.

"Don't bloody know, Yank. You don't look so pure yourself. Besides, none of our chaps could speak German."

David guided the bomber around the congested areas to avoid the flak guns until they safely passed the Dutch coastline, heading out to sea. David began homing on the radio voice steer-signals from Boxsted.

"Pigskin! Rastus blue-two. Bandits, three-o'clock."

"Gotcha, Rastus. Just keep'er heading the way you are now and you'll see the coast shortly." David turned toward three ME-109s dropping on the wounded bomber. They were lined up in a row, each ready to make a firing pass.

David pushed his throttle through the gate, pulling up to an intercept angle on the leading Messerschmitt. His thumb waited on the firing button as the Hun's wings rapidly filled the bars on his sight pip. His blood raced as he sped toward another life and death encounter. In a matter of seconds, it would be over. His lips were white, drawn tight against the buffeting wind. His eyes squinted through the goggles. Every fiber in his body strained, like a coiled spring wound tight. His muscles flexed in anticipation. He felt a queasiness in his stomach, but had no time or thought for it.

The Messerschmitt's wings filled the bars on his sight pip and he fired. The silence was deafening. He was out of ammo. David sat, still climbing in attack, stunned. His squeezed the trigger down on the firing mechanism again and again as he closed with the Messerschmitt.

The ME-109s split-essed and headed for the deck. David stared in disbelief as the Messerschmitts flew out of range, heading for the Fatherland.

"Say, Yank. That was the bloodiest damn thing I ever saw. Three to one and you scared the wits out of them."

"Not as scared as I was," said David over the "B" channel. "I was out of ammo."

"Pigskin, if we walk away from this one, I bloody well want to shake your hand. I must ask another favor, though."

"Ask away, Blue-two."

"Can you head us toward Manston? I don't know if anyone is alive in back, but should get them on the ground as soon as possible."

"You got it, Blue-two." David climbed higher for a better view. "Should be coming up in about ten minutes if you can hold that crate together."

"Made it this far Pigskin, but we'll need you to lead us in. I don't have any bloody airspeed indicator."

"Rastus Blue-two, landing flare just fired. Looks like they're waiting for us." David flew ahead of the bomber, lining him up with the runway. "What speed would you like over the fence, blue-two?"

"Can you bring us in at 120 mph?"

David dropped his gear and flaps, slowing to 130 mph. "Rastus, Blue-two. We're steady at one-thirty." He watched the bomber in the rear-facing mirror settle in behind him.

"Okay, Pigskin. Better stay at one-thirty. I don't think I've got any flaps!"

"One-three-zero it is, Blue-two." David flew a glide path toward the end of the runway. He crossed the threshold twenty feet off the ground and added power, climbing out of the bombers' landing path. "Good luck, Blue-two."

David circled downwind, watching what was left of the Wellington settle to the field. He held his breath as the bomber bounced once and swung to port. David crossed his fingers and clasped the St. Christopher medal that hung around his neck, hoping against hope. They'd been to Berlin and back. They had completed their mission. They had fought against far greater odds and had made it through.

David could only imagine what the bomber had encountered and how it continued to struggle for life. The gallant crew had entrusted their lives to the tough, battle-torn war bird and each other.

The bomber settled to the earth again and David could almost feel the pilot struggling against all odds to control the dying bird. As its air speed dropped, the damaged left gear collapsed under the weight of the bomber. The port wing dipped. The wing tip dropped slowly and slid along the ground. Part of the wing broke, trailing behind, hinged to the wing by a shred of metal. The bomber pivoted around the broken port wing in a slow arc. The right gear buckled under the side pressure. The bomber came to a stop, with its tail facing forward. A cloud of dust rose and settled over the Wellington.

"Rastus, Blue-two, Pigskin here. Bet you couldn't do that again."

"Tally ho, Pigskin. I can tell you for a fact, I wouldn't want to. Sure as hell is hard on the underwear. Where's your hangout, Yank?"

"Biggin Hill pub, The Station. See the old man, Hap. He'll know where I'm at."

"Okay, Pigskin. Thanks again for the help. Rastus, Blue-two, out."

David turned his Mustang toward Biggin Hill and felt a great weariness. His eyes drooped and he struggled to keep them open. Stabbing pain shot up his shoulders and he rested his arms on his knees. He knew he was only minutes from the field and yet it seemed to take forever before the field grew under the nose of his P-51.

David pressed his mike button and reported in to Biggin Hill control using the code name for the day. He could taste blood in his mouth and his ears were ringing from the wind whistling past the open canopy. Green patches of fields and farms flashed past his wings as he dropped lower in preparation for landing. David talked out loud to himself, trying to stay awake. He was tired and wanted no mistakes. He circled the field, noting the wind direction and several vacant slots in the dispersal area. He turned downwind, entering the landing pattern. He dropped his gear and half flaps, rolling the spider wheel to trim the nose. Final landing check, GUMP: Gas on mains, boost pump on, Undercarriage down and locked, Mixture, full rich, Prop, ahead full.

David did everything by rote. Turning final, his left hand brought the throttle back. Two hundred feet, speed 130 mph and settling. Speed 100 mph; he brought in full flaps. He crossed the threshold and the ground rushed up. "Power back all the way and hold'er off. Stick back, hold'er off," he said, talking himself down. He felt a thump as the wheels touched and stuck solidly to the ground. He rolled straight ahead, eyes looking out the port side, juggling the rudder pedals to keep the P-51 rolling in a straight line.

David taxied slowly toward the dispersal area. He stepped on the left brake and gunned the throttle, spinning the P-51 around in its parking area, facing out.

"Holy Shit!" clamored Woody as he crawled up the wing beside David. He took note of the missing canopy and the numerous bullet holes. Then, he saw David's bloody face grinning up at him. "Holy Shit! Where yea hit? Medic!" he screamed, looking for the ambulance.

"Hold on, Woodpecker. I'm okay. Just a scratch on the eyebrow. Bleeds like hell," David said, hanging his earphones on the side and slipping his bloody leather helmet off. "T'ain't nothing a few ales and a little sleep won't cure. But, I got a complaint about the shoddy condition of the Mustangs you guys expect me to fly," said David, grinning up at his brother-in-law.

"David...I got some really bad news ta tell yea." Woody stood on the wing alongside David sitting in the cockpit.

David looked at his brother-in-law's ashen-white face and felt a cold twisting in his gut. Something he dreaded and feared more than anything else. "What? Just tell me. Is it Millie? Something's happened to Millie!"

Woody looked off in the distance, unable to look at David while he spoke, almost in a whisper. Tears poured from his eyes unchecked. "There was this bombing raid," he choked, unable to talk.

David popped his safety straps open and stood shakily in the cockpit alongside Woody. Frightened, he placed his shaking hand on his brother-in-law's shoulder. "And?"

"One ah the bombs made a direct hit on the operations room at Detling. Everyone inside was killed!"

"But Millie wasn't working! It was her day off!" stammered David, relieved.

"Sorry David, but I checked wid one ah her girlfriends. She'd traded shifts wid one ah the other WAAFs so she'd have the time off when yea was home." Woody sat on the wing holding his head between his knees. "She was there!"

"No. No! You're wrong, Woody. She wasn't there. She couldn't be." David unbuckled his parachute, letting it drop to the ground, and stumbled off across the field pulling his gloves off and letting them fall. "You're wrong, Millie's at home. I know she's home...you'll see. Millie, I'll be home...just as soon as I fill out my reports...I'll catch the first train, Millie...."

Detling

"Ain't no reason for yea going out to Detling," said Woody, as they stepped down from the train at Victoria Station. "There's nuthin' yea can do out there. Face the facts, David. She's dead. The bomb made a direct hit. It went right down the entryway and exploded inside the operations room. Everyone working in there was killed instantly."

"I'm going, Woody," said David. He shouldered his kit bag and headed for the connecting train to Detling.

"I'm going wid yea."

"No, Woody." David stopped and turned to face his brother-in-law. His face was grim and drawn. He shivered as they stood facing each other in the damp, cold fog. "Woodpecker, I got to be alone for a while. I've got to find her and bring her home. I've got to say good-bye. I'll see you when I get back to London."

"I should be going wid yea. At a time like this, yea ought not be alone. She was me sister, remember?" Woody's bloodshot eyes were wet, threatening to spill over. "I'm staying at the Overseas League. If I'm not in, check at the Eagle Club. Me girl, Patricia McCartney, is one of the volunteer workers. She'll know where I'm at."

A muffled train whistle came out of the fog, sounding like someone blowing a horn in a barrel. The cars lurched and banged into each other as the train crept slowly into the station. The engine wheezed and huffed like a tired, old fat man trying to extract himself from a deep soft chair. The locomotive sat quietly belching out occasional puffs of coal smoke. An oiler scurried around the engine, lubricating the slides with a long-spouted oil can.

The conductor called "Board," and passengers scurried from the station, climbing into the waiting cars. Train men blew their whistles and began shutting doors. With a ringing of the bell, hissing jets of steam and grinding of the great iron wheels, the locomotive lurched forward. The cars jerked, stopped, then began moving slowly from the station. David stepped onto the moving platform leading into the car, turned and waved to Woody. Fog enshrouded the passenger cars as they picked up speed, plunging into the cold, black misty void.

David sat outside, on the steps of the car, not wanting to burden himself with the noisy milling throng of passengers. He felt like a victim of motion, always leaving something or somebody. Where was he going? Was there some divine destiny he was headed toward? Some purpose to what was happening? What was he chosen for? If only he knew, maybe he'd be able to make some sense out of everything that had happened!

He'd left his home and his family, but it was ordained that he leave them and make his own way. He'd go back again, but only for a visit, never again to stay. David felt as though he'd abandoned Joker and Chief. A real quarterback would never desert his teammates, yet things happened so fast, as though he were on a merry-go-round that never stopped. How many other pilots from his squadron had been discarded like broken suitcases? He'd lost track.

Millie was dead, and now he was going on without her. To what purpose? When he got back to base, he'd strap himself in his Mustang, in addition to eleven other pilots, several he didn't even know, to go out and kill. Who were they killing? Was he responsible for slaying someone's husband, some child's father?

And for what? Why were they exterminating these people? For someone they didn't know, for someone they didn't love. New pilots would be flying the positions where Robin, Bernie and Hans had flown. It was as though they'd never been there, as though they were only numbers. When your number was up, operations would call another number.

He and Millie had never seen their baby. Now it was gone. He wouldn't wake up from a bad dream with Millie snuggled alongside him. A small, pink, cuddly bundle between them. Did she go to join Binkie? Was that her destiny? Was he only an intruder? He felt dejected and utterly alone -- exhausted. He didn't want to go on alone anymore.

Why did Millie make him promise to go on without her? Did she know something was going to happen? Did she have a vision? Were they now bound, like Chief and he were? David wondered if he'd see Millie in a vision, like he'd seen Chief. What would be their medium, their channel of communications? He was Rain-in-the-Face. Would the spirits of his blood brother intercede? He clasped the St. Christopher medal, along with his single dogtag, in one hand. They'd become his totem, his bonding to his beloved. It was a small spark of hope, something to turn to when all else failed. Tenaciously, he clung to the one hope he had left.

David closed his eyes and thought of Millie. He saw her sitting naked in the bed, facing him with her legs crossed. He looked into her green eyes, burning with fire. Her mouth was drawn tight. He smiled to himself as he pictured her button nose and the freckles on her face and chest blushing a deep red, matching her hair.

A shadow clouded the image and he heard her voice, "You promised me!" and the voice faded.

Tears flowed from David's eyes and he cried out in anguish, "I can't!"

Millie's image appeared again, smiling at him. "This I pledge to you. I will be with you always." David reached out, but was greeted only by the cryptic, wet, cold fog.

"Taxi!" David shouted, as a cab crept by in the fog.

It pulled over to the curb and stopped, the driver rolling his window down. "I be off duty, but for an airman, I'll bloody well drive you any time. Hop in, sir -- where will you be off to?" asked the elderly driver. He should have been long past the age where he had to drive a cab, and especially in such fog.

"The Eleventh Group Operations," said David, giving the old man directions. He tossed his kit bag into the back seat and climbed in. The cab was warm and the driver seemed friendly, reminding him of his grandfather. He'd only been to the operations where Millie worked once, when they'd been giving a tour to some of the R.A.F. fighter pilots.

"Sir, I don't know if you're aware," said the driver hesitantly turning in his seat to face David. The skin sagged in baggy pockets on his tired face and he looked exhausted. "The operations building was bombed. There's nothing left but a smoking pile of rubble."

David sat quietly, waiting as though he hadn't heard. Then he looked at the driver impatiently. "Can we get going? My wife is a WAAF working in the operations. She's expecting me."

"Sir, I'm very sorry. If your wife was working there today, she was...," the driver said, speaking slowly and enunciating his words distinctly. "The operations room was bombed this morning. A bomb hit the underground entrance smack-dab center. It penetrated the operations room, exploding inside. Everyone working in there was killed. The building above collapsed into the basement operations room. There is nothing, not a bloody thing left there but a pile of rubble."

"I know you're off duty, but I'm really in a bit of a rush. Look, I'll pay you double if you'll just drive me to the operations and drop me there. Millie, that's my wife, has a lot of connections and I'm sure she'll be able to get a car."

The driver turned forward, shaking his head and engaged the gears. The car crept slowly through the fog, almost like a blind man feeling his way along a wall in a strange room. "You sound like a Yank," said the driver, trying to comprehend his strange passenger.

"Yes. I guess my accent gives me away," said David, half smiling to himself. He needed someone to talk to, and the old man seemed like a good listener as he gave a brief synopsis of his life as a squadron leader in the R.A.F.

"You are in a good outfit, the 71st. One of the best, I've been told. Isn't the 71st squadron all Yanks?"

"Well, not exactly. We've got a couple of Canadians, and I understand one of our new replacements is from Mexico. By the way, did I tell you my wife is Irish, and her brother is the rigger on my Mustang?"

"Small world," said the old man wearily. "I am afraid this is as far as I can go with the motor car. You will have to foot it the rest of the way."

"Thanks," said David, counting shillings from his wallet.

"Taxi is free," said the tired old man. "It is the least we can do. By the way old chap, I am Sir Henry Bickford. Didn't catch your name."

"David Hampton, sir, and I'm obliged."

"Forget the Sir. It is more of a formality nowadays. My friends all call me Henry. Look, lad, it's coming on dark. Why don't I just put up my feet and take a short snooze? I'll be waiting on you when you're ready to go back. Won't be any more taxis running this late."

"Thanks, Henry. I'll be coming back with my wife."

"Well I am kind of tired anyway. I'll take a short nap. If you're not back when I wake up, I will just head on home. Okay?"

"Okay, Sir Henry," David stammered as he shouldered his kit bag and picked his way through the bomb rubble. There were piles of bricks and broken concrete scattered helter-skelter and every surface was covered with broken glass. Jagged ends of timbers protruded from piles of rubble that had once been a building. Men and women with masks worked side by side clearing a passageway through the street. It smelled rotten, as though raw sewage were running through the streets. Several buildings stood like skeletal structures, missing walls on one side, leaving the rooms exposed and open.

Where was the operations? Everything was changed. Most of the buildings were damaged, but still standing. Smoke hung heavily in the air. It smelled of burning garbage and rotten flesh and he covered his nose and mouth with a hankie. His stomach rebelled, but he'd eaten nothing to throw up. Fire and rescue crews, all masked, picked through the broken buildings looking for bodies.

David saw a blue-suited Bobby giving directions and he stumbled toward the tall uniformed officer. "Pardon me," interrupted David, "but can you tell me where the Eleventh Group Operations is? I thought it was right here. I must've gotten turned around."

"You're bloody well not turned around, old chap. I'm afraid that pile of rubble you're looking at is the operations. There's nothing left. Going to bulldoze it over as soon as we can get a crew free. Got to bloody well protect against an epidemic, you know. All the dead bodies...."

David dropped his bag, staggering over to the pile of rubble that had once housed the underground operations. The walls and ceiling over the ops room had been made of reinforced concrete, enough to withstand a bomb blast. Millie had shown him the thick roof and surrounding blast walls. If only he could find the entryway leading down. He began throwing broken pieces of concrete, digging in the debris with his bare hands.

It began to sleet, but David did not notice. He worked alone in the dark, his hands raw and bloody from digging in the rubble. Then he came to a huge slab of concrete that could not be moved. He dug to the side and encountered more slabs wedged together. Rusty bayonets of steel reinforcing rod protruded from the concrete and locked the pieces of broken rubble together as if they'd been welded.

David wept in frustration, pounding the cold wet concrete impasse with his torn hands. His body jerked convulsively in sobs of defeat. He'd never known defeat. They'd been beaten before, but never defeated. Only a few feet away lay his wife and baby.

Chilled and exhausted, David sat huddled in his excavation. He began to realize the hopelessness of finding any survivors. Millie was gone and with her the dream. How could there be a dream without her? The baby he would never see, who would never play in the yard with a white picket fence. He didn't even know if it was a boy or a girl. All the things Millie had bought; the crib, the clothes, and the teddy bear he'd brought.

The operations had been built to withstand a direct bomb blast, but not from inside. The room would have been an inferno. The blast had pushed the walls out and the structure above collapsed into the underground room. Anyone not killed by the blast would be buried under tons of rubble.

David held his head in his hands, bent over, huddled in a ball. His body shook uncontrollably as he wept. Millie was only a few feet away, but she might as well be on the far side of the world. Had she lain bleeding and wounded? Or was she killed instantly, blown to pieces? He'd never said good-bye. He tried to remember if he'd told her he loved her...he knew now that Millie was gone, but he could not accept her death. He felt drained, but found relief in letting go.

The human psyche began its healing process. Where would he go from here? He had no idea except that now he was alone. He was alone before he'd found Millie, so what was the problem? But he was not alone, for their spirits were bonded. David heard voices coming from out of the dark and climbed from his hole.

"Sir Henry, you'd best wait out here. It's frightfully dangerous in there."

"Nonsense, constable. I saw a lot of this in the Great War, you know!"

"Sir Henry!" called David. "Stay where you are. I'm coming out."

"Here's his kitbag," called the constable, picking his way slowly through the rubble.

"What in the world would you be doing out there, David?" asked Sir Henry.

David stopped to catch his breath. "I had to know for certain, Sir Henry. I couldn't rest until I knew for sure that Millie was no longer alive."

"You'd best come along with me, lad. We've a big, empty, house. With the war and all, only the Misses and me there now." Henry had had his own share of grief. He felt useless, so he drove cab, the only contribution he could make to the war effort.

"You've already done enough," David said.

"Nonsense. I won't hear of it. Let's be off then. The woman does get on some whenever I'm late. Be the dickens to pay!"

"You and your wife are alone, Henry. Did you have a family?" asked David, shouldering his kitbag, bidding the constable a good evening.

"Did," said Henry. "Three boys and two girls. Only the one girl left that we know for sure."

They walked in silence, picking their way slowly down the blacked out street. David sensed there was more to Henry's story, but did not want to pry. He thought of Millie and how happy she'd been when she told him she was going to have their baby. Sir Henry and his wife had five children. If Millie had lived, they would have had the family they'd planned. The farm was a good life, a place to raise a family. The children grew up learning responsibility, for each had his own chores. David had taken a large part of the burden from his father. He'd felt guilty about going off and leaving his dad to take on his share of the farm while he went off to fly.

If his coming to England and enlisting in the R.A.F. would keep his brothers and sisters from the horrors of war, then it would be worth it.

Sir Henry continued, "Bertrum, he was the first born. Cocky devil. Joined the R.A.F. Then came the two girls. First Wanda, then Melissa. Last, the twins, Anthony and Alexander."

"You must have had a house full when they were all home," said David, thinking of his own family back on the farm.

"Bertrum would have graduated from Oxford in the spring, but he felt he had to give it up until the war was over." Sir Henry stopped to rest for a moment and catch his breath. "He was killed taking off in his Spitfire. Shot while still on the runway. I was told a fuel tank exploded."

David closed his eyes in pain. He thought of the many fighters he'd seen blown up. All they were, were numbers. But all of a sudden, a number had taken on a human form, a face. A face of the pain and grief that death inflicted on the loved ones left behind.

"Both the girls joined the WAAFs. Wanda fueled planes at Biggin Hill. She was killed when their barracks was bombed."

David remembered Raymond telling them how they'd carried out the girls' bodies...the parts: arms, legs, a hand, a body without a head. He saw the face of the WAAF refueling his Spitfire, streaked with blood and dirt. Her eyes had been large and moist from the pain and grief they'd witnessed but could not comprehend.

"Anthony went into submarines. He was fascinated with electronics and was one of the best sonar men England had, so I've been told."

"Had?"

"I understand they had fired two fish into a German freighter in the North Sea. That's the last anyone heard from them. Missing in action was the official notice...Alexander was a navigator on a Wellington that went down over France. Another missing in action notice."

"I was shot down over France and escaped back to England," David said, hoping to bolster the old man's hopes.

"Well here's our motor car. Couldn't have gone much farther," said Sir Henry, climbing heavily behind the wheel. He wheezed, trying to catch his breath while fumbling with the ignition. His foot stomped the starter and the gears ground slowly. "Damn fog! Going to be a real pea-souper for the next two or three days."

"How do you know about the fog?"

"By the smell. I can always tell by the smell. It's coming from the sea. You can smell the sea! Seaweed washes up on the beaches and an occasional dead fish; then there's the salt air. Sea air has a smell all of its own...now if only we can find our way. Tell me about your escape from France."

"I bailed out and came down in a vineyard. A farm couple took me in and put me in their barn. The farmer went to turn me in to the Germans while the wife helped me escape. She put me in touch with the resistance. The underground passed me along from agent to agent."

"How did you come to actually get out of France?"

"I was given a Greek passport and put on a merchant ship. They transferred me to a British frigate somewhere in the Channel."

"I'll have to ask Melissa to do some checking around," mumbled Sir Henry, leaning forward, straining to see the road in front of the car.

"Melissa, that's your other daughter in the WAAFs? What's she do?"

"Flies planes from the factories out to whatever base they are going to. She's the wild one. A real Tomboy. Damn near got shot down once," Henry chuckled. "Bringing a Mustang into a field just as it was being attacked by some Messerschmitts. Dove straight at'em. The Krauts thought they were under attack and turned tail for home."

"Tell me something if you will, Sir Henry."

"If I can, David."

"You've lost a son and a daughter and have two more sons missing in action. How'n the hell do you handle it? What can you do? What do you do?"

Sir Henry drove quietly for a while and David thought he'd overstepped his bounds. Maybe he didn't have the right to ask such a question. He thought of Millie and hid his face in his hands.

"It doesn't ever go away, David...the pain. After a while, it just aches like an old wound that acts up every time it rains. It doesn't ever go away. Some days, I don't think of it for hours at a time and then I'll see something of Bertrum's or Wanda's or one of the others and it all comes back. Like when I picked you up today at the station. I saw your disbelief and felt it just as the day we were notified of Bertrum's death. I wouldn't believe it for a long time. I even made a journey to the base where he was killed."

"I'm sorry, Sir Henry. I never knew. All I could think of was Millie lying hurt and trapped. I don't know how to deal with her death."

"You live one day at a time, David. When we finish this war, then we can put the dead to rest. It's why I drive cab. I needed something to do, to make some contribution to the war, no matter how insignificant."

A house loomed in front of the car as Henry braked to a stop. "We're home, David. Grab your bag." He shuffled up the walk banging the door open and calling, "I'm home, Mother."

Henry opened a door in the entryway leading into a large walk-in closet where he hung his coat on a hanger amongst a rack of clothes. He placed his hat on the shelf that looked as if it belonged in a mens' haberdashery, for the variety of headgear. Henry took David's coat and hung it for him. "Sorry, don't have a butler or cook, with the war on and all. Anyway, it's just Annie and I, so we manage to do for ourselves."

"Well it's about time. You worried me to death traipsing about in this dreadful fog. Don't know when I've seen it so bad!" Henry's wife was a head taller than him, with soft greying hair that hung in bouncy curls. Her wire-rimmed spectacles, balancing half way down her nose, made her look like a country school teacher. She tilted her head down to look at him over the tops of her glasses. Her eyes were brown and soft like David's mother's eyes. Though her face was wrinkled, it did not make her look old.

"I brought some company, mother. Have you fixings for two hungry soldiers?"

"Oh. Land sake's," she said in a high-pitched, squeaky voice. Her face was pale, as if she'd seen a ghost. "Are you from Bertrum's squadron?"

"No ma'am. I'm David Hampton. I'm with the 71st squadron at Biggin Hill. My ah, wife ah, she...."

"Annie, David's wife was working in the operations here in Detling. Yesterday," said Sir Henry, his voice quivering. "He came to make arrangements, but all for nought."

"Oh my. Oh dear, whatever can we do for you? David, is it?" asked Annie wringing her hands together in her apron. Her dress was elegant, not one for the kitchen or house work.

"Mother," Sir Henry addressed his wife, "The lad is hungry and tired. Could you fix a little something for us?" With that, he turned and took David by the arm. "Come, David, we'll slip into the study for a pint of bitters."

The study was a high-ceilinged room finished in a dark reddish-brown wood. The walls were lined with book shelves on two sides. The third wall was luxuriantly made up of arched windows reaching from floor to ceiling and looking out over a garden terrace. The chairs were heavy, leather-covered, the kind you could sit in and almost disappear. The floor was oak, highly polished and adorned with a large oriental rug. A fireplace set in grey handcut stone covered the fourth wall, and David stared at the military pictures that dignified the mantle. "Sir Henry, are these pictures of you?"

"Here's your bitters, David. Ah, yes. Most of them anyway. That was the Great War. I lost a lot of good friends...this was my older brother," said Sir Henry, taking the picture down from the mantle. "He was always looking out for me, the baby. Tommy was gassed in the trenches. One of his men had lost his gas mask and Tommy, gave the lad his own. Tommy ran through the trenches toward supply for another...I found him the next day...lying on his back in the mud, arms and legs stuck out in different directions. His hands were curled like he was trying to claw his way out. Gas is a lousy way to die, slow and agonizing. Tommy's tongue was swollen in his mouth and his eyes were bugged out of their sockets...staring up at nothing."

"Don't you hate the Germans? I mean, how do you catch and punish those who committed such atrocities? Where does it end, or does it ever?"

"Those people who fired the gas shells, the ones who dropped the bomb on Detling, the pilot who shot Bertrum; they're only soldiers doing what they were trained for. Just like we are. Just because they're led by a few crazies, does not make them bad people, David. They are just like us. They fall in love, get married and have children. They have pain and grief and fear. Eventually, we will get to the crazies who started this. Then we can put an end to it...until another fanatic gets in power and it starts all over again. I suppose I ought to care about them being punished. But I do not. I am so tired of war, I just want it over. Punishment is not our job," said Sir Henry. "In any case, there will be other people who will see them brought to justice."

Annie came into the study carrying a tray ladened with cheese, crackers and bowls of steaming soup.

"Whatever happens, it will not change anything," said Sir Henry. "It will not bring Bertrum or Wanda back. And it will not bring your wife back, David...or all the others."

Annie stood stiffly behind Sir Henry, like a lighthouse on a desolate rock, a beacon of hope to wayfarers, her hands affectionately caressing his shoulders. "Yesterday was our anniversary. Henry and I have been married forty-five years. And I am grateful for every day we have been together. All the time you had with your wife, David...no one can take those good times away from you. You will always remember them and be glad that you were lucky enough to have had them."

The front door opened with a bang and a high-pitched voice boomed down the hall. "Mum. Sir Henry, I'm home. Hello. Anybody home?" Footsteps sounded outside the study.

"We are in here, Melissa. We have company," said Annie, opening the door and greeting her daughter with a warm hug.

"Didn't think I'd find my bloody way home in this dreadful fog." Melissa rambled on nonstop in a deep British accent. David thought she looked like a pixie, though her slacks and shortie jacket did nothing for her figure. She was short and well proportioned, but not skinny by any means. Her short brown hair bounced as she walked, as if she were on a pogo stick. She bobbed around the room with pent-up energy, helping herself to crackers and cheese from the tray. She stuffed them in her mouth without missing a word, finally making her way over to her father. She bent and kissed the top of his balding head, "Sir Henry," she addressed him, "And how goes the battle?" She turned without waiting for an answer.

"Oh, you did say you had company. Jolly good evening, sir. I'm the brat daughter, Melissa." She crossed the room to David extending her hand to shake his while wiping crackers and cheese from her mouth. Her face was small, with sharply chiseled features, and her mouth was wide, the focal point on her face. She was not ugly, but would not win any prizes at a beauty contest. She wore no make-up, but her face was flushed and vibrant.

David stumbled to stand, setting his soup and bitters aside. He took her hand in his, shaking it, somewhat embarrassed. "David Hampton, with the 71st at Biggin Hill."

"Pleased to meet you, sir." Melissa turned toward her father, swooping down for more crackers and cheese. "Just delivered a new Mustang to the 71st," she said, stuffing her mouth while she poured herself a cup of tea. "Hell, Henry, you should've seen this Mustang sitting on the side of the field! It was shot to shit."

"LADY MELISSA!" Annie said, "We do have a gentleman present!"

"Mum. You know I don't like being called that! Anyway, there was this P-51 shot all to pieces and the canopy was missing. One side of the fuselage was bare bones, I mean the aluminum sheeting was ripped right off. I don't know how the pilot got back to the field. If it had been me, I would have gone over the side. It had some kind of goofy ball emblem on the side with lettering of 'Pigskin,' whatever that is."

"That Mustang was mine," said David.

The room was silent except for Melissa choking on her tea. "Guess I put my big foot in my mouth that time," said Melissa.

David, always alert to a little friendly jousting, said, "I really don't think your feet are that big and besides, that Mustang was a hell of ah mess."

Annie smiled, quietly sipping her tea, as Melissa for once had nothing to say.

"Jolly good, old chap," said Sir Henry. "Now if you ladies do not mind, David and I will be having a bit of scotch and our evening cigar."

"Yeah," said Melissa standing up and stretching. "I could go for a couple shots of scotch myself."

"MELISSA!" said Annie in a tone of voice that left no doubt as to her meaning.

Sullenly she followed her mother from the room, closing the study door behind her and calling provocatively as it closed. "Ta-ta, Mr. Hampton. See you bright and early."

"I like mine with a little ice and a splash of water," said Henry, setting two glasses on the bar.

"That'll be fine with me, Sir Henry."

"'Henry' will be jolly fine, old chap...titles seem so pompous with the war on and all. Death and pain have no boundaries, you see."

"Guess my mother was too strict. Habits are hard to change, Henry."

"That didn't hurt did it? Takes a bit of conditioning is all." Henry completed the drinks, walking around the bar with the two glasses and handing one to David. "Here is to the bloody end of Hitler and his crazies."

David raised his glass, clicking it against Henry's, "And the safe return of Anthony and Alexander."

"My fervent prayer and we will never give up hope. Help yourself to a cigar, David," said Henry, selecting one for himself from a cedar box on a side table and offering the box to David.

"Thanks, Henry. It's the one thing I really miss." David removed the wrapper and sniffed the cigar, smelling the deep, rich tobacco aroma. "Havana?" He closed his eyes and rolled the cigar over his tongue, tasting the sweet tobacco before striking a match. The Havana burning in his hand gave off a fragrance that brought back memories of more pleasant times.

"That it is. Can not secure them anymore, even on the black market. I was fortunate in being able to make a substantial purchase before the Blitz. Needless to say, I hoard them more closely than any other war rationed items." Henry puffed quietly, sitting in one of the oversized leather chairs, savoring the fat Cuban. He sipped his scotch while David paced nervously.

"Henry," said David, pausing momentarily.

"Yes, David."

"I, ah. I want to have some kind of memorial for Millie. A marker or something to show where she lies. Something to keep the memory, that she didn't die in vain." Tears ran unchecked as David stared into the glowing coals in the fireplace. "The name Millie Hampton will not be forgotten." He sipped his scotch and took a long draw on the Cuban, while faces flashed before him.

"I think I know what you mean, David. I do have a substantial influence in these parts, when necessary. I know that the disaster crews plan to level the operations area. I think," said Henry, puffing on his cigar and exhausting the smoke slowly, "that it should be turned into a memorial park."

David turned, waving his cigar. "With flower gardens and park benches and walkways with trees everywhere."

Henry added, "And a memorial stone with the names of all those who died in the operations room."

"I think," said David enthusiastically, for now he had some direction, some purpose; "that it should include all the service men and women from Detling who've given their lives. I've got some savings I'd like to put toward it."

"David, we owe you a debt of our lives. For without you Yanks helping, there might not be an England. If you would let me, I would consider it an honor to see to this memorial. It's the least we can do for you and the rest of our Yank friends. I can assure you, your wife, Millie Hampton, will not be forgotten."

"I don't know what to say, Henry. I've never met anyone quite like you."

"It is really quite simple, David. Just say 'yes.'"

"Yes," said David without hesitation. He turned to Sir Henry and raised his glass in salute.

"I think that this calls for another. How about you, David?"

"I concur," said David, smiling as he walked with Henry to the bar.

"I dare say, that smile is very becoming to you, David." Henry poured a liberal amount of scotch into each of their glasses. "This calls for a celebration, such as it may be under the circumstances. I get the feeling that you are an organizer, David, a promoter. And wherever you go there will be a trail of your having been there. I am certain that this park will be only one of many marks you will leave as you travel down the path of life. And now, I bid you a good evening. You may use Bertrum's room. Top of the stairs, first door on your right."

"A very good evening to you, Henry. I think I'll just sit for a spell and enjoy my cigar," said David, sinking into the plush leather chair and holding his glass up.

David sat in front of the fireplace watching the burning coals, sipping his scotch. He let it roll around his tongue, savoring the flavor as it burned down his throat. His stomach felt warm and relaxed and the feeling spread through his body. The room lights were dim and he gazed into the glowing embers of the fire. Smoke from the Cuban curled upward slowly and David drifted into a disembodied, mesmeric state.

He heard the soft, guttural sound of the medicine man chanting a prayer to Wakan Tanka, the Great Spirit of the Sioux. Shadows from the dying fire danced across his aged wrinkled face. His hair was a dull lead-gray color and hung in long braids in front of his rounded shoulders. A breast-work of bones, beads and decorative quills covered his sagging chest. He sat cross-legged in a pair of faded blue jeans. Worn and ripped moccasins covered his tired feet. The smell of sage and juniper from the Dakota Badlands seemed to fill the room.

Rain drummed against the windows outside, beating a sound of voices against the window. Rain-in-the-Face closed his eyes and saw the medicine man wave his pipe over the brilliant embers. The smoke drifted up and Joker sat beside him laughing. His eyes sparkled and he had a large wad of bubble gum which snapped and popped as he chewed with his mouth open. Chief sat opposite Joker on a buffalo robe, smoking quietly on the pipe the medicine man had passed him.

They all rose when Millie walked toward them. She wore a dress of white deer skin that hung past her knees. Long tassels on the bottom of her dress danced rhythmically as she walked. The soft buck skin clung to her body like a second skin, molding every curve. Her dress shimmered in the pale light as she approached, like a ghostly apparition drifting toward them. An elaborate decoration of porcupine quills fanned across her rising and falling chest. Tall, matching deer skin moccasins adorned her feet and were molded to her calves as if they were a part of her body. The moccasins were decorated with beadwork and fringed with wolf fur. As she walked toward the fire, her feet seemed to float, not touching the ground. She sat between Chief and Joker on a plush pile of buffalo robes. The top robe was from a sacred white buffalo.

They turned, looked at David and waved. He watched them, trying to understand what they were saying and reached out toward them. Millie patted the robe beside her and beckoned him to join her.

The medicine man passed an eagle feather over the glowing embers and smoke swirled up. The apparition faded and David called out, "Wait!" Something had disturbed his sleep, and David sat up with a start.

"Oh. Hello there," said Melissa. "Scared the bloody 'ell out of me for a moment there. Henry don't think ladies should drink scotch." She walked over to the dying fire carrying a drink carelessly in her right hand. She wore a long robe that hung to the floor, almost covering her bare feet.

The front of the robe hung open and her left hand in the pocket waved as she gestured while talking. A flimsy gown under the robe accentuated the firm, erect breasts rimmed with dark brown rosettes. Melissa sat on the stone hearth in front of the glowing coals, her bare legs stretched out and crossed in front of her.

"Well, your secret is safe with me," said David, coming awake and sipping his drink. He resented her intrusion having disrupted his vision, and he wished she'd leave. He wanted to be alone, to communicate with Millie, and she was like a chip of sawdust under the eye lid.

Melissa sat up, crossing her legs under her, elbows on spread apart knees, and resting her head on her hands. "You know what really pisses me off? I mean, here we are flying every type of plane built, but we WAAFs can't fly combat! Bullshit. I can fly just as well as any man. But, it's too dangerous. I might get my prissy little ass shot off."

"We need ferry pilots too," said David. "It's a little different when someone's shooting at you. You don't know what real fear is until you've seen your best friend going down in a burning wreck, screaming while he burns to death trapped in the cockpit. Or a brother has his guts shot out while hanging helpless in his parachute. You need to hear the sound of bullets ripping into your kite or bouncing off your bulletproof windscreen. There's not much glory flying a fighter. Most of the time you're just trying to keep from getting your ass shot off and joining the growing number of heroes."

"If only I'd had ammo in the Mustang I was delivering when those Krauts started strafing the field," said Melissa, taking a slug from her scotch. "Sure as fuck, I'd have sent those three bloody bastards back to the fatherland with one way tickets."

"You have to smell death," said David, "to taste it, to live with it. You wake up in the middle of the night with the cold sweats and pretty soon your guts turn into knots every time you climb into the cockpit, then you might become a fighter pilot."

"For your information, Yankee Doodle, my brother's Spitfire blew up in a ball of fire on takeoff. Wanda was killed when a Kraut bomb blew up her barracks...I just happened to be in the area and helped carry bodies from what was left of their building. I found Wanda," said Melissa getting up and walking to the bar. She sloshed scotch in her glass not bothering with the ice or water. Sitting back on the hearth she drank half the glass of the raw amber liquid, letting it settle her nerves. "First I found her head. It was blown off her body. Then I found one hand and half her arm...I knew it was hers from the finger...It had a ring on it like mine." Melissa turned the ring around on the little finger of her right hand. "Sisters' rings, she called them."

David sat half numb, wondering if there was anyone who'd not been a victim of the blood letting. "I'm sorry. I didn't know. I guess each of us lives in the small part of the world allotted to us. When you encounter what we've been through, it's difficult to imagine anyone else having gone through the same or worse."

"Shit. Now you're going to turn into a fucking philosopher. You damn near sound like Henry," said Melissa, draining her glass. "Eat, drink and be merry, for tomorrow you die. Don't know where I heard that, but it's my motto. Shit. My glass is empty and I'm just starting to feel good. How 'bout filling your glass, fly-boy?" said Melissa padding barefoot back to the bar, her gown open.

"I've still got some," said David, drawing on his cigar. It had almost gone out and he sucked on it, bringing the glowing end to life.

"Let me have a draw on your cigar," said Melissa, walking over toward David from the bar. She held her drink out front and bent her head, sipping from the glass as she walked. Her leg brushed David's hand holding his glass as she reached for his cigar. She took a couple of puffs, inhaling deeply, and gave the cigar back to David. "Christ, does that taste good. I'd take one of my own, but I think Henry's got them numbered. Miss it right off the bat, 'e would."

"You can have the rest of mine," said David.

"No. Thanks anyway. Good old Henry would shit if he walked in now. He's from the old school, you know. Good girls aren't supposed to drink or smoke and sure as hell not fuck. So what is left us?"

Disgustedly, David felt his penis pushing against the crotch of his pants. His wife hadn't been dead forty-eight hours and here he was alone in a room with a nearly naked woman who obviously wanted to have sex. He had to get out of there while he could. He was a guest in Sir Henry's home, sitting in his study, drinking his liquor and smoking one of his cigars. Being seduced was one thing, but not in his host's home and certainly not with this mouthy child. He stood clumsily, embarrassed by his erection poking the front of his pants out like a tent pole. "I think I'll turn in. It's been a long day."

David was heading toward the door when Melissa leaned back, her bare legs exposed. "My room is the next one past yours," she said smiling and wetting her lips seductively with her tongue. "The door's unlocked."

Blushing, David closed the door quietly, but not before he heard her call, "Ta-ta. See you around, Yankee Doodle."

David tossed fitfully in the strange bed. The scotch had helped and he would have liked another, but he couldn't stay in the room alone with Melissa. He chuckled thinking of Hap back at The Station. Some day he'd have to concoct an elaborate story for the old man. He rolled over in the huge bed that was far bigger than any he'd ever slept in. He felt lost in it and thought of Millie and their last evening together. They could've had fun in a bed such as this one. He pulled a pillow into his arms, buried his face in it and wept.

Exhaustion finally won, and he slept fitfully. David dreamt of the briefing room. Millie was conducting the briefing. She flipped the cloth cover back on the briefing map and turned to a room filled with women. "This is the dream," and she turned with a pointer indicating a farm house with a white picket fence around it and flower gardens. He heard the sounds of children's voices and the briefing map turned into a playground. He saw himself walking across the lush green grass in the yard, holding a woman's hand. The woman had no face. It was blank. Puzzled, he turned toward Millie, but she had vanished. He looked back at the room full of women who'd come to fill out applications for the dream, but their faces were all blank.

David looked back to the dream chart, but it was changed. There was a blank outline of a woman and, to the side, a chart labeled, FILL IN THE BLANKS. He turned to the audience of blank faces waiting expectantly, then he began marking the chart. HAIR: Strawberry blonde, shoulder length. EYES: Green and sparkling. NOSE: Button nose, small and slightly turned up. LIPS: Full, dark red and moist. FACE: Round, cheeks bulging like laughing bubbles with lots of freckles.

David looked at the faces in the audience but they were still blank. When he turned back to finish his chart, it was Millie's face that'd filled the blank spaces. He heard Millie's voice, "You promised to live the dream."

"No. I can't. The dream is gone, I can't." He clutched the pillow in his arms crying, "I can't. I can't." David awoke and sat up in the bed trying to place where he was.

"David," called Henry from the hallway. He knocked again, "David, are you awake? Breakfast is ready."

"Yes," David called. "Be with you in a minute," he said, struggling into his pants and shirt.

From the stairs he heard voices and Annie called, "David, we're in the breakfast nook." David followed the voices and walked into a bright room with a small round table already set for breakfast. Melissa sat on the far side sipping a cup of hot tea, but with her robe closed and tied. "Please be seated, David," said Annie, pouring him a cup of tea. "Will you be having a bite of breakfast? I'm afraid all we have is kidney pie and potatoes with biscuits."

"That'll be fine," said David. "Millie'd fixed that quite often."

"David," said Annie sitting beside him with her tea. "We have lost four children and it has been quite lonely...you being here has helped ease the pain. We would like to have you stay with us as long as you like. Henry and I both feel like you are a part of us."

David sipped his tea and forked a piece of pie into his mouth, chewing most of it before answering. "I'd like that very much and you have a beautiful home, but I've got to pack Millie's things from the apartment and put them into storage. I won't be needing the apartment anymore."

Henry put his hand on David's arm, "When you have your affairs all taken care of, we would be honored if you would come and stay with us. Besides, you and I have some business to tend to."

David smiled and said, "As soon as I can arrange a three-day leave, I'll ring you up, Henry. But I don't want to be sitting around doing nothing. I did come from a farm and am used to working."

"Oh, we have plenty you can do," said Annie smiling happily as she cleared the dishes from the breakfast nook.

"Well, Mother, I had best be bringing the car around. David, I will drive you into the station," said Henry. "And, if there's anything else we can do...."

When David and Melissa were alone, she said, "I guess I was a little obnoxious last night. I'm sorry. I mean, I didn't know about your wife. I'm just sorry. I hope we can still be friends?"

"Hell, yes," said David, holding out his hand to shake. "And next time you're in Biggin Hill, come by The Station, ask the old man, Hap. He'll know where I'm at, and I'll buy you a scotch and a cigar."

"Deal," said Melissa taking David's hand in hers, gripping it firmly. Still holding his hand she stood and kissed him on the cheek, then fled from the breakfast nook, leaving David sitting alone and wondering.

A Loner

Six days of bereavement leave passed and David felt as though he'd been walking in another of his nightmares. He was adrift in a lifeboat, alone on the ocean not knowing where he was and with no means of propulsion. He'd packed Millie's things and shipped them home for his dad to put in storage until he returned. The landlord had already found someone to move into their apartment. It was as if Millie had never existed. All trace of her had been removed. She was gone, but not forgotten, David vowed, clutching the St. Christopher medal tightly in his fist.

David was ready to return to base, to something familiar. The Station had been unusually quiet and he'd sat alone in his corner sipping a scotch and smoking a cigar. He knew his blood brother watched over Millie's spirit; he'd seen them together with Joker and the medicine man. Chief was the godfather of their unborn child. Was that why they were together? Would their child be born in the spirit world or would he remain forever in the womb? If it were born, he now knew that he would see it with Millie, but he must live the dream.

David finished his drink and slipped out quietly, alone. They were flying to Scotland in the morning for training on some new equipment, and he was ready to get back in the air, back to something familiar.

The drone of his Mustang's engine had a hypnotic effect on David as he led his squadron toward Scotland. It felt good to climb back into the P-51 again, like greeting an old friend. Even though it was a new kite, it was still a Mustang. They'd faced death together and in turn had killed. He had a fondness for the machine, for he'd certainly abused it and still it had saved his life.

Though the Mustang smelled new, it had an old familiarity like the tractor back on the farm. He'd spent many days driving the tractor, plowing, disking and cultivating. Then there was the fall harvest when the family all worked together as one. He and the P-51 had a bonding like his family, and now they were going to learn some different tactics. David remembered his dad bringing home a new piece of equipment and how everyone gathered around while he explained its use and how it worked. Only now, the equipment was four newly-installed 20mm cannons, two in each wing.

The long cannon barrels protruded from the wings like lances and gave the sleek Mustang a clumsy, ugly appearance. Bombs would be hung from the wing shackles when they got to their training station. They would fire the new cannons on drone targets and ground targets such as tanks and trucks. They would practice dive bombing with five hundred pound bombs attached to each wing. Their training would be learning a new way to kill, he thought bitterly.

Nervously, David scanned the skies. Though they were too far north for German fighters to reach them, scanning was a habit, like breathing. Rapidly his eyes searched an imaginary block of space and moved on to the next block. He flew the P-51 subconsciously; trimming, adjusting power, checking his map. They were following the coast along the North Sea, and David scanned ahead for Scarborough, his next check point. He glanced at his wing man flying a few feet off his wing tip. The Canadian waved and David gave a salute back. Behind Lance flew the new kid, Jose. The Mexican joked, "I love dos Americanos. Dey sing my song, 'Jose, can you see...', and everybody stands up."

David grinned to himself, then the smile froze on his face. Something flashed out over the North Sea. A reflection of sunlight like a signal beacon. He locked his eyes on the area and began his methodical search of the block. There were shadows on the water, then David saw a dozen Junker bombers. They were sneaking in from over the North Sea, flying only a few feet off the water to avoid detection. All the defense watches were down on the Channel facing France. The bombers were sneaking in undetected, coming in behind the coastal watchers. David didn't even know if there were watchers this far North.

"Pigskin, Red-one. Bandits two-o'clock low. Turn on me, line abreast for a strafing run." He switched his radio back to "A" channel, "Control, Pigskin, Red-one. Twelve bandits approaching the coast just south of Scarborough. We're attacking."

"Pigskin, Red-one, control here. Shall we scramble a backup?"

"Control, you'd better scramble'em. We've been refitted with 20mm cannon and nobody's used'em yet. Don't know what we can do, if we can stop them. Pigskin, out."

"Very good, Pigskin. Backup scrambled, listening out."

David switched back to his "B" channel, "This is Pigskin, pick your targets and give'em everything you've got. We'll see what these cannons can do." David was keyed up, his finger tensed on the firing trigger. Just a little closer. The Mustang screamed as its three metal propeller blades went supersonic. They plunged seaward in a near vertical dive, wind whistling around the canopy. Reaching maximum speed, the P-51 buffeted and David eased back on the throttle. A few drops of oil had leaked unto the Allison engine and he could smell the hot oil as the engine heated up. He dove toward the leading Junker, attacking from its forward port quarter. His ears felt the pressure from the steep descent and he held his nose, blowing out to clear them. The steep dive angle would put them above the Krauts' normal line of vision.

David centered his sight pip on the lead Junker. It was a crossing deflection shot and he placed the first ring in his site pip on the wing root, leading the JU-88. Five hundred yards and closing at four hundred miles per hour. He tightened his finger on the trigger, firing the four 20mm cannons. The P-51 bucked, as if he'd run into severe turbulence. Lances of fire shot out of the Mustang's long cannon barrels. Fumes from the twin-cannons' burning gun powder seeped back into the cockpit. It was a smell of the hunt, as they closed for the kill. He could feel his heart pounding in excitement, and blood surged through his veins in anticipation. Sweat broke out on his face, running into his eyes unnoticed.

Less than two hundred yards. David watched the tracers from his cannons arcing downward toward the Junker. The white lances seemed to wrap around the bomber's nose. Hot cannon shells hit the water and exploded in vaporous geysers. The nose gunner swung his gun toward the Mustangs. Cannon shells hit the nose of the bomber and it exploded in a shower of glass.

David saw the shocked look on the face of the Junker pilot before his glass canopy disintegrated. He could see daylight through the holes in the JU-88 where his cannon shells were striking.

David released the trigger, jerking back on the stick. The P-51 climbed up over the Junker. A fireball rose up from the Junker, engulfing the Mustang. The force of the blast drove David down in his seat. The engine coughed and sputtered. Where in the hell was the water? He only had a few feet above the sea to maneuver. All he could see was a wall of yellow flame. He ignored the searing heat inside his cockpit, concentrating on his instruments.

Wings level, his nose was up in a hard climb. David leveled the nose and broke out in the clear. He advanced the throttle and the Allison responded. He snapped his head around, looking for the Junkers. He rolled hard to the port and pulled the stick back in his lap. The Mustang flew in a tight turn a few feet off the water. Tracers shot past his canopy. Instinctively David jinxed, rolled hard right, leveled and kicked the rudder left while jerking the stick back then forward. He kept flying an irregular jinxing pattern, looking for the Junkers.

His eyes followed the stream of tracers that searched for his Mustang. Six hundred yards out three JU-88's were heading back to sea. David centered his sight pip on the trailing Junker, ignoring the occasional ping of bullets striking his P-51. The Junker's wings filled the bars on his sight pip and his finger clamped down on the trigger. The Mustang bucked from the recoil of its cannons. Ribbons of fire reached out, looking lazily for the fleeing Krauts. Cannon shells disappeared inside the trailing Junker. The bomber nosed down, striking the water. It bounced once and broke in half. The two separate pieces turned, flipped into the air and spun, striking the water and skipping back into the air.

David thought of how, as kids back home, they'd skip flat stones across the farm pond. They'd count the skips trying to see who'd get the most skips before the stone sank.

The last two Junkers were fleeing across the North Sea, flying so close to the water that wakes were created by their propeller tips disturbing the surface. David was sighting on the closest bomber. The Junker's starboard propeller struck the water, pulling it down. The wing tip hit and the Junker cartwheeled, breaking into pieces. In less than a second the crew had been killed and the bomber destroyed. One careless mistake and it was over. How many families would be notified that their husband, their father, their brother was missing in action? All because of one crazy fanatic in power.

The last Junker came into his sight pip. The distance closed between them, but the German was no longer firing back. David could see the gunner's face looking back at him from the rear gunnery station. The face had no features, just blank staring eyes, like his dream; he could fill in the face with what he wanted it to be. It was as though the German had resigned himself to his fate and sat waiting for the inevitable. David closed to within fifty yards of the JU-88.

David thought of Henry: "They're people just like you and me. They're fathers, brothers, and have wives, mothers and children. They have families and love and hate, hurt and die same as we do. They're just doing a job, same as we're doing ours." He eased his throttle back and raised the nose of his Mustang. He fired a warning burst over the bomber's canopy with his cannons. Frantically, the gunner waved something white, like a rag or piece of paper.

The Junker pulled up and dropped his gear, turning towards the English coast. David slowed further and took up a position below and a hundred yards behind. "Red-two, this is Pigskin. Where you at?"

"Hey Pigskin, we're just over the coast wrapping up the turkey shoot. We kind of lost you when your P-51 disappeared in the explosion."

"I'm about five miles out, escorting a Junker back."

"What? What'n the hell're you doing?"

"I'm bringing in the spoils of war. I got me a Junker," said David. "They surrendered, Lance, and I'm escorting'em back to the nearest airdrome."

"Pigskin, y'all think that's a good idea?" drawled Dixie. "Shit, ah mean it could ah been the same sneaky bastards that bombed Detling."

"I'm right behind'em and got my finger resting on the trigger," said David through gritted teeth.

"Green-one, I think you'd better waste'em. They ain't nutt'n but a bunch of worthless friggin' Krauts," said Storm'n Norman. "Three seconds on your firing button, Pigskin. That's all it'll take and we'll be done with these fucking square-heads."

"What's the matter with you guys?" said David. "Haven't you ever heard of the Geneva Convention? They surrendered. If I shoot'em now, it'd be murder."

"Y'all think them frigging Heinies'd give y'all ah break if'n they was the ones behind yah?" asked Dixie. "Y'all muddled up, Pigskin. Y'all forgetin' Joker an Chief? Or, maybe they's killing Miss Millie was just an accident?"

David's eyes watered and tears spilled uncontrollably. They had no right. He was the quarterback and called the plays. His hand tightened its grip on the stick, his finger caressed the trigger nervously. Images of ghosts from the past danced before his eyes. He tried to make out what they were saying, but their words were unintelligible. He groped for his St. Christopher's medal with his left hand and clutched it tightly. Nothing would change whether he shot the Krauts or not. Nothing would bring Millie back. Nor Chief or Joker.

Norman maneuvered his Mustang alongside David. "You're tired, Pigskin. Take a rest. Let me burn these fucking Krauts and we'll get on to Scotland!"

David looked at his friend and shook his head, no. He spoke through clenched teeth, his face contorted in bitterness, "I'm still the quarterback. I'm calling the shots. You want to be on my team, you'll play my game. Now get back to your position."

"Blue-one, you get on the Junker's tail. I'll lead'em into Scarborough. I checked with control, and they want the Junker intact as long as the Germans are willing to give it up without a fight," said Pigskin, backing up his play with a call from the bench.

"Y'all needn't worry, Pigskin. I'm on this fucking Kraut like two ducks making love."

"I'm switching over to 'A' channel, everybody monitor," said David. "Scarborough control, this is Pigskin flight, we're five miles out for landing."

"Pigskin flight, you are cleared to land," control paused, then continued. "with your escort. We have a reception committee for your chap's party."

David lined up with the main runway, checking in his rear-facing mirror. He moved his head around trying to find the bomber in the small, flat, rectanglar mirror. The Junker looked menacing, flying right on his tail. It was as though he was before a firing squad with a target pinned over his heart. He wasn't sure they were out of ammo just because they'd quit firing. He had to force himself to fly straight and level. It was hard not to start jinxing, out of the Germans' line of fire. He'd never been this close to one that wasn't firing at him or one he was attacking.

A mile from the field he pulled up and watched the JU-88 slow for its final approach. The bomber's landing speed was slower than the Mustang's. "Pigskin, Red-one. Everyone form on me, and we'll circle the field and land. We're going to need some fuel and ammo."

"Blue-one. Maybe I'd better stay behind Heinie here in case he tries something funny."

"He's too slow, Dixie. You'll stall out. Besides, where's he going with twelve P-51s less than a mile away?" David pulled up to pattern elevation and began circling the field. He watched the bomber approach the threshold of the runway. He glanced in his rear-facing mirror. His squadron was lined up behind, following his lead.

David started his turn on the far side of the field to downwind, paralleling the runway. He glanced down to see if the bomber was clear of the runway.

"Pigskin! The Kraut's flying across the field," yelled Dixie over the R/T.

David rolled his Mustang over and slammed his throttle through the gate pushing his stick forward. "Get that Kraut bastard! He's still got his bombs!" David screamed into the radio.

Large hanger buildings loomed ominously on the far side of the field. They were Spitfire assembly plants. The Junker was a thousand yards ahead of David. He couldn't wait or the Junker would be dropping its bombs. He clamped his finger down on the cannon's trigger. Nothing happened. He was out of shells.

David shrieked into his R/T, "Shoot that frigging Kraut. Now!" He tried his trigger again, but his cannons were silent. Desperately, he pulled his trigger on the 20mm cannon again and again. He jerked back on the elevators and kicked in left rudder trying to overtake the Junker, but his range was too far.

Eleven streams of 20mm cannon tracers swept out from the attacking Mustangs, crisscrossing the gap to the Junker. David watched in horror as the first bomb was released from the belly rack of the Junker. It dropped slowly, tumbling end over end. The bomb disappeared into the roof of the first hanger building.

A second bomb dropped from the external wing racks when the first bomb exploded inside the Spitfire factory. The sides of the building seemed to expand outward like a kid's balloon being blown up. Showers of glass flew outward. The building collapsed in on itself. Smoke appeared and then a blinding flash of fire.

The Junker was climbing, trailing smoke. A string of small bombs dropped from the belly bay. The JU-88 banked hard to port over a row of buildings on the south side of the field and released a second string of bombs from the belly bay. The Junker then turned hard to starboard away from the line of falling bombs.

One of the Mustang's cannon shells found the Junker and fire blazed from its left engine. Something dropped from the belly, and a parachute blossomed immediately. A second and a third chute appeared. The JU-88 dove, leveled out above the trees, turning out to sea. The bomber's engine blazed, looking like a Roman candle. Its fuel tank exploded, and the wing separated from the Junker. For a moment the bomber seemed to fly on one wing, then it rolled and plunged into a row of trees.

David circled the burning pyre. Though he was sick to his stomach, he had to admire the German pilot. The Krauts fooled them completely; it was like a new football play that no one had seen. The execution and timing had to be perfect, and it was a play that'd been thought up in a moment of desperation. David tried to reason it out. They'd had three choices as he saw it. Had they landed, they would have safely spent the rest of the war in a

British prison camp. They could have ditched at sea and hoped for a German patrol boat to pick them up. They had chosen their only other alternative, to fight to the death.

David turned, leading his squadron back to the field. Columns of black smoke marked the aerodrome. He was low on fuel and would have to complete a combat report. He worried about the outcome. What would he say in the report? It had been his decision to bring the bomber back, even though control concurred. It had been his decision. No one had thought about the bombs, only of killing four more Germans. If he'd listened to Dixie, none of this would have happened.

Fires burned out of control in the hanger buildings. David slowed on final, leading his squadron in for landing. Black smoke rolled across the field, partially obscuring the runway. They had no choice. They were out of fuel. Wind gusted across the field, and David held his approach for the upwind side. He crabbed into the cross wind, lowered his gear and put down half flaps. A gust caught his Mustang, and he turned into it. Air speed 120 mph; he didn't want to slow too soon with the wind. Gear down and full flaps, he flew the P-51 in with power. Over the fence he reduced his power slightly. Speed 100 mph. He rolled his ailerons into the wind and straightened the P-51 out with his rudder, dancing on the controls to compensate for gusts. His left main wheel touched down, and he eased his nose forward, planting both main wheels firmly on the grass.

A WAAF waved David's squadron into parking and climbed up on the wing before he shut his engine down. She was dressed in mechanic's coveralls and had her hair tied up in a bandanna. A streak of grease was smeared across what could have been considered a pretty face. "Stay with your kite, sir. Control wants you gone as soon as we can get you refueled," she snapped, her mouth contorted in a sneer.

"We'll need rearming. Kind of thought we'd get a bit of a rest," said David, unfastening his safety and climbing out on the wing.

"Don't have shells for cannon on this base," said the WAAF bitterly. "Your squadron let a single German Junker bomb our field. More than three hundred people were working in those hangers. Don't wear out your welcome here," she snapped. She spun on her heel and marched stiffly away.

David jumped down from the wing of his Mustang, laying his parachute on the port main wheel.

"What the hell's going on?" stormed Dixie, walking over to Pigskin. "If y'all'd finished that Kraut when you'd had ah chance, wouldn't none ah this happened!"

"It's my fault, I never thought about their bombs. I should have kept the squadron behind him until the bomber was on the ground." said David, his face drawn. Horrified, he watched the hangers burn.

"It's a damn good thing you talked to control before we brought that Kraut in or we'd be in deep shit," said Storm'n Norman, walking over with his chute flopping against the back of his legs. "I mean, hell, they wanted that Kraut kite. Well they got it. So Pigskin, what're we going to do now?"

"Let's get the hell out of here and on to Scotland." said David worriedly, as he turned and headed for his kite. He strapped on his chute and climbed up on the wing.

An old man working as a fitter helped him with his safety straps then tapped him on the shoulder, "Good luck to you, sir."

"Thanks," said David. "After what happened today and that WAAF sergeant chewing me out, I'll need it."

"Oh, don't mind her, sir. She's got the rag on full time, if you know what I mean. Snippy little vixen. Ever since her old man was left behind at Dunkirk," said the fitter, ignoring the burning hangers across the field. He'd obviously seen worse disasters than a few hangers blown up. His round fat face grinned a near-toothless grin. "Hell, he's probably shacked up with some French wench. Least ways, that's what I'd be doing if I had to come back to that!"

"Well, I was wondering if I'd forgot to brush my teeth this morning, or what?" said David, still in shock over the bombing. Where were his guides? Had the spirits abandoned him? Where had he failed? He'd called the play and it failed -- they'd lost the game because of him.

The old man chuckled, "Off wid you now, fore she comes back for another bite." The fitter jumped down from the wing like a young kid and marched around to the front of the Mustang, giving David the start-engine signal.

David sat alone in The Station with a half empty glass of scotch in front of him. They'd completed their training in Scotland on the use of the cannons in the Mustangs and learned the new techniques for ground strafing. The dive bombing was completely new to them, and their accuracy had astounded everyone at the training base. Their new targets were now going to be enemy troop movements, trains, bridges and fuel depots. Anything and everything that the Germans could use would be destroyed. David was tired. It seemed like he never had a chance to rest...ever since Millie....

How long had it been? Less than two weeks and yet it seemed like Millie had never existed. As if she'd only been a fantasy of his imagination; except he had the St. Christopher medal, the one tangible thing he had to show that she had even been a part of his life. He drained his glass and banged it on the bar signaling, Hap for another.

"You can't talk anymore?" said Hap contemptuously.

"Need another drink, barkeep."

"Name's Hap, to you. I'm not barkeep, nor your mother."

"You going to gimmie 'nother drink, or what?" said David. One more drink and he would drift into a fog -- then he could be alone. Then he could rest. "Hap," he said with resignation.

"This a one-sided conversation, or can anyone jump on the iceberg?" asked Raymond, sliding up on the stool next to Pigskin. He puffed slowly on his pipe, looking at Hap through a blue haze of smoke, then glancing at Pigskin out the sides of his eyes.

"Jeez. All right. One more and that's it. This ain't a nursery for mamma's babies," said Hap, grabbing David's glass and filling it with scotch.

"Old man's kind ah crotchety tonight," said Raymond after Hap went down the bar to wait on another customer. Slowly puffing on his pipe and sipping his ale, he waited quietly for David to respond.

David gulped his scotch, spilling some on the bar and down the front of his shirt. "I mean, who in the hell's he think he is, Spike? The King of England, or what? So big friggin' deal, he shot down a couple of Krauts with his sling shot, and now he's David going after Goliath."

"No," said Raymond, "he's just like you. Hap came to England from Wyoming and enlisted in the army. In the Great War, he flew the finest fighter built. Not only that, he was the best. So you see, Pigskin, both of you came to England to help fight in a war. You both were pilots flying against the invading Huns. You both flew the best aircraft England had at the time and are the best pilots in your own squadron. Each in his own time."

"Well, what right's he got getting on my case? He's not my mother, for Christ sake," David argued.

"Pigskin, I think he's jealous."

David gulped some more scotch and sat thinking about what Raymond had said. He was drunk and knew it, but tried to act sober. "What'n the hell's he got to be jealous 'bout, Spike?"

"You don't know him, do you, Pigskin?"

"Who'er you trying to shit, Spike? Hell, I know Hap. He brings us our drinks every day. Pokes into your lives and struts around like a father confessor." David drained his glass and banged it down on the bar.

"As you know, I've been taking notes on Hap for a story." Raymond puffed on his pipe. "Not only was he the leading Ace during the Great War, he lost his wife and two kids to the war as well."

"How'd he lose'em to the war? The damn war was fought in France." David swayed on the bar stool.

"Giselle was French. You know how Hap's always kidding about 'those French babes?' Well, Giselle would have put the best of them to shame. Hap showed me her picture once. She was something else," said Raymond puffing on his pipe. "Just from her picture, she was prettier than anything I've ever seen. She made Rita Hayworth look like a high school kid. They had a son, five, and a daughter, three, and Giselle was expecting their third child. Giselle wanted to be with her mother and father until after the baby was born. So she went back to France while Hap continued fighting the Bosch."

"Why'd she go back to France when there was a war being fought there? Sounds kind ah dumb to me," David mumbled into his empty glass.

Raymond struck a match and held it to his pipe, puffing until it relit. "They were a long way from the fighting at the time and thought they were safe. The Germans made an end run around a supposedly impregnable line, and there was a complete collapse of the entire French front. The leading elements spearheading the German advance are the toughest fighters anywhere. The thugs, the street fighters, brawlers, criminals; you name it. They're given uniforms and weapons and turned loose on society. It'd be like turning a weasel loose in the hen house," Raymond said.

"What happened, Spike? Were they shelled or gassed or what? David was somewhat sober as he listened to Raymond.

"From what the neighbors found after the Boche had left, Giselle was dragged out in the yard. Her clothes were ripped off, and she was beaten and raped. Probably by every German there. The two children and her mother and father must've tried to resist. Their bodies were found in various parts of the farm yard bayoneted. They'd been stabbed repeatedly and left in the yard bleeding while Giselle was raped." Raymond sucked noisily on his cold pipe. He struck a match and puffed, drawing the fire down into the pipe, rekindling the sweet-smelling tobacco.

"Guess I kind of know where the old man's coming from now," said David, staring into his empty glass. "But, why's he always coming down on me?"

"He likes you, Pigskin. In his mind, you're the spittin' image of his son that was murdered. He knows what you're going through, and the only way to survive is to be tough. Hell, you're the quarterback, the leader, you know what it's like. You get knocked down and you pick yourself up and keep driving down the field. No matter what the opposition, what the odds are, you pick yourself up and keep fighting."

"You two look like a couple of old women, sitting there gabbing away by yourselves," said Hap, shuffling over and leaning opposite them on the bar chewing on a toothpick.

Raymond tapped his pipe in the ashtray, knocking out the cold ash and replacing it with fresh tobacco from a leather pouch in his jacket. "Solving world problems, Hap."

"Hey barkeep," said David, banging his empty glass on the bar. "Got any that hot, black shit you keep under the bar? I got to fly in a few hours, better pour down a couple cups of coffee." David grinned at Hap seeing he'd roused a spark of fire in the old man. "Hap," he added.

"'Spects I might, boy. Lemme just rinse my teeth off with it first," said Hap, slipping his teeth out and smiling at them with his toothless gums. He headed down the bar carrying his teeth in one hand.

The steady beat of the Mustang's engine was soothing to David. His head throbbed with a massive hangover even though he'd been sucking oxygen since he'd climbed into the P-51. The Channel passed rapidly, only a hundred feet below, dark and sinister looking. The waters churned up like an angry demon reaching up, trying to grasp them and drag them down to a watery grave. The clouds above them were a sickly greenish-yellow, rolling restlessly as a thunderstorm built over the Channel.

They were flying in a coffin box. Death waited them at every turn, but then what was life but a short journey toward the inevitable? Once you accepted that fact, there was no more fear of death. David no longer cared if he lived through the war. He could not imagine going home, back to the farm. It would never be the same. He grasped the St. Christopher medal Millie had given him and heard her voice: "We promised each other with our pledge of love. You must live the dream."

Rain pelted the windscreen of David's Mustang, sounding like the medicine man tapping his drum to some incantation. The squadron flew on, visibility dropping to less than a quarter mile. David flew on instruments and the rest of his squadron followed his lead, each flying only feet off the wing of the plane ahead. When he glanced down the only thing he could see was the churning water below; then the bull appeared through the driving rain. The bull had a chip missing from one horn. It looked at David then swung his head around and headed off to the left. He heard someone call

"Pigskin" and heard Joker's hoarse laugh. Leading the squadron, he banked to port, following Chief's totem. He imagined he could smell smoke from the medicine man's red-clay pipe as they drove on through the pounding rain.

The sky lightened and the French coast appeared bright and sunny as they broke out in the clear. David led the squadron up to a thousand feet for better visibility as they left the Channel behind. Green vineyards passed below, and David thought of Monique and Father Paquette and wondered if they were still alive. After the war...if he made it.... He scanned ahead for any possible targets. They flew over a hay field, and David thought of his mom and dad back on the farm.

Funny, David thought, why was the field cut? It was too early for hay, unless..."Pigskin, Red-one, let's swing back and look at that last field again. I think the Germans might be using it for an airfield."

David rolled the Mustang to port, standing it on its wing. He felt the g forces from the turn and thought bitterly about being taken off active air combat for ground attacks. Would he ever again battle the yellow-nosed devils? How would he find the one who'd murdered Joker? The field loomed ahead; it had clear approaches on both ends for takeoffs and landings. Dark silhouettes, looking like hay stacks, bordered both sides of the field. David dropped his nose and dove, leveling out above the trees.

At tree top level, David could see what had been hay stacks were camouflaged ME-109s. "Blue-one and Green-one, take the left side," said David into his R/T as he lined up on the right side of the field. Rows of grapes flashed below in a green blur as they streaked in over a vineyard. David worked his ailerons and rudder pedals together lining his sight pip up with the first Messerschmitt. The ME-109 grew until it filled his sight bars and he fired his 20mm cannons. Four streams of burning white hell scribed paths down to the stationary targets.

It was like shooting ducks in the Dakota corn fields. Mallards would fly in to feed and gorge themselves until they had difficulty flying. David pulled the nose up and fired on the second target. The ground passed in a blur a few feet below. On target, he fired again, pulled up, turned, dropping his nose, centered and fired again.

A tower of fire rose directly in his flight path. Like a genie appearing magically out of a bottle, it jumped out at him. David banked hard to his port. He stood the P-51 on its wing until it was perpendicular. His left wing tip was only inches from striking the ground. The fields passed in a blur of green and brown. He was too close to avoid the boiling tower of fire. Heat blistered the paint on his P-51 as he plunged into the red inferno. The plexiglass canopy crazed, turning it cloudy. The inferno, like a vacuum, sucked all the oxygen from the air. Inside the firestorm, the Mustang's engine quit. David choked, unable to breath. His lungs felt as though they would burst. Clumsily he fumbled for his oxygen mask. He sucked greedily on the mask feeling the cooling oxygen instantly soothing his burning lungs.

Instinctively, David looked to his instruments and leveled the Mustang. Then he was clear of the fire. The thermal updraft from the fire had carried him up a thousand feet and he dove to regain his airspeed. The P-51's three-bladed propeller labored, then began to windmill faster and faster. David pumped the primer and advanced the throttle slowly. The ground was coming up alarmingly fast. All he could see was a blur of green out the forward windscreen. He was too low to bail out; he'd have to try and belly land.

David pulled the nose up and jerked the release catches of his canopy. The wind caught the three paneled canopy and ripped it from the Mustang. He pumped the primer again and again, the Allison sputtered and labored gasping for oxygen like a drowning victim. The controls felt mushy and unresponsive. A hedge row of trees loomed ahead and seemed to grow taller and taller the closer he came. He pulled back on the stick and felt a buffeting as the wing approached the stall point. He slammed the throttle through the gate to full emergency power. Instantly the twelve-cylinder Allison responded.

David eased the stick forward, gingerly playing the controls as the P-51 picked up speed. The wall of trees became an impossible barrier. David banked slightly and aimed the Mustang so the cockpit would pass between the two largest trees. He grabbed the flap handle and jerked it upward, dropping his flaps full. The Mustang jumped up as though it'd been kicked from behind.

Stick back, the Mustang struggled over the trees. The three-bladed metal prop chopped a path through the tops of the green canopy. He was in the clear. The P-51 stalled and rolled to his left. David pushed the stick forward and stood on the right rudder. Torque from the straining Allison started to roll the stalled fighter. David eased the throttle back to half, and the P-51 straightened out. Again the ground rose to greet him like a bride from the wedding bed. It had some magnetic force drawing him down. He thought of Millie running through a throng of people, in the crowd-packed London station, to embrace him. The temptation was real, in a second it would be all over, and they would be together again.

David heard voices: "You promised to live the dream," Millie admonished.

"You got to be tough boy if'n yea goin'na make it," Hap said, his face scrunched up.

"When you're down, you got to pick yourself up and start all over again," Raymond coached.

He was the quarterback and he had the ball. He automatically jerked the stick back and slammed the throttle full forward. The P-51 seemed to leap upward driving him down on his seat pack parachute. The tough fighter struggled to stay in the air. The heavy P-51 sank lower. A cushion of air between the ground and his wing buoyed him up like an inflated rubber raft.

David nursed the controls, trying to hold the Mustang in the air. Green leaves and vines flew up into and over his open cockpit, as the metal propellers chewed a path through the tops of the grapes. David eased the stick back, drawing the flaps up in increments. At the far end of the field he climbed up and rolled on his side, looking back at what could have been his burial sight. A row was torn through the grape vines as though an excavator had dug a ditch through them.

David rolled out and looked around for the rest of his squadron. He was alone. The R/T was dead. He turned toward the Channel and climbed into the protection of the towering cumulus.

The Dream

"Hey boys," said Raymond, greeting everyone in The Station in his deep bass voice, a pipe clamped between his teeth. He hung his English flat hat and top coat on the coat rack by the door. "I hear you had quite a mission."

"Hell, y'all should ah been there," said Dixie. "Those Squareheads never got off the ground."

"Wiped out the whole damn squadron, Spike," said Norman, signaling Hap for another ale. "Shit, it was just like a training run. We caught 'em sittin' on the crapper. They never got off a shot, and we didn't get so much as a scratch."

"Except for Pigskin," said Lance. The Canadian sat sipping his ale and lit a cigarette.

"Dis is true," added Jose. "If me and dis Canadian had been behind him...well, I'd be on a one way trip back to Mexico."

"Where is Pigskin?" Raymond knocked the cold ashes from his pipe and drew a pouch of fresh tobacco from the pocket of his tweed jacket. "He should be in on the celebration."

"He's down the end ah the bar, talking to the dead, he is." O'Leary sat his mug down and puffed on his cigar before continuing. "We got separated after the fuel depot blew up in his face."

"Separated, shit," said Lance. "We all figured he was a goner. I mean, the last thing we saw, his Mustang disappeared in a ball of fire. O'Leary brought us back across the channel."

"And we was damn lucky to make 'er. Fog down to the water she was. Had to land at Hawkinge and still don't know how we found that." O'Leary took a sip of ale. "Waited almost six hours for the blaming fog to lift before we could get back."

The Canadian chuckled to himself, "And when we landed, there sat Pigskin's Mustang. Burnt black as hell. His canopy was crazed from the heat, what was left of it and he had grape vines packed up in the engine. Claims Millie brought him back; he never saw the runway until his wheels touched down."

"You believing that shit?" said O'Leary puffing his cigar. "You're gettin' as daffy as he is, fly'n round in this bloody fog wid some spook whispering in his ear."

"All right, O'Leary. Maybe he is feeling a little battle fatigue, but aren't we all? Besides, his kite was sitting out there hours before we showed up," said Lance, defending Pigskin.

"Congratulations on a successful mission and everyone making it back," said Raymond. "Hap, set the boys up a round on me. I'll mosey on up and see if I can join in on the seance."

Pigskin sat with his elbows resting on the bar, his chin propped on his hands. His eyes were closed and a mug of ale sat in front of him, untouched.

"This a private sitting or can anyone join in?" asked Raymond sliding his mug down the bar and climbing up on a stool next to David. He struck a match with his thumb nail and sucked noisily on the pipe, puffing blue smoke as the tobacco relit. "Heard a rumor you brought Woody some Mustang parts. The way I hear it, you flew them in."

David spread his fingers apart on his left hand and looked between them at Raymond. "Just a vicious rumor, Spike. Don't believe a word of it." He put his hands down, his eyes bright, laughed and sipped his ale. "You wouldn't believe anything that pack of mealy-mouthed novices told you, would you?"

"You know me, Pigskin. I write the story no matter what. Of course, I always try to go to the source. But if the source isn't available or won't talk...well, I write with what I have," said Raymond.

"Tell me what you think you know, and then I'll tell you what happened," David replied.

"We pretty much figured out what happened after the fuel depot blew up in your face; need a few descriptive phrases on how you rearranged the French country side. What I really want to know is how you found your way back to the field. We were fogged in, I mean thicker'n pea soup right down to the ground," said Raymond. He drew a couple of quick puffs, "And you actually landed in this crap. Hell, the sea gulls were walking!"

"I don't want to talk about it, Spike. Okay?" said David, turning his mug nervously in his hands.

"No, it's not okay. If there's some psychic phenomenon or spiritual manifestation, I want to know about it. Come on Pigskin. This is Spike. There's nothing you can't tell me. If you don't want me to write it, say so, but I want to know how you flew in when nobody else could. Pretend we're in the locker room." Raymond sucked noisily on his pipe, keeping the ember burning.

"Millie brought me in, Spike."

Raymond puffed quietly on his pipe, blowing blue smoke up towards a model fighter.

"See," said David. "You think I'm crazy too!"

"No. I'm just trying to visualize what you've told me. Does she tell you to turn right or descend and bring the power back or what? Can you hear her voice? Have you seen Millie?"

"I've seen her, Spike. I've also seen Joker and Chief." David sipped his ale while Raymond puffed quietly on his pipe. "Chief is my blood brother, you remember. I am Rain-in-the-Face. Crossing the Channel, we ran into a thunderstorm. Rain was beating against the windscreen and I couldn't see the water below. Chief's totem, a bull, appeared and headed off to our left. I turned, following, and we broke out in the clear, right on the French coast."

"So, you followed this totem symbol you saw in the sky, and it led you out of the bad weather. What kind of a symbol does Millie have?"

David pulled the St. Christopher medal from inside his shirt and held it in his hand. "Millie gave this to me. She said it would always bring me safely back to her. It would protect me, and she would be with me always."

"You know, Pigskin, that the boys in your squadron don't exactly believe this talking to the spirits. They think you're going a little wacky, know what I mean?"

"They're just scared, Spike. Half the time, they're scared shitless they're going to be dead before noon. The rest of the time they've watched so many die they don't give a damn."

"Every man in your squadron has at least one kill. They didn't get those because they were scared," said Raymond. "A little fear can give you a lot of respect and caution. Hell, if I was going up to face someone in a shoot out, I'd be scared shitless. I don't know how anyone does it day after day, wondering if today is the day your number will come up."

"I don't mean scared of fighting. They're scared of dying. When you have a fear of death, you make mistakes. It only takes one mistake and it's all over." David sipped his ale, rolling it around his tongue tasting its bitterness, then spoke quietly. "I don't believe there's anyone among us who knows no fear. When a Sioux boy becomes a man, he must first learn to put aside his fear of death. I went forth on such a quest."

"So David, tell me how you became a man," said Raymond, sucking on his cold pipe.

And David began....

It was one summer that I spent with my grandfather in the Badlands on the reservation. I set forth with my pony on my journey as a boy and returned a man. I had a buckskin bag of dried jerky grandmother had shown me how to make, and a water flask, and I rode from his place before the sun awoke. I rode all day, munching on the jerky and sipping water, stopping only to rest my horse. That evening, I made a small fire with my flint and steel and rolled up in my deer skin robe. It was a clear night, and I lay there shivering alone. At sunrise, I awoke chilled and ate some jerky. Through the summer, my body had grown lean and sinewy, and my muscles rippled like a taut bow string. The world took on a sheen of newness, of magic, a timelessness in which I absorbed all being through my pores.

I felt a sense of yearning and my pulse quickened with a newfound sense of adventure. What would I encounter? Whom would I meet? What dangers lay ahead?

Sunset reigned over the rolling hills, and for the first time in my life I surveyed the many-hued event unhindered. I went most of the day without water, and sitting alone before my fire, I consumed the last of my jerky. My pony looked a little worse for wear. The second day ended without a single encounter with man or a dangerous animal against whom I could test my manhood.

I slept fitfully and the old familiar Badlands sounds no longer soothed my ears. I awoke to find the morning filled with soreness and thirst. My enthusiasm and confidence were quickly fading. Perhaps this was only a boy's folly, and I was not yet ready to be a man, I thought.

At two hands before noon, I found a small creek and quenched my thirst, but my stomach complained at the lack of food. At least my pony had plenty to eat, and he drank from an alkali creek.

My trek continued, but the sun seemed to beat down harder and my joints ached. My buckskin breeches rubbed skin raw, and my pony kept trying to turn around and go home. The sun rested once again, and I slept on the hard cold prairie grass. The dawn found me with my tongue swollen and dry and a terrible emptiness in my belly. My pony had wandered away during the night. I found enough strength to walk until I found my pony back at the watering hole and dragged myself astride. My pony had eaten the green grasses around the water hole and showed fresh strength. We wandered aimlessly throughout the day, alone and adrift on the vast prairie, but I grew weaker by the hour. I pursued my manhood, but now I was pursued by death. I thought of someone finding my bleached bones here on the prairie as I trudged wearily toward the setting sun.

I was never to be a warrior. I would meet death as a child and then I fell, too weak to rise. My pony whinnied, and I struggled to roll over. I raised my head and saw two feet, clad in moccasins, standing before me. Above the moccasins hung fringed buckskin breeches. I was certain my mind was playing tricks on me as I gazed upward. A mighty warrior stood before me, arms crossed over his chest-plate of wooden beads, muscular shoulders bare. I felt his dark penetrating eyes staring at me, looking through me. The face was a wooden mask with a fierce, hooked nose. I struggled to my feet and stammered. The warrior handed me an animal skin containing water, and I grabbed it, pulling the stopper and desperately sucking the water. The stranger grabbed the skin and took it from me.

"You have no discipline, boy!" said the warrior. "And you think yourself ready for manhood!"

I looked down with embarrassment at the reprimand. My eyes fixed themselves on the powerful man's moccasins, and I asked him who he was?

"Do you not know me?"

I shook my head, benumbed and confused.

"I see you have a pony," said the stranger. "If you let me ride behind you, I will share my water and help you find that which you seek."

How do you know what I seek, I asked?

"A wise warrior knows many things. Perhaps I know you better than you know yourself."

I reached for the water skin and his eyes glinted with bemusement as he handed it to me. This time I drank with self-restraint. And I said, We shall camp here and ride at first light.

"No," said the Warrior, "I ride at night."

We mounted as the sun's last rays painted the horizon with shades of red and orange. To the east stood the huge disk of the full moon. "One more thing," said the warrior mounted behind me. "You asked who I am. That is something every warrior must know. It is something you must know. If you do not guess who I am by the time the moon sets, I shall kill you and leave your body for the coyotes."

I looked down and saw a large obsidian hunting dagger in the warrior's hand. Its formidable blade gleamed in the moonlight, almost as bright as the warrior's eyes. I felt a deviance, a flame bursting brightly, something that had been waiting years to come forth. I kicked the pony in the ribs and we headed across the prairie into the unknown. I called over my shoulder, Where do we ride?

"To the land where warriors walk with pride -- and fools cower in fear."

How long will we ride? I'd asked.

"Until you tell me who I am -- or until the moon sets!"

I thought that if I asked some questions he might reveal his identity. What is your tribe? I asked.

"All who ever lived and all who shall be!" came the voice from behind me.

What do you hunt?

"I hunt all who live, lest they hunt me."

You travel alone; have you no companions?

"Every wise warrior is my companion. Cowards and fools dwell without my comfort."

And which am I? I stammered.

"You are neither, but you shall be either a wise warrior or a dead fool by the setting of the moon!"

As I racked my brain trying to search for the fearsome stranger's identity, the moon had begun its descent. You seem a powerful warrior, I said. You must be at the same time famous and feared by all who have heard your name.

"I am known to all. Most fear me. Few know me as friend." The warrior's hand went to the hilt of his dagger, as though I'd overstepped my bounds and he was tired of me; then he answered, "I am friend to all, for I am a part of each person's being. Those who fear me, fear their own being. Those who know themselves, ride with me at their shoulder."

The moon sank toward the western horizon and I was weary. I said, Let us rest!

His reply was, "Your rest is all too close, boy! See? The moon is two fingers above land. Soon you shall rest forever!"

I felt something shouting from the depths of my soul. No! I shall live.... Ahead a blanket of silver mist rolled across the prairie, and I felt cold fingers of fear clutch at my heart. What is that? I asked.

"It is the boundary of your existence," said the warrior. "See, you have almost reached it. Soon I will show you the rest of your being! You shall see the glory of who you really are!"

The moon lay half buried in the mist. The warrior's hand drew the deadly dagger from its sheath. One powerful arm reached around my throat. The dagger glittered in the moonlight. The warrior brought it to full height above my head, ready to plunge. "Now you shall know me, my friend!"

A powerful urge to live pumped through my veins, and in that moment a man and warrior was born. YOU ARE DEATH! I shouted out.

I sat drained, watching the moon slide into its misty crypt, and the sun burst over the horizon. Gone were death and the boy. Yet, they ride at my side, the side of a warrior.... And with that, David ended his story.

Spike put down his pen and relit his pipe, puffing slowly. "That's some story, Pigskin. I don't think I've known anyone who has faced and overcome death as you have. So how does the rest of the squadron overcome their fear of death?" Raymond asked.

"Each must face it in his own way. Only a fool says he isn't scared. But when you're afraid of dying, you do stupid things. When you're so mentally and physically tired, self-preservation takes over. You freeze on the controls. You forget to look behind or watch the sun. You get tired of jinxing when there's no enemy in sight. A pilot who's scared of dying is as good as dead."

"What about Millie," Raymond asked.

David sat quietly for several minutes, staring emptily. It was as if he had been transported to another time and place, in a dream world. He closed his eyes and felt the St. Christopher medal. He could visually picture Millie in the distance, waving to him. Beckoning to him. "She wants me to follow her," David said quietly not opening his eyes. "I don't know where to go, but she always comes to me when I'm in trouble. Sometimes in a dream, she'll reach out to me."

"How about flying? How'd you land in the fog?"

"I just did, Spike. I knew the runway was there and flew the Mustang in and landed." David sipped his ale, then set the half empty mug on the bar and slipped down from the stool. "Got to go. We're flying in the morning."

"Pigskin, I don't think anyone's flying in the morning. We're fogged in tighter than a bull's ass in fly time. The forecast's for it to last several days."

"I'll be flying! See you, Spike." David stepped from the noisy, smoke-filled Station into a cold wetness. The fog sent a driving chill through him like a knife. He turned his jacket collar up around his neck and stuffed his hands deeper in his pockets. The fog closed in around him as though he was in a room with no doors and someone had shut the light. He could smell the sea, the salt air and sea weed. It was as if he were standing on the beach. He stumbled along in the dark toward the barracks like a blind man. This is what it must be like to be blind, he thought. He could only see a couple of feet ahead as he followed the curb, stumbling alongside the road.

David tossed restlessly in his bunk. He could hear Millie's voice, but could not understand what she was saying. He looked around but could see nothing. He was in a cloud, flying in circles going nowhere, burning fuel.

He could hear the tribe's holy man chanting the Yuwipi (Spirit Calling). He'd only heard it a couple of times, when the chief of the tribe had passed away and when a baby became sick and died. It was a ceremony calling in the spirit beings of deceased ancestors. It was calling the spirits for wisdom and guidance to predict, find or protect. David imagined being in the clouds, he looked down and saw a farm through a hole in the clouds. He rolled over and descended in a tight spiral through the hole. It was the Wilson Farm. The one his father purchased for him and Millie.

David descended further and saw a woman and three children lying scattered around the yard. As he dropped lower he saw that the woman was naked and bleeding. His eyes scanned the yard as he circled. The children were dead. They'd been stabbed, reddish-purple holes in their chests and stomachs still oozed fluids. Flies, attracted by the blood, buzzed around the open wounds to feast and lay their eggs. He saw the woman closer. She was several months pregnant. Blood trickled from her breast where a single jagged wound had ended her struggle. She had no face.

David leveled out and flew toward his father's farm. A column of black smoke rose over the trees, and he climbed higher. His dad's barn was on fire. His father and brothers were in the yard with a garden hose trying to extinguish the fire. Out of the corner of his eye, David saw a flash of a Messerschmitt diving from above. It was a yellow-nosed ME-109 with a schnauzer emblem on the side. The pilot looked at David, grinning as he dove on the farm. Reddish-orange flames spewed from the wings of the Messerschmitt. Plumes of dust rose where bullets struck the ground. His father clutched at his throat, blood squirting between his fingers. His brothers ran to their father's side and fell wounded. David saw his mother run across the yard. Her white print house dress, the one with a pattern of flowers, turned red with blood. David screamed, but could not hear any sound. He dove at the Messerschmitt.

David awoke sitting on the floor shouting, struggling to escape the entanglement of his blankets. A light snapped on, blinding him, and he stared around the room wildly.

"Pigskin! What's happening? I thought someone was getting killed in here," said Norman, standing in the hallway in his skivvies, shivering. "You okay?"

"What time is it?" asked David, looking around confused.

Norman squinted at his watch trying to make out the time in the dim light, "Zero-three-hundred."

"Ah, Jeez."

"Go back to sleep, Pigskin. Got another three hours before we have to get up."

"Can't sleep anymore after that dream. I'll see you at breakfast, Norm," David replied.

David sat on the edge of his bed shivering. No one would fly today. The damp moist air seemed to penetrate everything. He could not rest until he found and destroyed the yellow-nosed Messerschmitt with the schnauzer. Was the dream a message, a vision? Was someone trying to tell him something? The Nazis must be stopped. They must be destroyed so they could never wage war again.

David grabbed his towel, stepped into his wooden clogs and headed for the showers. He felt driven...for what purpose...toward what goal? He knew deep in his heart that Hitler was the crazy person driving this insane war machine. The only way to end the war was to destroy Hitler, and he had to be stopped here in Europe. Hitler was a disease; like a gangrene or a cancer which spread uncontrolled until it destroyed the whole body, or in Hitler's case, the whole world. David felt it was hopeless; he was only one pilot and there seemed to be an endless number of German pilots. Were they only numbers too? Hans didn't come back from mission today, Herr Cap-e-tan. Shall we call up another number?

David hung his towel on one of the hooks along the wall and stepped into the shower. It was the one time there weren't at least ten guys trying to shower at the same time. He adjusted the knobs until the water was hot, and the shower filled with a cloud of steam. He stepped under the shower and let the hot water drive the chill from him. It felt good, and he closed his eyes letting it spray in his face.

He was Rain-in-the-Face. Who would show him the path? Who would be his guide? Then he heard Millie's voice, sweet and bubbly -- yet distant. "I will be with you always." He would live up to his promise to Millie, he would start filling in the blank faces.

David thought of Melissa. He chuckled to himself as he thought of her and his family. He tried to picture her back in Minnesota on the farm, with a passel of kids surrounding her. She'd never survive the culture shock. And yet there was something, a raw energy that was undeniable. There was a magnetic current that kept drawing him to her, and he was finding her irresistible and exciting. They were both pilots; maybe together they might fly passengers. They could start an airline. It was a dream, or at least a beginning.

Rain pounded against the barracks. David pulled his rain slicker over his head in the darkened entryway. The cold biting rain, whipped to a frenzy by a hard metallic wind, tore at his slicker. He leaned into it like a car banking on a steep curve. With each step, he sunk down into the mud, until he reached the walkway. It was like spring breakup on the farm; the fields would be a sea of mud. Trying to take off from the soggy field with a loaded Mustang would test his skills to the limit.

David slipped through the blacked-out entry into the mess tent. It was warm and steamy, and the smell of cooking food made his stomach grumble. The lights were all off except in the corner nearest the kitchen where fitters and riggers were sipping hot tea. David flipped his poncho over his head and draped it across the back of a chair to dry.

"Pigskin!" called Woody getting up from the far table and walking around to David. "What'n the 'ell are yea out and about for in this lousy weather, in the middle ah the night?"

Woody's uniform was covered with mud and his hair was rumpled, looking as if he hadn't slept in several days. "Hi, Woodpecker. Just checking to see if you've got my kite ready to roll," said David, pouring a cup of tea.

"Yea're bloody funny Yank. Yea'll not be ah flying anywhere in this crap. Anyway, we had to scrounge around to find yea a kite. The one yea brought in was burned to ah crisp. We scrapped 'er for parts."

David held his mug of hot tea in both hands, feeling the warmth take the chill from his bones. "I hope it's got cannons," he asked glancing at Woody. "I'm starting to like'em."

"No such luck, Pigskin. It's back to the fifties for yea. It's a kite we put together from all the scraps yea've been bringing us. Yea'd probably flown every part ah this one at one time or the other. Be just like one ah yea old birds," chortled Woody.

"It's got drop tanks?"

"The boys are out putting the finishing touches on 'em now. And, that's not all. Yea remember that crummy rear-facing mirror yea keep complaining 'bout?"

"Yeah, so what'd you geniuses come up with?"

"I told'em there'd be no flying today, but they wanted it ready anyway. Seems as though there happened to be a wrecked Spitfire everyone's been pilfering parts from. Da boys jus' happen to have one of those nice outside mirrors which has been installed on top ah yea windscreen this very morning."

"That's a crew I'll buy a few pints for when I get back," said David, grinning and sipping his hot tea. "Damn, burned my lip."

"Slop's on," called one of the cooks.

"What I wouldn't give for a good steak, about four eggs and a plate of fried potatoes," said David, standing in the chow line with Woody. The riggers and fitters, finished with David's P-51, stood in line behind them waiting with their metal trays. Their uniforms were covered with mud and smelled of aviation gas. Their hands were black with grease and cracked from working in the cold.

"Just close yea eyes, Pigskin, and picture back home. Yea mamma's bringing our plates in now. Ah, can't yea just smell it? Fresh strawberry jam on hot biscuits."

"You're getting a bit daffy, Woodpecker, it's still bully beef and gravy," David retorted.

"Daffy, is it? Must be ah hanging around yea to much."

"Had another dream. Couldn't sleep after that. This time the Krauts were in the United States."

"Well, David me boy, they'll be in England a hell of ah long time before they'll ever get to the States. So, I don't think yea have to bloody well worry about it."

"It was the Abbeville boys, the ones with the yellow-nosed Messerschmitts. The ones who murdered Joker," said David, as though he hadn't heard Woody. "The farm Millie and I were buying...there was a woman and two kids lying murdered in the yard...only, the woman had no face. I mean she had a face, but there was no mouth or nose or eyes. It was just blank."

Woody sipped his hot tea thinking about what David had told him. "Maybe it's someone yea'll marry. Yea just don't know who."

"That's what I was thinking, but why am I dreaming about the farm I was buying and my father's farm? Everyone in my dream was killed. It must be a warning or an omen. The Nazi warmongers must be destroyed. I can't rest until Hitler is either killed or captured!"

"Well, I'm ah betting yea'll be ah resting today. The field is a swamp wid all this rain. Besides, yea're not fighting this war alone. There's a few English alongside yea. More than one has lost loved ones to the Germans." Woody poked at his food, going through the motions of eating. "I lost a sister yea'll remember."

In his mind, David saw the image of Millie smiling at him, happy and content. "I know. I lost a wife and baby."

"Join the team, Pigskin. Don't be a loner. One of these times yea luck's going to run out. Then we lose one of the most experienced fighter pilots in England." Woody stuffed food into his mouth and continued. "This is going to be a long war, Pigskin. We've got a lot ah new pilots coming in every day. Green as grass they are. Guess what's going to happen to them? The Heinies are going to paint more British flags on the side of their Messerschmitts."

"What'er you getting at, Woodpecker?" asked David, sipping his tea, his food untouched.

"Yea've killed more'n yea share ah Bosch, Pigskin. You'll not win this war single handed. The squareheads are building planes five times faster than yea can shoot'em down." Woody talked excitedly, his mouth stuffed with food. "Stay here and train pilots, Pigskin. Yea'll kill more Nazis by sending ah hundred trained pilots up than yea ever could wid sending these green kids."

David thought of Sir Henry and Annie doing everything possible to further the war effort. Then he pictured Melissa. Was it her face filling in the blanks? He saw her with a little girl, holding her hand and felt a twinge of guilt. "I'll think about it, Woodpecker. It's just that I can't walk away from this dream. It's haunting me and I can't seem to put it to rest."

"Yea know, Pigskin, there are a lot of us who've lost loved ones and yet we've never killed a Kraut. Me boys worked all night fixing a kite fer yea. This is how we kill the Huns. We do our job so the rest of the team can do theirs."

"I'll think about it, Woody!"

"In the meantime, yea'll be risking our losing a valuable tool needed to win this damn war."

"I said I'd think about it," said David again. "Better get over to the briefing room. I want to take a good look at the weather. See you on the line, Woodpecker."

"Let me know what yea decide, Pigskin. I got me a bit of influence. I'll put a word in fer yea."

Disheartened at being grounded, David stood staring at the dispersal area. His Mustang was parked on the edge of the muddy field. "Hey Pigskin," called Norman sloshing up to David, his poncho snapping in the wind-driven rain. "Saw some ducks walking back there."

"Hey, Storm'n Norm. Looks like another day sitting around the alert hut."

"Well now, that ain't all bad, I mean it's warm and dry and you aren't getting bounced all to hell and gone or shot at," said Norman. "Pretend you're back on the farm. It's just another day you can't thrash the wheat."

"And," said David, still staring down the soggy field as they walked toward the briefing hut, "if it keeps up, the wheat may rot in the field and we could lose the entire crop."

"Shit. Never thought of that, Pigskin. Well maybe it'll let up and we'll go this afternoon," said Norman looking at his boots sinking in the mud as they plodded on, leaning into the wind. "Be ah bitch, though, trying to get a loaded P-51 rolling in this crap."

"Shouldn't be a problem, Norm, this wind will make up for it. Look't that lorry flying through the slop. If whoever that is can get a lorry rolling in this mud, should be a piece of cake for us."

"Look out. The damn fool's going to splash the shit out'a us," said Norman jumping out of the way.

"It's Woody. What the hell's going on, Woodpecker?" asked David, as the lorry slid to a stop alongside them.

"Get in Pigskin. Bogey coming across the channel. Operations wants someone to take a look. I said yea were the only one crazy enough to try in this crap."

"I'm going with you, Pigskin," said Norm, climbing in the back.

"Thought you wanted to have a day of rest," remarked David. The lorry spun, spraying mud and water heading toward their Mustangs.

"I think the wheat's drying. Besides you're too damn crazy to be let loose alone and I'm the only one that can keep up with you," said Norman grinning.

"All right, Storm'n Norman," said David, jumping down from the still-moving lorry. "Start your engine, I'll meet you at the end of the field."

David struggled to pull his poncho off in the gusty wind. A rigger handed him a rag to wipe his boots off and helped him up on the wing. One of the fitters opened the canopy. "Here's your chute, Pigskin. I put it inside last night to keep'er dry."

"Thanks," mumbled David slipping the chute on and climbing into the cockpit. He lifted the left side panel on his canopy and latched it. One of the riggers lifted the right side up and he reached up and pulled the top down into place and latched it. He wiped his face and hands with another dry rag the fitter had miraculously produced. They were a part of his team, keeping him going. David ignored the rain drumming on the plexiglass as he concentrated on fastening his parachute straps and adjusting the tighteners. Even though they were uncomfortable, he pulled the straps tight, remembering his last bail-out. David snapped his safety straps into the release latch and plugged in the oxygen, sucking on the mask to check its flow. He pulled his helmet on and turned the radio to "B" channel.

David primed the P-51 and gave the thumbs up signal that he was ready. Brakes set, prop and mixture full, he nudged the throttle and pushed the starter buttons. He felt rather than heard the meshing of gears as the starter engaged. The Allison engine turned over slowly and he waited counting eight blades, then turned both magneto switches to on. The engine fired and quit. David gave it another shot of prime and pushed the starter impatiently. The Allison caught. David eased the throttle back to idle and signaled the fitter to remove the power cord and chocks.

David advanced the throttle and the Mustang shuddered, but did not move. He shoved the throttle full forward until the P-51 grudgingly began to roll. He started a down-wind turn, and a wind gust caught the tail, swinging him back into the wind. He gunned the throttle and tried again. He could not turn down-wind. Unless he could get to the end of the field, he wouldn't have enough room to take-off. He ran the throttle in full and stood on his right brake and rudder. The P-51 shuddered and slid forward in the mud as though it were on ice. Frustrated, David brought the throttle back.

David felt his aileron control jerk in his hand and looked out at the back of the wing. Woody and three of his men stood in the driving rain pointing at the tail; then the fitters stumbled over to the tail and began pushing it around so he was facing downwind. Woody signaled David to taxi and they would hold the tail down and steer.

David eased the throttle and felt his tail rocking back and forth, but he was not moving. He advanced the throttle slowly. The P-51 did not budge. He was stuck in the mud. Agitated, David jammed the throttle to full power and the Mustang lifted from the mud and began rolling. He eased the throttle back to half, enough power to keep the heavily loaded fighter moving.

David taxied slowly past Norman's position and saw his crew struggling with the tail of his Mustang. It was a total team effort. Without the riggers and fitters they couldn't taxi to the end of the field. He couldn't see the men back there, but he could feel them pushing and pulling the tail to keep him taxiing downwind. He could only imagine them slipping and sliding, falling, covered with slop from the prop blast and soaked from the driving rain. They didn't have to do this, but they did, and he began to understand Woody.

At the end of the field, Woody's men turned him into the wind, and he brought his throttle back to idle. David looked out as the men rounded the port wingtip and waved. He swung the left panel of his canopy open and shouted over the shrieking wind. "See you at The Station tonight. Drinks are on me." One of the men waved his hand in the V-victory sign, but David could not make out who it was. All he could make out were round white spots of eyes looking up through mud covered faces.

"Red-two, you there Norm?" David called, looking at the P-51 along-side.

"Ready to roll, Pigskin. Think we'll get loose of this mud?"

"Start with fifteen degrees of flaps, Norm. When the tail comes loose, dump in half flaps," said David.

David ran his throttle in full and the P-51 shuddered, started to move and stopped. He jammed his stick full forward and jerked it back, while kicking his rudders full left then right trying to break the wheels loose from the sucking mud. Streams of water raced over his canopy from the prop blast. He rocked the nose forward again and a gust of wind caught the P-51, lifting the tail. David stood on the right rudder and the P-51 began to roll. He eased the elevators forward holding enough pressure to keep the weight off the tail wheel. He fed in left rudder, turning into the wind.

David watched the midpoint of the field slip past. He struggled to keep the tail clear of the mud. Each water puddle dragged his speed down, but he could not steer clear of them. Where was Norman? Did he get started? He pulled in half flaps and eased the stick back to compensate. He lost a little speed through the added drag, but made up for it with more lift. The end of the field rushed at him like a defensive tackle at the snap of the football. It was like a draw play, and he was quarterbacking a Moorhead Minnesota high school football game. He was in the pocket and the field opened up before him.

A stone fence bordering the end of the field began to grow awesomely. He was ten knots short of flying speed, but there was no longer room to stop. He heard the Joker's hoarse laugh. "You can do it Pigskin. Go for it." David jammed the throttle through the gate to full power. He eased the elevators back slightly and felt the P-51 settle. The Mustang was loaded heavier than he'd ever flown. How much added weight was there in the rebuilding? He had full fuel plus two drop tanks. The tail and belly must be loaded with a couple hundred pounds of mud. He jerked the flap lever to full flaps and pushed the nose forward. The Mustang broke free of the ground, but he did not have flying speed. He hung between flying and stalling. He flew on ground effect; a cushion of air compressed between the wing and the ground was all that held him up. David pulled the gear lever up and pointed the nose at the stone fence. If he pulled up too soon he would stall and drop into the wall. Why was the gear coming up so slowly and the fence coming at him so fast?

David watched the stone fence grow, coming at him like an angry fist thrown at his nose. Then he saw the bull and heard Chief call, "Sink or swim." A vision of a gravel pit flashed through his mind. It was where they'd gone swimming as kids. He couldn't swim and everyone taunted him. "Jump in," called Chief. "If you can't swim, you'll sink and then walk out." He'd jumped and sank, but he fought back to the surface and swam. He jerked back on the elevators and the Mustang flew. He cleared the fence.

He was in the clouds before he could level the nose. His eyes automatically scanned the instruments. He felt the Mustang's prestall buffet and the controls felt sloppy. David leveled the nose and eased his flaps up ten degrees. Grudgingly, the airspeed increased two knots, then three and four.

He eased the flaps down one notch at a time and the airspeed built slowly. He rolled the trim back and began a gradual climb. "You there, Norman?" called David while concentrating on his instruments.

"You mean did I leave the earth? Told you I was the only one could keep up with you. However, I'm in the soup about a half mile behind. Guess we won't be making a tight formation climb, eh."

"Climb heading zero-nine-zero degrees and switch to "A" channel. I'll see you on top." David switched his radio and called. "Control, Pigskin flight of two, airborne."

"Okay, Pigskin leader. Fifteen plus bandits mid-Channel heading northwest, angels twenty, vector zero-niner-five, bluster."

Turbulent winds blowing in from the North Sea buffeted the Mustang and David fought the controls. His heading drifted, and he turned back to his course. The airspeed fluctuated and he adjusted the trim and power. The Mustang's climb speed indicated five thousand feet a minute climb, then dropped to five hundred. It was like riding an elevator in the Empire State Building. He held his attitude constant and let the P-51 ride the turbulent up and down drafts.

"Pigskin flight. Control here," squawked David's head set.

"This is Pigskin," answered David.

"Bandits, angels twenty, twelve-o'clock."

"Pigskin, roger. Let us know when they're six-o'clock." said David. "Norm, Pigskin. I'm leveling at eighteen. Stay in the soup and let'em pass over us."

"Roger, Pigskin. Level at eighteen."

The sky was lighter and the turbulence had settled down to a light buffeting. David adjusted his power for cruise flight and rolled the trim to hold the Mustang level. He armed his nose guns and checked his sight, ready to fire; his wing guns were hot on the ground. They'd had too many malfunctions with the arming switches, so they flew with hot wing guns all the time. He tightened the parachute straps and waited in nervous anticipation. The radio crackled in his ears and he jumped. "Pigskin flight, bandits six-o'clock, angels twenty."

"Norm, switch your fuel and drop the aux tanks. We'll do a chandelle and break out of the cloud right behind them."

"Roger Pigskin, tank dropped -- executing the maneuver."

David switched his fuel back to the mains and pushed the release button on top of the control stick dropping his auxiliary tanks. There was a bang below him as the tanks broke free from the wing shackles and the P-51 leaped ahead. He ran in full power and the Mustang climbed like an eagle on a rising thermal of air. He pulled up in a tight climbing turn, reversing his heading. The clouds grew brighter. He squinted his eyes at the blinding brilliance.

David popped out of the clouds into clear skies like a watermelon seed squeezed between a kid's fingers. He leveled the nose and brought his power back, scanning the skies. The flight of bombers was less than three hundred yards ahead. "Where you at, Norm?"

"Just breaking out, Pigskin. Holy shit. The sky's loaded with Heinkels."

"Must be at least thirty of 'em. Pick a target and start shooting, Norm. Let's see how many Krauts we can send back to the Fatherland." David turned toward an HE-111 and centered his gun sight on the exposed belly. The belly gun position was empty. The gunner must be sitting up above, he thought. He eased in a little left rudder and centered his sight on the wing root. He closed undetected to a hundred yards and fired his fifties. The wing spar broke and folded back.

David did not wait to see the results. He rolled hard right and slammed the throttle through the gate to full power. He centered his sights on another Heinkel and squeezed the firing button. White streaks of fifty caliber tracers arced a path from the Mustang, ripping into the port engine of the bomber. Black smoke trailed from the engine followed by orange flames flickering out around the cowling.

David released the firing button and jammed the rudder to the floor, snapping the ailerons full left. The Mustang did a complete roll, placing David below the bombers. The Heinkels dove helter skelter for the protection of the clouds.

Closing from the rear port quarter, David sighted on a Heinkel three hundred yards away. The top gunner fired his single machine gun. White flashes winked up, pinging harmlessly off the windscreen. The fat, dark green bomber grew in his sights until it filled his windscreen. The German jinxed the heavily loaded bomber. David touched the rudder, shifting the orange sight dot from the German cross on the side of the fuselage to the Kraut top gunner. He touched his firing button and cordite fumes poured into the cockpit. Six streams of fifty caliber slugs shattered the glass of the gunner's compartment. He released the firing button, shifting the P-51's sight pip to the wing root. The wing filled his windscreen. He held the firing trigger for three seconds. Bullets tore football size holes through the wing as they dove into the cloud.

Engrossed with killing the Heinkel, David had closed with the stricken bomber which was now buried out of sight in the cloud. For an instant he felt shocked, as if someone had thrown a pail of ice water in his face. The Heinkel was less than a hundred yards ahead, hidden in the cloud. He pulled the power back to cruise and brought the stick back into a climb.

A loud bang came from the floorboards below him. The Mustang lurched to port throwing David sideways. He was still flying. He moved the stick back then forward, left and right, checking the controls. Everything worked. He broke out in the clear and began searching the skies for more targets. "Where you at, Norman?"

"Above you Pigskin."

"I think I hit a piece of wing off the last Heinkel. Better check my underside, Norm."

"Dropping below you, Pigskin. Your right landing gear looks a little funny. It might be jammed. Maybe you'd better try it."

"I think I'll wait until we get back to base, Norm. Just in case it is jammed. I don't want to get it stuck down yet."

Ahead of them a fire ball erupted from the clouds. "Looks like we might get to claim a couple probables, Normie. Let's make one more sweep for any stragglers and head for the base."

"By the way, Pigskin, I got four kills. How about you?"

"Guess I owe you one, Norm. I only got three. Next thing they'll be calling you Top Gun, squadron leader," said Pigskin, thinking that Norm would be a good leader to take his place if he went into training like Woody suggested.

"Not likely, Pigskin. Nobody will ever take your place."

"Nobody's indispensable, Norm. There's somebody waiting to take over our positions, right now. Maybe not as good, maybe better!" David thought about the day he became squadron leader. He'd been stuck with it. 'Either take it or we can find someone who can.' He still smarted over the biting words. Yet, if they were killed today, where would their mark in history be? Would they only be a score in some dusty forgotten record books? However, if he trained a hundred pilots to do what he was doing -- "Hey, Storm'n Norman, how about taking the lead? Let's see if you can find the field."

"Bullshit, Pigskin. My mamma didn't raise no ordinary dummies."

David rolled on his back and sucked the elevators back into his lap, diving straight toward the clouds. "See you at The Station, Normie. I'm buying."

"Pigskin, damn you! Don't you pull this fucking bullshit on me! Listen, asshole, you get the hell back up here. Climbing out in this shit's one thing, but groping around in it looking for the field is a bunch of crap. Pigskin, do you hear me?"

David picked up his mike and sang, "Oh, say can you see, does that star spangled banner yet wave?" He smiled to himself as he switched channels. Norm was going to be a good leader. Now, if only he could put the dream to rest.

"Millie. Where are you, Millie?" David sighed. There was no sign from her. No direction, no guidance. Maybe Millie's spirit was leaving him and the nightmares would end. Was that a part of the dream? The spirits would help him for a short time, then he would continue on his own. But, Millie said that she would be with him always. How could he live their dream with someone else? Their dream was dead, and so was Millie.

The clouds thinned and David searched for a familiar landmark. The base of the clouds had risen to eight-hundred feet. Rain hammered on the windscreen, and the P-51 bounced as if it was on a roller coaster. The field came up slowly, and David, bucking the wind, dropped his nose adding full power. The Mustang screamed as he pulled up over the field. He slammed his ailerons and rudder full left, working the elevators. The P-51 rolled once, twice, three times. Once for each kill.

David pulled up, circling the field for a landing. The commander would be furious. Pilots were prohibited from doing victory rolls over the field. They'd already lost too many pilots and planes. What the hell, thought David. It might be the last chance he'd get.

The landing flare arced up and blossomed in a green star cluster shooting out miniature flares. Someone's been roused out of a warm dry building David thought, grinning to himself. He eased the throttle back and brought in half flaps. He pushed the mixture and prop full forward, boost pump on high. His hand pulled the gear lever out, and he heard it drop free and lock. The P-51 lurched sideways. Only one gear had dropped, dragging him to starboard. A red flare arced up over the field canceling the landing.

David ran his throttle in full and leveled out over the field. He retracted his gear and brought his flaps up to a quarter. His radio blasted away, "Pigskin, yea only got one leg," said Woody. "Yea'd best keep'er up an belly in. Might be better anyway wid dis bloody mud."

"Okay, Woodpecker. You're calling the shots." David lined up on the field and brought the throttle back. The speed dropped to eighty and he added flaps. The Mustang seemed to hang suspended in the air, rocking back and forth. David pushed the throttle forward a little, keeping a safety margin. He crossed the end of the field nose down and high, but he had lot of room. He pulled in full flaps. It felt as if the P-51 ran into a brick wall. He added more power to keep from stalling in the gusting winds. Slowly he walked his way down, closer to the ground.

David was halfway down the field and still fifty feet in the air. He eased the elevators forward and was sucked in by a downdraft. He tried to catch his descent, but was too slow. The P-51 hit the soggy ground solidly. There was a sickening thud as the propellers dug in throwing chunks of mud. The Mustang lurched sideways, sliding to a stop.

David jerked the throttle back, but the engine was already dead. He was on the ground, wondering how or why? By all rights, he should have been dead long ago. He reached up and shut the electrical switches, then cut the fuel. He shut off his radio and hung his headset up on a clip on the right side.

"Yea know how many bloody hours we spent fixing this kite?" shouted Woody, wading through mud to the grounded Mustang. Mud slopped over his boots, and he looked up, grinning like an Irish leprechaun, his eyes wide and round,. "And don't think everyone on base didn't see yea roll three times. Including the old man. Where's yea bloody wing man? What happened to Norman?"

"Ah, Storm'n Norm's coming along. Little training exercise -- seeing if he can find his way home alone. As for the kite, fix her up and I'll get your boys three more Krauts." David patted the side of the Mustang like his pet horse. "Good ol' girl. Okay Woodpecker, let's get this mess cleaned up and head for The Station. I think I'm owing a few rounds. Besides I need to talk to the old man about a training position."

"Hot damn," chortled Woody as they bounced and slid across the soggy field in the lorry. "I'll get working on it fer yea right away. That's the transfer, mind yea."

Melissa

The Station was noisy with pilots, fitters and riggers celebrating. The air was blue and smelled of cigarettes and cigars. Snooker balls clicked in the back game room. "Here's to Storm'n Norman, Top Gun," someone shouted, raising his mug in another toast.

David sat alone at the end of the bar. He gazed at the pictures hanging on the walls, and thought of Sir Henry and the pictures on his fireplace mantel. By unspoken word, the corner had become his place, as if reserved solely for him...and him alone...by himself. Since Millie had brought him back in the fog when no one else could fly, most of the pilots shunned him. He was the quarterback -- their leader, but that was all. He sipped his scotch and thought of Millie. It would be their first anniversary...one year...they would have been married a year come Friday. How long would this war last? He missed Joker's hoarse laugh. The big clown was always kidding around, pulling some kind of mischief or prank.

"Fill your glass, Pigskin?" asked Hap. "Seems as though 'Top Gun' is buying fer everybody. Even someone he's referring to as, 'Asshole'. Now, you wouldn't know anything about that?"

"Top'er off, Hap. Wonder who he could be talking about?" said David, smiling at the old man.

"Tell me more about it," coaxed Hap. "I want to know all the bloody details. Right from the horse's mouth, so to speak."

"Well, Normie, I mean, 'Top Gun,' seems to be taking care of that department. Anyway, I don't want to rock his boat," said David, sipping his scotch.

Hap turned, heading back down the bar mumbling to himself about all the abuse he had to put up with.

David closed his eyes and shut out the noise and the carousing. He thought of Chief and all the nights they'd spent camped out hunting. The hours sitting around a campfire. He missed those times. Now, there was never a time you could be alone, except when flying. Even then, someone was following. Looking to him for direction, for guidance. He would train them. Teach them how to survive and how to kill. They were scared kids.

Most of them would still be going on to college if it weren't for the Bosch. Or, in some cases, they would still be in school. No one was asking for proof of age. England was desperately short of pilots, any pilots. No one cared if you were Indian, or wore reading glasses. That was how the three of them came to fly with the R.A.F. Now Joker and Chief were dead.

The celebrators' whoops and laughter changed to cat calls, whistles and low seductive offers. David looked up and saw that it was Melissa who'd walked into The Station. She was dressed in a flight jumper and wore little if any makeup. She didn't need it. Funny, thought David, how much she'd been in his thoughts lately and now she was here.

"Hey baby, how about joining me and helping in the celebration?" said Norman, stepping out in front of Melissa.

"I don't think so, sailor," she retorted, deftly sidestepping him.

"Hey! I'm a fighter pilot. With the R.A.F., you know!"

"Oh, sorry," said Melissa. "My mistake. You just look like someone who's missed his ship."

"Whoa, Normie baby, I think you've just been shot down," said Lance. Laughing, he raised his mug in a salute to Melissa as she walked by.

"Well I'll be damned! I believe you're right, Lance. Must be one of those Canadian cold fronts moved in."

Melissa walked up to the bar with short bouncy steps, rolling her hips as she walked. She knew she was sexy-looking and took full advantage of it. "You must be Hap, the dirty old man?" she said, smiling at Hap and reaching across the bar to shake his hand.

"Which one ah these bloody scum bags you been talking to?" said Hap, trying to look indignant, but still holding her hand.

"Why, all of them," Melissa said, looking miffed. "Actually I'm a horny old witch in disguise, and I'm looking for a dirty old man."

Hap pulled his hand back holding it close to his chest, as though she might grab it. "Was a time I'd ah whirled you around the floor. I'd ah danced your socks off, Miss."

"From what I hear, it wouldn't have only been the socks. I've just heard so much about you; I'm glad I finally get to meet you in person. I'm Melissa. Most of my friends call me Missie."

"Well Missie, I sure hope I'm one of them," said Hap with a grin that split his wrinkled face. "What can I get you?"

"Actually, I'm looking for Pigskin. He owes me one. He said, if I was ever in the neighborhood to check with Hap at The Station. That you'd know where to find him."

"Now what in the world you ever want with him? He's mean, cantankerous and has no respect for an old man. Just jealous ah my record from the Great War."

"Yes, that sounds like him all right. Well, first of all, he promised me a drink and besides, he's kind of sexy."

"Well, I'll be damned," said Hap standing there with his mouth open and clicking his false teeth up and down. "That's him sitting by himself at the end of the bar."

Melissa searched the faces along the bar, then she saw David sitting alone. "Now the fun begins," said Melissa, adjusting the strap of her black shoulder bag and taking her cap off. She tossed her head, brushed her hair carelessly with one hand and sauntered down the bar toward David. Smoothing on some lipstick, she rubbed her lips together. "Hi, stranger. Six months no see."

"Melissa," stammered David. "Hot dang. What're you doing here?"

"You promised me a scotch and a cigar, remember?"

"Yeah, seems as though I remember something like that. Hap," called David without taking his eyes off Melissa. "Hap, this is my friend, Melissa. You remember, the one who ferries planes from the factory."

"Seems as though you described her a lot differently," said Hap, his face beaming as he watched David squirm.

"Just exactly how did you describe me, David?"

"Well, ah. That you were a WAAF and that, ah, you delivered airplanes. Just a little slip of a thing, or something like that."

"Weren't nutt'n like that at all," said Hap, his arms crossed and resting on the edge of the bar. "It went something like this. 'Hey Old Man. You should see this gorgeous babe I met with the big gazoombas.'"

David's face flushed a deep red as he stammered, "It didn't have anything to do with you, Melissa. I always make up a story, to keep the old man happy. That's all."

"So," said Melissa unbuttoning her jacket and thrusting her chest out. "You don't think I have big gazoombas?"

David's mouth sagged open trying to speak, but no words came out. Hap howled with laughter, pounding his hand on the bar. Melissa held the edge of the bar with both hands laughing uncontrollably, tears streaming down her face.

"Jeez, you guys. What's this, some kind of a set up?" asked David, slipping his finger in his shirt collar and stretching it out trying to cover his embarrassment. "Besides, old man, we need another scotch. For Melissa. See, I didn't forget."

"And a cigar," added Melissa, wiping the tears from her cheeks.

"Make that two cigars, Hap. Not those cheap bar cigars, the good ones you keep stashed in the back," said David, looking at Melissa wiping tears from her eyes. "So did you fly in a new Mustang?"

"Yeah. Did you scrap another one?"

"Well, not exactly, but the one I've been flying has been put together with parts. Had to belly land when one gear wouldn't come down."

"How'd that happen?" asked Melissa sipping her scotch.

"Kraut bomber came apart in front of me. I didn't get out of the way in time," said David.

"You do live a charmed life, David. By the way, Sir Henry asked if I'd look you up. He's been expecting you. Seems as though you've given him a spark of life, something important to do besides drive a cab. I don't know if it's the park, or having a job to do that has some meaning to it, or if you've filled a void for him."

"I've been meaning to go back, but Detling still holds a lot of painful memories for me. Soon," said David. "Soon. I may be going into training new pilots, giving them some combat flying experience before they go up against the Germans. So, I'll have some free time."

"Here's your cigars. Mind you, they don't come cheap," said Hap, resting his arms on the bar. "Now back in the Great War, we pilots kept the party going until daylight, then went out and kicked Kraut asses."

"How about a couple more scotches, old man, and save the ancient history," said David, reaching over and rumpling the old man's sparse hair.

Hap grumbled loudly as he took their glasses to be refilled.

"I can see it's going to be one hell of an evening," said David.

"Night," said Melissa tossing down half of her glass of scotch. Slowly, she opened the wrapper around the cigar and smelled it, taking her time. "Would you be so good as to light a lady's cigar, Pigskin?" She puffed a couple of times, drawing the fire into the fresh Havana, then took a long draw, savoring the flavor. Head back and eyes closed, she exhaled slowly. "I'm staying the night and taking the train back tomorrow. I have a chit for a hotel room. Beats the hell out of sleeping in the barracks...alone...if you know what I mean."

"I, ah," David stammered. "Yes. That'd be great."

"I'm not a witch or a whore, David. I just want to be loved. We've lost so much, I feel life is getting away from me, passing me by. What if we were killed tomorrow? What difference will it make then? I," Melissa paused.

"I don't do this with just anyone. It has to be someone who has their head on straight, who knows what he's doing and where he's going, you know. Someone I could marry and live the rest of my life with...if I so choose."

"I've thought a lot about you since our evening in Sir Henry's study," said David, sipping his scotch. He puffed on his cigar thinking about what he was committing to. "I want a wife and kids and a nice home, someday. I'm planning on getting married again, but not right now, Melissa. Yes. I'd be honored to spend the night with you."

"Thank you, David. I knew you were special the first time I met you. I won't marry either until the war is over. No commitments, no regrets. Besides, you can check out the gazoombas and get the size right," said Melissa, raising her glass and proposing a salute. "Here's to love."

Their glasses clicked together. A bonding? A dream?

The hotel lobby was Spartan, as if carpenters had just left and the decorators hadn't shown up yet. The walls were bare. A small counter faced out from a door leading to a back room where a clerk slept. There were no chairs, couches or other furnishings in the lobby. David fidgeted nervously waiting for Melissa to check in and pick up the key.

Melissa banged the bell on the desk for the third time when a wheezy crippled old man stumbled from a back room still trying to pull one of the suspender straps up over his rounded shoulder.

"We'd like a room for the night," said Melissa, sliding the chit across the desk and filling in the registration book.

"The chit's only for one," said the ancient, with a puzzled look on his wrinkled face. His toothless mouth hung open and his wide rounded eyes looked up at Melissa like an owl's.

"I'll pay for the extra. How much?"

The old man looked first at Melissa then at David, both in uniform. "Hell, for you kids, the chit's sufficient." He closed the registration book and turned, taking a key from the rack behind the desk and sliding it across the counter. "Checkout's by nine a.m." he said, turning and shuffling back to his room behind the desk, quietly closing the door behind him.

David kissed the top of Melissa's head as they ascended the creaking stairs arm in arm. A single light bulb dangled from a black cord, glowing a dirty yellow, barely lighting the hallway. They squinted at each door in the dim light, reading the room numbers. "Here it is," said Melissa as she fumbled with the key. The door swung open into a blackened void. David fumbled along the wall feeling for a light switch. "Oh," said Melissa. "Here, David." She pulled the string dangling from a light bulb in the middle of the room. The bulb glowed a dingy yellow, not enough light to cast a shadow.

"Well at least it has a bed," said Melissa, feeling the lumpy mattress and setting her shoulder bag on it. There were two chairs beside the bed and a small wooden dresser. A toilet and rust-stained sink stood alone in one corner.

"If I'd known," David said, looking around the bare room, "I think I could have come up with something better than this for our first night."

"It makes no difference, David," she said, walking over to him. She wrapped her arms around his waist and buried her face against his chest. "We're together, and that's all that counts for now."

He held her close, her face against his chest. The top of her head came up to his chin. He breathed in deeply, smelling her hair and the perfume she wore. He couldn't quite place the scent, but it smelled of fresh blossoms in spring. Melissa turned her face up to his, standing on tiptoes. Her lips eagerly searching found his and they kissed slowly, passionately, like the wind blowing across the water -- first a ripple, then small waves and finally whitecaps crashing on the beach.

There had been other people in their lives. He'd had Millie and Joker and Chief. Melissa had had her brothers and sister. He was sure there had been other lovers before him. And yet, they were here now and suddenly she needed him, just as he needed her. Maybe that was all that was important. David held Melissa tightly, lifting her from the floor. His mouth crushed down hard against hers and she met him with eager abandonment.

David felt her tongue pushing between his lips and he opened his mouth slightly, enticing. Melissa fumbled with his belt buckle until it yielded. His pants dropped to the floor around his ankles, and she locked her arms around his neck. She wrapped both her legs around his and began slowly rubbing her pelvis against his throbbing bulge. He shuffled toward the bed, his pants still wrapped around his ankles and lowered her gently onto the lumpy mattress.

He slipped his hand down and cupped her breast. He could feel the nipple growing hard beneath his caressing fingers. Melissa fumbled with the buttons on her blouse and reached around, releasing the catch on her bra. David fondled one breast and then the other. Their lips sealed together, tongues probing, discovering each other.

Locked together, they rolled on their sides, and David slipped his hand down her bare stomach searching for the clasp on her flight pants. Her hand guided him to it and he opened the fastener, slipping her slacks down. Melissa lifted up from the bed momentarily, helping him slide her garments down around her butt and kicking them off her legs onto the floor.

"Millie. Oh, Millie darling," mumbled David into her ear as he kissed the side of her neck.

Melissa went limp for a moment. "What? What did you call me? David, what did you call me?" She arched her back and heaved upward, throwing him off.

He tried to hold onto the edge of the bed. Melissa gave his shoulder a shove and he slid off onto the floor. "I'm Melissa," she screamed, kneeling on the bed, looking down at him. "Melissa. Say it, damn you. Melissa."

"Melissa," stammered David sitting naked on the floor. "Melissa, I'm sorry. I, I just don't know what happened."

"I'm Melissa. Millie is dead." She sat up, naked in the middle of the bed, her clenched fists pounding the mattress. "I'm Melissa, alive in flesh and blood. Get out of here."

"Melissa, listen. Give me another chance," said David, holding the edge of the sheet in front of him. "It hasn't been that long, and I'm still trying to forget, to put it behind me."

"Out of my fucking room, David. I won't be a punching bag for your dead wife. I'm Melissa! Melissa! Melissa! Now get the fucking hell out of Melissa's room and take your dead wife with you," shrieked Melissa. She turned, throwing herself down on the bed, pulling the blankets up over her head. She lay face down sobbing into the pillow as David dressed quietly and slipped from the room.

The Anniversary

"Woody! You better come here," called one of the fitters.

"What'd yea have, laddie?" asked Woody, striding up to Pigskin's Mustang.

"Well, ah. It's Pigskin, Woody. Sittin' in his P-51...drunker'n ah skunk."

Woody climbed up on the wing and lifted the canopy. "Whoa. What 'ave we got here?" Woody waved his hand to clear the air.

David looked up waving a scotch bottle. "Hi ya, Woodpecker. Care for a little eye-opener?" He hiccupped and drained the last of his bottle. "Oh, oh. You're too late Woodpecker. Let's go to The Station and get the old man up...have a real celebration."

"Come on, Pigskin. I'll help yea out. Got to get some coffee in yea."

"No, wait, I got to fly. Millie's waiting for me."

"Yea're too drunk to fly. Yea can't even stand up."

"Hell, I can fly this ol' P-51 standing on my head, with my eyes closed," said David, reaching up to turn on the master switch. He reached for it three times before he could place his finger on it.

Woody reached in and shut the switch off. "All right, Pigskin, let's go get yea some coffee," said Woody, unfastening David's safety harness. "Come on boy. Bail out."

"What?" said David, grasping the sides of the cockpit and trying to stand up. He lurched over the side and rolled out of Woody's grasp, tumbling off the back of the wing.

"'E's passed out, Woody," the fitter observed.

"Well good for 'im." said Woody. They each picked up an arm and dragged David to the lorry. "Let's load 'im in the back of the lorry."

"Be a little rough bouncing around back there," said the fitter.

"Be good for 'im. Sides, don't want 'im throwing up in the front, now do we?

David moaned, holding his head. He opened his eyes cautiously. "Where am I?" The room looked familiar but he couldn't remember from where.

"It's about time. Come on, Pigskin. Get up and take a hot shower. We'll get some chow in you...and a few gallons of coffee."

"Normie? That you, Norman?"

"Yeah, Pigskin. It's me. Now let's get crackin' or we'll miss chow."

"You go ahead, Norm. I don't feel so good."

"Bullshit," said Norman, reaching down and jerking the blanket off David. "Get your drunken ass in the shower. Besides, you'll feel a lot better with some food in that empty stomach. Don't know what we can do about the empty head, though."

David rolled over and sat on the edge of his bunk holding his head. "Jesus Christ. I'm not going to make it!"

"In the shower, Pigskin. Or we'll drag you in and turn the cold water on."

"Okay, okay. I'm going." David stripped and grabbed his towel, heading for the showers. The hot water felt good and he stood with it beating down on his face. His head pounded and his stomach churned.

He could hear the pounding of drums. The voice of the ancient medicine man ran through his head. 'You will be known as Rain-in-the-Face.' The old man had sat quietly staring into the deep red coals of their campfire, meditating. 'Rain-in-the-Face, I see a great warrior...leading men into battle. Many enemies will die before your lance. Many of your warriors will journey to the happy hunting grounds. Always remember who you are and the spirits will lead you.' He puffed on the hand-carved, stone medicine pipe. A puff of smoke swirled around his head. The specter vanished as he had appeared.

"Remember, the spirits will lead you," David mumbled to himself.

"Come on, Pigskin. You taking a nap in there or what?"

"Just communicating with the spirit world, Normie."

"Very funny, Pigskin. You just spent twenty-four hours in the spirit world. You know, you got Hap all fired up. He's strutting around The Station like a young bantam-rooster. Claims Melissa picked him as her first choice...course he couldn't leave. Had an obligation to mind the store...take care of his boys so to speak."

"Storm'n Norm, you been hanging around that dirty old man too long. You're starting to sound like him. Let's go."

"Pigskin, you don't look a hell of ah lot better, but you sure smell better. How about filling Normie in on the big kill."

"Don't know whatever in the world you're talking about, Sailor."

"Okay. You don't have to get nasty about it. Guy's got to try. Never know what turns some of these babes on. Score, score, score. Just like football, eh Pigskin?"

"Yeah, Normie. Look, I don't feel like bully beef and biscuits. I'll see you at the briefing," said David, heading for operations.

David walked toward the operations tent, shivering in the cold morning air. He had his collar turned up and his hands shoved down in his jacket pockets. He had the hangover of hangovers and only in time would he feel better. He wasn't sure what he'd done, but drinking didn't help. He heard someone calling his name and turned.

"Pigskin. Captain Simpson wants to see you in his office."

"What's up?" asked David, turning and heading toward the CO's office. Clerks always knew what was going on. He wondered if Simpson had put him on report for not making the morning formation.

"Don't know, sir, but his mustache was twitching more than usual, if that means anything."

"Thanks. Guess I'll just have to find out, maybe someone put starch in his shorts," said David, walking over and knocking on the captain's door.

"Enter."

David opened the door into the bare office, sauntered in and stood at a lax attention. The Spartan office reminded David of the army hospital room. "Flying officer Hampton reporting as ordered, sir," said David, trying to present a good image though he still felt dizzy and his stomach was churning.

"What's this transfer crap, Hampton?" asked Simpson without looking up. "Getting cold feet, Yank?"

The sarcasm in his voice could have made ice, thought David. "No, Sir. It's just that...well these kids coming in as replacements are being killed without a chance. I believe the purpose to us Yanks being here in England is to stop the Germans. Begging the Captain's pardon, but if these green pilots don't get better training, you'd better start studying German. Sir."

"You're lucky, Hampton. There's a letter here from the Wing Commander asking for your transfer or you'd be spending the rest of the war cleaning latrines. You're out of here Monday morning. In the mean time, I don't want any more of my kites wrecked." Simpson's face was red, as though his shirt collar was too tight. His mustache twitched spasmodically as he stood and handed the transfer papers to David. "You're on the flight line until then. Dismissed," Simpson shouted across the table at him. David did an about-face and marched from the room.

The Station was dark, with only a bar light on. Hap hummed to himself as he stood polishing glasses.

It was a quiet time with only David sitting in his corner at the end of the bar, an untouched mug of ale in front of him. His head bobbed up and down as if keeping beat to some imaginary music.

"Hey, Hap. Kind ah quiet. Yea're not gonna get rich like this," Woody chortled.

"Hump," snorted Hap. "I got Pigskin buying rounds for the house. 'Sides I got everything I need right here. Clowns coming in to entertain and depositing all their pounds with me."

Woody slid up unto the bar stool next to David, "Hear yea been entertaining the old man and buying rounds too. What's the occasion?"

"Tomorrow's Friday," snickered David with a spacey look.

"So. It comes every week. Follows Thursday, yea know." Woody drained his mug of ale, banging the empty mug on the bar, signaling Hap for another.

"It's our anniversary. Millie's and mine. We've been married a year tomorrow."

"David," said Woody shaking his head, "Millie's gone. She's been dead for more than six months."

"The baby's kicking...it's due any day now," said David, as though he were talking to himself. "Millie's all excited, says she's got something special planned. It's our anniversary you know. Probably a party or something."

Woody sat quietly, shaking his head.

David mumbled to himself, drunkenly. "We'll be back together soon. Real soon..."

The smell of sea was in the air. There was no dawn; the sky gradually became lighter. Dark, moisture-laden clouds blowing in from the North Sea carried the bite of winter. The briefing had been a rehash of earlier briefings. 'Eagle Squadron to lead the bombers to the target area, the rest of the squadrons to cover the bombers.' He thought of Father Paquette, 'David, give up this quest to kill the German who murdered your friend.' After this weekend it would be over. He would go to a training squadron and teach kids how to kill. If he was lucky, maybe he could also teach them to be warriors.

He sat in his Mustang waiting for the start-engine flare, his cockpit check complete. More waiting. What was the problem? The weather was lousy; maybe they would stand down and he would spend his last three days sitting around the alert hut. He thought of Melissa, and the dream. Maybe she wasn't going to be a part of the dream. Had he just picked the wrong person, or was there ever going to be a dream?

David jumped as the start-engine flare burst over the field, jarring him back into reality. Woody was signaling him to start his engine. He pushed the primer three times, cracked the throttle, and turned the fuel boost pump on high. He hit the start switch on the front panel, automatically counting propeller blades turning slowly. At eight blades he turned the magneto switch to both and the Allison engine caught with a loud cough. The prop blast swirled into the cockpit and David closed the hinged canopy, turning the latches shut. Riggers pulled the starter dolly clear, giving the V-Victory sign.

David taxied downwind and each of his pilots turned in behind him in loose formation. He turned into the wind and waited for clearance. Two more days of combat flying and he would transfer to training. He wondered if he would ever play football when he got home, or would they put him on the coaching staff. Maybe he would be a good coach.

The take-off flare blossomed into a green star cluster lighting up the base of the clouds. David pushed his throttle forward with his left hand while holding the stick slightly forward with his right. The wind was strong and gusty and the Mustang responded like a frisky puppy wanting to play. He was airborne before he crossed the mid-field point and he leveled the P-51, retracting the gear and bringing the flaps up gradually. He rolled the elevator trim and set his throttle for cruise-climb.

David turned the Mustang, leading his flight into the black abyss. They hit a solid bank of clouds like going through a curtain into a blackened room, as if someone had shut off the light switch, turning day into night. The heavily loaded Mustang jumped around like a fallen leaf in a gusty wind. He fought the controls, trying to hold a constant climb attitude.

David turned his cockpit lights up full. He thought of the pilots he'd lost trying to make a formation climb in severe turbulence and flashed his navigation lights signaling the flight to split and climb on their own. All he could do was hold his attitude. It was like riding a roller coaster. Once you began climbing on instruments, you were at its mercy; all you could do was ride it out. The rate of climb registered two thousand feet a minute, then dropped to a thousand feet a minute descent.

Gusts of wind slammed into him. He felt as though he'd been sacked by a three hundred pound linebacker. Rain ladened with ice pellets beat on his windscreen, sounding like bullets ricocheting off the bulletproof glass. A thin layer of ice began building on his windscreen and David checked the heater on his Pitot tube and turned on his windshield alcohol. He did not want to lose his airspeed indicator if he picked up a load of ice climbing. A loud bang in front was accompanied by an engine vibration. David's eyes scanned the panel rapidly. De-icers dripped alcohol onto the propeller blades. Ice broke loose, banging into the cockpit.

David could feel Millie's presence, imagined he could hear her voice, "Soon, David. Soon!"

"What?" David called out, confused. It had seemed so real. It was real. It was Millie's voice, it was their anniversary. David's mind filled with thoughts of Millie and all their good times together...of their baby. David had always thought it would be a boy...a son, a pal...Millie was just as sure it would be a girl. David didn't really care as long as it was healthy, but their speculation made it all the more fun.

David heard Millie's voice. "Soon. We'll be together soon! It's our anniversary today, David."

David shook his head; the altitude must be getting to him, he thought. He checked for moisture in his mask and the gauge on the oxygen bottle. Still plenty and the connections were okay. The sky lightened and he squinted his eyes against the brilliant glare of the sun. "Pigskin, Red-one, on top, circling."

"Rog, Pigskin. Red-two pulling into position behind you."

"Red-three, on top. Gotcha in sight."

One by one the Mustangs popped into the clear and formed up. David turned his flight toward the rendezvous. They climbed silently in cold, clear, smooth air. Frost formed on the inside of his canopy and he scraped it nervously with his gloved hand. Black specks ahead rapidly grew into the Wellingtons they were to escort.

David called the bomber group, "Rolly-Polly, this is Pigskin with little friends, your six-o'clock high, for top cover." It never hurt to let the bombers know where you were. Some of the bombers' gunners were so nervous, they shot at anything that came within range.

"This is Rolly-Polly, roger that Pigskin. Sure glad to have little friends with us."

To David, they appeared like fat, wallowing pigs on the farm. Rolling around in the mud, exposed and helpless. Probably it would be his last mission and he was assigned to escort bumbees on a milk run.

David eased the throttle back and trimmed the Mustang for a slow cruise, matching the P-51's speed to that of the bombers. He smiled, thinking proudly that his squadron was always picked to lead the group. His eyesight was exceptional. He could see enemy fighters long before anyone else. Nervously he wiped the frost from the canopy, seemingly for the thousandth time. It was the worst time. The waiting time. They could be attacked at any second, from any position. Then there was always the lucky shot, where you blew up without ever knowing. Here one second and gone the next.

They were over France. The farms below showed green patches through a break in the clouds. From twenty-four thousand feet they looked like the patchwork quilt his grandmother had made. From altitude, the pattern of farmland could have made a picture jigsaw puzzle. They were small farms, not like the farms in the Red River Valley that ran for miles; fields of wheat, flax, beets, corn and alfalfa. Greens and yellows and brown, plowed or cultivated, sections of pastures dotted with cattle. He wondered if he would ever see it again and felt a pang of regret.

They flew into a wall of building cumulus clouds. The towering columns rose to forty thousand feet, drawing moisture from the North Sea and mixing with cold air ridging down from Finland. The anvil shape, topping the vertical wall, warned of severe winds aloft. The moist warm air from below rushing upward was like vertical shafts of air trying to fill a vacuum. Lightning flashed deep inside the cloud. Ice formed on the windscreen and David had only a small hole, heated from the engine, to look through.

They should have been back in the clear. The building column swallowed them up like a sea gull gorging himself with a fish. David stared into the greenish void and saw an image in the distance. It was the medicine man walking in the pouring rain. He was chanting an incantation in a voice David could not understand. He leaned heavily on his walking stick and turned wearily toward David. "Rain-in-the-Face. Trust the spirits, they will guide you." The image turned, walking into the abyss.

He saw the tall gangly form of Joker pointing and he looked in that direction. A bull stood in the distance snorting and pawing impatiently. The tip of one horn had a piece missing. David turned his Mustang toward the bull, heedless of his flight following. The bull turned, running into the dark, greenish void. Lightning flashed, striking his wing, blinding him. He blinked, trying to focus his eyes on the instruments. He heard a voice, "Soon, David."

"Millie. Millie, is that you?"

"Soon David, we'll be together forever." The voice sounded weak and distant, as though it were going away from him.

"Millie? Where are you, Millie?"

The clouds lightened and they broke out in the clear. David began scanning and wiping frost from the inside of his canopy. He looked down for a fraction of a second then froze momentarily on the controls. They were over a flight of Messerschmitts.

"Pigskin, Red-one. Bandits twelve-o'clock low." David switched his fuel selector, turned his boost on high and pulled the release lever on his drop tanks. He heard a bang below and the Mustang jumped upward, free of the drag from the auxiliary fuel tanks. He pushed the stick forward, diving on the Germans. David armed his nose guns, touched the rudder, centering his sight pip on the lead Messerschmitt and pulled the trigger. The Mustang bucked convulsively from the recoil of six machine guns. It was music to his ears. Burned gunpowder seeped into the cockpit, and he inhaled deeply. It was a tonic, pumping adrenaline into his veins. A wisp of black smoke poured from the engine of the ME-109. A flame flickered from under the engine cowling, then burst like a forest fire exploding in a spruce tree, wrapping around the Messerschmitt.

David slammed his stick to the right and pulled it back in his lap while kicking the rudder to the floor. Blood drained from his head; he was blacking out. He leveled out behind an ME-109. It filled the bars on his sight pip. His finger clamped down on the trigger for three seconds. Flames shot out of the Messerschmitt's engine like a rocket being fired. The Hun's canopy flew back and he rolled out the side, into a wall of fire.

A parachute popped open. Jerry had managed to escape the burning pyre. A calmness settled over David. He thought of Ralph hanging help- lessly in his parachute while his murderer closed and fired. David would not waste ammunition. He wanted to hear the Hun scream. He turned the Mustang toward the Kraut. The German had a pistol in his hand and was firing at him. He heard the ping of a bullet glancing off his protective wind screen. David opened the throttle and trimmed the nose. He played the rudders and ailerons. Another harmless ping and David thought, if his wing tip caught the shroud lines on one side of the German's parachute...he would be no better than the Hun butcher who'd killed Joker. He pulled up in a steep climb and circled, watching the Nazi's parachute drifting slowly earth- ward. David felt nothing, but he was not a murderer.

A shadow flicked across his canopy. Instinctively, David slammed the controls hard to the left and jerked the elevators back into his lap. White flashes snapped by, inches over his canopy. Bullets impacted the armor plat- ing in back of his seat and he felt a sharp pain in his back where they hit. He heard a metallic pinging of bullets punching holes in the aluminum fuselage behind him. David threw his Mustang on its side, rolling, turning, jinxing.

He glanced in the rear-facing mirror Woody's boys had mounted above his windscreen; the Messerschmitt was on his tail. Again bullets ripped into his wing and he pulled into an even tighter turn. He strained with both hands, holding the control stick back.

David felt his vision greying as the g forces built. He dare not let up on the controls or the Hun would finish him. They turned like a pair of mated eagles, each trying to tighten the circle and come in behind the other. Was this to be his fate? His joining with Millie? If that was to be, then so be it. But first there was one more Kraut to finish. They'd killed Millie and the baby; now they would pay.

David snapped his head back looking for the Messerschmitt. He pulled on the control stick with both hands and dropped in ten degrees of flaps, tightening the circle even more. The square-winged ME-109 with a yellow nose began to form in his sight pip. He saw a schnauzer emblem on the side of the ME-109's cockpit. This was the one. This was the murderer who killed helpless pilots hanging in their parachutes, the devil who shot downed pilots, floating in their life vests, in the Channel. The leader of the feared Abbeville boys.

David held the control back and slowly closed on the German. He could see the pilot looking back. He wasn't grinning. The German knew it would only be seconds. The Mustang could turn inside the Messerschmitt. One more turn.

The tail of the Messerschmitt crept into his sight pip and David's finger slipped into position over the trigger. The German looked back over his shoulder, eyes wide behind his goggles. David touched the firing button. The Mustang jerked from the recoil of its six fifties. His sight pip was empty. He stared in disbelief, into an empty sky. The German had snap-rolled to the right, dropping into a vertical dive.

David pushed the stick forward until the Mustang was diving straight down. The fleeing Messerschmitt was again in his sight pip. Unconsciously his hand pushed the throttle past the gate. The P-51 swooped after the German as an eagle diving on some unsuspecting prey, but the Hun butcher knew it was Pigskin after him. The avenger. The debt would be paid in full.

He would not escape. The P-51 could turn tighter and dive steeper and faster than the ME-109. The fleeing Messerschmitt headed for a building thunder-head, seeking protection in the cloud. The Hun rolled and David followed. The ME-109's wings gradually filled David's sight pip. He squeezed off a two-second burst. He was two hundred yards and rapidly closing on the Abbeville assassin. David watched his heavy fifty-caliber shells disappear inside the fuselage. The Hun's nose pitched up. David was wired; his heart was racing and his muscles responded instantly. He closed to a hundred yards. The Messerschmitt covered his sight pip. White glycol streamed from the Messerschmitt's engine and David laughed deliriously. The German murderer was as good as dead. Joker could rest in peace. David hoped death had not come too fast -- that the pilot would know what was happening. He wanted him to see the football on the side of his kite, to know it was David who'd killed him.

The German jinxed hard to the right and David followed; they plummeted like a pair of tango dancers in a tight embrace. His sight pip swept the length of the Messerschmitt, then centered on the schnauzer emblem. David checked his coordination, that his needle-ball was centered. Then something snapped in his mind. He screamed, "You mother-fucking whore! Eat this, Nazi shithead!" His finger clamped the trigger to the control stick as if he could actually squeeze more from the heavy machine guns. The schnauzer emblem disappeared under hundreds of fifty-caliber bullets, and still he held the trigger down. The Messerschmitt came apart like pieces of a paper bag shredded by a double-barreled shotgun blast. Black smoke spewed from the cowling.

David's guns were silent, though his finger still held the trigger down. The ME-109 leveled out, heading for the cloud column. Pieces of the stricken craft flew back, to flutter down like giant black snowflakes. The clouds swallowed the burning Messerschmitt.

Elated, David spiraled down below the towering cumulus and waited for the broken Messerschmitt to drop out of the cloud. He would make sure the Hun was dead. David vowed there would be no escaping.

"Millie!" David shouted, "We're free."

The Messerschmitt came silently out of the cloud, trailing black smoke. The pilot slumped forward in the cockpit. Flames flickered under the cowling.

David, wild with joy, circled slowly below. He did not look above. He did not see the burning ME-109 hurling from the clouds. He did not see the black smoke trailing behind.

The German lay slumped over the controls. Flames lapped up through the floor of the Messerschmitt. The body was soaked with leaking gas. The gas vaporized, mixing with oxygen pouring into the cockpit. The cockpit ignited like a bomb. The body burned, but there was no screaming. There was no pain, for it was already dead. Dead; but still it seemed to direct its own funeral pyre.

David glanced up just as the yellow-nosed spinner of the falling ME-109 impacted the Mustang's Allison engine.

The two gladiators clung to each other like two exhausted boxers in a clinch, spinning out of control. David smelled the burning flesh in the Messerschmitt and could feel the intense heat from the fire raging out of control in the ME-109. He struggled to open his canopy, ripping and tearing at anything he could grasp. He tore the release handle out of the jammed canopy of the P-51.

Where were the spirits to guide him? Was this then to be his joining with Millie? Instincts and self-preservation prevented him from taking the easy route, of quitting. He was not a quitter. Not on the football field nor in the cockpit. He would fulfill his promise to Millie. He would live the dream. He was a warrior. He ripped open the release on his safety harness and began kicking at the torn firewall mounting.

The burning pyre spun out of control and David could see red. He knew he would soon lose consciousness. He was a Sioux warrior; he put the pain and fear from his mind. With a rush of herculean strength, he bunched his muscles and kicked outward with his feet. A twist of the spinning wreckage finished tearing the Allison engine free from the Mustang. Suddenly David was sitting in his seat with nothing in front of him. He dove forward, like an Olympic diver off a springboard. He was free-falling in a nose-down dive when a fuel tank in the Messerschmitt exploded. In the span of a millisecond he was entombed in a ball of fire.

Rain fell on his face and he could hear voices:

"You will be called Rain-in-the-Face. You will be led by the spirits; follow the guidance of Wakan Tanka."

"You promised to live the dream," Millie whispered.

"You got to be tough boy if'n yea goin'na make it," Hap admonished.

"When you're down, you got to pick yourself up and start over again," Spike coached.

David tried to open his eyes, but they hurt and all he could see was a blurry mist as though he was looking through a sheet of water. Then he heard Joker's voice, like an echo in one of the canyons in the Badlands: "Pigskin, pull the rip cord."

David felt, groped for his "D" ring, grabbing and jerking downward with both hands. There was a sharp sound like a balloon popping, then a searing pain through his groin. He swung quietly, gently swinging back and forth. He could hear the rain beating on the top of his parachute, but could see nothing. His eyes were still clouded. Thunder rumbled in the distance.

He closed his burning eyes and in the far distance envisioned a bull with long horns. One horn had a chip missing from its tip. It turned to follow a white buffalo calf into the black abyss.

*****

Epilogue

Room 325
Savoy Hotel
London, England
November 15, 1941

THE SATURDAY EVENING POST
Editor: Richard Wilson
Waterway Blvd
Indianapolis, Indiana

Dear Richard:

"Does that star spangled banner yet wave?" That
was the last thing David Hampton asked me yesterday. I
thought a lot about it as I watched him take off leading
his eagle squadron. The clouds gobbled them up, but I
stood riveted to my spot at the end of the runway, thinking about the three Americans.

There were three when they came to England. Now
there is only one. They were a very important part of
the fighting force stopping Hitler from world domination.
They helped save England; now he wants to know if his
flag still waves? Are his home and his loved ones safe?

David Hampton didn't return from his mission today.
He was in a mid-air collision with a burning
Messerschmitt. There was a fiery explosion. No para-
chutes reported. He is listed as missing in action.

"When will Roosevelt send us troops?" he asked once. "When will they realize that England is only a stepping stone to America? 'Does that star spangled banner still wave?'"

There was a ceremony at The Station last night. We placed David Hampton's mug on the top shelf, upside down. A shelf reserved for those who have completed their last mission.

Yes, David; that star spangled banner still waves, over the land of the free and the home of the brave. Thank you for helping keep it that way.

Sincerely,

Raymond Burrel
War Correspondent, England

Afterwards

"Never in the field of conflict was so much owed by so many to so few."

WINSTON SPENCER CHURCHILL

Allied pilots who took part in the Battle of Britain:
July 10 -- October 31, 1940

Pilots		Killed in action
1822	R.A.F.	339
56	Fleet Air Arm	9
21	Australian	14
73	New Zealand	11
21	South Africa	9
2	South Rhodesian	0
8	Irish	0
7	American	1
141	Polish	29
86	Czech	8
26	Belgian	6
13	Free French	0
1	Israeli	0

German losses during the Battle of Britain.

	Killed in action
Bomber crews	1176
Stuka crews	85
Fighter-bombers	212
Fighter pilots	171
Missing crews	1445

Glossary

ABBEVILLE: Town in France, an air base for the elite German.Fighters.

AILERONS: A control on an aircraft that provides lateral control.

ARMY AIR CORP: The first aircraft units the United States formed. It later became the Air Force.

ARTIFICIAL HORIZON: A gyro driven instrument that tells the pilot the attitude of his aircraft.

ANGELS: Code used to give the altitude of incoming enemy aircraft.

BATTERY TROLLEY: External power for starting aircraft.

BIGGIN HILL: British fighter base.

BBC: British Broadcasting Corporation, a radio station.

BLENHEIMS: British bomber.

BLITZ: An intensive aerial attack.

BLITZKRIEG: Violent rapid surprise attack by both air and ground forces.

BLOODED: Having killed an enemy.

BLUSTER: Climb at the fastest speed possible.

BOBBY: British policeman.

BOGIES: Enemy aircraft.

BOCHE or BOSCHE: Slang term for German soldiers.

BULLY BEEF: Dried beef.

CANOPY: Covering over the cockpit of fighter aircraft.

CHANDELLE: An abrupt climbing turn in which an airplane exchanges airspeed for altitude and reverse of direction.

CHEVRONS: Patch on uniform designating rank.

CHESTERFIELD: Couch.

CORDITE: Gun powder.

CO: Commanding officer.

COMBAT POWER: Extra engine power for limited time.

CIRCUITS AND BUMPS: Take-off and landing practice.

DETLING: Base for 11th group operations.

DINGHY PACK: Case with small inflatable rubber raft.

DISPERSAL AREA: Outlying areas around an airfield where aircraft are parked.

DOPE: A finishing paint on fabric aircraft.

DORNIER: German bomber also called the flying pencil.

DRAW PLAY: Football maneuver.

FITTER: Mechanic.

FLAT: Apartment.

FLAK: Exploding shells which leave cloud of burned powder when they explode throwing out small pieces of steel. "Flak alley," refers to a concentrated area defending a military installation.

FOCKE-WULF: German fighter also called FW-190.

FUEL BOUSER: British fuel truck.

GLYCOL COOLANT: An anti-freeze in the radiators of fighter aircraft.

GREAT WAR: World War I.

GREYING OUT: When a pilot begins to loose consciousness from excessive centrifugal forces of his aircraft.

HEINKEL, HE-111: German bomber.

HUN: Slang for German.

HURRICANE, HURC, HAWKER HURRICANE: British fighter plane.

IAS: Indicated Air Speed.

JERRIE: Slang for German soldier.

JINXING: Flying in a constantly changing attitude. Up, down, left and right making it difficult for an enemy aircraft to fire your aircraft.

JUNKER, JU-87: German built bomber.

KIT BAG: Overnight bag or suitcase.

KITES: Fighter aircraft, planes.

KRAUT: Slang for German soldier.

LANDED IMMIGRANT: Newly arrived foreigner.

LITTLE FRIENDS: Friendly fighters' identification to Bombers.

LIQUID COOLED: The engine is cooled with an anti-freeze.

LUFBERRY CIRCLE: When attacked, a maneuver where a group of planes fly in a circle, each protecting the aircraft in front of them.

MAE WEST: Inflatable life vest.

MARIE CLAIRE: Code name for a French underground group.

MEDICINE MAN: Priestly healer among the American Indians.

MESSERSCHMITT, ME-109: German built fighter.

MILES MASTER: British training aircraft.

MIA: Missing In Action.

MPH: Miles Per Hour.

MUSTANG, P-51: An American built fighter.

NISSEN HUT: A prefabricated building, used as a barracks.

NEEDLE-BALL/AIRSPEED: Basic instruments for blind flying and control coordination.

PITOT TUBE: A tube that measures relative air speed.

PROP WASH: Wind generated by a turning propeller.

R.A.F. Royal Air Force, the British air force.

R/T: Radio Telephone.

READY ROOM: Waiting room for pilots waiting for orders.

RHUBARB: A low-level fighter mission to destroy any enemy positions or possible enemy supplies.

RIGGER: Mechanic.

ROLLS-ROYCE: Twelve cylinder engine used in the Hurricanes and Spitfires.

RPM: Engine speed as Revolutions Per Minute.

SAFETY BOX: A quick release device a pilots safety straps are fastened into.

ST. ELMO'S FIRE: A flaming phenomenon sometimes seen in stormy weather at prominent points in or on and aircraft, discharge of static electricity.

SCRAMBLE: A rapid deployment of fighters.

SCHNAUZER: A breed of dog.

SHILLELAGH: An Irish oak stick, or walking stick.

STUKA: German dive bomber.

SPITFIRE: British fighter.

THE STATION: The fictitious name for a British pub.

TIE DOWNS: Anchor in the ground for securing aircraft.

TOTEM: Something that serves as an emblem or revered symbol.

TRACERS: A shell, the inside loaded with phosphorus which burns leaving a white burning streak, marking the path of the bullet.

TUBE: Underground rail or subway station.

VECTOR: Magnetic bearing given to fly to a specified point.

VIC: A formation of three fighters.

WAAF: Womens Auxiliary Air Force.

WAKAN TANKA: The Great Spirit, the Supreme Being, of the Sioux.

WATER CLOSET: A bathroom or toilet.

WELLINGTON: British bomber.

WILLI-WAW: Strong sudden gust of wind.

WHITE BUFFALO: Sacred symbol of the Sioux.

YELLOW NOSED 109: Refers to Messerschmitts with the nose cowling painted yellow, the most feared German fighters.

ZERO-ZERO WEATHER: When there is no forward or vertical visibility due to some weather such as fog.

Behind Enemy Lines

BOOK II

Book II continues the saga of David Hampton.

David, his face burned and eye sight blurred, finds himself deep inside Germany. A Jewish partisan finds him and takes him in, tending to his burns. A Jewish doctor and his daughter keep him hidden in their attic. Gestapo raid the farm and arrest the Jews. David is taken captive with them and shipped by cattle car to a Nazi death camp. He escapes and reverts back to his Native Wisdom to elude his captors. He joins a resistance group and steals an FW-190, bringing the war home to the Nazis inside Germany.

He begins to live the dream.

THE LAST MISSION

May be ordered from:

Four Directions Publishing
P.O. Box 18085, Duluth, MN

55811
(218) 729-7509

Send $16.95 per book, plus $2.50 for mailing and handling. Add $16.95 plus $1.00 for each additional book. Check/money order only.
Please remit in U.S. Funds.

Name _____

Address _____

City _____ State _____ Zip _____

Phone number _____ - _____

Thank you.